LEADER OF LIBERTY
TALE OF AMERICA'S FIRST SPY RING

Perrie Patterson

Copyright © 2022 Perrie Patterson

All rights reserved. No part of this publication may be reproduced, distributed, or transmitted in any form or by any means, including photocopying, recording, or other electronic or mechanical methods, without prior written permission of the publisher, except in cases of brief quotations embodied in reviews and other noncommercial use permitted by copyright law. For permission requests, contact the author.
www.perripatterson.com

AUTHOR'S NOTE:

Although this book is a work of fiction, details of the American Revolution, including letters, events, dates, and locations are accurate. To enhance readers' understanding of the period, I've added more historical information to the back of the book along with photos from my personal tours, and information on books I used for research. I've tried to create an interesting work of fiction that blends a fictional story with historical facts regarding the Culper Spy Ring and the American Revolution. I enjoyed traveling to New York City and many locations on Long Island to research this novel. Please see the listings at the end of this book for more information on tours as well as books featuring the American Revolution and Washington's spies!

The cover photo was taken on May 24, 2022, at The Old '76 House in Tappan, New York, where Major John André was held prior to his execution. I truly enjoy taking my own photos for my book covers. The back-cover photo was taken in Setauket, New York on May 29, 2022, next to the Three Village Historical Society and the Thompson House.

The cover graphics and title design were created by Victoria Buckley——@vabz303@googlemail.com. The title font is American Scribe and was inspired by Timothy Matlack (1736-1829). Matlack was a clerk in the Pennsylvania State House, and was the scribe charged with writing the Declaration of Independence out in a large legible hand, as he was known for his penmanship. Matlack was involved with the Second Continental Congress and was also elected to Philadelphia's committee of inspection.

ISBN# Amazon paperback #9798370225604

ISBN# IngramSpark paperback for retailers #9798218132101

ISBN# Barns and Noble classic hardcover #9798823163934

Kindle version available on Amazon

THIS BOOK IS DEDICATED TO:

MY NSDAR CHAPTER, CHESTATEE RIVER OF CUMMING, GEORGIA

AND TO ALL THE DAUGHTERS' BELONGING TO THE NATIONAL SOCIETY DAUGHTERS OF THE AMERICAN REVOLUTION.

FOR YOUR TIMELESS SERVICE AND VOLUNTEER EFFORTS THAT HELP TO KEEP OUR HERITAGE AND AMERICAN HISTORY ALIVE FOR FUTURE GENERATIONS, AND FOR YOUR LOVE AND SUPPORT OF OUR MILITARY, OUR VETERANS, AND THEIR FAMILIES.

GOD BLESS AMERICA!

As we may every moment expect the arrival of the French fleet, the correspondence with the Culpers will be of very great importance— *George Washington*

1

September 1769, Long Island.

Pattersquas estate was magnificent. Mary loved exploring the rooms in her Uncle Richard's large home. She felt each grand room she explored held its own secrets. As she stopped in the doorway of the enormous ballroom, her eyes took in the thick curtains surrounding the enormously tall floor-to-ceiling windows. It was early morning before sunrise and the room was dark and felt daunting. Quietly, she stepped into the middle of the floor. There in the center of the large, open space, she felt small. She wanted to look up to see why the room made her feel so tiny. Slowly, her eyes moved upward, her head tilted all the way back, and everything looked so high, far away, and untouchable.

Suddenly, her sister called out,

"Mary! Where are you?"

Mary jolted forward, catching herself before tumbling onto the dark wood floors. She took a deep breath, then ran from the room. She went to the front of the house and from the window saw her sister on the spacious front porch, watching as the carriage approached.

Mary opened the heavy front door.

"I'm here," she called to her sister, Kitty.

Her sister turned around. "Where were you?" Kitty moved closer. "Are you okay? You look like you've seen a ghost."

Mary nodded. "I'm fine. I was just looking around the ballroom. It felt odd to be in there alone in the dark. The ceiling is so high. Then when you called for me, I was startled."

Kitty rolled her eyes, then flung a lock of her long blond hair over one shoulder. The carriage pulled up to the front of their uncle's estate and stopped. Their older brother, Nicoll, hopped down from the bench where he had been sitting and turned back to speak to Jeb, the driver.

"A fine pair of horses those are," Nicoll said.

Jeb nodded. "Yes sir, they is. Only the finest for Master Floyd."

When Nicoll saw his sisters about to step into the carriage, he rushed over to get in front of them.

"Make way," he said. "I'm the oldest. I get to sit by the window."

With one of his long arms, he moved Kitty aside and clamored into the carriage.

Then Kitty moved in front of Mary.

"I'm next oldest," Kitty said. "I get the other window."

Mary crossed her arms, squinted her eyes, and poked her lips out. Behind her she heard the voices of her mother and father. Turning around she saw her mother was holding her baby brother, Lucas. Mary's father was talking with his brother, Uncle Richard, and Liza, the slave-girl Richard had requested to help care for the baby while his brother's family visited was following them.

Mary stepped up into the carriage and squeezed in between her brother and sister, careful not to mess up the large bow holding back her mousy-brown ringlets. Most of the time she hated being younger, and today was no exception. Mary watched as her father helped her mother into the carriage before he entered. Cecil, one of the slaves on her uncle's estate, came from around the corner of the house and waved. When he saw that Liza was about to step up into the box seat, next to Jeb, he rushed over to give her a hand. Mary thought about how nice he was to offer to help, just like her father did for her mother. Mary glanced at Nicoll. At twelve he acted like he hated girls. Kitty never seemed to mind that Nicoll never asked her to join him to race their horses in the meadow or go fishing down at the creek back home. Mary always asked to tag along, and most times Nicoll would say no, but Mary would follow him anyway because she thought her brother was a lot more fun than Kitty.

The carriage began to move, and Mary could see the sun was starting to rise on the horizon. The wheels on the carriage rumbled over the uneven ground, jostling Mary into Nicoll's sharp shoulder then to the left into Kitty's lap. The windows of the carriage were open to let in the cool, early-morning air, but with the entire family packed tightly inside, it quickly grew warm. Mary, thinking the family was in for a day-long journey, tried her best to fall asleep. Her eyes slowly closed as she watched her father, who sat across from her, remove his snuffbox, take a sniff, and put it back into his pocket. As Mary drifted off, she could hear her mother's cooing over her baby brother in a soft, soothing voice.

When Jeb called the team to a halt, it awakened Mary from a dream.

Jeb hopped down from the box seat, then he helped Liza down before opening the carriage doors for Mr. and Mrs. Floyd and the rest of the family to exit.

"Take the team for water and a rest," William Floyd said to Jeb as he stepped off the carriage.

"Yes'er," Jeb answered.

After Mary stepped down, she looked around and saw they were stopped in front of a white church. People and families were mingling around. Her mother handed the baby over to Liza, then took her father's arm as they began to walk up the path to the church entrance. Liza was following when suddenly Mary's mother stopped and turned around. Liza stopped too but didn't turn; instead, she softly rocked Lucas.

"We expect you all to be on your best behavior," Hannah Floyd said, then looked at each one of her children before continuing toward the church. Mary watched as her parents were greeted by other church members on their way inside.

"Is this Uncle Richard's church?" Mary asked her siblings. "Why don't I see him?"

"This is the Presbyterian church," said Nicoll. "Uncle Richard goes to the Anglican church. And we're in Setauket now."

Mary's family had traveled the day before yesterday from their home in Mastic on the other side of Long Island to arrive in the town of Brookhaven, where her father's brother lived at his Pattersquas estate, named for an Indian tribe. All Mary knew was that her father wished to meet with someone he knew in town and also visit with his brother. Mary now wondered why they hadn't gone to Uncle Richard's church since they were staying in his home. But after their long, early-morning carriage ride, Mary thought they must be visiting more family or friends.

"Come on, Mary," Kitty urged. "I want a seat by the window. Stop stalling."

"I'm not stalling. I just never get told anything," Mary argued.

"You're too young to know anything," Nicoll said as he quickly walked past the girls and stepped into the church foyer.

"I am not too young!" Mary interjected. "I turned nine last week." But Nicoll was too far away by then to hear her. "How old does he think he is?" Mary thought. He was just twelve. But he acted too big for his britches sometimes. Kitty was eleven, but they both treated her like she was the baby. Mary's shoulders slumped, she stared at the ground a moment, then continued into the church.

When Mary and Kitty caught up with Nicoll inside, he was standing with a group of about six other boys; some seemed a little older than Nicoll. Mary stopped to ask her brother something else, but Kitty grabbed her arm, pulling her along. Mary turned back around, curious as to what the boys were laughing at. They looked like they were taking turns twisting each other's arms and watching their skin turn bright red. It seemed like it might hurt, and Mary didn't think it would be anything to laugh at, but she didn't always understand boys.

Once inside the sanctuary, Mary saw that her parents were speaking with the minister at the front of the church. Liza was sitting on the very first pew up front holding Lucas. There was plenty of room on the bench for Mary and her siblings, but Kitty pulled her over to the pew opposite Liza, where she slid up against the open window.

Mary watched as the minister excused himself from the conversation with her parents and walked up the stairs to the podium and took a seat. Her parents sat down next to Liza. Mary turned to look for her brother, who she found was sitting in the back row with the group of boys they had seen near the entrance. Kitty was daydreaming out the open window, but Mary was too short to see out. All she could see in the distance were a few gravestones from the church cemetery.

The minister's voice broke through the hushed whispers and voices around the room as he commanded each individual's attention. "Our passage today comes from the Psalms," he began. "In your Bibles, turn to Psalm 119:71 and let us stand together as we read God's word."

Mary watched Liza, who was still holding Lucas. As Liza stood, she carefully snuggled the baby and softly patted him on the back. As Mary's mother stood, she glanced at Mary and Kitty and smiled. Mary smiled back and tried hard to pay attention as the pastor read the scripture.

"It is good for me that I have been afflicted," he read. "That I might learn thy statutes." With that, he closed his Bible and said, "Let us sing a glorious song unto the Lord with the hymn 'All Hail the Power of Jesus's Name." Kitty found the hymn book, turned to the right page, and held it out in front of Mary as the song began. When Mary glanced up at Kitty with a confused look, Kitty put her finger on the right spot on the page and continued to sing. Mary soon joined in, but after singing five hymns, she was ready to sit. And when Lucas started to fuss, she watched as Liza put her finger inside his small pink mouth and he began to suck. But she knew that trick would only last so long. Mary was also hoping the sermon wouldn't last much longer.

A while later, Mary's head snapped up, and she realized she had dozed off. The pastor was leading the congregation in the Lord's Prayer, and Mary quietly joined in, saying the prayer almost in a whisper. After the Doxology had been sung, the minister held out both his arms and said, "Go into the world telling others of the love of God, the grace of Jesus, and the forgiveness of sin. Hold fast to the word of God, study it daily, take his word to heart, pressing it upon your lips and sealing it into your consciousness forever. Amen." His arms fell back to his sides, and he smiled. "It is a great honor to invite you and yours to dinner on the grounds today in celebration of my son, Benjamin, who will be leaving in the morning for Yale. We invite you to stay and enjoy the meal, give Benjamin your best, and enjoy the fellowship of friends and family. You are dismissed."

The congregation began to shuffle its way through the doors and into the bright sunshine. Mary noticed her brother following the boys he had been sitting with. Only one boy didn't go with them outside. Mary heard him say, "Abraham, tell the others I'll catch up." Then he walked to the front of the church, where Mary's parents stood next to the Reverend. Mary and Kitty walked over to their mother, who took Lucas from Liza and told her it was time to feed him. Their mother then turned to go into a small room off to the side of the pulpit. But first she said to Liza, "The church has prepared something for you and Jeb. You can come with me to get it."

Liza nodded and followed.

"Mary, Kitty," their father called. "Let me introduce you to Reverend Tallmadge, and his son Benjamin."

Kitty walked closer to their father and curtsied, so Mary did the same. Minister Tallmadge engaged with them what Mary knew to be small talk, and her father congratulated Benjamin.

"I'm grateful for your support, Mr. Floyd," Benjamin said. "Father told me that you provided some books and supplies for me. Even some spending money. I'm more than thankful for your help, sir."

Mr. Floyd shook Benjamin's hand and grasped his elbow. "It's the least we could do for such a fine young man." With that, Mary's father glanced at her and Kitty.

"Girls, let me introduce you to Master Tallmadge."

Just as Mary and Kitty said hello, a boy ran into the church, almost bumping into an elderly gentleman, and rushed over to Benjamin. "Come on, Ben," he said. "Austin is holding your place in line. You'll want to get the best pick of the food."

Benjamin looked shyly up at his father as if to ask permission to be excused.

"Go, go," the minister said, shooing the boys with both hands. "After all, you're the guest of honor today." Benjamin's friend turned to leave. "But . . ." The Reverend held up his right hand, and the boy stopped in his tracks. "Caleb, please slow down, take your time, and enjoy the day. Try not to be in such a hurry."

"It was very nice meeting you," Benjamin said to both Kitty and Mary. "Mr. Floyd," he added with a slight bow, then the boys took off quickly down the aisle and out the front of the church.

"Since their mother died a few years ago," the Reverend began. "it's been hard on me and the boys. And we are grateful to you, William, for supporting Benjamin and for being here to celebrate him today."

The Reverend looked down briefly and shook his head.

"You know," he continued. "a few years ago, when Benjamin was twelve, the president of Yale had told me Benjamin was ready for college. But I didn't feel *he* was ready. At least not so soon after his mother passed. I wanted him around for his younger brothers, as we were all still grieving our loss, and I didn't want him to be the youngest student."

The reverend chuckled. William nodded.

"I know he will make you proud," he said.

William placed a hand on the Reverend's shoulder and gave it a slight squeeze. Just then, Mrs. Floyd returned with a happy Lucas in her arms.

"Shall we?" Reverend Tallmadge suggested. He waved a hand toward the exit, allowing Mrs. Floyd to head toward the door to the waiting feast. Mary and Kitty followed her outside with their father and Reverend Tallmadge in tow. The lush green field across from the church was set with tables filled with food, and everywhere Mary looked were families sitting on blankets and quilts, laughing, and enjoying their meals.

After Mary finished eating, she said, "I need to find the outhouse. Can I be excused, Father?"

"I believe it's to the left side of the main building," Mr. Floyd said. "And then if you can find Jeb and Liza, have them bring the team around. We should be ready to leave within the hour." Her father gestured in Mary's direction for her to hurry on before lying down in the grass and closing his eyes. "Just resting my eyes for a bit, dear," Mary heard him say as she stood to leave. Kitty was holding Lucas now and ignored Mary.

Mary found the privy in a field to the left of the church just as her father had said. When she came out, she started down the hill behind the building. In the distance she could see horses grazing along with a few wagons and carriages, and she decided that must be where she'd find Jeb and Liza. As she made her way down the hill, she heard a ruckus and turned to look. There, near the horses, she saw her brother with his new friends. They were gathered in a circle cheering for something. As she made her way closer, she saw that two of the boys were rolling around like they might be fighting while the others egged them on. She walked a little closer to watch and wondered if she should get Nicoll's attention. Maybe he would include her in the fun. He probably wouldn't, but why should he have all the fun? Was rolling around in the grass fun? It must be, she decided, because these boys seemed like they were having a grand time.

Mary got right up next to her brother, but he didn't seem to notice. He and the rest of the boys were yelling and cheering so loudly they might never notice her. Then, in an instant, the two boys on the ground rolled in Mary's direction, and the crowd of boys opened up to let them pass. One of the boys pinned the other to the ground. But then he broke the lock and jumped up. They rushed toward Mary, knocking her down, and she fell backward into the dirt and mud. Quickly, she jumped up. The large hairbow holding back her mousy-brown ringlets was askew, and her dress and shoes were splashed with mud.

"Hey," she yelled. "That's rude."

The boys hadn't noticed because they were still rolling on the ground and tugging at one another.

"You," she tried again, this time a bit louder.

The cheering stopped, and the boys turned to look at her. Even the two who were rolling, fighting, and grabbing each other stopped to look.

With her hands balled in tight fists at her side, Mary told them angrily, "You knocked me down. Look what you did!"

One of the boys on the ground stood. "I'm sorry. We didn't see you there. It was an accident." As soon as the words were out of his mouth, the boy he was fighting with lunged at him, gripping him about the waist and taking him down to the ground. The rolling around continued. Mary looked over at her brother, but Nicoll wouldn't look her way. She squinted her eyes, drew a breath, and pouted.

"I apologize on their behalf, Mary."

The boy she'd met inside the church, the Reverend's son, had made his way over to her.

"Here." He handed her a handkerchief from inside his vest.

She took it from him and began to wipe the mud from her shoes.

"Thank you," she said. Then she turned to look back at the commotion. "What are they doing?" she asked.

Benjamin looked at her curiously. He cocked his head to the side, just like her dog back home sometimes did. Mary thought he looked nice, and thoughtful. His light brown eyes were flecked with green and looked soft and kind.

"You mean wrestling?" Benjamin asked.

"Is that what it's called?"

He laughed. "Yes. It can be somewhat barbaric, I guess. Definitely not for girls."

Mary's eyes got big. "Humph! You sound like my brother."

She dramatically placed both hands on her hips, turned on her heel, and stormed off toward the wagons and horses to find Jeb and Liza. Before she got there, she saw Liza heading her way. Liza stopped in front of her.

"What happened to you?" Liza asked.

Mary looked down at her dress, sprinkled with splatters of mud. She turned around and pointed to the group of boys. Now, she could see the one named Caleb being carried on the shoulders of two of the other boys. "I guess he was the winner." Mary shrugged, then noticed she still had Benjamin's handkerchief in her hand.

"Liza?" Mary asked. "Do you think I'll ever get noticed by boys? They never seem to want to include me in their games."

"What? Noticed? That's not something you need to be worried about. Boys will notice you soon enough." Liza smiled. "Where did you get that?" She pointed to the handkerchief in Mary's hand.

"Benjamin Tallmadge gave it to me. He's the one the picnic's for. He leaves for Yale tomorrow."

"Well, there. You see. He noticed you," said Liza.

Mary giggled. "I've noticed how Cecil looks at you. I think he walks by the kitchen just so he can talk to you."

She watched Liza's lips form a soft, bashful smile as she looked down at her hands.

"That ain't anything I want to talk about."

"Maybe you'll marry him," Mary said.

Liza shook her head. "Naw, I'm too young, for that."

"How old are you, Liza?"

"About thirteen. Come on, your mamma gonna be worried about where you is."

Together, they walked toward the carriage, where they found Jeb hooking up the team of horses. Mary asked to ride up in the box seat with Jeb and Liza, mainly so she could get a good view of Benjamin Tallmadge, who she had decided, might be the nicest boy she had ever met.

2

September, 1769, Yale

    The moon was shining on the water as Benjamin, his older brother, William, and their father made their way down the hill from their home to their boat. Benjamin had packed cheese and apples for the trip, wrapping them in cheesecloth, which he'd tied in a knot. He placed the package into his knapsack, which hung low over his shoulder, then helped his brother load the trunk onto the boat. Silently, they pushed the boat off from the shore and the three travelers hopped inside. William took hold of the oars and began to row as they made their way across Long Island Sound to the next town over from their home in Setauket. There, Benjamin would catch the ferry that would transport him to Connecticut.

    Their movement across the water was swift, and Benjamin felt a gentle breeze. Somewhere up ahead, a fish jumped, and Benjamin wished he could stop to fish. But there was no time for that if they wanted to make the ferry. He would miss fishing with his brothers. But he knew his older brother, William would look after the younger ones. And they promised to write to him. He knew they'd probably write to him with tall tales about fish they'd caught, and it would be something he'd enjoy reading. Benjamin's father was sitting at the bow, and he began to say a prayer.

"Father God," he began, "we give praise to you for this day. We thank you for your many blessings. And we thank you for the opportunity, Benjamin has been given to attend my own alma mater. We ask that you bless him and his studies while he's there. Take him under your wing and guide him through his days. Lead him not into temptation, Lord, but remind him of your grace and goodness. Amen."

Benjamin and William both said, "Amen" as well.

The three sat in silence for the next few moments as the sun started to peek from the eastern horizon. Benjamin was grateful this day had finally come. A few years ago, when he was twelve, the president of Yale had told his father he was ready to attend, that he was accomplished in his studies, largely because of the role his father had taken in his education after his mother passed. Benjamin knew he had excelled in his studies, predominantly in the classics, but his father had thought he was too young to attend Yale at twelve and had kept him home another two years. At least now he would be close to the age of the other boys.

Soon they were able to see the dock a few hundred feet ahead. William rowed more vigorously, churning the water up along the sides of the boat. As they grew closer to the dock, Reverend Tallmadge waved to the ferry captain. William guided the boat close to the dock and tossed a rope onto it before hopping out to tie up the boat. Benjamin and his father heaved the trunk up onto the dock, then the two of them climbed out of the boat. The Reverend pulled Benjamin into a strong embrace.

Then Reverend Tallmadge wiped his eyes with the back of his hand. "I love you, Son."

Seeing his father's emotion tugged at Benjamin's heart. "I love you too, Father."

His father reached into his pocket, removed several shillings, and handed them to Benjamin.

"For the ferry and the coach."

Before Benjamin took the money, he grasped his father's hand, and their eyes met. "I'll do you proud, Father," he said then turned to his brother.

William reached for him, and the two brothers embraced. William whispered to Benjamin,

"You know it's okay to sow some wild oats while you're there. And I don't just mean going to the local tavern with your mates."

This made both brothers snicker and lightened the mood.

"Well, I guess it's time for me to go," said Benjamin.

With that, he leaned down, picked up his trunk, and carried it over to the ferry. After stepping on board, he set the trunk down and waved goodbye. The ferry captain pushed off, and Benjamin watched as his father and brother become smaller and smaller in the distance. He wasn't sure what lay ahead for him, but leaving his brothers and father behind felt strange—yet exciting at the same time. He would write to them as soon as he could.

About two hours later, the sound of the ferry's bell and the captain's voice announced their arrival. Quickly, Benjamin leapt to his feet, picked up his trunk, and made his way to the edge of the ferry. After handing the captain some money, he walked toward the street. Soon, he found a parked stagecoach, and Benjamin asked if the driver was going to New Haven.

"It depends, Son. How much you got on you?"

Benjamin hesitated a moment, then he said,

"A shilling, sir."

The driver nodded and said, "Wait around a few minutes. We might have another headin' that way, then it'll be worth my time to go that route."

Benjamin set his trunk down and sat on it to wait. Soon, a lady with a young son approached the coach driver and asked if he was heading to New Haven. The driver said he was, and she and her son got on board. Benjamin quickly placed his trunk on the back. After securing it, he stepped inside the coach and introduced himself to the lady and her son. During the five-hour ride Benjamin shared his excitement about spending his next four years at Yale. And the young boy talked about helping his father at his blacksmith shop. The boy eagerly pulled out a small metal cross from his pocket to show Benjamin.

"My father made it for me," he said. "This too, for my sixth birthday."

He reached into his pocket again, removed a small wooden soldier, and held it in the air.

"Those are mighty fine indeed," Benjamin said.

Soon the boy fell asleep in his mother's lap, and Benjamin took the opportunity to pull out an apple from his bag to have a bite to eat. With the boy sleeping and his mother occupied with her sewing, Benjamin didn't feel the need to continue with small talk, so he pulled a letter from his bag and reviewed the information on where to find the dormitories. He also studied the map his father had drawn of the Yale campus.

Several hours passed before the coach came to a stop in town, and the driver opened the door for his passengers to exit. The lady offered up two coins, and Benjamin handed him one, grabbed his trunk, and began the walk toward Yale.

When he spotted a church steeple, he knew he was close. Once he finally arrived, he was hot, sweaty, and exhausted. The large building next to the church came into view, and Benjamin headed in that direction, remembering his room number in the dorm. He hurried toward the stately building named Connecticut Hall. Climbing the stairs, he made his way to the second floor and found the door to his room ajar. Benjamin heard voices coming from inside, so he rapped on the door.

The conversation stopped, followed by the sound of shuffling. Then a tall fellow with light brown hair, blue eyes, and a scar across his forehead opened the door wide.

"Hello. I'm Nathan Hale. You must be Benjamin Tallmadge," he said.

Benjamin nodded. "I am."

"Welcome." Nathan waved a hand to invite Benjamin into the room.

Looking around, Benjamin saw a set of beds, each flanked by a desk. Another boy rose from where he sat at one of the desks.

"Hello. I'm Nathan's brother, Enoch."

Benjamin set his trunk down, and the three boys shook hands. Enoch was tall like his brother, Nathan, and both were close in age to Benjamin. After a few pleasantries and stories from his journey, Benjamin began to settle in.

"We want to introduce you to some of the others," Nathan said. There's talk of going to Hickok Tavern later. That is, of course, if you're up for it after your long day."

"That sounds fine," Benjamin said. "I also hope to write a letter tonight, letting my family know that I've arrived safely."

Just then, there was a knock on the door. Nathan got up to answer it.

"Ah, James. Come in," Nathan said. "Let me introduce you to Benjamin Tallmadge, my roommate, who's just come from Long Island."

James extended his hand toward Benjamin. "James Hillhouse. Good to meet you."

Benjamin shook the young man's hand, and Enoch began to gather his things to leave.

"I might head over to the library for a bit of reading," Enoch explained. "That way, we can let Benjamin get settled."

"Right," James said. "Why don't we all meet up later at Hickok Tavern in town. I believe there are a few others planning to be there tonight too."

The boys agreed on a time to meet, and Nathan, James, and Enoch left Benjamin to unpack and write his letter home.

3
1769 Long Island

Mary was told she had to clean her dress and stockings after her unfortunate fall in the mud. As she was scrubbing, Liza came by.

"You need me to do that?" Liza asked.

"No," Mary answered. "I almost have it. And this too." She pulled from the water the white handkerchief. "It looks almost white again," she said proudly. "But look at my fingers." She curled her soapy fingers into claws and growled at Liza. "Grrrrr. My skin is old and wrinkled." Mary made a scary face while holding up her hands like tiger paws. "Am I scary?" she asked.

Liza laughed and held up her hands to playfully mimic Mary. When their giggles died down, Liza helped Mary take her things to the clothesline. The sun had begun to set, casting the sky above them in a rich, pink glow. Mary plucked a clothespin from the line and stared at the sky before she began to skip around in a circle. Holding the clothespin high in the air, she said,

"I've turned the sky pink forever."

A bunny hopped nearby and with her clothespin, Mary pointed to it.

"And I will turn all the bunnies pink."

Liza took a clothespin and moved closer to where Mary stood, pointing to a tall stalk of Queen Anne's lace. "And I will turn all the flowers pink."

Together, the two skipped around the clothesline, naming what they saw and turning it all pink. Soon they grew tired from skipping and they both plopped down onto the grass giggling. Mary loved that Liza paid more attention to her than her siblings ever did. She was growing fond of Liza and wished more than anything that Liza could go with them when they left her uncle's estate to return home to Mastic.

Mary and her family had only been at Uncle Richard's home for about five days, and she'd especially loved the tales her father and her uncle would tell in the evenings when they'd gather in the study. Sometimes they would even play a round of checkers. Uncle Richard might be missing his son, Benjamin, who was away in London, and his daughter, also called Mary, who had recently been married. But having family around seemed to be cheering him up.

Uncle Richard had been teaching Nicoll to play chess, and Mary wished she could learn. But her bossy brother had shooed her away from last night's game, saying it was too complicated for her. Uncle Richard also had a library full of books and told Mary that he'd find some books for her that had belonged to his son. That morning, he had given her a copy of *Gulliver's Travels*, and she was excited to start reading. She wondered if Liza would like to read it with her.

Uncle Richard had brought Liza in to help with Lucas. But she usually worked for one of Uncle Richard's friends in a nearby town called Oyster Bay. Mary hated to think about leaving Liza next month when they had to return home to Mastic.

Liza was lying in the grass and was looking up at the pink-cast sky.

"Liza?" Mary asked.

"Yes?"

"Do you want to read *Gulliver's Travels* with me?"

Liza laughed and shook her head. "I can't read it. I don't know how, but you can read it to me."

"I can teach you how to read. That is, if you want me to."

Liza looked a bit nervous but nodded.

"But don't tell anyone that you're teaching me," she said. "I don't know what others like Master Floyd would think. My real master, Samuel Townsend, might not mind, but you can't be too careful."

Mary shrugged, not sure what Liza meant. Since Liza was older than Kitty, and Nicoll, Mary wondered why Liza had never learned to read.

"Stay here. I'll go get the book," Mary told Liza before running off into the house.

When Mary returned with the book, she sat down on the back steps and began to open it.

Liza made her way over to where Mary sat.

"Wait," Liza told her. "Let's find a place in the stables to read— not here. I mean if you're really going to try to teach me, that is. I don't want you to get into trouble or nothin'."

Mary shrugged and closed the book.

"Okay," she said and stood.

Together they walked into the stable and found a stack of straw bales next to a stall door. They sat with their backs up against the bales, and Mary opened the book. She pointed to each word as she read it slowly, then let Liza have a turn reading the same words. A few minutes later, a noise in the back of the barn made them jump.

Mary dropped the book on the ground.

Liza placed a finger to her lips.

A moment later they heard whistling and realized it was just Cecil, who had come to muck out the stalls. Mary sat back down and opened the book to the page where they had left off. When Cecil walked out of the stall, he noticed Liza, who was still standing.

"What you doin' here, Liza?" Cecil asked, walking toward the girls.

Mary stood and held out her book. "We're reading *Gulliver's Travels,* and I'm teaching Liza to read."

Liza looked at Mary and shushed her. "I told you not to say nothin'."

"Ooops. Sorry, Liza. You won't tell anyone, will you, Cecil?"

"Nah," Cecil said with a smile. "It's always good to see you around here, Liza. Don't let me keep you. I've got to get the stalls cleaned before Jeb and I bring in the horses for the night. So just go 'bout your business; don't mind me." He smiled at Liza.

Liza grinned but turned her eyes back toward Mary.

Liza sat back down, and they read a few more pages until Mary heard Nicoll calling for her.

"Ugh," Mary said with a snort. "Wonder what he wants." Just as the words left her mouth, she heard Nicoll yell, "Time to eat. Don't be late."

Liza stood and offered her hand to Mary to help her up.

"Maybe we can come back here and read again tomorrow?" Mary asked.

Liza glanced at Cecil, who had come by to get a bundle of hay from the stack next to them.

"Yeah, maybe we could come back tomorrow and read some more," she said to Mary, but her eyes caught Cecil's.

Later that evening after dinner, the family retired to the library. Liza took Lucas from his mother and made her way up the stairs to put him to bed. Mary's father and Uncle Richard both enjoyed smoking pipes after the evening meal. Mary watched carefully as her father filled his pipe with sweet-smelling tobacco and lit it with a match while taking deep puffs. Soon a circle of smoke surrounded his head, filling the den with a comforting, familiar scent. Since it was still early September, it wasn't cold enough for a fire, but the smoke from the pipe made the library feel cozy. Even Nicoll was being quiet and respectful as he set up a game of checkers with Kitty. Their mother was embroidering a new outfit for Lucas. Uncle Richard went about lighting his own pipe, and when Nicoll finished setting up the game, he asked his uncle,

"Can you tell us some more stories about whale fishing?"

"Ah, is it the thrill of adventure that you seek?" Uncle Richard asked. "Or is it the joy of conquering the whale?" He chuckled. "Let me see if there's a good one I haven't shared." He sat back in his large dark red velvet wingback chair and pondered for a moment.

Just as he began a story, Liza wandered down the stairs.

"Liza?" Uncle Richard called, "could you make us a pot of tea and bring us some of those wonderful cookies you made earlier?"

"Yes'ir, Master Floyd."

Mary remembered tasting one of the cookies after breakfast, and they were the best things in the world. She *had* to find a way to have her mom keep Liza around even after they went home next month. With Lucas so young, Mary was sure her mother would love having Liza go home with them. As she settled back onto the couch to listen to Uncle Richard's story, she knew in her heart she would do everything she could to convince her mother and father to take Liza home with them.

Mary must have fallen asleep during the story because she woke up to her father lifting her from the couch. Her partially eaten cookie fell onto the rug. As her father carried her to the room she shared with her sister, Mary said, "Wouldn't it be wonderful if Liza could be with us forever? At least until Lucas is older?"

Her father smiled. "Liza lives with the Townsend family over in Oyster Bay. They might want her back home soon. And Liza might not want to leave to go somewhere new."

"But I'm going to ask her, Father. And if she says yes, then you'll let her stay with us, right?"

"We'll see, child. We'll see. Sleep tight."

4

February, 1770, Yale

Only a few candles flickered in the darkness of the tavern. The wintery wind howled outside as snow fell thick and heavy onto the ground. Benjamin and his classmates sat at their favorite narrow wooden table in front of a large stone fireplace. The fire cast an ominous glow onto the faces of his friends. Pewter pints of ale sat half emptied and warm in front of each of them as they competed to see who could recite the most lines correctly from Homer's *Odyssey*.

It was Enoch's turn, and Benjamin watched as he uncrossed his ankles and removed his feet from the table. Enoch stood and recited. "Outrageous! Look how the gods have changed their minds about Odysseus—while I was off with my Ethiopians. Just look at him there, nearing Phaeacia's shores where he's fated to escape his noose of pain that's held him until now." Enoch bowed with one hand held behind his back, while the other hand made royal-looking flourishes.

Everyone but Enoch had to take a drink, and then it was time for someone else to complete the next line, so Benjamin stood. If he were to get it wrong, he'd have to drink all of his ale, and these boys had already had their fill.

"Come on, Ben," Nathan said. "I hope you get this one wrong. We need to get you good and drunk. After all, today is your fifteenth birthday!" James, Enoch, Nathan, Stephen, and Noah all cheered.

"To Benjamin!" they said in unison.

Nathan leaned toward Benjamin over the top of the table.

"Now, what say you? Can you complete the quote, or shall you drink a pint?"

Benjamin stood, cleared his throat, and began. "Still my hopes ride high—I'll give that man his swamping fill of trouble!"

"Blast!" James Hillhouse shouted. "He got it correct. We all take a drink except Master Benjamin."

The others took deep drinks while Benjamin watched them keenly to make sure they all did. Afterward, they slammed their cups onto the table, and Nathan turned around to look for the barmaid to bring them another round. But before he could call for her, the blustery winds flung the tavern door wide open with a loud thud. Snow flurries began to float onto the tavern floor, then a man stepped into the tavern and announced, "Paper just arrived." He slapped the stack of newspapers down on a table and left just as quickly as he had arrived.

Enoch walked over, picked up a copy and brought it back to the table. He silently read the first column while James ordered another round from the tavern owner's wife.

"Bones of me! Heaven have mercy," Enoch said. "A boy has been killed in Massachusetts. Shot by a Tory merchant named Ebenezer. They're saying that a Patriot riot was started by Samuel Adams, and the merchant was trying to stop the angry crowds from destroying his shop." As Enoch set the paper down, a silence fell around the room. All eyes were on Enoch as they contemplated what they'd just heard.

"When was this?" Nathan asked.

"Three days ago," Enoch answered.

The boys' faces grew solemn. Then Enoch said, "There's unrest in Boston for sure."

"Let it not come to us here," Nathan added.

"But what of liberty and freedom?" Benjamin asked. "And of a man not having a king telling him what he can and cannot do?"

"Aye, agreed," said James.

"Alas," Stephen said, "what of angry mobs stirring up politics with discourse? Is hurting the innocent the way to bring about change?"

"Boston is becoming known for burning effigies, and for brawls in the streets," Enoch said. "Where it will lead is unknown."

"What good can be done by stripping a man of his clothes," Stephen asked. "slathering him with burning, hot tar and as he screams in pain, then covering him with feathers? Will scaring and mocking a man change his vote? Or bring him into comradery with the other side?"

"Nay," Noah said. "A horrible suffering indeed."

The rest of the boys murmured in agreement as their pints were again filled to the brim, and the game continued. But after another round of quoting *The Odyssey*, they stopped to debate what each thought about whether ladies should receive college educations.

"Should they not have an opportunity to choose their level of education?" Benjamin asked.

"Some may want to do more than cook and sew and raise children," Nathan added.

"Such radical ideas, my boys," James said with a chuckle.

After a while, the tavern owner, thinking they'd had too much ale, told them they should be getting back to campus. The six of them donned their coats and hats, made their way out into the snow, and began their walk back. As they approached the school, James said, "We should start a club. A private fraternity for those interested in discussing the classics, debating literary topics, ideas, and philosophy."

"Fantastic," said Nathan. " A secret society. What shall it be called?"

"Let's each say a letter, and from that form the name," James said. "I'll start. *L*."

Nathan said, "*I*."

"*N*," said Benjamin.

"Noah threw out, "*O*."

Stephen added "*N*."

Benjamin choked back a laugh. "That one's been said."

"The Linonia Society," Enoch suggested.

"Then that's what it shall be," James said.

As they approached campus, they stopped next to the library wing, and Enoch lifted a hand and said, "To the first members of this new society."

"Hear, hear," the others cheered.

James bent down and picked up a rock. "Reach down and find something," he told the others.

That was harder than it might have seemed because of the snow covering the ground. But the five boys each found rocks of their own and held them up.

James tapped Enoch on the shoulder with his rock. "I hereby induct you into the society of the Linonia," he said. Then each of them with his rock in hand tapped another on the shoulder. Afterward, Nathan tossed his rock high into the air, and the others did the same. Unfortunately, a few of them crashed through the windows behind them.

"We better go," Enoch said.

Bent over with laughter, the boys began to run.

As they made it to their rooms, they had hope that no one had seen them.

5

March 1770, Mastic Long Island

The doctor placed Lucas in his mother's arms, then silently left the room, closing the door behind him. William Floyd was waiting for him at the bottom of the stairs. Mary peeked around the corner of the hallway to listen.

"I'm afraid only time will tell," said the doctor. "He's in God's hands now."

God's hands, Mary thought. "Well, that's a good thing, I guess," she whispered to herself, then watched as her father shook the doctor's hand and said,

"What do we owe you for the visit, Doctor?"

"Nothing. Nothing at all," the doctor said solemnly. "It's hard enough for me to take a call from a family with a sick baby. I know how heartbreaking this is. Especially for Hannah. Send word if you need me again. And please take care of Hannah, especially if . . ."

The doctor's words trailed off, and Mary wondered what he meant by "especially if." She watched her father walk outside with the doctor, then went to meet him when he came through the door.

"Goodness, Mary." Her father was startled to find Mary standing near the doorway when he came inside. "What are you doing up? You should be in bed. I know these past few days have been hard for you with Nicoll and Kitty both in quarantine—*and* your mother and the baby. But you need to mind yourself these days, and we'll all try to get through this smallpox outbreak, hopefully without any more of us getting sick."

Her father closed the door behind him and locked the bolt across the top then took a seat at the table. Mary watched as he put both hands on either side of his head and bent down over the table. Just then Liza came down the stairs. William jumped up from his seat and went to her.

Liza shook her head.

"Nothin' changed," she said. "Ms. Hannah, she so tired she can hardly stay awake. She tried feeding him again, but they both asleep now. He felt hot, so I've come to get a damp cloth to lay over him."

Mary's father nodded, and Mary followed Liza to the kitchen, where Cora, their cook was chopping carrots and potatoes for the next day. The only light in the kitchen was one small candle sitting on the cutting block. Mary watched as Liza found a rag and dipped it into a bowl of water, wrung it out, then turned around, bumping into Mary.

"What you doin' in here?" Liza asked.

Mary shrugged. "I heard the doctor say Lucas was in God's hands now. That's good, right?"

Cora stopped chopping for a moment and looked at Mary. "Yes, it is a very good thing. You don't need be worrying youseff about grown people business, child. But you can pray; we can all pray. We can always pray." With that, Cora began chopping again and started humming a hymn, a song Mary recognized.

Mary followed Liza toward the stairs. When they passed her father, his eyes were closed and his head was down. His lips were moving, but no sound was coming from him. And Mary knew he was praying too.

∞∞∞∞∞∞∞∞

The following morning, Mary woke on her pallet on the floor of her father's study to the sounds of sobbing. She hadn't been allowed upstairs since the sickness began, but she often snuck up there. She tiptoed up the stairs to her parents' bedroom and found the door cracked open. She peeked through the opening to see her mother holding Lucas and crying. Her father was sitting next to his wife with his arms around her. Liza was standing next to the bed with Cora by her side, both with tears streaming down their cheeks. Mary wanted to burst into the room to find out what was happening, but she was afraid of being yelled at. So she went back downstairs, rolled up her pallet, placed the bundle to the side of the fireplace, and waited.

Soon Liza and Cora made their way down the stairs. She heard Liza say, "I'll go find John and tell him so he can get started."

Started on what? Mary wondered.

"Liza," Mary said, running over to her.

Liza turned to her, and Mary saw the sadness in her eyes, and her tear-stained cheeks. And Mary knew in her heart what Liza was about to tell her.

"He's gone, Mary. He's gone to heaven."

Liza covered her mouth with her hand, then fled the room.

Mary's shoulders crumpled; she shook her head as silent tears rolled down her cheeks. But how? she thought. If he was in God's hands, how is he gone? How could God let her baby brother die? He was only eight months old. Didn't God love him? Is Momma being punished? All these thoughts flooded Mary's mind until she couldn't think anymore. Instead, she dropped to her knees and cried. Cora found her curled up in a ball and wrapped her strong arms around her. Cora held her for a long time as Mary's tears flowed.

"It'll be all right, child," Cora said. "The Lord gives, and the Lord takes away. We don't understand his ways, but we know he's good. He's always good. We're all his children, and we are all loved by him."

"But I want to know why, Cora!" Mary's shoulders shook. She sniffed, then wiped under her nose with the back of her hand. Her breath came from deep, open-mouthed gasps. "I want God to tell me why he let my baby brother die."

"Then you best talk to God about it. The more you talk to him, the more you learn from him." Cora picked up one of Mary's hands and brought it to her chest. "Just like you're talking to me now. You just tell him what's on your heart. He know. He already know. But he wants you to tell him."

Still holding Mary in her arms, Cora began to gently rock back and forth. "Same way you want your best friend to tell you everything, tell God what's on your mind. You'll feel better. His peace will come."

Cora continued to rock Mary, then she sang an old spiritual, a song Mary had heard John and the others who worked on her father's farm sing. Her voice started low and mournful as the words "Swing low, sweet chariot" filled the air around them. Soon, Mary felt a little better.

Later that afternoon, John, Silas, and Henry went out with Mr. Floyd to an oak tree in the far corner of the field, close enough you could see it from the bedroom windows along the back of the house, and they dug a small grave. After it was ready, the men spent the rest of the day placing a knee-high picket fence around it.

The next afternoon, Mr. Floyd had the minister come out to the house, and they buried baby Lucas. Since Nicoll, Kitty, and their mother were still too sick to leave their quarantine rooms, they stood and watched from the upstairs bedroom windows. Mary, Liza, Cora, and Cora's young daughter, Joli laid flowers on top of the tiny coffin before it was lowered into the ground. Mr. Floyd kissed Mary on the head, then he began shoveling dirt onto the tiny coffin. Liza took Mary by the hand and led her back toward the house.

"What will happen now, Liza?" Mary asked. "Will you go back to Oyster Bay and live with the Townsends again?"

"I suppose," Liza said with sadness in her voice.

∞∞∞∞∞∞∞∞

A few days later, Kitty and Nicoll were well enough to leave their bedrooms, and they came downstairs for the first time in weeks. Their mother stayed in bed, and Mary was told she just needed some time. Now Liza had gotten sick, and was in quarantine, and Mary hadn't been able to see her in days. But Mary was glad to be able to go back into the room she shared with Kitty.

In the bedroom, she stood looking through the window, where she could see Lucas's grave. It had a nice fence and a tall wooden cross that stood next to the oak tree.

Mary wiped her eyes; she hoped Liza would be okay. She turned from the window, went to her dresser, and opened the top drawer. Inside was the Bible she and Liza had been reading together in the early mornings. Before anyone in the house was awake, Mary and Liza would meet in the kitchen before Liza's chores and read by candlelight. Now, Mary lifted the Bible from the drawer and held it tightly against her chest. She squeezed her eyes shut.

"Please, God," Mary begged, "I don't want to lose Liza too."

She stood quietly, holding the Bible to her chest and waited for God to respond. She didn't hear anything, but she felt a closeness, a sense of comfort, as if she weren't alone. As Mary went to place the Bible back into the drawer, something caught her eye. The small white handkerchief with the initials "BT" was folded next to the spot where she kept her Bible. She picked it up and held it for a moment before wiping her cheeks with it. "I'll always be friends with Liza," Mary whispered. "No matter what—even if she has to go back to Oyster Bay. She's my forever friend."

Mary put the handkerchief and the Bible back into the drawer and left the bedroom. As she started down the stairs, a rider approached the house.

"It's the post," Nicoll called.

"Don't go out," Mr. Floyd said. "You've only just started to feel better." Instead, Mr. Floyd went out and met the rider.

Cora came out from the kitchen with a bowl of scrambled eggs and a plate of biscuits. She set them down and scooped some food onto plates for Nicoll and Kitty. After William walked back inside with a few letters in his hands, Mary watched him walk into his study. She snatched a biscuit from the plate and left the table to see her father. From the doorway of his study, Mary watched her father read a letter. A smile appeared on his lips, and it made her curious.

"Who's it from, Father?"

He looked up, a smile still on his lips, and said, "Master Tallmadge. He's written from Yale."

"What does it say?" Mary stepped into the room and close to her father's desk.

"Ah, apparently the boys have been up to some mischief and there have been a few broken windows. And he goes on to say he's excelling in all his classes, and he's joined a literary debate club, something of a secret society." He looked down at the letter. "He's also just gotten over the measles."

Mary smiled, glad he wasn't sick anymore.

Her father reached for the quill on his desk, then took a sheet of paper from his drawer.

"I shall write his father in Setauket to let him know I'm happy to pay for the window repairs, seeing how serious and studious Master Tallmadge is. I'm sure the boys meant no harm."

Her father chuckled. Then he said something under his breath, and Mary strained to hear it, "At least it was harmless fun," her father said. "Unlike that unfortunate situation with the mob that led to five men in Boston being killed. And it's only been a few weeks since that young lad was killed. God help us."

Whatever her father had meant by the whispered comments, Mary was glad Benjamin Tallmadge's letter had made her father smile. He finished writing his own letter quickly, and Mary watched as he heated the wax, then took the seal from his drawer, placed it in the center of the wax, and pressed.

"Have you eaten?" he asked Mary.

"Just a biscuit."

"Come, Let's sit down and enjoy the meal. You must keep your strength up."

As they left the study, Mary took her father by the arm. "Father, I hope Liza doesn't die too," she said earnestly. "And if she has to go back to Oyster Bay once she's well, I want to make the journey with you."

As her father patted his daughter's small hand, he didn't answer, but he smiled.

6

New Haven, Connecticut December 1773

The elegant home of the very prominent merchant and mayor of New Haven, Roger Sherman, was filled with the smells of Christmas. He was hosting a Christmas Eve gala in his home for some of the more promising men in the recent graduation class at Yale. Benjamin Tallmadge, James Hillhouse, Nathan, and Enoch Hale were a few of the attendees. The smell of pine filled the air. Greenery and garlands lined the windowsills, chandeliers, and staircase banisters as well as the long banquet table where they would soon sit for supper.

Benjamin couldn't help but notice the beautiful young ladies in attendance. He hoped he'd be seated next to one and the conversation would be agreeable. As luck would have it, he soon found himself seated to the right of a lovely young lady named Alice. Benjamin observed Alice's posture and air of confidence, which stirred in him an interest to learn more about her. He was charmed by intelligent women who were not only graceful but could match him in conversation about current events and books. To his right was Enoch, and to Enoch's right a lady named Emma. It seemed Mr. Sherman's wife, Rebecca, had made sure there were equal amounts of ladies and eligible gentlemen this evening. Nathan and James, across the table from him, were engaged in conversation with the ladies seated next to them, and the room was filled with lively chatter.

Soon, Mr. Sherman stood from his place at the end of the table and proposed a toast.

"Let us drink to these young lads who have such promise in their futures," he said, with his wine glass in hand. "Graduating Yale is a grand accomplishment. And what fine futures they each hold. Huzzah!"

The guests around the table shouted, "Huzzah!"

With that, everyone tapped their glasses together and drank. Quickly, servants came to refill their drinks, and the meal began as Mr. Sherman carved the turkey. But after a few drinks, James's lips had been loosened enough to turn the table talk to news from Boston. Just weeks ago, they'd all learned of what people were calling the "Boston Tea Party."

"The Sons of Liberty are heroes, are they not?" James said. "They're showing the king what they think of taxing us. It's horribly unfair."

Most nodded in agreement.

Benjamin spoke up. "The East India Tea Company has created a monopoly. The Boston colonists have proclaimed their frustration with Britain for imposing taxation without representation. They've shown the king that tyranny won't do. Just think what will happen if this government-created monopoly extends to include other goods in the future."

Alice, the young lady sitting next to Benjamin, asked, "What if the Tea Party was not the act of a lawless mob, but instead, these Sons of Liberty were carrying out a principled protest, which might be the only remaining option the people of Boston have to defend their rights?"

"Hear, hear!" Nathan said.

Benjamin smiled at Alice. "Well said." He was very impressed with this young lady and planned to talk with her more. He was also filled with hope that he might have an opportunity to dance with her later.

"Maybe we should stop drinking tea altogether," Emma said then giggled. "That should help. Anyway, it's Boston that's dealing with unfair taxation, right?"

"No," said Mr. Sherman. "Great Britain wants its money. I'm afraid all the colonies will be in for a struggle, not just Massachusetts. We may have a fight ahead of us."

His wife changed the subject. "It's Christmas." Rebecca raised her glass. "The most joyful time of the year." She smiled broadly at Mr. Sherman. "Shall we toast to good health, and happiness and forgo talk of taxes, mobs, and the king for the rest of the evening?"

With another toast and another round of drinks, the table conversation became lighter as the boys entertained the ladies with their wit, jokes, and stories.

James tapped his knife to the edge of his glass. "A bit of humor, if you will, to add to the merriment." Taking a theatrical stance, he cleared his throat and pulled his shoulders back. After a quick glance around the table to make sure he held everyone's undivided attention, he began. "A man was sitting in the window of his local tavern when a fishmonger passed with his son. 'Buy my soals,' he cried. 'Buy my son's.' The man in the window replied, 'Ah, you wicked old man. Are you not content to sell your own soul, but you must sell your son's too.?'"

This brought a roar of laughter from the men at the table and shy giggles from the ladies. As their supper drew to a close, the gathering moved to the parlor, where a string quartet played Christmas music. When the quartet finished playing "God Rest Ye Merry Gentlemen" and began "The First Noel," Benjamin turned to Alice.

"Would you dance with me?" he asked.

She blushed and curtsied then held out her hand to him. Delicately, Benjamin took her hand in his and led her to the middle of the floor. He placed his other hand around her waist, and they began to dance. Soon, the other boys headed to the floor to dance with the ladies they'd been paired with at the table.

At the stroke of midnight, Mr. Sherman tapped his glass to gather everyone's attention. "It's Christmas morning! Shall we sing?"

Several servants gave out candles. With a few of them already lit, the guests touched their candles to one another's until each one held a flame. In the glow of the candlelight, their song started quietly and softly, growing louder as they began to harmonize. "Silent, night, holy night, all is calm, all is bright . . ."

After a few carols, the carriages arrived to take guests home. On the way out the door, Benjamin stopped and thanked Mr. and Mrs. Sherman.

"I've had a most festive evening. You are very gracious hosts."

With that, he gave a short bow and moved outside, eager to speak with Alice again. When he saw her coming down the stairs, he moved to take her by the hand.

"I've waited to speak with you, if I may," he said.

"Certainly, Master Tallmadge. I've enjoyed your company this evening."

"It would please me to start a correspondence with you if you're agreeable."

A look of shyness fell over her face as her eyes fell away from his briefly, then she looked back up.

"I would also enjoy that."

His smile grew wide as Benjamin kissed her hand and bowed. Together they walked to her carriage, and he bid her adieu.

∞∞∞∞∞∞∞∞

Stars twinkled in the cold, crisp darkness of the Christmas-Day sky as Benjamin and three of his closest friends made their way from the Sherman home to the tavern to celebrate some more. Once they were seated at their favorite table near the large stone fireplace, they ordered pints of ale and their celebration continued.

"Ah, Pythias, you shan't leave me!" Nathan joked, using the nickname he had given Benjamin.

Having had several rounds of beer, the boys were in a most joyous mood.

"Damon, my loyalty is to you always," Benjamin said, calling Nathan by his Greek nickname.

When the tavern owner's wife stopped to fill their cups once more, she looked at Nathan and Benjamin with a question in her eye. Having known them as regulars these past four years while they'd studied at Yale, she was curious as to why they'd suddenly begun calling each other by different names. "Who are Pythias and Damon?" she asked.

Nathan answered. "In Greek legend, Pythias and Damon illustrate the Pythagorean ideal of friendship. Pythias is sentenced to death on a charge of plotting against the tyrannical Dionysius the First of Syracuse. But first, he asks Dionysius to allow him to settle his affairs. Dionysius agrees only because Pythias's friend Damon asks to be held hostage in his stead, and Damon will be executed should Pythias not return. When Pythias returns, Dionysius is enamored by the love and loyalty they have for each other, and he frees them both." Nathan glanced at Benjamin. "Using the nicknames is our symbol for our friendship and loyalty."

Benjamin lifted his pint to Nathan.

The tavern owner's wife smiled at them.

"Friendship is like gold, they say. A true friend is a treasure," she said before walking away.

"Tell me, Benjamin," Enoch asked. "Will you continue correspondence with Alice after moving to Wethersfield to teach? Or will you amuse yourself with the local female crowd once you're in your new Connecticut home?"

"I think I shall keep it going as long as she is in favor," Benjamin responded.

"And you, brother." Enoch turned to Nathan. "You've flirted with the best of them this past year and at supper earlier. What say you?"

"First, I'd say I'm certainly in favor of female company. As a teacher, I prefer a well-educated lady." He chuckled. "We shall see how things line up once I prepare to move to my new Connecticut home in Moodus. Mind you, it's thirty miles south of our family home in Coventry. Alas, I will be lonely at first."

As the boys talked and reminisced about their four years together, they made plans to correspond in hopes of staving off any loneliness moving to their new towns might bring.

Just before dawn Benjamin said his final goodbyes to his friends then made his way toward the stagecoach that would take him to Bridgeport, Connecticut. From there a ferry would carry him to Port Jefferson on Long Island, where his father would be waiting on the dock to take him home for a few weeks before he started his teaching job in Wethersfield.

7

New Year's Day Mastic Long Island 1774

Mary poked her head inside her mother's bedroom to see Kitty draped in the new fabric she'd gotten for Christmas. It glinted when the light hit it in just the right spot. Curious about the new dress Kitty would be getting, Mary made her way into the room.

"Are you making a gown for Kitty to wear to a ball with that new fabric, Mama?"

Her mother nodded. "I am."

"I'm going to Uncle Richard's birthday gathering in Brookhaven in a few weeks," Kitty announced.

"Can I go too, Mama?" Mary asked.

"I'm afraid not," her mother answered. "This is a social gathering. It will be mostly grown-ups and young ladies who are old enough to begin courtship. Your brother and Kitty will go together. Jeb will take them in the carriage. They'll stay a week with Richard and meet his new wife."

"But I'm almost thirteen. I'm old enough," Mary complained.

Kitty laughed. "You are *not* almost thirteen." She turned up her nose and said, "Your birthday is at the end of August. That's a little over six months away."

Mary didn't appreciate her sister's sarcastic tone. She made a growling sound low in her throat, then she sighed. "Ugh. I'm twelve and a half, right, Mama?"

Hannah Floyd took out the pins from between her teeth and looked at Mary.

"It's not your time yet, dear. There's no reason to rush into anything. Kitty is fifteen. She'll soon be sixteen, and it's time for her to start going to balls and parties."

"I'm going to ask Father." With that, Mary turned and stomped out of the room and down the stairs to find her father in his study.

She then stood in the doorway, watching as her father peered at papers on his desk and made notes in his ledger. She cleared her throat to get his attention.

"Ah, Mary. Come in," he said.

"Father," Mary said. She stopped in front of his desk and waited for him to look up again.

"Yes, child?"

"Kitty and Nicoll are going to Uncle Richard's for his birthday party in a few weeks, and I'd like to join them. And maybe Liza could come and help with the party too. Maybe Richard's new wife could use extra help for the party." Mary's voice got higher and more fervent as she spoke. "And I would love to see Liza. We've only spoken through letters the past few years since she went home to Oyster Bay. It would be so nice to see her again. And, of course, to see Uncle Richard, and Cousin Benjamin too."

Mary had been only nine the last time they'd visited Uncle Richard's Pattersquas estate, and Benjamin had been away in London.

Her father chuckled. "I'll need to speak to your mother about this. But I don't see a reason you shouldn't be able to go with Kitty and Nicoll. It appears it would mean a lot to you."

Mary smiled then ran around the desk and flung her arms around her father.

"Thank you, thank you, thank you, Father. I can't wait to write to Liza and tell her." She paused and studied her father for a moment. "And Father?"

"Yes?"

"Could you ask Uncle Richard to speak to Mr. Townsend about Liza? To see if she could come to Brookhaven for a few days to help with the party?"

Mary's father placed his hands on either side of her head and touched his forehead to hers. "My dear, you know you have my heart wrapped up tighter than brand-new rope on a bed frame. I'm worried about the man who falls in love with you."

Mary smiled and nuzzled her chin into the sleeve of her father's jacket. "I'm so happy, Father. This day couldn't get any better."

Her father kissed the side of her head and said, "Oh, just you wait, dear. Cora has a fine New Year's meal planned for us this evening."

Mary pulled away from her father's embrace, bounced up and down on her heals then said, "I've got to write to Liza." Leaving the room, she stopped in the doorway and turned back around. "And don't forget to write to Uncle Richard."

William Floyd, shook his head, let out a short laugh and said, "Nay, I won't forget."

∞∞∞∞∞∞∞∞∞∞∞∞

    Three weeks later, Mary stood taking in the sights and sounds of her uncle's birthday party. The formal gowns donned by the women looked more regal than anything Mary had seen before. Tall vases of flowers sat elegantly on tables; the smell of cooked goose filled the room as did the familiar sweet smoke of her uncle's pipe. The birthday festivities held excitement for Mary, and her eyes grew big as she watched her sister twirl on the dance floor. Her brother was on his best behavior, and Mary thought she should warn some of the young ladies that he was a stinker, but she was in too good a mood for that. She was standing near the hallway that led to the kitchen, hoping to catch sight of Liza.

    Her sister had given Mary her old stays and a dress that didn't quite fit Kitty anymore. The stays caused a tremendous tightness around her ribs, but Mary knew in order to wear a lovely gown, she must get used to the discomfort and learn to breathe slowly and steadily. Her mother had given her a pair of gloves and a small pouch-like purse that dangled from her wrist. Mary hadn't known what to put inside the purse, so she had tucked in the handkerchief Benjamin Tallmadge had given her years ago. And her mother had bought her a new ribbon and loaned her a gold locket to put on it. The ribbon matched the blue trim of the gown she wore, and the locket settled in the hollow of her neck. These new items made Mary feel quite grown-up.

    Every few beats, Mary's eyes darted from the dance floor toward the kitchen; she was determined to catch Liza walking past. Grand-looking servers in fine suits passed her with trays. Everything smelled wonderful. One server walked close, and Mary recognized him.

    "Cecil!" she called.

    He turned and smiled at Mary.

"Mary, it's good to see you. When did you arrive?"

"A few hours ago. We got here just before the guests began to arrive. But we are staying a few days. I got to come with my brother and sister."

Cecil lowered the tray he was carrying in front of Mary so she could choose something from it. Everything was tiny and bite-sized. Some were topped with rosemary, or maybe it was thyme; Mary wasn't sure. After she took one, she looked at Cecil with uncertainty.

"Just pop it into your mouth, and chew quickly," he said.

Mary almost choked trying to swallow it, and when another server walked past with a tray of small glasses filled with a dark liquid, Cecil took one and handed it to Mary. After taking a sip, she made a sour face.

"Ewww, that's so bitter. And the other was not good either."

"Sorry 'bout that. That was port; the other was fish eggs. I need to take this tray around. I got to keep the guests happy." Cecil smiled and turned to leave.

"Wait," Mary called after him. "Have you seen Liza?"

"I did see her, but she's been out on the back porch washing dishes. Master Floyd has more guests here than plates and forks."

Mary nodded and let Cecil get back to work. Then she decided to sneak outside to find Liza. Mary squeezed her way through the many guests who were dancing and others who were talking with each other. Quickly, she made her way to the front of the house and out the door, then she took off in a sprint around to the back. There on the porch, Liza was sitting on a stool between two large tubs filled with water. Underneath one of the large tubs was a small fire to heat the water. Mary watched as Liza washed glasses and plates in one tub, which was filled with soapy water, then set them into the other tub where the water was clear.

"Liza!" Mary called.

Liza looked up, shocked to hear her name. Then she recognized Mary running toward her. Liza stood and wiped her hands on her apron. The two girls collided, holding on to one another like they'd never let go. When Liza pulled away, she looked at Mary and said,

"Mercy, you've grown over these last three and a half years, sure enough." Liza shook her head in disbelief. "It's good to see you."

"I'm glad it worked out that we could be in the same place again. And that Uncle Richard was willing to ask Mr. Townsend for a favor. I'm just so glad you're here!" Mary bounced a little on her heels with excitement.

Well, I'll be out here until I get these washed up. Then Lotty will need me in the kitchen when it's time to get the supper and the cake ready." Liza chuckled. "Heck, they even got Cecil dressed up and walking around with fancy trays tonight."

"I saw Cecil. He told me where I could find you."

Liza smiled, sat back down on the stool, and started scrubbing another dish.

"Well," Mary said. "Doesn't he look handsome tonight?"

Liza gave Mary a bashful look. "I suppose he does."

Just then, two riders approached the house from the far-left side. Mary peeked around to see them as their horses came to a trot, heading to the hitching post and water trough. As Mary looked carefully, she thought one of the figures looked familiar, but it was too dark to really see.

"You better go back inside and enjoy the party," Liza told her. "Soon they'll seat everyone for supper."

"How are they going to do that? There are seventy people in there," Mary said.

"I think Lotty told me there were fifty-eight invited." Liza laughed. "It probably seems like more. There's going to be a surprise outside in a few minutes. Master Floyd's son told us about it, and when everyone is outside, we're going to add more chairs and tables to the dining room. It will wind all the way through into the next room. That's why I got to get all these dishes washed. Master Floyd had to borrow some from the neighbors up the road. His new wife had some dishes with her when they married. But they were still afraid they were gonna need more."

"All right, I'll see you later then." Mary bent down and hugged Liza again, careful not to get water on her dress. Then she stepped off the porch to make her way around to the front of the house.

"You look beautiful tonight, Mary," she heard Liza say as she turned the corner.

The two men she'd seen ride up to the house had just finished tying up their horses and were walking up the front steps. Could it be? Mary thought. She'd have to get much closer in order to find out. Careful not to draw attention to herself, Mary snuck back inside while the two gentlemen were being greeted by Uncle Richard's wife, Elizabeth.

The men then made their way through the crowds toward the far side of the room where they stopped to watch the dancing. Mary watched as they chatted with another guest, and when one turned his head just so, Mary knew in an instant it was Benjamin Tallmadge. My, how he'd grown so much taller and more handsome too. His dark hair was pulled into a short ponytail at the back of his neck and tied with a black ribbon. Mary's stomach did a somersault, and she felt like the breath had left her lungs. Once she gathered herself, she had to figure out a way to speak with him. She was curious after all.

A moment later, the other Benjamin, her cousin, tapped on a glass to gather everyone's attention. Soon the musicians stopped playing and the crowds turned to Benjamin Floyd. Mary had only met her cousin a few times, and that was years ago. He was much older than Mary and her siblings. After getting married, he had taken over most of Uncle Richard's business operations, even expanding some of them into Oyster Bay—or so Mary had heard.

"Greetings!" he began. "I'd like to thank you all on behalf of myself and my family. We are honored you are here to celebrate this momentous occasion as my father turns sixty. I have something special planned before we sit and enjoy our meal. So if you would indulge me, please head out the door and around to the back."

Murmuring and whispers erupted as the crowd made their way into the hallway and out through the door. Mary found Kitty and walked with her outside. After Benjamin Floyd led them toward a field along the back of the house, Mary was startled when a sound like a gunshot rang out. She took hold of Kitty's arm and gripped it tightly. But then to everyone's amazement, colorful explosions appeared in the winter sky; pops of gold and red rained down like water, but they looked like fire. Mary let go of Kitty's arm and drew her hand to her mouth as she took a breath and held it in astonishment.

"Isn't it beautiful, Kitty?" she asked.

"It is. It truly is the most wonderful thing ever," Kitty said.

After the glorious fireworks show, her cousin Benjamin led the crowd back to the front of the house, and they made their way inside and into the dining room. Mary hesitated as she searched the crowds for Benjamin Tallmadge.

"Make haste," Kitty called to her from several feet ahead. "I'm anxious to see who I'll be sitting next to."

Mary caught up with Kitty as they walked inside. There, she saw not only the large dining room table that usually sat fourteen, but more tables had been added, creating an "*L*" shape that continued into the next room. Small name cards sat at each table setting, and mismatched candlesticks were ablaze, casting a brilliant glow down the center of each table.

Mary found her name near the very end of the joined tables and noticed most of the older guests had been seated in the original dining room. Next to her, at the very end of the table, was her cousin Benjamin, and across from her was her brother. Nicoll was seated next to a girl who was probably Kitty's age. Next to the girl was Kitty, and on the other side of Kitty was—

"Oh." It slipped out of Mary's mouth before she realized she'd said something. Seated next to her sister was Benjamin Tallmadge.

Suddenly, Mary felt hot. Her stays felt even more uncomfortable. And she was a bit angry too. What would Kitty talk to him about? She had to find a way to speak with him herself. About what, she didn't know, but she was determined she would figure something out.

All through dinner her cousin engaged Mary in small talk. Not wanting to seem boring, she talked with him about the animals on her farm, including the sheep and cows. She told him about her favorite horse and the books she'd read. But Mary also kept her eye on Kitty and watched as she flirted with Benjamin Tallmadge. At least it would be easy later for Mary to find out all about their conversation—since Kitty was somewhat of a braggart.

When it seemed that supper was coming to a close, her cousin stood and made a toast to his father. Soon everyone was standing with their wine glasses in hand as Cecil strolled in carrying a large cake glowing with what looked like a hundred candles. Cecil walked slowly into the next room where Mary couldn't see him, but she figured the cake would be placed in front of Uncle Richard and that soon everyone would get a slice.

Not long after everyone finished their cake, a string quartet began to play a lively tune, and a few gentlemen led ladies onto the dance floor. Mary watched her brother offer his arm to the young lady he'd been sitting next to, and they began dancing. Benjamin and Kitty continued talking, but instead of taking Kitty's hand for a dance, Benjamin gave her a short bow. Mary watched Benjamin approach a man and greet him as "Colonel Nathanial Woodhull." They spoke for several minutes, and the friend Benjamin had come in with joined the conversation before they made their way to Uncle Richard.

They must be getting ready to leave, Mary thought. Now or never, she decided. She squeezed through the crowds and dancers and made her way through to the front door. By the time she got to the bottom step, Benjamin Tallmadge and his friend were at their horses.

"Mr. Tallmadge," Mary almost shouted.

He turned toward her and waited as she approached.

"I, um, I . . ." There had been no time to plan what to say. She thought quickly and opened the velvet pouch on her left wrist.

"Here," she said, handing over the white handkerchief. "I washed it."

The other man was gathering the reigns for his horse, about to put his foot in the stirrup, when Benjamin said, "Hold on, Abraham."

Benjamin walked closer and took the handkerchief from her. After glancing at it, he looked into Mary's eyes. "Mary Floyd?" he asked.

Mary nodded. "Yes. Father read your letter to us back in the fall, when he told us you'd just graduated from Yale. Father was always glad to hear from you. He said you have plans to teach school in a town in Connecticut."

"Yes, that's right. Soon, I'll be in a town called Wethersfield preparing students for college." He handed the handkerchief back to Mary. "Keep it. It seems you've taken good care of it over the years. And grown into a fine young lady." His light brown eyes seemed to shine in the light from the full moon, sending tingles all the way down to Mary's toes. "It was good to see you again, Mary, and your sister too this evening. Please give your father my regards."

With that he turned to his friend Abraham, who had been waiting for him, and began to gather the reigns to his horse.

"Wait," Mary called. "Could I write to you?"

"Pardon?"

"Well, if you were to write to Father, maybe I could add a letter with his reply. I remember Father reading in your letter about how you might be lonely, not knowing anyone in your new town. I love getting letters. They make me feel better if I've had a bad day."

Benjamin smiled. He let out a short laugh then said, "Of course. Good evening, Mary Floyd." And with that, he climbed onto the saddle and rode off.

8
Late January, 1774

Mary talked her uncle into allowing her to ride to Oyster Bay with Liza and Jeb as long as Nicoll agreed to go with them. Mary was hoping to personally thank Mr. Townsend for allowing Liza to be a part of their lives over the years. Even though Liza had come to Uncle Richard's originally to help Mary's mother with baby Lucas, Mary had been grateful she had gotten to know Liza years ago before her baby brother died. Now, once again, Mary felt gratitude to Samuel Townsend for allowing Liza to help out at Uncle Richard's estate. Mary was more than grateful for Liza's friendship. She always listened to Mary, whether Mary was lamenting or dreaming or wishing or going on and on about something she knew her sister would find completely unimportant. Mary believed Liza to be her truest friend.

During the carriage ride, Mary shared with Liza that she had seen Benjamin Tallmadge at the party the evening before. She whispered it to Liza because Nicoll was sitting across from them inside the carriage, and she thought he might only be pretending to be asleep.

"He was sitting next to Kitty at dinner." Mary continued to whisper the story into Liza's ear. "It made me very jealous. So I decided that I just had to talk to him before he left. When I saw that he and his friend were getting ready to leave—oh, I think his friend is called Abraham— anyhow, when they set out to leave, I found him next to his horse and I got his attention."

Liza pulled away from Mary and stared at her for a moment before she spoke. "I swanny, what was you thinkin'?"

Nervously, Mary glanced over at Nicoll, hoping Liza's words wouldn't disturb him. Satisfied, Mary leaned back into Liza, cupping her hand around Liza's ear. "I took out the handkerchief—the one he'd given me a long time ago—and handed it to him. I told him that Father always enjoyed his letters, and I asked to write to him, and he was agreeable."

Liza shook her head and made a tsking sound. "If I ain't heard it from you, I don't know if I'd believe it or not. But I suppose I've knowed you long enough to know you will do what you gonna do." She chuckled. "So, what you gonna say when you write to him?"

Mary shrugged. "Don't know yet. I asked Kitty what they talked about at dinner. She said it was about Yale mostly. And Benjamin asked her what her favorite book was. And he asked if she'd read any of the classics. Of course, Kitty said no. But I'm going to ask Father about them, and I will read them so that I can write to Benjamin about how much I enjoy reading the classics."

Liza burst into laughter at that, which woke Nicoll. He scowled at the two of them, which caused Mary and Liza to giggle even more.

Soon the carriage arrived in front of a large white saltbox house with a covered front porch. As Mary, Liza, and Nicoll stepped out of the carriage, they left footprints in the snow, which had started to fall heavily. Jeb took the horses and carriage to the stables while the others made their way inside the house.

As soon as Liza stepped inside, a girl about Kitty's age ran to her.

"Liza, you're back."

Liza nodded and turned to Mary. "Phebe, this is Nicoll and Mary Floyd. Two of the children in the family I've helped with over the years in Brookhaven and Mastic."

Nicoll looked at Phebe. "I'm almost seventeen, ma'am," he interjected.

Phebe smiled at Nicoll, and her words bubbled out of her. "Welcome to you both. Liza has said so many wonderful things about your family. It's so nice to finally meet you."

She escorted them further into the parlor, where Mr. Townsend met them.

"Welcome," he said. "I'm Samuel Townsend. It seems the weather has taken quite a turn. You're welcome to stay here for the night rather than trying to head back to Brookhaven in a snowstorm."

Just then a teenage boy about the same age as Nicoll appeared. Mr. Townsend introduced him as his son David. Another girl came into the room and was introduced as Sally.

"It's nice to meet you both." Sally greeted Mary and Nicoll, then turned her attention to Liza. "I'm glad you're home. We've all missed your cinnamon cookies. I dared to make some the other day," she said.

Phebe and David giggled, remembering the odd-looking cookies their sister had made.

"It's good to be home," Liza agreed. "I'll go see if Susannah needs any help in the kitchen, and I'll bring out some tea."

When Liza left, Mr. Townsend's wife, Sarah came down the staircase.

"I see we have company," she said. And Mr. Townsend began the introductions. Mrs. Townsend took Mary's hand in hers and told her how nice it was to finally meet the Mary Liza loved so dearly.

Mrs. Townsend asked them to be seated, and Mary and Nicoll sat down with her on the couch. Mr. Townsend sat in a tall chair near the fire. David walked to the fireplace and added another log. Phebe sat at a table, and Sally joined her. Sally told the guests about her father's work as a merchant, adding that her older brother, Robert, took care of most of the business from a shop located in Hanover Square in New York City. The shop sold items that their father's shipping business brought into the colonies.

The sun was setting, and the room grew dark. Soon, only the glow of the roaring fire gave any light. Susannah, a tall, thin, older black woman came around and lit two candles, and Liza came in with a tray of tea and cookies.

"Supper will be ready shortly," Liza said, setting the tray on a table near the window.

Later, during their meal, Mary couldn't help but notice her brother talking to David about his riding skills and how fast his horse could go. Then he went on and on about the biggest fish he'd caught. Mary knew he was trying to impress Phebe, who did engage with Nicoll a time or two. Mary was much more interested in hearing Mr. Townsend talk about how his ships sailed to foreign places in order to bring goods into the colonies for shop owners to sell.

Mr. Townsend turned to Mary and Nicoll and said, "I'll send my best rider to Brookhaven tomorrow with word letting your uncle know you're safe. As long as this snow keeps falling like it is tonight, it'll be a few days before the carriage will be able to make it back."

Mary nodded, and Nicoll said, "Thank you, sir. We appreciate your hospitality and the food."

"Of course," Mr. Townsend said. "Your family has taken such good care of Liza over the years; it's the least I could do. Anything you need at any time, our family is here for you."

Nicoll smiled, and Mary felt grateful for new friends—and even more thankful she could have extra time with Liza. They could read together, and Mary could even help Liza practice writing words, something they'd only had time to start on. During their correspondence, Mary had mailed Liza the alphabet and some practice pages. Then when they met again, Liza had been proud to show her work to Mary.

∞∞∞∞∞∞∞∞∞∞

Two days later, the sun was shining brightly, and the snow had begun to melt. Jeb had been staying in the cabins in the far back part of the property, where Liza said the slave cabins were. After breakfast, Liza led Mary and Nicoll out toward the small cabin where Jeb was. An older man came to the door, and Nicoll asked to speak with Jeb.

"Jeb, I believe the snow's melted," Nicoll explained. "Best to get the horses ready for travel."

Jeb nodded. "Yes'ir, I'll get to it."

When they turned to head back to the main house, Mary took Liza's hand. "Keep writing to me through Mr. Townsend's correspondence," she said. "Or even through Phebe's. If she writes to my brother, add your letter with hers."

Liza smiled at Mary. "I'll be proud to."

Together, they walked into the kitchen, and Liza began to pack Mary, Nicoll, and Jeb some food for the trip. Later, when the team was hitched and the carriage was waiting at the front of the house, it was time to say goodbye to the family Mary had grown so fond of. Mary said goodbye to Sally and

Phebe with brief hugs. Then she turned to David and said goodbye before reaching for Liza.

"I'll miss you the most," she said.

Mr. and Mrs. Townsend shook hands with Nicoll as Mary stepped up into the carriage and scooted next to the window. Mary watched from the carriage window until she couldn't see the house anymore.

9

September, 1774, Wethersfield Connecticut

Benjamin was beginning to adjust to his new environment. He had taken up residence in the town's late Presbyterian minister's home, which was known as Lockwood House. The house stood next to a building called Hospitality Hall, which was the scene of many social events in town. Benjamin had made the acquaintance of many prominent members of this community, including Silas Dean, a Yale graduate, lawyer, and prominent merchant. He also befriended a young businessman, named Jeremiah Wadsworth. On many a night, Benjamin found himself enjoying the town's social gatherings and flirting with its most attractive young ladies. On some days, teaching made him weary, and letters from his dear friend, Nathan Hale, who always signed them "Pythias," lightened his mood tremendously.

One morning, Benjamin wrote back.

The Reception of your Epistle has sensibly increased my happiness, as perhaps any on accidental circumstances which hath happened to me since my first arrival. Although my company and present condition is far from tending to melancholy and dullness, yet in a place where few intimate friends, or even acquaintance are at first to be found; that absolute contentedness of mind which is so necessary to true happiness is not so readily obtained. But perhaps I am more than commonly delighted with the perusal of such friendly epistles. Indeed, I know of no one circumstance which would tend more directly to make me contented in any particular place than the correspondence which I should hope to maintain with some of my most intimate friends. That which has for some time subsisted between you and myself, I desire may never have an end . . . yet I hope you will by no means suffer your pen to be in dullness . . . so long as you can both be contributory to my advantage and happiness.

But in such company of the ladies of Wethersfield we have not only the advantage of friendly intercourse . . . but it may also be rendered very useful and instructive—the female part of this place, you have often heard, is very agreeable.

Yours, Damon

Benjamin folded the letter, then took his pin from his lapel—the one the members of Linonia had crafted and worn during their years at Yale. After heating some wax, he placed the pin in the center to seal the missive with the mark of friendship. He got up from his desk and gathered his coat and hat and made his way down the street in the cool September morning air to the place where he received and sent out his posts. Upon entering the shop, he ran into Silas Dean.

"Ah, Benjamin," Silas greeted him. "What say you, young man?"

"Good morning, Silas. Just leaving a letter and gathering any posts I might have on my way to the school."

"Well, I implore you to join me at the tavern on Main Street tonight. Others will also be in attendance. I'm leaving for Philadelphia in the morning. The First Continental Congress has been scheduled. Twelve of the colonies will be represented. I don't know how long I'll be away."

"I see," said Benjamin. "I'll be very interested to meet you tonight."

∞∞∞∞∞∞∞

Later that evening, Benjamin made his way from the schoolhouse to the local tavern in the heart of Wethersfield. There, he found a man barring entrance to the front door.

"State your name," the man instructed.

"Benjamin Tallmadge."

The man moved and allowed Benjamin to step inside. The room was filled with men's voices that were loud, boisterous, and excited. He walked into the crowded room and soon, Silas and Jeremiah noticed him and called him over.

"Gentleman," Silas said. "This is young Benjamin Tallmadge, the schoolmaster and school superintendent. A fine Yale graduate, a good Presbyterian, and a Whig."

Several men reached out and shook Benjamin's hand, welcoming him into the group. Others raised their pints of ale in recognition. Benjamin found a seat, and soon Jeremiah called the meeting to order. Then Silas began his explanation of the importance of the first meeting of the Continental Congress in Philadelphia.

"We shall be meeting behind locked doors in Carpenter's Hall," Silas said. "I don't know how long I'll be away. But I do plan to send a missive stating the conclusions from the debate. I'm curious to know what ideas I might share from you with the other delegates. For we must exchange ideas in order to organize ourselves as a unit against the power by which we feel we've been held hostage."

A man stood up and said, "We shouldn't pay Britain back for the tea. I say, we ban imports from Britain. The king's idea of closing off the Boston port and bringing the colony under even more British control calls for denouncement. I say we join with Massachusetts, help them out with the goods they can no longer receive because of this unfair taxation and British rule. The royal governor doesn't represent the colonies."

Another stood and said, "My family has been living here since the year 1636. My grandfather was one of the founders of this city. We've done fine until now. The king has no right to take away our rights, tax us, or keep our businesses from thriving. We've no need of him."

Benjamin spoke up. "I agree we should unite the colonies in order to stand against Britain. I also agree we should ban all trade between the colonies and Britain. It will only be through solidarity that we have any chance against the most powerful country in the world."

Silas asked, "And what if these proposals from the congressional delegates bring war?"

Several gentlemen stood and cheered, while others banged their canes on the wood floor.

When the jarring cheers died down, a man in a back corner said, "Any attack against one colony is the same as an attack against us all. We shall fight for our liberties."

"Hear, hear," the rest of the group shouted.

When Benjamin left the meeting, he felt unsure of what results might come from the Continental Congress, but he knew in his heart it was right to stand up to England against their unfair rules and taxes. He would stand with his fellow colonists in support no matter what that might mean for their future.

10

September, 1774, Mastic Long Island

  A fox scurried across the field in front of the house, and Mary's dog, Moses, ran after it, barking the whole way. Mary, who had come outside to see her father off, watched Jeb steer the horses and carriage from the stables toward the house. A moment ago, she had stopped by her father's study to see him packing papers and quills into a bag. Her mother was with Cora in the kitchen preparing a basket of food for her father and Jeb for their trip to Philadelphia. A few weeks ago, her father had told them about the meeting of the First Continental Congress, which was to be held on September 5 for delegates from all the colonies except for one. Father had told them Georgia was to remain on the side of the king.

  Mary's father explained that Georgia had opted out for various reasons, the main one being they still wanted Britain's protection from the Indians. And the goods coming into their shops and towns from England had made their colony quite wealthy. Mary's father had told her the Georgians didn't want to upset the applecart or bite the hand that fed them.

  Now her mother and father stepped out onto the porch where Mary was sitting, followed by Nicoll and Kitty.

Her mother gave her father a kiss, then Mr. Floyd hugged Kitty. He next turned to Nicoll. "You're in charge; do me proud, son," he said. "I don't know how long I'll be away, but expect a letter from me soon. I'll keep you as up-to-date as I can."

Nicoll nodded then hugged his father.

When Mary stood, her father smiled at her. "My dear Mary," he said. "I will miss our evening talks while I'm away, but you can write to me." He turned to look at her siblings. "All of you may write to me."

"Father, what will you do while you're in Philadelphia?" Mary asked.

"Will there be any grand balls to attend?" Kitty added.

Her father shook his head. "I don't know about any grand balls, Kitty. I do know that what we as delegates will be discussing and the decisions to be made will be very serious. The consensus after deliberation will hopefully leave us prepared to negotiate peacefully with the king."

"What would be the worst that could happen, Father?" Nicoll asked.

"War with England," their father answered. "A result we hope would lead us to the freedoms and liberties we as Americans are entitled to. And justice when it comes to the rules Parliament holds us to."

"Freedom, liberty, and justice," Mary repeated. "Oh, Father, I hope it ends satisfactorily." Mary threw her arms around her father and held on, lingering for a moment.

William Floyd looked at his daughter. His eyes held a vision of hope fused with concern.

"Freedom offers up many choices," he said. "It allows for a keen sense of awareness of what might be most beneficial and brings with it responsibilities." He turned toward Nicoll and Kitty and continued. "Freedom is also the ability to accept all outcomes without blaming others or life circumstance, or luck. The amount of freedom one might experience could be based on the degree of responsibility one takes with the liberty they are offered, and together with fairness, equality, and justice come the values of freedom. A greedy king an ocean away should not have the right to say that some should have more than others. Instead, there should be a choice for a man who owns his land, produces his own crop, and makes his own way. A choice to live free, to enjoy liberty, and hold justice with great esteem, that is what is hoped for."

William's children nodded, then Nicoll spoke,

"So our liberties could be abused by those in power. But if the congress is not able to win the dispute with the king and if we were to go to war and win, we might forever be free?"

"Aye, son, but the price of that freedom is continued vigilance. It is not a right bestowed upon us by man; instead it is of Divine Providence."

Hannah Floyd moved toward her husband. Mary stepped away and stood next to Nicoll, and Kitty.

"It's time to get going, William," Hannah said. "Remember, you need to be in Brooklyn tomorrow to collect Simon. You both need to be in Philadelphia on time."

"You are correct, my love. I shan't make Mr. Boerum or myself late."

Mary took hold of her mother's hand as the four of them watched her father enter the carriage. The words he had spoken about freedoms, liberties, and justice now resonated in her heart and made their home in her memories. When the carriage was out of sight, they all went inside and sat at the table for breakfast.

"I'd like to go to Philadelphia," Mary said. She picked up a biscuit and added some jam, then set it on her plate. "I'd want to hear what all the delegates have to say."

"They're going to say, take a stand against Britain," Nicoll said. "Show them we won't tolerate unfair taxes and treatment. We don't want to be told what to do by some king an ocean away."

"I bet there are fine balls in Philadelphia," Kitty added. "Really grand." She looked up dreamily.

Mary tried to see what Kitty was staring at, which seemed to be nothing but air.

"I wonder," Kitty continued, "how long will Father really be gone. How could we find out if there will be any balls going on while he's there?"

Their mother shushed Kitty, but Mary decided that if Kitty planned to attend a ball in Philadelphia, Mary would most certainly not be left out of that.

∞∞∞∞∞∞∞∞∞∞

Mary snuck out of the house before dawn and headed out to the barn, where she saddled her favorite horse, the one she called Spot. She was a beautiful chestnut mare with a white streak between her ears and muzzle. Mary softly ran her hand along Spot's left flank before placing her foot into the stirrup. Then the horse trotted slowly out of the stable before Mary nudged her with both heels, and the horse took off at a fast gallop.

Mary slowed Spot down as they approached the oak next to Lucas's grave. Then she brought the horse to a stop and climbed down, leaving Spot to graze. She climbed over the short fence surrounding the grave and sat down next to the tall wooden cross that had Lucas's name carved into it along with the dates of his birth and death.

It had been three weeks since they'd heard from her father. Their last correspondence from him had come in a package. Included were new ribbons for Kitty, a knife for Nicoll, and two books for Mary. Mary had been glad to receive *The Iliad* and *The Odyssey,* both by Homer, but she desperately wanted to know what was taking place inside Carpenter's Hall in Philadelphia; she was especially concerned about her father's interest and place in the congress. Were things going as well as he would like? As she sat in the grass next to her baby brother's grave, she began to pray for her father, for what she was unaware of, and what possibilities the future might hold for the state of their colony.

Mary's prayer began, "Mighty God, be with Father and the other delegates in Philadelphia so they might make the best decisions for our future. Oh, God, I don't understand everything that has taken place in Boston or those things that have now caused Father to be away, but I do want what's best. I trust you, God, to lead Father and the others to know what to do. And please let us hear from Father soon. Amen."

Mary climbed back over the fence and walked to a place near the woods where a cluster of Queen Anne's Lace was growing. She used her strength to pluck the stubborn but beautiful weeds from the ground then walked back to the gravesite and laid them across the stone at the base of the wooden cross.

"Bye, baby Lucas. I'll see you later," she said before gathering Spot's reins and stepping into the stirrup.

Mary kept Spot to a slow pace, as she watched the sun rise over the horizon. When she got closer to the house, she could see a rider coming up the road with his horse at a fast trot. Her dog, Moses, was running after him and followed as the rider made his way up to the house.

"Woe, Spot," Mary said and pulled back on the reins. She waited and watched as the rider got closer to the house. When he stopped and got down from his horse, she recognized that it was her cousin, Benjamin Floyd, and she began to fear the worst. She squeezed her legs to signal Spot forward and the horse was soon galloping at full speed toward the house.

By the time Mary got to the front of the house, Benjamin had already been escorted inside, and Moses was lying by the front step. Quickly, she tied Spot to the hitching post next to Benjamin's handsome black stallion, who was drinking deeply from the trough. She ran up the front steps and quickly swung the front door open, causing it to hit the wall with a loud thump.

"Mary, what on earth?" asked her mother, who was standing with Benjamin in the foyer.

Benjamin turned around to look at Mary. He bowed slightly and smiled, but her mother's look was fierce.

"Sorry, Mama," Mary said.

Her mother shook her head, then led Benjamin into the main room and asked him to have a seat.

Cora walked in from the kitchen.

"What can I get for you, Master Benjamin?" she asked.

"Coffee, if you please."

"And bring some biscuits," Mary's mother added.

Seeing as how her mother hadn't told Mary to leave, Mary sat down on the stool next to the fireplace and waited on Benjamin to explain his sudden visit.

"The reason I've come," he began, "is that I wanted to make sure you are aware of how the meetings in Philadelphia are progressing. It's been brought to my attention that the discussions are taking longer than expected. There's been a bit of a standstill. As you know, some members of the delegation are wanting to side with Great Britain, while others are talking about committing treason."

With that, Mary's mother took in a deep breath.

Nicoll walked into the room and asked, "Treason?"

Benjamin looked up at Nicoll, then he turned to look at Mary's mother.

"I believe I know which position my husband has taken, Benjamin, and we stand by him. We believe in having our freedom."

Benjamin nodded. "I know," he said. "I received correspondence from him yesterday. The missive was dated three days ago. I thought I might have the most current information and wanted to tell you in person."

Cora approached with a pot of coffee, cups, and biscuits on a tray. She sat the tray down on a table in front of Hannah and began to pour coffee into the cups.

"I also wanted you to know where I personally stand," Benjamin added. "I favor the King."

Mary heard Nicoll take in a breath. He was standing behind Benjamin but facing his mother and Mary.

"For now," Benjamin continued. "I believe it best to allow England's rule over the colonies. I feel it gives us much security."

Cora handed Benjamin a cup of coffee and a small plate with a biscuit. He accepted it and told her thank you before taking a sip.

By that time, Kitty had made her way downstairs.

"I thought we might have guests," she said.

Benjamin stood and greeted Kitty. "It's lovely to see you again, Miss Kitty. I was just bringing news to your mother about the talks and goings-on at Carpenter's Hall in Philadelphia."

"Oooh, wonderful," Kitty said. "Have you heard about any grand balls? I should love to attend one."

Benjamin cleared his throat and looked at Mary's mother. "I'm sorry. I have not."

"That's not why Cousin Benjamin has come," Mary's mother said. "Why don't you stay for breakfast, Benjamin? We were just about to sit down and eat. It would do you good before you have to make the journey back to Brookhaven."

"That's very kind of you," Benjamin said.

"Son," Hannah told Nicoll, "take Benjamin's horse to the stable and have one of the hands give him some hay."

"Yes, ma'am." Nicoll left the room and went out the front door.

Mary saw that Cora was setting bacon, eggs, gravy, and biscuits on the table in the dining room. When Cora was done, she walked into the main room and said, "Breakfast is ready."

After they were seated, Benjamin asked to say a blessing. Hannah nodded, so he led them in a short prayer of thanksgiving. Soon, Nicoll was back and made his way into the dining room to join them.

"Mother," Kitty said, "if we can't go to Philadelphia, could we at least host a dance and a party here? Our house is grand enough for a party. It could be a masquerade ball. Fall is almost here. Please, Mother. We could invite family from Brookhaven too." Kitty smiled at Benjamin.

Benjamin glanced at Mary's mother, who sat stirring her coffee as if the cup held more interest than those who sat next to her.

"Nicoll and Mary could help with the decorations," Kitty continued. "The newspaper told stories of Pope Night celebrations held in Boston in early November. Remember, Nicoll? You read stories from the paper about the costumes they wore. And how they would go door to door asking for treats."

"A Pope Night celebration—with a bonfire, costumes, and treats?" Nicoll asked. "I don't know. I have work to do in the field with the herd. I have crops to gather, and I have to keep on top of the help, letting them know, they can't slack off while Father is away. There's no time for parties."

"But, mother," Kitty urged. "We don't know when Father will return."

With that, their mother finally removed her spoon from her coffee and set it on the table, then looked from Nicoll to Kitty. "We won't have any type of raucous celebration with a theme inspired by a rebellious mob. We may not agree with Parliament or the King's treatment of the colonies, but we don't need to host a party in protest."

"Mother, it would only be a fall celebration," Kitty pleaded. "It's only rebellious if it happens in Boston. Here, a Pope Night celebration would just be harmless fun."

Benjamin spoke up. "A party is always a good way to create and expand political or economic interests. You might find a time when you need a neighbor." He chuckled. "Let's say one with certain connections. A hospitable social gathering is always a good way to remain on friendly terms with your guests. But maybe not one with the theme of a rebellious Pope Night. Either way, what's happening now gives us pause and brings much uncertainty, and welcoming others into your home, regardless of which side they might stand for, should bring some form of unity."

Mary's mother took in a deep breath and nodded. "We'll see what we can put together in the coming weeks. Cousin Benjamin might be right; a masquerade ball might be just the thing we need during so much uncertainty."

11

October 31, 1774, Wethersfield Connecticut

Benjamin's letter from Silas Dean was still folded in his hand. After reading it he'd known there would be no turning back. What England would decide to do from here would determine the future of the colonies. The missive had arrived yesterday, and was dated October 26, the final day of the gathering of delegates in Philadelphia. Benjamin knew Silas would be home soon, and a meeting would be called at the town's tavern.

Benjamin placed the letter in the drawer of his desk, then pulled from the drawer a single sheet of paper. For several moments he stared at the blank page. He ran his hands through his hair, and with a sigh, he leaned back in his chair. He was full of emotion, and his mind was filled with heavy thoughts about the brewing war with England. Oh, how he wished he could have a long talk with Nathan and his friends the way he once did at Yale, or even speak with his older brother, William. Instead, he looked back at the empty page and picked up his quill. Soon his thoughts turned into words as he began to pen a letter to his old friend and roommate.

I consider our country a land flowing with milk & honey, holding open her arms, and demanding, assistance from all who can assist in her sore distress. A Christian's counsel must favor the latter. Before a commanding officer can deploy us and bestow upon us orders, we are first subject to our Holy and Just God. We are bound by God's will and his Holy word. Because without God's guidance how could we best serve our cause to the best of our abilities. For our holy religion, the honor of our God, a glorious country and happy constitution is what we have to defend. We shall all be ready to step forth in the common cause.

Later that evening, after Benjamin had penned letters to Nathan; his brother, William; and his father, he made his way to the tavern on Main Street. Once again, outside the door was a man standing guard.

"Your name, sir?" he asked.

"Benjamin Tallmadge."

The man moved aside to let Benjamin pass. Upon entering the tavern, Benjamin sensed the mood was more subdued, calmer, than before, and maybe even fearful. Looking around the crowded tavern, he found a seat at the end of a table and waited.

Soon, Jeremiah Wadsworth called the meeting to order.

"As you know we've gathered to hear the news from the delegation in Philadelphia," he said. "After two months, there has been a resolution."

Silas made his way through the door, in a rush. Quickly, he walked to the center of the room. A negro man who had come in with him, took Silas's coat and hat and placed them on a chair. Silas opened a small trunk and removed some papers from within. The room was silent as Silas cleared his throat, and Benjamin could feel his muscles tense with anticipation. Silas looked at the papers in his hand and began to read.

"The First Continental Congress held a meeting of delegates from twelve of the thirteen colonies to respond to Parliament's punitive Intolerable Acts, and coercive actions." Silas looked around the room. With his next statement, he confidently raised his voice. "And therefore signed the Articles of Association. Together we worked to create a common plan, and our intentions are as follows: to stop all importation of goods from Great Britain beginning on December 1, 1774, unless Parliament should rescind the Intolerable Acts. And on December 1, 1774, there will be a nonimportation of slaves." Murmuring broke out among the crowd in attendance.

Silas continued, "Committees of observation and inspection are to be formed within each colony to ensure compliance. If Britain fails to repeal the Intolerable Acts; we will no longer export goods to Britain after September 10, 1775. This Congress has agreed to meet again in May. It is hoped that by then, Georgia will have decided to join us."

Silas handed the papers to Jeremiah, who took them to the entrance. The tavern owner met him at the door with a hammer and nails, and together they posted the declaration to the outside of the tavern for public view. The crowd in the room began to talk among themselves.

Silas made his way over to where Benjamin was sitting.

"Ah, Benjamin Tallmadge, my dear boy," he said. "It's good to see you again. Aye, it's good to finally be home again as well."

Benjamin offered Silas a seat next to him. "So, it appears things went well, and good things were accomplished in Philadelphia," he said.

"Nay. It took almost two months. Every day for hours on end. The delegates were divided, I tell you. Some wanted to appease the king." Silas leaned in close to Benjamin. "But Samuel Adams, Patrick Henry, Roger Sherman, and John Adams believed the task at hand was to devise a statement of the rights and liberties of the colonies. With the ultimate goal being to end the abuses of parliamentary authority and to retain the rights which were guaranteed under colonial charters and the English constitution." In a whisper, Silas added, "Those four men deny the authority of Parliament. And believe Congress needs to develop a completely new system of government, independent from Great Britain." Silas rapped his fingers on the table. "Independence from England."

Benjamin knew those words would by some be considered treason.

Silas said, "The delegation will convene in May once Parliament has had time to receive and review the documents." Silas placed his hand on Benjamin's shoulder as he stood to leave.

"Good evening, Silas," Benjamin said as Silas took his leave of him.

12

November 1, 1774, Mastic Long Island

Hannah showed Mary how to finish the lace on the masks they'd made for the party that evening. Mary was excited to be working on such beautiful accessories. Outside, Kitty helped Nicoll haul wood he'd chopped for a bonfire.

The room upstairs where Mary and her mother were busy sewing had the windows cracked open a few inches. A fall breeze blew in, but the weather hadn't yet turned cold enough to snow. And the rain had held off for at least another day. The evening's festivities should be spared any poor weather.

Through the open window, Mary could hear Kitty ask, "Can we make torches to line the path up to the bonfire?"

"I'll have to call some of the field hands up to help with that," Nicoll answered.

Mary was glad Nicoll was being so accommodating. Normally, he wasn't as helpful. Mary thought it was because he knew he'd be in the company of many young ladies this evening and would have his pick of who to dance with.

Cora and her young daughter Joli had been busy for days making pies and cookies for tonight. Cora had only let Mary and Kitty taste a small sample of her treats.

A while later, Kitty called from downstairs, asking for help moving the furniture.

"Mother, Mary, come down, please."

Mary and her mother met Kitty at the bottom of the steps.

"What do you need now, Kitty?" her mother asked.

"We need to move the furniture so that it's against the wall and there's room for the fiddlers to stand," Kitty explained.

"Have you asked Nicoll to help with this? Or some of the farm hands?" her mother asked.

"Nicoll said he can't spare anyone with the crop being harvested. He fetched John to help with the torches that will line the pathway up to the house. They're working on those now."

Mary moved into the large room. "We can do it ourselves, there's not much to move," she said.

Together the three of them moved the couch and the two tall wingback chairs against one wall. Then they moved a small table and two more chairs to a corner next to one of the fireplaces. Kitty looked around at the newly created large open space flanked on either wall by fireplaces. The room next to it was the dining room, and the table there would be filled with the lovely pies, cookies, and desserts Cora and Joli had been making. Kitty walked into the dining room and stood.

"Mary let's go pick flowers for the tables. And pick some pumpkins to set around for decoration," Kitty suggested.

Mary nodded. "Okay."

The girls headed outside, and their mother went back upstairs to finish sewing lace around each of the girls' masks. She could hear Cora in the kitchen singing a soulful spiritual as she worked. Soon Hannah was finished with the details on each mask and headed down to the kitchen to check on Cora's progress with the food for the evening.

She entered the kitchen to the glorious sights and smells that filled every inch of space.

"Cora, everything looks wonderful," she said.

"Mm-hm. Yes'm," Cora answered before turning back to chop radishes and carrots. "I sent Joli and Stephen out to the bay to gather fresh oysters. They left before sunup. They should be here with a bucket of oysters within the hour." Cora turned back around to look at Hannah, who was sneaking a sample of one of the cookies on a tray. "I didn't ask Master Nicoll's permission before I sent them. I know he was worrying himself about not having enough help for the harvest with all he needed to do for the party too. It'll get done. No need to worry."

Hannah nodded.

"Master William won't be disappointed in him whenever he returns," Cora said and smiled at Hannah.

"No," Hannah said. "I agree. Mr. Floyd won't be disappointed. The harvest will get done, and the flocks have been taken care of since he left."

Mary and Kitty came bounding through the back door into the kitchen with handfuls of wildflowers.

"Can we put these in a vase?" Kitty asked.

Their mother moved to the cupboard and opened it. Inside she found a large pot. "Here," she said to Kitty. "Take this to the well and fill it with water."

Later that evening, the girls had on their finest dresses, and each sister held a satin mask trimmed in lace. Kitty's mask was yellow, and Mary's mask was purple. Each girl wore a satin ribbon around her neck that matched the color of her mask.

Together, they made their way down the stairs to see if they could help finish the preparations. Hannah, Cora, and Jolie were setting desserts, cheeses, apples, carrots, and more on the long table in the dining room. Mary and Kitty's large bouquet of flowers sat in the middle, and on either side were two large candelabras, both aglow with candles. Two hefty pumpkins sat next to the candles.

"It's beautiful, Cora," Hannah said.

"It is. Miss Kitty will be pleased."

Kitty, having overheard, Cora and her mother, made her way farther into the room. "I love everything." Kitty gave her mother a hug.

Mary began wandering around the table, carefully looking at every item. A smile lit up her whole face. She was grateful her mother had agreed to host a party.

"Nicoll is out lighting the torches now," Cora said.

"Yes," Kitty said. "He plans to light the bonfire once the guests arrive."

As the women put the finishing touches on the table, two riders made their way toward the house. The girls glanced out the window, where they could see Nicoll walking back to the house with a lit torch in his hands. The torches he'd lit along the path up to the house were starting to glow as the sun began to set. Soon their guests would be arriving. The two men stepped down from their horses, tied them to the hitching post out front, and made their way up to the house. They both carried small matching cases on their backs.

"They must be the fiddlers," Kitty exclaimed.

Kitty and Hannah went to the door to greet them. The men bowed and introduced themselves, and Hannah led them into the large main room where they'd be playing. The two musicians set about opening their cases and tuning their instruments. Nicoll set the lit torch in a stand near the bonfire and made his way inside. He stopped to greet the musicians before making his way upstairs to freshen up.

By the time he returned downstairs, lively music filled the room, and the sounds of horses' hooves rumbled up the path. Their guests had begun to arrive. Kitty, Mary, and their mother made their way to the foyer near the door to greet them. Nicoll went outside and took the lit torch from its stand and lit the bonfire he and Kitty had prepared earlier in the day. The fire started to pop and crackle and soon grew into a triangular orange glow that was reflected in the windows along the front of the house and danced on the walls inside the great room.

The girls greeted each guest while wearing their masks, which were tied on with matching satin ribbons. Many of the ladies also had masks with them. Cora made the rounds with offerings of ale and cider. Lively fiddle music filled the room.

Once all the guests had arrived, Kitty and Mary made their way into the large room, which was now filled with dancing and lively chatter. Soon, a carriage pulled up to the front of the house. Mary's mother opened the door to see who it could be, and William Floyd stepped down from the carriage. Hannah ran to greet him, and William enveloped his wife in his arms and kissed her.

"You're finally home," she said.

He smiled. "That I am. And being greeted so warmly and with a festive party on my behalf is most welcoming."

Hannah laughed. "Kitty wanted a masquerade ball."

"Ah, I see. Shall we?" He held out his arm, and together they walked inside to enjoy the festivities.

Mary was the first to spot her father walking into the great room with her mother. Quickly she ran to him.

"Father," Mary said. "I missed you so."

Her father reached out and hugged her. "And I missed you."

Soon, Nicoll and Kitty came around and greeted their father. The party became livelier, the joy of a family reunited overflowed, the music sounded better, the dancing felt more splendid, and the food and drink tasted more delicious.

Hannah pulled her husband close. "Cousin Benjamin came a few weeks ago with the news."

Her husband looked into her eyes. "Yes, he wrote me. I know my letters sounded happier and more jovial than you might have expected given what was taking place. It was a long two months." He kissed his wife's hand. "We've stated our rights as we see them to the king and to Parliament. We have plans to stop trade with Britain. Those punitive laws passed by Parliament after the Boston Tea Party are highly unfair. It isn't right, Hannah, them taking away all of Massachusetts' self-governance and rights." He scoffed and shook his head. "They're trying to make an example of Massachusetts, thinking they can reverse our resistance to parliamentary authority. We've sent our response to the king, and the Congress will reconvene in May. Until then, let us enjoy ourselves."

William led Hannah out to the dance floor, where they danced happily with their guests—with no idea that before the delegates returned for the Second Continental Congress, their country would be at war with England.

13

Wethersfield, Connecticut April 1775

Benjamin sat at his desk grading papers at the end of a long school day. Once finished, he pulled out the post he'd picked up that morning on the way to the schoolhouse. When he opened a letter from William Floyd, a second missive fell out. Turning it over, he recognized it was a new letter from Mary. A smile formed on his lips as he unfolded the paper and began to read about the mischief she'd been up to in recent days. Her letters often left him smiling. She'd tell him about something funny her dog had done or how she'd helped her brother build a trap to catch a fox that had been stealing their chickens. She'd also told him her impressions of the Homer Classics her father had given her recently, and he had enjoyed reading her thoughts on both.

He gathered paper to begin a return correspondence, then realized he had another letter he'd not yet opened; it was from his friend Nathan. Reading Nathan's letter, Benjamin learned his friend had taken a new teaching job and had moved from Moodus to New London, which Benjamin knew to be a larger and more progressive city. Nathan's letter also brought a smile to Benjamin when he read about the two women that Nathan seemed to be courting in tandem. Nathan's letter went on to discuss the town meetings he was attending on a regular basis and the liberty pole that had just been erected in New

London's town square. All of these were gathering places where men would proclaim their rejection of the Crown and talk about their ideas for independence, the concept growing stronger each month. Nathan closed the letter with a quote from the play Cato, written by Joseph Addison. *How beautiful is death, when earn'd by virtue! Who would not be that youth? what pity is it That we can die but once to serve our country! Portius, behold thy brother, and remember Thy life is not thy own, when Rome demands it.*

Nathan signed his letter using his nickname, Pythias.

Benjamin started a response to Nathan's letter with his own quote from Cato. *The ways of heaven are dark and intricate; puzzled in mazes and perplexed with errors.* He went on to tell his friend that the correspondence between him and Alice had recently ended. Mostly because Benjamin had not found the time to visit her in New Haven as much as she thought he would. But he added he believed that she at last had found someone new. He finished his letter with the latest news he'd learned of Boston, and he remarked on the unrest they all were feeling as they waited on word of the king's response to Congress.

∞∞∞∞∞∞∞

Cold weather soon gave way to spring. The days grew longer, and flowers began to sprout up from the ground that had recently been covered in inches of snow. April was a beautiful time in Wethersfield. Benjamin was spending a lot of time at Hospitality Hall dancing and enjoying the company of the town's fine young ladies.

But on a late April morning, a rider rode hard and fast down Main Street, blowing past Benjamin, who was on his way to the schoolhouse. The rider stopped in front of the tavern and jumped from his horse.

"To arms, to arms!" the horseman shouted. "The war has begun. It is time to respond to the call for men and arms. Blood has been shed in Lexington and Concord."

With that he climbed back up on his horse and took off quickly for the next town.

The men who had heard the horseman's cries began to gather at the liberty pole. Benjamin joined them and learned some were planning to leave immediately for Boston, while others talked of gathering a militia.

"There is a great need to gather arms," one man said. "To be primed and ready to defend our lands, our homes, our businesses, and our lives."

"It's only cowards who stand with England," another said.

Benjamin looked at his pocket watch. He was going to be late if he stayed any longer. He tipped his hat to the men and walked on. As he walked toward the schoolhouse, Benjamin knew he stood for the decisions made by Congress; he also believed that some with close ties to England wouldn't care to break the alliance with the mother country. In Connecticut, it was obvious where most stood, and that was to unite with Massachusetts and continue to fight for justice.

Benjamin closed the school for the season in May after hearing the results of the second Continental Congress. He was feeling apprehensive, knowing the colonies would soon declare independence. Upon ending school for the year, he made plans to head home to Setauket to visit with his family, because with war approaching, he was unsure when he'd see them again. Before leaving, he penned a letter to Nathan leaving no doubt which course he had chosen.

America, my friend, at the present period, sees such times as she never saw before . . . the great wheels of the state and constitution seem to have grown old and crazy; everything bids fair for a change . . . How soon a great, flourishing and powerful state may arise from that now stigmatized by the Name of Rebels, God only knows. The prospect however for the same seems to be great. But that we ought at present to desire it is far from being clear. We ought by all means to prepare for the worst, and then we may encounter danger with more firmness and with better prospects of success.

A month later, Benjamin would be offered a lieutenancy and a regimental-adjutant position by Colonel John Chester, whom he had met in Wethersfield. Chester had urged him to put aside his books and teaching and take up the sword, all of which Benjamin would do at the ripe age of twenty-one.

14

Mastic, Long Island June, 1776

Mary came through the back door and into the kitchen to find Cora making a cake. She set down on a chair the bouquet of wildflowers she'd picked for the party.

"Oooh," Mary cooed. She walked over to where Cora was stirring batter in a large bowl, picked up a spoon, and stuck it into the batter to take a taste. "Is this Nicoll's birthday cake for tomorrow?" she asked while reaching into the bowl again.

Cora smacked her hand. "It is. Hands out. You'll have your share of cake tomorrow."

Mary huffed. "If Nicoll or Kitty knew it was being made already, they'd be in here trying to taste a sample too."

Cora laughed. Mary could hear their newest fortepiano being played from the next room and knew Kitty was practicing. Mary rolled her eyes. She hated to play the piano and had only learned two songs. Kitty, on the other hand, absolutely loved practicing and played every day. Kitty had turned eighteen last week, and the piano had been a gift from Uncle Richard, his wife, and cousin Benjamin and his family. Mary knew Kitty wanted to impress everyone tomorrow evening.

Mary's own birthday was just a few months away. At the end of August, she would turn sixteen. Although, unlike Kitty, she didn't know what she wanted to ask for—certainly not fine dresses from Paris or a piano. But letters from her friends were like gifts from Heaven to Mary.

Leaving the kitchen, she made her way past Kitty's piano-playing and into her father's study to look for paper so she could write some letters. It was her favorite thing to do besides . . . well, maybe, riding her favorite horse and reading books. She usually only wrote to Benjamin Tallmadge and Liza. She hadn't received any mail from Benjamin in the past several months. She'd last heard from him in May, and another reply had come in January, almost five months ago.

What Mary knew was that Benjamin was leading troops in the war. But the battles so far had been far away in Massachusetts, or they seemed far away to Mary. She knew Nicoll wanted to join the Patriot army. She'd heard her father and Nicoll arguing about it one night a few months back. Nicoll was turning nineteen, and he was ready to enlist, but Mary's father was reluctant to allow him to leave. Nicoll would probably wear their father down, and in his heart, William knew his son would one day join. After all, William was a Patriot. Mary's entire family were believers in the cause. Her father had been a delegate for both the First and the Second Continental Congresses, and he'd only just returned a few weeks ago from the second meeting.

Mary found the paper she needed and walked up the stairs to the room she and Kitty shared. She sat down at the desk that faced the open window, where she could see Lucas's grave in the distance. She took her quill from the ink bottle and began to write to Liza. She told Liza all about Kitty's birthday last week, and her gifts, including a special one her father had said was still on its way from Paris. She wrote about how her father had gone to Setauket to meet with several gentlemen. He then planned to meet with other well-known Patriots in Port Jefferson, another port city just on the other side of Setauket. He would then return home tomorrow evening for Nicoll's birthday. Mary decided to finish the letter later in order to add any news about tomorrow's events and to explain what type of cake Cora had made for Nicoll.

∞∞∞∞∞∞∞∞∞

The next afternoon, Mary kept watch for her father. She even rode Spot down to the water's edge to look for him. Her father's estate spanned over four thousand acres, all the way to the river on one side and south to the ocean. Easing Spot through the trees along the river, Mary led him to the bank for a drink. She watched as an egret walked along the bank searching for fish. She dismounted and let Spot drink her fill from the cool river waters. Soon she heard voices coming from the south, and she could tell the unknown people were heading her way. Slowly, she moved Spot away from the riverbank and over into the brush close by. As the newcomers seemed to grow closer, Mary recognized her father's voice. Excited, she left Spot and walked back to the bank, where she could now see a whaleboat approaching.

Mary waved her arms, and her father stood in the boat and waved back. After the boat came to a stop at the bank, her father got out and came to Mary with his arms outstretched.

"You're a sight for sore eyes," he said.

Mary returned the hug and said, "I'm so glad you're home."

They turned to watch a man pull the boat up onto the bank before tying it to a tree. After securing it, he gathered a few packages and stepped out onto the bank.

"Caleb," William said, "this is my youngest, Mary."

Caleb took off his hat and bowed. "Nice to meet you."

When Mary returned the greeting, she was struck by something familiar about him, but she wasn't quite sure what. She gathered Spot's reins, and her father took the packages from Caleb and secured them to the saddle before the three walked to the house. Before her father and Caleb made their way inside, her father removed the packages from the saddle, and Mary took Spot to the stable. When she returned to the house, her father and Caleb were sitting in the main room with her mother, and sister. Cora brought in tea, and Mary sat and joined in on the conversation. Soon Nicoll came in from tending to the cattle and the estate's large flock of sheep.

William stood to greet his son with a robust hug. They slapped each other on the back with huge smiles on their faces.

"Happy birthday, son," William said. "I've brought you something." He turned and picked up the longest package from the floor and handed it to Nicoll. "It arrived from France a day ago, the same as the gift I'd ordered for Kitty's birthday. Both of them are from Paris."

Nicoll took the wrapping off to reveal a fine, gleaming Charleville Musket. The look on Nicoll's face was one of pure joy. And this gift let Mary know her father intended to allow Nicoll to fight in the Revolution if he chose to do so.

"Thank you, Father," Nicoll said. He set the musket down and hugged his father once again.

William laughed. "So, one of the reasons I was needed in Port Jefferson was not only to receive my order from France but on the way, I met with some men in Setauket about any updates from the war." He sighed and sat down. "I'll be heading back to Philadelphia in a few weeks. The delegates will meet again."

Mary felt distressed. "You must leave again Father?"

Caleb cleared his throat and turned to look at William. With his head turned to the side, Mary realized why he had seemed familiar. He was the same Caleb she'd seen seven years ago running into the church in Setauket to encourage Benjamin Tallmadge to get in line with him for food. The same boy who'd won the wrestling match, who had been hoisted onto the shoulders of another boy as he claimed his victory.

"I'm afraid, I do, child," said Mary's father. "The committee is meeting now to propose a Declaration of Independence, and each state must have at least two representatives present to vote once the final draft is completed. It will be the most important vote to date. We will vote on declaring our independence as we decide to become thirteen united states." William stood and lifted the other package from the floor. "This is for you, Kitty. A late birthday gift."

"Oh, Father," Kitty cried. She took the package from him and opened it to find a beautiful French-made gown. Kitty gasped. "It's . . . it's unbelievable. Thank you, Father. This is the best birthday ever."

"I guess it's not every day one turns eighteen," her father told her with a chuckle. "Or nineteen," he said, glancing at Nicoll, who was inspecting the musket with great care.

"Caleb," Hannah said, "won't you stay and join us for supper? We have quite the meal planned to celebrate Nicoll's birthday. And Kitty will entertain us on the piano."

"Thank you, ma'am. I'd be honored to stay."

∞∞∞∞∞∞∞∞∞∞∞

Later that evening, the table was set with fish, oysters, and game hen along with apples and pears picked from the estate's orchards. The beautiful cake Cora had made sat on a stand on the buffet along the wall. It was topped with a few of the wildflowers Mary had picked the day before. The rest of the flowers filled a vase in the center of the table.

Mary's mother lit the candelabras, then called everyone into the dining room. She showed Caleb where to sit, then everyone took their places. William held out a hand to his wife on one side and his son's on the other. The group held hands around the table as William led them in prayer. Once everyone had been served, William shared more about his plans to leave for Philadelphia in a few weeks.

"I don't know how long I'll be gone," he said, "but I would like to invite you to go to Philadelphia with me, Kitty."

Kitty's fork hit her plate with a loud clank. Quickly, she stood and ran to hug her father. "I can't believe it. Really?" she asked.

William nodded. "I've already spoken to your mother. She's agreed."

Kitty made her way over to hug her mother. "Thank you," she said with tears streaming down her cheeks.

When Kitty was back in her seat, Mary looked from her father to her mother, thinking they'd obviously forgotten something. Before Mary could voice her question, her father spoke.

"I've spoken to Dr. Gerardus Clarkson and his wife, Mary. Both are prominent citizens, and theirs is a fine Presbyterian family. Dr. Clarkson is a well-known physician in Philadelphia. They have children around Kitty's age—several fine sons whom she may find agreeable. The family will host Kitty during her time in Philadelphia."

"What about me, Father?" Mary finally asked.

Her mother and father looked at each other then at Mary. "Your mother and I did speak about you making the trip," her father said. "But after several discussions, it was decided this is Kitty's time. You will have yours soon, dear."

Her father's voice was calming, but his words felt like knives in Mary's chest. How much she wanted to go to Philadelphia to be a part of the excitement, the city, and the fine parties and balls she'd only dreamed about. But on the other hand, her sister was older. She knew it would be wrong to complain. It was so unlike Mary to hold her tongue when she thought something was unfair, but this time she would. Her shoulders slumped. Being the youngest wasn't always fun.

After dinner, Caleb took his leave, and Nicoll walked with him back to the boat at the riverbank. When Nicoll returned to the house, Mary was sitting at the desk in her room in front of the open windows. A small lit candle sat next to her as she finished the letter to Liza, telling her about how she had remembered who Caleb Brewster was and about the gifts her father brought. And, of course, the news about Kitty going to Philadelphia and the family she would stay with there. Mary folded the note and wrote Liza's name on the outside. It would be placed with another note Nicoll would write to Phebe.

She heard Nicoll open the door, his footfalls stopping short of the staircase. Then she heard her father's voice as he and Nicoll spoke.

"Caleb has been able to keep a keen eye on the goings-on along the harbors from the East River down to Port Jefferson and across the Connecticut coastline," Nicoll said. "A Patriot frigate has been commissioned and is named the Trumbull, and Caleb believes two more will be built within the year."

Although she couldn't hear her father's response, Mary could sense the significance of that news and what it meant for the future—especially the next few months, when her father would join in the voting for the new Declaration of Independence. It was in that moment Mary vowed to pray for those who were risking everything for a chance at freedom. And she asked God to gift her with the knowledge of how she might be of service.

15

New York, July, 1776

Benjamin Tallmadge was stationed near Wall Street. The street had gotten its name many years before from a tall wooden wall built by the Dutch colonists to defend themselves against Indian tribes and British troops. Although the wall was no longer in place, the name had stuck, and the area had become a bustling center for trade because of its close proximity to the port and docks. This is where Benjamin was training and drilling his recruits. He was short on experience but long on enthusiasm, and he had received guidance and military knowledge from more experienced officers. Being the intelligent scholar that he was, he'd read up on the subject, allowing him to come off as quite prepared.

With his current location being so close to family in Setauket, Benjamin decided to pay them a visit.

The fifty-mile trip took three hours by horseback, although the ride on Denyse's Ferry allowed his horse some rest before they arrived on Long Island. Then the horseback ride down the densely tree-lined path of Gnarl Hollow Road proved to be a respite from the hot July sun. A thick path of pine needles led up to the house, and his childhood home was a welcome sight. He dismounted from his dapple-gray mare, led her to the trough for a drink, then made his way to the front door.

The Reverend Tallmadge was taken aback upon seeing his son in full uniform. He stood in the doorway silently taking in his son's appearance. Benjamin's older brother William and one of his younger brothers, Samuel, had enlisted in the Patriot cause as well. Once, the reverend gathered himself, he greeted Benjamin.

"Son." His father reached for Benjamin, and they embraced. The older Tallmadge choked on his words before he finally said, "Come in."

Benjamin removed his tall, plumed dragoon hat and took his sword from its scabbard and set them on a table near the door. He followed his father into the next room, where they sat across from one another. Benjamin's new stepmother, Zipporah, and his youngest brother, Isaac, who was thirteen, came in from out back, where they'd been cleaning fish. Upon laying eyes on Benjamin, Zipporah ran over to grasp him at the neck, and kissed the top of his head. Benjamin stood and wrapped his arms around her. His younger brother looked on in awe.

"Oh, my dear boy," his stepmother said. "Look at you in this fine uniform. How long are you here? Can you stay for supper? We've caught two black sea bass."

Isaac proudly held up the pail to show Benjamin.

"I'm stationed in the city training my regiment," said Benjamin. "I can stay for a few hours, and a meal would be welcomed. That sounds like a feast."

Soon after that, the family table was filled with more food than Benjamin had seen in months. Isaac sat to one side of him, and his brother John, almost nineteen, was seated across from him. As Benjamin's father moved to lead the family in a blessing, they grasped hands around the table.

"Amen," they said collectively after the blessing had been said.

When Isaac asked for news of battles and war, the Reverend Tallmadge tried to steer the conversation in a different direction as often as he could.

"After I read the Declaration of Independence to my troops," reported Benjamin. "I could feel such enthusiasm, such zeal for the cause of freedom, and liberty from England. No longer are we dependent on the mother country. We now depend on God and the conduct of the Patriot army." He paused. "We have resolved to conquer or to die."

Benjamin's father nodded solemnly. "Our prayers surely go with you and your men, son."

Later that evening, Benjamin said goodbye to his family, mounted his horse, and headed back to New York. Upon entering the city, he made his way toward Broadway, and as he approached the wide road, he could hear loud cheers. A mob had gathered in the park at Bowling Green around the tall marble and bronze statue of King George III. Benjamin pulled his horse to the side of the road. He watched as soldiers and other men wrapped ropes around the statue, bringing it down as the cheers grew louder. Soon the replica of King George and his horse fell to the ground in pieces. "Turn these pieces into musket balls and bullets!" someone shouted from the crowd.

Benjamin guided his horse away from the mob and made his way to camp, his mind filled with thoughts of the imminent British invasion and attack by General William Howe, the British army's commander in chief.

∞∞∞∞∞∞∞∞

Just over a month later, two hundred British warships sat along the shores of the East River between New York City and Long Island. On the morning of August 22, General

Howe's cannons could be heard as he started moving troops to Long Island from Staten Island, where they'd mustered for weeks. General George Washington, having decided to split his troops between New York City and Long Island, had sent ten thousand men to Long Island to erect a series of forts on the high ground known as Brooklyn Heights. England had sent just over thirty thousand troops, thinking they could end the skirmish quickly.

Benjamin's regiment was the first to cross over from New York City into Brooklyn on Long Island. He and his men settled in and prepared for the first official battle with bloodshed since American independence was declared. General Howe shuttled a total of twenty thousand troops from Staten Island to Long Island, keeping around ten thousand on Staten Island. General Washington split his army, sending ten thousand to Long Island, and keeping ten thousand in New York city. With a combined twenty thousand British soldiers—and with ten thousand Americans—it would be the largest battle to take place during the entire Revolution.

When Benjamin and his troops advanced to meet the enemy, he gave voice to his thoughts. Under his breath, he asked, "Lord, am I willing to set my mind to attempt the life of a fellow creature?"

The action soon commenced. Through gunfire, smoke, and the boom of hundreds of rifles fired, there wasn't time to think, only to reload and continue shooting. The fighting continued at intervals throughout the day until the Patriots could no longer man their ground against the more numerous British troops. They then retired to their forts in the village of Brooklyn.

A Maryland militia group of about 270 men had arrived to help. The Maryland militia helped to hold off the British for just a bit longer. After two days of fighting—with little to no sleep and a huge loss of men—the outlook was devastating. Before all seemed lost, Colonel Chester arrived from Washington's council amid a rainy downpour to give Benjamin some news.

"There aren't enough men covering the Jamaica Pass," Chester began. "The Regulars have found a way through the pass and will close in on us on the left flank. Washington plans to ferry everyone—the entire encampment—back across the East River."

Benjamin nodded.

"You and your men will stay here and keep watch," the colonel continued. "At ten o'clock, troops will begin to retire in such a manner that no chasm can be found. As one regiment leaves their station, the remaining troops will move to the right and left to fill the vacancies. Washington will take his station at the ferry to superintend the embarkation."

Chester took his leave, and Benjamin remained especially alert, given that he and his men would be the last to make their way to the ferry. With the rain pouring down on him and a lack of sleep, Benjamin grew anxious. The dangers ahead consumed his thoughts, but he still had the power of prayer. As he stood watch that night, he prayed aloud but softly. "Lord, God, the East River is a mile wide and has a rapid current. And we are up against the strongest, most well-disciplined army, nearly three times as numerous as ours. Their fleet is capable of stopping our navigation, and the obstacles we face are most formidable. But only in you I place my hope and trust. Amen."

Before dawn broke, Benjamin's regiment was the only one still on duty. A dense fog rose and settled over both the British and American encampments. It was a fog so thick a man could scarcely discern anyone six yards away. Benjamin acknowledged the density of the fog and its location as a peculiar providential occurrence. Soon he received orders to leave the lines, and he was thankful to bid the trenches adieu. When he reached the ferry, the boats had not yet returned from their last trip, but they soon appeared through the fog and would take him and his whole regiment to New York City. As Benjamin and his men boarded one of the boats, he watched General Washington step into the last boat. Benjamin had left his favorite horse tied to a post at the ferry, and once he reached the other side, he began to deeply regret not taking his mare aboard. At the time, his only thoughts had been to get his men across to safety. With the fog still as thick as ever, he decided to request leave to make a return trip with volunteers to get his horse.

"Sir, if I may," Benjamin said to Colonel Chester. "I've left my favorite horse behind. May I ask for a few volunteers to go back over with me? I'll guide the boat myself."

After being given permission, Benjamin and the volunteers boarded the boat they'd just gotten out of and began the trip back across the East River. Quickly, Benjamin loaded the horse. By this time, however, the British had taken notice and began to fire as the ferry left the shore. Thankfully, Benjamin and his men were far enough away that they were not hit.

Stepping foot on safe ground once again, Benjamin reflected on the providential appearance of the fog that may have saved at least seven thousand from being captured. He was eternally thankful to God, but also to Washington for the bold and wise measures taken to remove his army to safety. They would now be allowed to fight another day.

16

August 30, 1776, Mastic Long Island

Mary woke just before sunrise. It was the morning of her sixteenth birthday, and as she gazed out the window of her bedroom, she was thankful the winds and harsh rains had finally passed. She dressed in the dark, then made her way down the stairs. Her dog, Moses, greeted her at the bottom step with his wet nose pushed against her hand until she gave him the attention that he wanted.

As she made her way into the kitchen, Moses tagged along beside her. Mary opened the back door, and Moses bounded out onto the porch and down the stairs, chasing after who knew what. Soon, she saw Cora and Joli making their way from their quarters toward the main house.

Mary sat at the table and nibbled on an apple from the bowl of fruit in front of her. Cora was startled to see Mary sitting in the dark room when she walked in.

"Mercy, child," Cora said, trying to catch her breath from the scare. "My bones are weary enough without you giving me such a fright."

Mary giggled. "Oh, Cora. Good morning to you too."

Joli shook her head and smiled at Mary. "Today's your birthday, ain't it?" she asked.

"Yes. It is a most beautiful day too," Mary responded. She gazed out the window to the east, where the sun had begun to rise. Her face beamed with joy, as she wondered what the year might bring now that she was sixteen. There could be parties, balls, and, possibly trips to Philadelphia with Kitty and her father. She missed them, and she hoped the war with England would not last long.

"Days ago, you told me what kind of cake to make. You ain't changin' yo mind about it now, I hope," Cora said, then turned around to gather some buckets from the cupboard. She handed them to Joli, who left to fill them at the well.

"No," Mary answered. "But I thought I'd help."

"I see. Well then, you best start by gathering eggs from the henhouse."

Cora reached up to the top shelf and pulled down a large round basket and handed it to Mary.

"Be careful reaching in. Yesterday I caught a rat snake."

"I will."

Mary took the basket and headed out the back door. Seeing Moses, she called him over, and together they made their way to the henhouse. Mary gathered nine eggs without seeing any snakes, for which she was grateful. Returning to the house, she set the basket down on the table next to a bowl of strawberries Cora had just finished chopping. A bag of flour was opened, and a small container of fresh milk sat near it.

"How many eggs would you like for the cake, Cora?" Mary asked.

"Three. And if you gathered enough, I'll use the rest for breakfast. Your mama should be up and ready to eat soon."

Mary divided out the eggs. As she did, she thought about how quiet the house had been these last three weeks with her father and Kitty in Philadelphia. Nicoll had signed up with the Suffolk County Militia to fight for the Patriot cause and defend their towns, land, and shores. He was working closely with Caleb Brewster, making rounds from Long Island to Connecticut, across the sound and back.

"Here," Cora said. "Take a spoonful of sugar, a cup of flour, and a little of this milk, and mix it all together in this bowl."

Cora handed Mary a wooden spoon, and Mary began to mix the ingredients. "When should I add the eggs?" she asked.

"Smooth out any lumps you see first."

Mary stirred until everything looked slick and smooth. She picked up an egg, but before she cracked it, she thought about how her mother had taught them to tap a tiny hole into the bottom of an egg. Then they would let it drain, and later they would use the empty shell for decorating.

"Cora, do you remember how when Kitty and I were little, we loved to paint the shells of the eggs after we'd drained them?"

"Yup, I remember those days."

"Can I do that with these? I want to decorate them and use them on the table tonight for the birthday dinner. Nicoll promised when he left that he'd come home on my birthday. I hope he does."

Cora dug around in a drawer, looking for something. "Yes," she said. "It's your birthday. Do what pleases you." Cora smiled, then handed Mary a large sewing needle and a small wooden mallet. "Be careful not to crack it too much. Be gentle."

Mary took the tools and began to tap softly. A hole a little bigger than the needle tip appeared, and Mary held the egg over the flour and sugar to let it drain. It took a while for the liquid to leak out, but shaking it helped.

"Child," Cora said. "tap a hole into both ends, then blow out the insides." Cora chuckled softly.

Mary nodded.

Finally, the contents of all three eggs were added to the mixture, and Cora told her to add the strawberries next.

Joli came back into the kitchen with two buckets full of water. "Mmm, it smells so good in here," she said. She left one bucket of water in the kitchen, then took the other upstairs to pour into the washstands.

After Mary poured the mixture into a pan, she placed it over the fire to bake. Then Cora showed Mary how to make the icing. After she'd done that, Mary's hands were crusted over with the white substance. She wondered what would happen if she put some icing over the holes in the eggs. Would it harden enough to fill in the holes? She decided to try it. With a knife, she added a small amount of icing to fill in the holes in one of the eggs, then she set the eggshell aside to dry.

"Cora, what will happen if the icing hardens before we can ice the cake?" she asked.

Cora had told Mary how they would make the icing but didn't realize she'd forgotten to tell her they'd finish with the icing once the cake had cooled. "We'll just add some butter to it and a little milk. It'll soften up again," she said.

Cora had finished scrambling eggs for breakfast and set those on the table just as Mary's mother came in to check on everyone.

"Good morning," she said. "I must have slept later than I thought. Looks like you've been busy."

She walked over to Mary and gave her a hug. "Happy birthday, love."

"Thank you. Look, Mama. I'm going to decorate these." Mary held up an empty eggshell. "Remember how you taught Kitty and me how to drain the eggshells so we could save them for decorating when we were young?"

Her mother smiled. " Yes. And I see you've already got a birthday cake baking. It smells delicious."

Mary's mother sat at the table, and Mary joined her for breakfast.

"I'm hoping Nicoll remembers to come home tonight," Mary said.

Her mother looked up from her plate. "So do I."

Just then a postrider rode up to the house. Quickly, Mary stood.

"Father's desk will have money for the post," her mother said.

Mary ran down the hallway and into her father's study, where she opened several drawers almost at the same time in search of a few Spanish dollars. European money held more value than their own Continental coins. With those in hand, she ran out to greet the postrider. He handed her two letters, and two small packages.

When Mary handed over the money, he said, "Them's already paid" and rode off.

Mary looked at the postmarks on each one. One was from New York; she wondered who that was from. Another had come from Philadelphia; she knew that was from her father or Kitty. Then Mary looked at one of the packages and gasped. "Oyster Bay!" She ran back inside to show Cora, Joli, and her mother.

"Look." She held out the letters and packages for them to see. Before sitting back down at the table to finish her breakfast, she untied the string and tore the brown paper from the package from Oyster Bay. Inside was a handmade nightcap trimmed in satin and lace. Mary looked at it carefully, wondering if Liza had made it herself. She noticed her own initials were embroidered along one edge, and there was something sewn into the seam. She found a loose thread near the seam, which she pulled, loosening the edge. With that, she was able to see that a piece of paper had been rolled up and stuck inside. She stood up from the table and walked into the kitchen to find the needle she'd used on the eggs. With her back to Cora, Joli, and her mother, she carefully used the needle to retrieve the note, which she read eagerly.

Dear Mary,

Happy Birthday. I made this for you. Liza

It made Mary smile, and she thought it was unique that Liza had placed a note inside the edge of the lace on the nightcap. She thought she might write Liza back and tuck a note inside one of the empty eggs she planned to decorate. But then she decided that gift might not last long, considering how long and hard the postrider had to travel—unless she could find a small container and some padding for the egg. Well, she'd come up with something just as unique to send to Liza later. For now, she had more letters to read.

As Mary sat down to open the rest of the post, her mother picked up the nightcap.

"This is lovely," she said. "What else do you have there?"

Mary opened the next package and found it was a book from her father. She showed the book to her mother and read the title, "*Moll Flanders.* This shall keep me busy today." She opened the book to see that on the first page, her father had written a note wishing her a happy birthday.

Cora checked on the cake, then she and Joli worked to get the icing soft again by mixing and adding a few ingredients to it.

Mary opened the next letter and found it was also from her father. Another note fell out, labeled "To Mary." Her mother took the letter, and Mary took her note and opened it.

"It's from Kitty," she announced.

Mary set Kitty's note aside and looked at the last letter. It was addressed to her father, but he wasn't here, and neither was Nicoll. "Can I open this one, Mama?"

Her mother was busy reading the letter from her father and simply nodded.

Mary cracked the seal on the letter and opened it to find a note with her name written on the outside. The other letter was written to her father, and both of them were from Benjamin Tallmadge. Her cheeks flushed red, and it felt as if something was inside her stomach-turning flips.

"Your father says he plans to return home soon, but he's not sure if he'll make it for your birthday." Her mother held up the letter. "But this is dated a week ago, so your father may be making his way home now."

"That sounds wonderful, Mama." Mary finished the food on her plate. "May I be excused?"

"I just remembered something, Mary," her mother said. "Come with me upstairs."

They left the table, and Mary followed her mother into her bedroom. There, her mother walked to a tall dresser and opened the top drawer. She pulled out a box and handed it to Mary.

"I was given this by my parents when I turned sixteen," Mary's mother said. "I'd almost forgotten about them. I gave Kitty the earrings that went with this on her sixteenth. And I saved this for you."

Mary remembered Kitty getting a beautiful pair of pearl and crystal earrings a few years ago. Enthusiastically, she opened the box, and inside was a short necklace made of tiny pearls.

"Try it on," her mother said.

Mary turned around so her mother could slip the necklace around her neck. Then she walked to the mirror above the dresser and admired it.

"It's so lovely, Mama. I love it. Thank you."

Her mother walked behind her and bent to kiss Mary on the cheek.

"Well, I'm headed to the garden to pick some vegetables for your birthday supper tonight. And to gather some flowers for the table."

After her mother left the room, Mary gazed at herself in the mirror for a few seconds before remembering she'd left her post on the kitchen table. She decided to leave the pearls on for the day—after all, it was her birthday—and went back down to read her mail.

When she got back to the kitchen, Joli was adding the rest of the chopped strawberries to the top of the perfectly iced cake.

"Ah, it's lovely," Mary said.

"I bet it tastes even better," Joli added.

Mary noticed a small box sitting on the counter near where Cora was cleaning the dishes. She walked over and picked it up. "This might just work," she said to herself.

"Cora, do you need this little box?" she asked.

Cora looked at Mary. "That old snuff box? I had some sewing supplies in there. Why?"

I thought I could draw on this egg and ship it to Liza inside the box. I could wrap it in some of the brown paper from the gifts I received today."

"Go ahead. I can find another old box around here."

Mary gathered the snuff box and an empty egg, stuffed her letters inside her book, and rushed up to her room. She placed everything on her desk, then took her quill and drew a flower on the outside of the empty egg. She set the decorated egg aside, then picked up the letter from her sister and read it.

Dear Mary,

I am having a lovely time at the home of the Clarkson family. Philadelphia has so much to offer. There are new things to see each day. The shopping is dreamy. We plan to attend the theater tonight. And I will be escorted by Mister William Clarkson. He's one of the oldest sons of Dr. Clarkson and is quite handsome. I don't know if I would ever want to leave Philadelphia, certainly not to return home to a secluded farm. There are boarding houses here, and I should plan to ask father about staying. I hope this letter finds you well. Have a very happy birthday.

Sending my love. Your favorite sister,

Kitty

Mary wasn't sure what to think about Kitty wanting to stay in Philadelphia and not return home, but she supposed she was old enough to make those decisions. Mary wondered when she would have her chance to do something equally exciting. She picked up the letters from Benjamin Tallmadge, which were dated a little over a week ago. Quickly, she read the one to her father, which gave details about the British troops and ships in New York Harbor. There were more details as well about General Howe's possible plans for an attack on New York. The information was disturbing to Mary. She'd never read many details about the war, and these seemed too close to home. She picked up her own note from Benjamin and began to read.

Dear Mary,

How lovely it is for you to remember to write to me. I apologize for not writing you any sooner. I've been recruiting and training my men and have had little time for correspondence. My new assignment in New York, gave me the chance to travel home to Setauket to visit with my father and stepmother, and I was able to see my two youngest brothers while I was there. It was a good visit. I hold a busy post in the army as things are becoming more involved. Your father has always been a great source of support to me, and I am thankful for him. And your letters too, of course. I hope this finds you well and that I might enjoy your company after the war has ended and America receives her liberty.

I am your friend,

Benjamin Tallmadge

Mary took the letters and placed them inside her Bible, where she kept all her other correspondence along with the handkerchief Benjamin had given her all those years ago. She thought she'd write him later after she gathered her thoughts. For now, she wanted to write Liza and thank her for the gift. She took out paper from her drawer and began.

Dear Liza,

It was most gracious of you to make me such a beautiful and personal gift. The nightcap will be treasured. I'll wear it each night and think of you and our friendship. It arrived on my birthday along with a book from Father. And also a note from Benjamin Tallmadge. His note came with a letter to my father, which I read too since Father is away in Philadelphia with Kitty. I hope Father returns home soon. Kitty's letter says she is making plans to stay in Philadelphia. I hope to go someday. News of the war from Benjamin Tallmadge to Father was quite distressing to me. His note to me was nice and told of being able to visit his family in Setauket since he was stationed in New York to recruit and train troops. Oh, I do hope he stays safe and in God's hands. Please remember to pray for him and for us all to survive this war. I do hope you are well. I miss you and hope to see you again. I decorated this eggshell this morning from some that went into my birthday cake. I shall hope you enjoy it.

All my love, your friend,

Before Mary could finish signing the letter, the front door burst open and she heard Nicoll shouting. "Mary, Mother, Father, Mary!"

"Upstairs," Mary yelled back.

Nicoll must have taken the stairs two at a time, because before she could blink, he was standing in her room.

"We must leave! Make haste!"

"What?" Mary asked.

"The Regulars are coming for Father. They're coming to kill or to take prisoner anyone who committed treason by signing the Declaration of Independence. You cannot stay here. They will kill the family, anyone they find. Where's Mother? Has Father returned from Philadelphia?"

Nicoll's words were flying at Mary so fast she could barely comprehend what was happening. She stood frozen.

"Did you hear me, Mary? Where are Father and Mother?"

"He . . . he . . ." She stumbled over her words as they tumbled from her mouth. "Father was planning to return soon. We just received a letter from him dated last week. But he's not here. Mother is in the garden."

"Gather your things, Mary. Make haste. We must leave Long Island."

Nicoll left her room and ran down the stairs, calling for their mother. Cora and Joli, alerted by the noise, ran into Mary's room.

"Child," Cora said, taking Mary by the arm. "What's happening?"

"Nicoll said the British are coming to kill anyone who's committed treason. Anyone who signed the Declaration, including their families, and we must leave immediately."

Cora turned to Joli. "Go to the cellar and pack as many jars of food into a crate as you can and bring them up."

Joli turned and ran down the staircase.

"Wrap your dresses inside the quilt from your bed and roll it up," said Cora.

Mary flung the door of her armoire open and threw dresses onto the bed. Cora began rolling them up inside the quilt.

"Take anything else you want and put it in your trunk." Cora pointed to the smallest trunk in the room. "I'm going to your mother's room to get her things."

Mary turned to the things on her desk. Quickly, she added to the bottom of her letter to Liza that they were running for their lives from the British. She didn't know where they were going so, she ended it there. She rolled the letter as small as she could and fit it inside the eggshell. She then placed the eggshell inside the old snuff box and quickly wrapped it in the brown paper scraps from her package.

She placed the small package, her Bible, and a few books into the small trunk, grabbed her rolled-up quilt, and rushed down the stairs as her mother was running up.

"Mary, go to the barn. Nicoll is getting a fresh horse. Jeb will pull the wagon down to the river. We'll get into the boat from there."

Mary rushed out the door, and as she did, she glanced into the dining room, where she saw her beautiful birthday cake topped with freshly chopped strawberries sitting on the table. She ran out the door, with the quilt dragging behind her under one arm. Under her other arm was the small trunk with her most treasured items. She could hear her mother shouting at either Cora or Joli to bury all the silver in Lucas's grave.

When she got to the barn, Nicoll tossed her quilt and trunk onto the back of the wagon. "Hop on," he yelled. Her mother and Cora came running from the house with Joli, who held a rolled-up quilt tucked tightly under one arm. In her hands, close to her chest, she carried a small crate of canned food. Mary's mother held one handle of a large trunk and Cora held the other.

"Did you go to Father's study and clean out any papers?" Nicoll asked his mother, who shook her head.

"I'll go," Nicoll said. He turned to Jeb, who was already in the box seat, with the team hitched to the wagon. "Help load the trunk onto the wagon," Nicoll said to Jeb. "Cora, find Stephen, and tell him to let all the horses go. Except to save one for me. I've got to ride back to Setauket and get word to Caleb that you'll be coming by boat. Tell Stephen to stay with the other men. Then you and Joli meet Mother and Mary at the shore."

"Don't forget to tell Stephen to bury all the silver," Hannah shouted to her son.

Cora and Joli ran alongside Nicoll. Mary could hear Cora shouting. "Joli, gather all the silver and wrap it in the bedsheets. I'll find Stephen and tell him where to bury it."

Mary and her mother sat on the back of the wagon, holding on to what little they'd brought with them. Jeb brought the team to a gallop, and they took off for the boat down at the river. When they arrived at the riverbank, Jeb unhitched the team and shooed the horses off into the woods. Then he helped Mary and Hannah into the boat and began loading the items from the wagon into it. Soon, they could see Cora and Joli running toward them. Cora was carrying a small trunk Mary recognized from her father's study.

"Nicoll said he cleaned out everything he could find that looked important from Master Floyd's desk, including some money. It's in here." Cora handed the trunk to Hannah. Cora and Joli climbed aboard, and Jeb pushed away from the shore.

"What about Nicoll?" Mary asked. "And the others?"

"The men's staying with the farm," Jeb said as he rowed faster, moving toward the ocean. "Nicoll said he was letting all the sheep and cattle loose. Then he gonna ride back to Setauket and find Mister Caleb or someone to let them know where to find us. Someone will come with another boat and take us to Connecticut. We just gotta make our way along the coast. When we get to the north end of the island, we'll make the turn toward Connecticut. We'll be okay from there."

Mary's mother took over rowing for Jeb while he took a rest, then Cora rowed before returning the oars back to Jeb. They'd been gone for hours by the time the sun set. Mary's mother took another turn at rowing, and Mary fell asleep.

When she woke, their boat was beached on an island. The sun was already up, and in the distance, she could see another boat heading their way. She just hoped it was someone on their side and not the British.

17

Fall 1776

General Washington removed the main body of his army to White Plains, taking possession of the high ground, a mountain called Chatterton's Hill. Benjamin and his troops worked to dig an entrenchment. Long poles with iron pikes upon them were supplied in place of bayonets. To the right, Chatterton's Inn was separated from the entrenchment by a valley and the river Bronx. Washington ordered General Alexander McDougall, along with one thousand men, to defend it.

A prior skirmish had ensued at Harlem Heights and Hell's Gate, where part of the brigade, under Brigadier General, James Wadsworth were engaged, and Major John Willis had been taken prisoner. Benjamin was immediately appointed to fill his station. At dawn Benjamin and his men learned the enemy was in full march to meet them. The German Hessian troops the British had brought over to fight with them advanced with musket shots, causing the American Continentals to withdraw behind stone walls. From there, they could pour destructive fire onto the oncoming enemy. When it became clear the enemy would advance further by entering the river, Benjamin ordered his men to retreat.

Benjamin was on horseback when he entered the river to head up the embankment and back to Chatterton's Hill. A horse carrying chaplain Benjamin Trumbull sprang up behind Benjamin's horse, causing the spooked animal to buck. The Reverend Trumbull's horse bolted, with the incident hurling both the reverend and Benjamin into the river. The men scrambled up the bank toward the American lines in hopes McDougall's troops would volley with the Hessians to protect them as they scurried to get away. The two men fled behind a stone wall as the Hessians entered the river. A volley from General McDougall's troops saved Benjamin from being captured, and he was able to remount his horse and immediately ride to headquarters to inform Washington of the situation on Chatterton's Hill. The startled Reverend, Trumbull managed to remount his horse while McDougall's troops continued their cannonade against the enemy.

Benjamin met General Washington in his tent. "Sir," he said as he removed his hat.

The general looked up and greeted the young Dragoon commander. Having Washington's full attention gave Benjamin pause as he took in the general's polished appearance. The commander didn't seem to notice Benjamin was muddy and dripping wet. He pulled his shoulders back then gave the full report of the battle at Chatterton's.

"Thank you, son. We shall prepare to remove our troops and stores up to North Castle."

Benjamin bowed and turned to leave the tent. Before he could exit, one of Washington's aide-de-camps, Colonel William Grayson, stopped him.

"I have news for you, sir," Colonel Grayson said. "Your brother William was one of the men captured and taken prisoner during the battle on Long Island. They're being held on a prison ship called the Jersey. And an officer from Knowlton's Rangers, Nathan Hale, was hung as a spy last week."

Benjamin froze in place. His brows knitted together, and he tightened his grip on his hat. "A spy? Nathan Hale? That can't be."

Colonel Grayson walked outside the tent and Benjamin followed. The colonel moved off to the side and took time to explain. "He volunteered to go behind enemy lines. He may have been caught by a ruthless British agent—a member of the Queen's Rangers, Robert Rogers. He was hung on September twenty-second at Post Road Park of Artillery in New York City. I'm sorry. I know he was a Yale graduate same as you. A good man."

Benjamin nodded. "He and I were great friends. He was a good man. Thank you for the news."

Benjamin left the commander's tent and made his way into the woods. His thoughts were reeling from what he'd just learned, and his heart ached. His mouth was dry, and tears ran down his cheeks. He came to a tree and leaned against it. As silent tears continued to fall, he began to pray aloud.

"Holy Father, I bid you come near to me in my time of sorrow. Oh, how grievous a day this is. What of my brother now in the hands of the British? Must he die in prison? And of Nathan, dear Pythias, who has been executed while Damon is still here, not able to take his place. Oh, to become Damon and exchange my life for that of Pythias as the story be told, for he would do the same in my stead. My heart breaks for my friend. My heart is in pain and anguish for my brother William. But I must take charge of these feelings and manage them with control. It is duty that calls me to a place and time where I must defend the honor of those who've perished before me. It will be by your divine providence that we shall defeat the British and gain our freedom. I pray, Father God, that you will give me your blessing, wisdom, and strength on this day and in this hour of my grief. Gift me with honor and a willingness to make sacrifices so I might lead my men into battle against the enemy. I pray that I might lead by your will. Allow me to leave my grief and go on in your service and in the service of my country. Amen."

18

Connecticut, September, 1776

After being rescued Mary, her mother, Jeb, Cora, and Joli were taken to New London in Connecticut, where an elderly Presbyterian couple gave them shelter. From there, Hannah sent a letter to her husband in Philadelphia, and Mary was able to send the small package to Oyster Bay. Hannah knew that her son Nicoll and Caleb Brewster had sent word to William in Philadelphia that they were safe in Connecticut, but she wanted to send a note in her own hand too. She also reached out to a cousin in Middleton, Connecticut, who arranged for a carriage to meet them and take them to the cousin's home. That's where they'd stay until William could secure a private home for them.

Connecticut was secure Patriot ground. Philadelphia was still held by the Americans as well, but they soon learned Long Island had been completely taken over by the British. Mary worried for Liza and the Townsend family. How were they faring? Had their home been overrun? Mary hoped Liza was safe. She hoped the package would arrive. But Liza wouldn't be able to write to her again until Mary sent a new letter letting her know of her new location. She hoped that if the British were in the Townsends' home, they wouldn't find out about Liza knowing how to read and write—just the thought of it worried Mary. What would happen if they knew?

Would Liza be in danger? As soon as Mary was able, she would figure out a way to get a message to Liza secretly with the hope of learning of her safety and that of the Townsends.

Her mother's first cousin, Alice Jones, made Mary and her mother feel welcome in her home. Her children were younger, and Mary tried to be as helpful as possible with the baby and two toddlers. Cora and Joli were a big help, and Jeb was put to work tending horses and mending things around the house and farm. Mary and her mother shared a room, and Cora, Joli, and Jeb were given space to sleep with the other slaves.

The home was only quiet after eight when the children were put to bed. At that time Mary and her mother would gather with Alice and her husband, Tom, in the great room. They sat by candlelight sewing, reading, or just quietly talking about news of the war. One evening, as Mary watched Cousin Alice making a dress for one of her children, she got an idea. Maybe she could make something and send it to Phebe Townsend. It could look like a gift, then inside the hem, a note could be added for Liza.

After breakfast the following morning, Mary asked her mother,

"Would it be possible for us to ride into town to shop for new fabric?"

"I suppose so," her mother said, sounding cheerful. "We could check on the post while we're there and see if we have anything from your father. It's been almost two weeks since we arrived in Middleton. I'm sure he's gotten the letter I sent. Originally, we did expect him home by now."

The next morning, Jeb dropped Mary and her mother in town. When they got off the wagon, Hannah told Jeb to come back around in about an hour to find them. Then she walked into the mercantile to check on the post while Mary watched the carriages go by and wondered what exciting things her sister would be up to this week in Philadelphia.

Her mother came out and said, "No mail. Shall we walk to the fabric shop now?"

Mary nodded and strolled along beside her mother.

Stopping outside the shop's window, Mary paused and gazed at a mannequin dressed in a fine gown of green silk trimmed with a wide band of white lace with a gold edge.

"It's so lovely," Mary whispered to herself before they walked into the shop.

Mary looked through all the fabric and finally chose a tiny floral cotton print. She purchased thread and a few sewing needles, and they walked back to where Jeb had dropped them off and waited for him to come around.

When they arrived back at the Joneses' home, a huge surprise was waiting for them. William was there. When he heard the carriage approach, he rose from his chair and walked out to greet his wife and daughter.

"Father!" Mary cried and ran to him.

"Oh, my child, it's so good to see you. Let me look at you."

Mary pulled out of her father's embrace and took a step back and turned slowly.

"Sixteen. My, my," her father gushed.

Hannah's eyes filled with tears as she took hold of her husband's hand.

"You're really here," she said. William pulled her to him, holding her like he'd never let her go.

"Are you going to stay with us?" Mary asked. "Or do you have to go back to Philadelphia?"

"I'm staying for a while, although I will be needed at Congress again. But when I do go back, I'm taking you with me."

"Really, Father?"

William looked at his wife and winked.

"Really," he replied.

∞∞∞∞∞∞∞∞

For the next month, Mary worked on the apron for Liza or Phebe. The note she'd put inside the hem would be for Liza, but she didn't care if her brother's sweetheart kept the apron as long as Liza got the message about where Mary was. As the fall weather grew colder, Mary's parents began to look for a house of their own in town. Soon they found one to rent, and they moved from Cousin Alice's home into their own space. Mary was thankful for the new place, and as soon as the apron was completed, she penned a letter to Liza, telling her where they were. She added that when her father returned to Philadelphia, she'd get to go with him. She asked Liza to write her back if she could, because she was worried and wanted to know she was safe.

Mary had no idea what had happened to her home and farm in Mastic, but she couldn't worry about that now. The most important thing was for the Americans to win the war.

When she finished with the note, she rolled it tight. Then, near the top of the waistband, she stitched a blue flower along the edge. When she was finished, she opened the hem of the waistband next to the embroidered flower and slipped the rolled-up note inside.

∞∞∞∞∞∞∞∞

The following month, Mary received a letter from Kitty. It announced that she'd be moving from the Clarkson home to a boarding house and planned to stay there for quite some time. Her letter hinted that she might get engaged to

William Clarkson but that he would finish his college degree first. Then near the bottom of the letter, Mary was excited to read that there would be a ball on the third Thursday in December, and Kitty wanted Mary to attend.

19

Philadelphia December, 1776

Congress recognized, after the distress of the fall campaign, that its military forces would need to be enlisted for longer terms of service. In the reorganization that followed, Washington authorized the raising of four light dragoon regiments. Like all early six-month regiments, Colonel Chester's command was dissolved in the new reorganization. Benjamin's regiment fell into this category as well, so he immediately enlisted in the new Continental units. His performances at the Battle of Brooklyn, and Chatterton's Hill had attracted notice from his superiors. Colonel Chester had already marked Benjamin as worthy of promotion.

Benjamin was offered command of the first troop of the Second Continental Dragoons, based in Connecticut, with his appointment having been approved by Washington. Benjamin's service continued with no break, and he brought in as recruits some of the infantrymen he had commanded in Chester's regiment. He then proceeded to Philadelphia, which was now known as the Continental capital, for instructions regarding raising and equipping the new regiment. There he received his captain's commission, signed by John Hancock, president of the Continental Congress, on December 14, 1776.

Hoping to spur enlistments, the Continental Army instituted a bounty system for those joining. This along with a fiery speech from Connecticut's governor, Jonathan Trumbull, that had taken place on the town green in Lebanon, Connecticut had brought in several thousand more recruits. Trumbull was the only colonial governor to support the American Revolution.

Benjamin walked into the tent of Colonel Elisha Sheldon, who was busy trying to procure supplies and necessities for his horses and men.

"You wanted to see me, sir?" Benjamin asked.

"Yes. I have orders from General Washington. He's written to me regarding a lack of supplies and a need to inoculate the army against smallpox."

"Yes, sir. I shall see to keeping my men well supplied as best I can. And I'll make sure to get my men inoculated if they've not already been exposed."

Colonel Sheldon gave a slight nod. "In the letter is a message from Washington I'd like to share. And Washington added some words from Governor Trumbull. These ideas might help you to engage your men and avoid any ideas of desertion that might be building among your troops. To quote General Washington, '"Three things prompt men to a regular discharge of their duty in time of action: natural bravery, hope of reward, and fear of punishment."' Also, Governor Trumbull's speech to all men in Connecticut seems to have resulted in new enlistments. Here, I made a copy for you."

Benjamin took the paper from Sheldon. "Thank you, sir. I shall be excited to read it to my men. And I will keep General Washington's words at the forefront of my mind."

"Oh, and one more matter," Sheldon said. "There is to be a ball organized by the Philadelphia Dancing Assembly on the third Thursday of this month. If that sort of thing interests you, I know several officers and commanders will be in attendance. That will be all."

As Benjamin left the colonel's tent to head back to his own, he began reading the speech by Trumbull that had inspired several thousand to enlist in the American cause.

In this day of calamity, to trust altogether to the justice of our cause, without our utmost exertion, would be tempting Providence... March on! This shall be your warrant: Play the man for God, and for the cities of our God. May the Lord of the Hosts, the God of the Armies of Israel, be your Captain, your Leader, your Conductor, and your Savior. —Governor Jonathan Trumbull Sr.

Upon reading the Connecticut governor's speech, Benjamin felt rallied, and infused with a new zeal. Already ambitious as well as enthusiastic and committed, he wanted to impress his commanders with his diligence, intelligence, and initiative. He strode back to his tent with his shoulders back and his head held high with a sense of purpose that would propel him as he would later lead his men into the throngs of battle. When he reached the tent, an aide-de-camp was waiting.

"Have you heard?" the man asked.

"What's that?"

"There's a ball to be held next Thursday. Several officers plan to attend. I should hope it would be of interest to you."

"Yes, I've just come from Colonel Sheldon's tent and was informed about it. I'll make plans to be in attendance."

20

Philadelphia, December, 1776

Mary, and her mother and father arrived in Philadelphia three weeks before the grand ball. William had business with Congress and spent many days away from Mary and Hannah. Kitty had just moved into a boarding house, and Mary and her parents rented a room in the same house. On most days, the family would breakfast together before Mary's father left for the day to attend Congress. After that, one of the ladies' most important tasks was getting ready for the ball. All three had picked out fabric and were measured for gowns, which they were anxious to try on. In the days leading up to the ball, Kitty, Mary, and their mother practiced the latest dances with the guidance of a teacher in order to get Mary feeling more prepared. Today, before their dance lesson, Kitty and Mary would be meeting their mother at the dress shop. They chatted fondly in the carriage ride over.

"I enjoy the minuet," Mary said.

"The allemande is the newest. I favor it," Kitty added.

"All that hand-holding?" Mary made a face.

Kitty laughed. "The point exactly."

"You can be such a flirt sometimes," Mary joked. "How does Mr. William Clarkson stand it?"

"The innocent flirting?" Kitty giggled. "I think he must enjoy it."

The carriage driver stopped and let the young ladies out in front of the store. They greeted their mother inside.

"Your gowns are ready to try on," the shop owner said, leading them into a back room.

There, three mannequins stood wearing the most gorgeous gowns Mary had ever seen.

Mary had chosen a pale blue silk, which was trimmed in lace. Kitty's gown was gold with rosettes and ruffles down the front, and their mother's dark-green dress was simpler but beautiful, nonetheless. After they all had tried their gowns on, the seamstress added pins where a few final adjustments were needed.

"I'm going to place the gowns back on the mannequins," the shop owner said. "Please look around for anything else you might need. I've just gotten in a shipment of silk stockings from France, some soaps, perfume, and parasols."

Mary, her mother, and sister changed back into their day dresses and made their way to the front of the shop to look at all the items for sale. Mary and Kitty each chose new stockings and a new bar of soap.

"What about new shoes, Mother?" Mary asked.

"Have you gotten new shoes lately, Kitty?" asked their mother.

"Father took me to the cordwainer not long after we arrived in early August. My shoes are almost four months old. I suppose they'll do."

"Mary does need new shoes. Can you show us the way to the cobbler from here?"

"I believe so. Do we have time before the dance lesson?"

"Yes," their mother said. "We didn't take as long trying on our dresses as I'd planned."

The owner came out from the back of the shop. "We can have your items delivered later today."

Hannah added the additional items to the order, paid, and gave the shop owner their address. They left the shop and walked two blocks to the cordwainer.

There, the cobbler fitted Mary for a fine pair of black leather shoes with a mid-heel and a large silver buckle across the top. He told her they would be ready next week. Which only gave Mary a few days to break them in before the ball.

∞∞∞∞∞∞∞∞∞∞

The day of the ball arrived, and each of the girls took time bathing in a deep copper tub. Afterward, their mother combed and braided each daughter's hair. For Kitty she created a fishtail along one side then pulled it, along with the rest of Kitty's long blonde hair, into a high bun and secured it with hair pins. Next, she braided some of Mary's hair—into two strips on either side of her part, then she pulled the long braids, along with the rest of Mary's mousy-brown ringlets, into a bun, letting a few ringlets spill out of the back.

Kitty put on her crystal and pearl earrings along with a simple necklace. Mary reached for the pearls she had received on her sixteenth birthday. She had worn them as they escaped to Connecticut and had decided she would treasure them more than any jewelry she might ever own.

She next slipped on her stockings, tying them with ribbon just above her knees, then slipped her chemise over her head. The girls helped each other with their stays and their stomachers, which matched their ball gowns.

Soon William knocked on the door.

"It's taking quite a long time in there," he said. "Is everything okay?"

"It is," Hannah answered. "It's just different from being at home and having Cora and Joli to help us dress. We're almost ready."

"The carriage should be here momentarily," Mary's father said. "I'll wait for you downstairs."

The girls' father was in awe when he saw his two beautiful daughters descend the staircase to the main room of the boarding house. He leaned in and kissed them each gently on the cheek. "The carriage is outside," he said. "I have the pleasure of accompanying the three most beautiful ladies in all of Philadelphia this evening." He took his wife's hand, kissed it, and held his other arm out for Mary and Kitty. Together they made their way to the carriage.

When the carriage driver let them out, Mary took in the grand scene before her. Her eyes roamed slowly to the glowing candles lining the steps as glorious music spilled out of the open doors. Dr. Clarkson greeted Mary's father as they made their entrance into the building. Formal introductions began as Dr. Clarkson introduced his wife and three of his sons to Mary and her mother. William took Kitty's hand and bowed.

The ladies were handed their dance cards with ribbons attached to them and they quickly tied the card's ribbons around their wrists, where the cards dangled like small trinkets. Hannah and Mrs. Clarkson were soon engaged in chatter. Mary's father and Dr. Clarkson were talking, and William had already led Kitty out onto the dance floor. Before Mary had too much time to feel left out, Samuel, one of the Clarkson brothers, asked her to dance. Mary nodded and hoped she could remember all the steps while at the same time keeping up an interesting conversation. The young man bowed and offered Mary his hand. She took it, and he led her out onto the dance floor.

"I'm very glad to finally meet the Mary Kitty has told us so much about."

"Oh?" Mary felt herself blush. The young man was near her height and had lovely blue eyes that matched his coat.

The music began and Mary tried hard to concentrate on the steps. She'd never been as musically inclined as her sister. *Right foot, step, point the other toe*, she said in her mind.

"Kitty would have us in stitches during supper some nights, telling us about some of your adventures. Catching toads and fish, and your impressive riding skills."

Samuel seemed pleasant enough, and he appeared to know quite a bit about Mary. She knew she needed to be engaging, but the dancing was taking a lot of her concentration. She kept a count going in her head. *One, two, three, four, five, six.*

"Uh . . . Oh, yes. Kitty and I have different interests, I suppose," she said. "And what about you, Samuel? What interests do you have?"

I would like to be a doctor like my father and brother, I think."

Three, two, three, four, five, six. Mary continued to count in her head. She tried to listen to what Samuel was saying but everything was a bit of a blur. She kept a smile on her lips, and every so often she would nod. Soon the dance ended, and Mary and Samuel bowed to each other.

"It was lovely to meet you and to have the first dance," Samuel said. "I know the rules are to only dance with the same person twice." He chuckled. "But, if you are agreeable, I'd enjoy finding you and asking you for a second dance later this evening."

"That would be lovely," Mary said as Samuel turned to walk away.

When Mary turned away from Samuel, she noticed that a group of Continental soldiers had arrived. They stood together in a circle, some of them talking, while others looked about the room, probably searching for an available dance partner. Mary was making her way through the crowd, watching the group of officers, when the side of her dress caught the edge of a table. Then she turned to find the most delightful assortment of cakes and desserts. There was also a tower of coupe-style champagne glasses arranged like a pyramid with golden, bubbling liquid flowing from the top-down, filling each glass as it spilled over. Curious, she picked up a glass and noticed nothing fell. With the coupe in her hand, she went to find her mother. On the way she stopped to talk with her father, who had just left a group of gentlemen he'd been engaged with.

Mary caught up with him just as a few soldiers were making their way onto the dance floor. She noticed Kitty on the arm of one.

"Are you having a nice time, dear?" her father asked.

"Yes, it's really quite entertaining."

Mary turned to watch Kitty, thinking her sister might dance all evening and end up with a full card while Mary might not get asked again. When she turned back to speak to her father, his back was to her, and he was engaged in conversation with one of the officers. She stepped closer, hoping to be introduced.

Her father turned to Mary, "There's my lovely daughter," he said.

Mary's eyes grew large, and her heart beat faster. Her palms became sweaty, and words caught in the back of her throat.

"Yes, it's nice to see you again, Kitty," said the officer.

What? Mary thought. He thought she was Kitty?

Her father wasn't paying any attention. "Excuse me please," he said. "I see James Madison. I must have a word."

He left Mary standing there with a look of shock on her face. She knew she needed to say something. But there, standing in front of her, tall and noble in a fine captain's uniform, was Benjamin Tallmadge. His hair was pulled back and tied with a black satin ribbon at the back of his neck. His kind eyes were gleaming, and he was smiling down at her, waiting for her response.

"Kitty's on the dance floor." Mary's voice sounded raspy and dry. "I'm Mary."

She drank some of the champagne from the coupe in her hand. Benjamin's expression changed from one of interest to one of curiosity. He cocked his head to the side and gazed at her quizzically.

"Mary. My apologies." He bowed slightly. "You look . . ." He paused, cleared his throat, and said, "It's good to see you."

Just then, another soldier walked up to Benjamin. "The ol' chaps are off to dance," he said with a chuckle. "I'd need a partner who wouldn't mind if I had two left feet."

Benjamin turned to his friend. "Mary, this is Captain Meade."

Meade bowed to Mary. "A pleasure, ma'am," he said. "I don't mean to interrupt. Were you two heading off to dance?"

Mary shook her head and Benjamin stumbled on his words. "Oh, uh . . . no . . . um, not at the moment."

"Ah, good," the captain said. "Miss Mary, may I extend the offer of the next dance? Would you do me the honor?"

Mary glanced at Benjamin, who looked slightly defeated, but he smiled at Mary.

"Of course, Captain Meade," she said.

Meade took the glass of champagne from Mary's hand and handed it to Benjamin with a grin. Benjamin nodded, looking slightly annoyed. Mary offered her hand, and Meade took it, leading her out to the edge of the dance floor.

When the current dance ended, they stepped out to the center of the floor. The music began to play for a contra dance. Mary was glad this type of dance didn't allow for much conversation. The dancers would be changing partners, executing hops and twirls, and performing a series of hand taps that reminded Mary of patty-cake.

When the dance ended, Meade bowed and said, "Thank you for the dance." He signed Mary's dance card and then asked, "Can I offer you refreshment?"

Mary nodded. "Thank you."

They walked to a refreshment table that boasted a large floral arrangement in the center. On either side were two large sterling silver punch bowls. Mary watched the captain fill two cups with punch, then she turned around in search of Benjamin. She spotted him on the dance floor with a young lady wearing a lavender gown. The lady wore a large ostrich feather in her hair, and Mary thought it looked silly. She was a bit angry that Benjamin had not offered her a dance.

Meade handed Mary a cup, and they moved off to the side to watch the dancers. Mary tried not to watch Benjamin the entire time, but that's exactly what she did. Meade tried to engage her in conversation about random things. She thought he probably noticed he wasn't holding her attention—until he said, "I'm aide-de-camp for General Washington. I write important dispatches for his excellency."

This got Mary's attention. "Oh, that's an incredibly important position."

With that, the captain beamed. "'Tis so," he agreed.

Kitty walked up from behind Mary with an older gentleman. "Sister," she said, getting Mary's attention.

"Mary, I'd like you to meet James Madison."

Introductions were made all around and the small talk began. Then an officer named Alexander Hamilton approached their group, and more introductions were made. A few minutes later, Kitty excused herself, and Mary felt someone step up behind her.

"Ah, Benjamin," Alexander said.

Mary turned around. She breathed in deeply, enjoying how close Benjamin was to her. He smelled of campfire smoke, wool, leather, and fresh soap. She wasn't listening as the men talked among themselves; she was more interested in why Benjamin had approached.

"I should apologize," Benjamin began, speaking to Mary. "I'm sorry I thought you were your sister. Obviously, you are not."

Mary smiled.

"You. . ." He paused a beat. "You look very lovely this evening."

Mary felt a blush creep from her chest to her throat. She glanced at the floor then returned Benjamin's gaze. Her eyes stayed locked on his longer than they should.

"Thank you, Captain Tallmadge," she finally said. "I'm sorry I've not written lately. We escaped with our lives and are now living in Connecticut. Father continues to have business with Congress in Philadelphia. Kitty has been living here for several months, at first with the Clarkson family, and now, she's decided she wants to stay on here and has moved to a boarding house. Mother and Father have rented a room there too while we are here in Philadelphia. Mother and I will return to Middleton within the week. I'm sure you haven't had much time for trivial things like letters lately."

"There are days that are long with some sleepless nights, yes. And the business of war takes its toll. But to receive a letter always brings joy. I have just been promoted as an officer of the Second Light Dragoons." The thought crossed Benjamin's mind that Mary might not understand the nature of his command. "We are a mounted troop of light horsemen. I myself ride a striking dapple-gray mare. I report to Colonel Elisha Sheldon. In fact, I will be stationed in Connecticut for the winter months."

"Stationed in Connecticut, you say?" Mary's father's voice startled her briefly. She hadn't noticed he'd approached, as she was so engaged in such pleasant conversation with Benjamin.

"We shall invite you to join us during the holidays," Mary's father said.

"I would be honored, sir," said Benjamin.

"Good, good." William turned to his daughter. "Your mother has taken a turn. She's not feeling well, and I've called for the carriage to be brought around. We shall gather your sister." He turned to Benjamin and bowed. "Captain Tallmadge. We look forward to your visit in Middleton soon."

Benjamin nodded. "Yes, sir. Thank you." He looked at Mary. "It was nice to see you, Mary." Benjamin bowed low, and Mary curtsied. Their eyes locked for a brief moment, and Mary felt flushed.

Mary's father offered his arm to his daughter, and together they walked away to find Kitty.

21

Connecticut, Late December, 1776

After returning to their home in Middleton, Mary's family had entertained several men from Congress over Christmas. Even Nicoll had made it home by Christmas and was planning to stay a few days.

Although planning for the festivities had kept the ladies busy, Kitty was anxious to go back to Philadelphia as soon as her father made plans to return, but until then there wasn't a moment to spare between all the cooking, baking, and cleaning. New Year's Eve was approaching, and they'd received word several days ago that Benjamin Tallmadge would make a stop to visit with them. For this, Mary was excited and nervous.

Their home smelled of fresh pine Mary and Kitty had gathered on Christmas Eve and placed along the fireplace mantle and at the center of the large dining table. Mary decided that for Benjamin's visit she wanted everything to be extra special, so she went out to clip holly with red berries to add to the pine garlands. For Christmas, her father had gifted her and her siblings with a bag of oranges, and Mary placed several in clusters among the pine and holly down the center of the dining table.

"That looks splendid, dear," her father said as he watched Mary add sprigs of holly and fresh oranges along the center of the table. "Everyone will be pleased."

"Do we have more guests coming, or is it just Captain Tallmadge?" Kitty asked.

"While I was in Philadelphia, I invited Mr. James Madison to join us over the holiday," her father said. "But I haven't heard from him."

"You invited James Madison?" Kitty asked.

"I believe he quite favors you, Kitty," her father told her with a chuckle. "He's a very respected man."

"He's quite old, isn't he?" Mary asked.

"Oh, I suppose he might be somewhere in his late twenties," their father said.

Kitty huffed, and Mary giggled.

Their father changed the subject. "Something smells delicious. I'll go have a look in the kitchen and check on your mother and the food preparations. Everything looks beautiful in here. Thank you, dear." He leaned down and kissed Mary on the top of her head.

∞∞∞∞∞∞∞∞

Later that evening, Benjamin arrived right before they sat down for New Year's Eve supper. Benjamin and Mary shared a pleasant greeting, then he retired with Nicoll and her father to sit near the fireplace while the ladies completed the final food preparations. When they were called to the table, Mary made sure to sit next to Benjamin. Kitty and her mother sat across from them. Their father and Nicoll sat at either end of the table.

Cora brought out a platter of turkey and placed it next to William. Joli brought in a bowl of potatoes and carrots along with a tray of sliced bread, placing them in the center of the table.

William asked everyone to bow their heads for the prayer. He reached out and took hold of Mary's hand and Hannah's. Cautiously, Mary held her hand out for Benjamin to take. When he took her hand in his, it felt as if her stomach had leapt into her throat. His hand was large and warm and made Mary feel safe while holding it. The sensation of holding hands with Benjamin was so strong that at first Mary didn't realize the prayer had ended. When she finally understood, she blushed and released his hand. But the smile Benjamin gave her didn't make her feel embarrassed; instead, it was a warm and inviting smile that turned her insides to liquid.

"So, Benjamin," her father said, "tell us how your post in Connecticut has gone so far."

Benjamin set down his glass of mead. "The winter months can be slow and not good for fighting when the weather is cold and rainy. So, in between battles, I've worked extensively to equip and train my troops in Wethersfield. I've erected a large circular arena for the purpose of training and breaking our horses to prepare for spring." Benjamin smiled. "I have no hesitation in acknowledging that I am very proud of this command. My troop mostly rides dapple-gray horses. Our saddle gear includes black straps and black bearskin holster-covers—and they look superb. When Washington commented on our exceptional appearance, I felt extremely proud."

"That sounds fine. Fine indeed," William said. "I know the winter in Valley Forge has been a harsh one for Washington and his men."

Benjamin nodded. "It has been. A lot of men don't have shoes. Food is scarce. I'm in constant contact with Jeremiah Wadsworth about the need to keep my men supplied and equipped. I know Washington bends the ear of Congress on this topic until it is worn. But Congress will be pleased to learn of the capture of one thousand Hessian soldiers. Washington and his men crossed the Delaware on Christmas night with a surprise attack on Colonel Rall and his men the next morning. Another bold move by General Washington and a victory for independence."

"Huzzah!" William said, lifting his glass.

Everyone at the table followed suit. "Huzzah!" they shouted in unison.

"Were any of our men killed or injured?" Nicoll asked.

"Very few," said Benjamin. "We had five injured. I believe only two deaths. Major James Monroe was shot, but I've been told he will recover. I received word from both James Madison and Alexander Hamilton."

"May Divine Providence continue to go with Washington," William said.

Benjamin nodded. "I believe Washington plans another crossing soon. May General Washington elude Cornwallis."

"To Washington." Nicoll held up his glass, and everyone at the table toasted.

"Has there been any news about your home and farm in Mastic?" Benjamin asked.

"Caleb Brewster and I scouted the area," Nicoll began. "There are British soldiers quartering there now. We tried to collect most of the horses that we let loose during the escape. I rode away on Mary's horse, and she was grateful to see Spot again on Christmas morning." Nicoll's smile lit up his face.

Mary smiled back. "And Nicoll said my dog was with a neighbor and is safe," she added. "His name is Moses, and I truly miss him too." When she turned to look at Benjamin, their eyes locked. His eyes were soft and his expression sensitive.

Benjamin smiled at Mary. "I know about favorite horses," he said, with all of his attention now focused on her. "I almost lost mine during the Battle of Brooklyn. After crossing the East River safely on one of the last boats, I regretted leaving such a fine horse and asked for permission to recross. It was a bold move, and we faced fire but were far enough away their musket fire couldn't reach us—and my horse and I were reunited."

"You are quite brave, sir," Mary said. Her heart pounded loudly in her chest, and she worried everyone could hear it. The thought of Benjamin risking everything to save his horse gave her goosebumps in the most perfect way.

Soon Cora brought out a cake and started to slice it. The aroma of butter and cinnamon filled the air. Once they each had enjoyed a slice of cake, William said, "There are to be fireworks at midnight in the town's square if you are able to stay, Benjamin. You may retire here for the night."

"That would be most agreeable. Thank you, sir. I shall stay until daybreak before returning to my post in Wethersfield." Benjamin turned to Mary and finished his remarks. "Your home is quite welcoming."

∞∞∞∞∞∞∞∞

Later, when Mary and Kitty retired to their bedroom, Mary fell back onto the bed, feeling overwhelmed with joy. Nicoll had left after their meal to head back to Fairfield, and Benjamin had been given Nicoll's room. Mary breathed deeply and let out a happy sigh.

"Is everything all right, Mary?" Kitty whispered.

Mary turned to face Kitty in the dark. "Perfect. Today has been perfect."

Kitty stared at Mary for a few beats. "You fancy him, don't you? The captain who's sleeping in the room downstairs." Kitty sat up. "Ahhhhh, my baby sister is in love."

"No. I am not," Mary said with determination. "What would you know of love?" she whispered. "Keep your voice down. I don't want Mother to hear us." She could hear her father snoring and knew at least one parent was asleep.

"Goodness, Mary. No one can hear themselves think as loud as Father's snoring is," said Kitty.

Mary turned away and settled her head on the pillow. "I'd rather not discuss this anymore this evening. Good night, sister," she whispered.

Mary rose before daybreak and dressed quietly so as not to wake up Kitty. As she tiptoed down the steps, she could hear the shuffling of feet in her mother and father's bedroom so she knew someone else would be downstairs soon. Mary was hopeful she would not miss Benjamin when he gathered his things to leave. When she entered the kitchen, Cora and Joli had just started making breakfast. Cora was rolling out biscuits, and Joli was gathering jars of jam from the shelf.

"Good morning, child," Cora greeted Mary. "Biscuits almost ready to go into the pan. You're up early this morning after a late night with all those fireworks and loud booms. Woke me from my sleep, I tell you."

Mary giggled. "Captain Tallmadge stayed the night. I don't want to miss his departure this morning."

"Oh, I see," Cora said.

A knowing smile graced Cora's lips as she turned away and began placing biscuits into a black iron skillet. Mary watched as Cora carried it over and placed it on the fire. Soon William and Hannah joined Mary in the kitchen, and a few moments later, Benjamin appeared in the doorway.

"Good morning," he said.

Mary turned to see Benjamin leaning against the doorpost dressed in his fine uniform. The brass buttons that ran down either side of his navy coat shone brightly and were offset by wide ivory trim. His knee-high black leather boots look freshly polished. The sword at his left side drew her attention to its large gold handle. He held his tall, plumed Dragoon hat under one arm. "I shall see about gathering my horse," he said while looking at Mary. "It has been a most pleasant stay."

"Stay and eat with us, won't you?" Hannah asked.

"The sun is rising, and I should get on the road and back to my troops."

"Can I pack you something to take on your journey?" Mary asked.

"That would be most thoughtful. Thank you, Mary." Benjamin added a slight bow.

Mary gathered some oranges, leftover bread, and a slice of cheese, and wrapped and tied the items into a square of cheesecloth.

"I'll go get Jeb and have him bring your horse around," William said.

"Have some coffee at least before you go, Captain," Hannah offered. "Please sit."

Benjamin sat at the table. Joli poured him a cup of coffee, and William walked out the back door to fetch Jeb about the horse. Mary carried the package of food to Benjamin. When he placed his coffee down, she handed him the package she'd prepared.

"Some cheese, bread, and oranges for the trip," she said. "How far is it from here to Wethersfield?"

"It's almost ten miles. I should arrive back at camp before noon."

William walked back inside. "Jeb is bringing your horse around now."

Benjamin turned to Hannah. "I greatly appreciate your hospitality. It's been a lovely visit."

"It's been our pleasure," Hannah replied.

Just then Kitty made her way down the stairs. "Oh, Captain. Good morning," she said. "Good to see you again."

Benjamin stood and greeted Kitty, then made his way into the front room of the house. Mary and her father followed. As they walked out onto the porch, they saw Jeb walking toward the house with Benjamin's horse. Benjamin turned and shook hands with William.

"Thank you, sir," Benjamin said.

"You are welcome anytime, son," William replied. "Safe travels."

With that, William turned and went back inside. Benjamin walked down the steps toward his horse. Jeb tied the horse to the post. Mary followed Benjamin down the steps. When he noticed she was there, he turned around.

"I will be praying for you, Captain Tallmadge," Mary said.

"I shall be grateful for that, Mary. I would be hopeful to continue our correspondence if it pleases you."

"Very much, sir. I would be honored. I do wish you safe travels and hope to see you again."

Benjamin turned to Jeb. "Thank you," he said. He placed his hat on his head then mounted his horse and tipped his head to Mary before riding away.

22

Summer/Fall 1777

At the opening of the spring campaign of 1777, Benjamin and his Second Continental Dragoons left Wethersfield where he had passed a gratifying and very busy winter—with military duties by day and pleasant interchanges with the town's inhabitants in the evenings. He left with some regret, having also been the town's schoolteacher and superintendent prior to the war. But he was also filled with military ambition and was panting for victory.

He and his troops moved from Connecticut into Morristown, New Jersey where Benjamin met with the commander-in-chief, who ordered him to move his encampment to a spot near Middlebrook, New Jersey. It was there General Washington again praised Benjamin and his detachment on their fine appearance. Within the next few days, Benjamin's mounted horse squadron, a lightly armed but highly mobile type of cavalry unit known as light horse—would be engaged in the Battle of Short Hills. General Washington immediately took precautions to procure strongholds in Middlebrook. General William Howe was disappointed in his plan to draw Washington into battle. Washington's men had alerted him that Howe had left behind equipment needed to cross the Delaware and thought it might be unlikely that the British were heading for Philadelphia. But

Washington called on the southern New Jersey militia as a precautionary measure. When Howe's army moved again, seeking to draw Washington into battle on open terrain, Washington refused the bait and remained in the hills.

Benjamin's light troops hovered near the rear, and once Washington had determined the course of the British, he put his whole army under march for the Delaware. Benjamin's recruits crossed the Delaware, as they slowly began their move toward Philadelphia, and halted in Germantown prior to the Battle of Brandywine. By this time, Benjamin had been promoted to the rank of major.

Washington was determined to strike the British before they reached Philadelphia. He deployed his men along the edge of Brandywine Creek. A full-scale battle ensued with Benjamin and his men in the thick of the fighting.

During the battle, General Henry Knox called out to Benjamin, "Major, the enemy has made it to the stone house. Place your dragoons across the road and secure a picket with a small unit of soldiers on guard. You must prevent the retreat of their infantry."

Immediately Benjamin led his squadron to a spot near Forty Foot Road, where they began to spread out, poised for attack. "Prolong the retreat," Benjamin commanded.

The line held for over thirty minutes before conditions became unbearable, and a retreat was inevitable.

From there, General Washington removed his armies to Pottsgrove, and Howe moved to the Schuylkill River, which gave the enemy an easy march into Philadelphia. A few days before, General Cornwallis and a column of Hessian grenadiers would enter Philadelphia, Congress would flee the city for safety in Yorktown.

Once the rebels had retreated toward Chestnut Hill, the enemy halted. Washington fell back to his quarters at Valley Forge, and the enemy took Philadelphia. Late in December of

1777, Washington stationed Benjamin with a respectable detachment of dragoons as an advanced corps to maintain observation of the enemy. Benjamin's duties were arduous, with him not being able to tarry long in one place with the British light horse continually patrolling the intermediate area. While on duty at two in the morning, Benjamin and his men were attacked by a large body of British light horsemen commanded by Lord Francis Rawdon. As the battle drew on, Benjamin and his men tried to retreat, but Lord Rawdon's men came around their flank, and three of Benjamin's men were ruthlessly killed.

Although Benjamin was on frequent picket duty to keep watch against the enemy near the Delaware and Schuylkill Rivers, he took time to write letters when in camp. In one letter to his friend Jeremiah Wadsworth, he lamented about the manner in which his men had been slaughtered.

Dear Wadsworth.

Notwithstanding the entreaties and prayers of the prisoners for mercy, the soldiers fell upon them with their swords, and after hacking, cutting, and stabbing them till they supposed they were dead, they then left them there, setting fire to the barn to consume any who might be in it. They also coolly murdered an old man of the house, first cutting and most inhumanely mangling him with their swords then shooting him. These were the Devils that murdered those lads of my troop. Wish to God I could take some of them to show them that we dare and will retaliate such unprecedented barbarities. We are ten miles in front of the army now and have not pulled off our clothes for eighteen days. We are in need of provisions and supplies enough to make an honest man desert, and I am told the cause of a great many leaving us.

I pray to God; you may not let us starve. Just when our prospects begin to be promising.

Benjamin closed the letter to his friend, sealed it, and left his tent to carry it to dispatch. On his way, he noticed someone on horseback entering their encampment. When he realized it was Lieutenant Caleb Brewster, Benjamin ran over to him.

"Caleb, what brings you this far?" Benjamin asked.

Caleb dismounted his horse, took him by the reins, and walked closer to Benjamin.

"I've news," Caleb said. "During the raid in Setauket, Colonel Richard Hewlett took over your father's church. They must have been informed we were coming because they had established a breastwork." Caleb raised one hand above his head. "The armored structure stood six feet high all around the church. Mounted atop were swivel guns. General Samuel Parsons ordered Hewlett to surrender. Hewlett refused, and for at least three hours we exchanged gunfire. My men and I placed a cannon on top of a large rock and fired upon them." Caleb grinned. "Remember that mountain of a rock we used to climb as boys? The one that faces the sound?"

Benjamin nodded. "What of Hewlett and the church?"

"They've taken over the church, even pulled gravestones from the cemetery to make shells and weaponry. Before we retreated and recrossed the sound back to Connecticut, Colonel Webb was captured."

"No other casualties?" Benjamin asked.

"No, but I've more intelligence. There will be a girl who has volunteered to go to Philadelphia to gather information about the British positions. Can you provide an escort for her near Germantown?"

"We can meet near there," Benjamin answered. "There's a tavern there called The Rising Sun. Who is this girl?" he asked.

"That I cannot say for sure. She'll be coming from Philadelphia and will need to meet you. She'll debrief you on any news about the enemy, then she'll need safe escort from there up to Princeton. Then from there, safe passage back into Connecticut."

"I'll see to it," Benjamin replied. "Within the next day, I'll plan to move a small detachment with me to Germantown."

With that, Caleb saluted Benjamin, gathered his horse, and left the camp.

23
Winter, Middleton, Connecticut, 1777

Mary was outside beating the rugs when the post arrived. The postrider handed her a letter and a small package. Her father had sent something, which Mary quickly opened and read.

She clambered up the front steps into the house. Oh, Mother," Mary cried. "Father and Kitty must leave Philadelphia immediately. Congress is being removed to a safer place. The British have entered the city. Father says he will return long enough to see that Kitty is home safely but will have to leave again."

Mary's mother took the letter from her and began to read it herself. "Praise God they will come back to us safe and unharmed."

Mary's mother took the letter with her and went back to the kitchen. Mary looked at the package in her hand. The postmark said Oyster Bay. She felt both joy and a bit of apprehension as she tore open the package. Inside she found three small sachets made from cotton muslin, each embroidered on one side with leaves and flowers. They smelled of sweet spices, cinnamon, oranges, and dried mint leaves.

Mary opened the note enclosed with the handmade gifts and began to read.

Dear Mary,

I hope this letter finds you and your family well. I wanted to thank you for your gift of the apron with the lovely small embroidered floral design along the edge which revealed to me your great friendship with our family and interest in continuing a correspondence with me and our beloved L. I shared your news and she was thankful.

Upon reading the first sentences, Mary realized that Phebe's letter was a bit abstract, talking in vague terms, and using only the letter *"L."* She thought this was odd but soon realized Phebe must be afraid someone might read her posts.

The letter continued.

We've made something special for you, your mother, and sister to keep close by. I hope the fragrance is agreeable. You will notice the stitching along the edge of one. A design by our friend that she hopes will implore you to further discover.

We send our love and best wishes. Always, Phebe

Quickly, Mary took time to look at the stitching along each sachet. Along the top and bottom edges of one, a whipstitch had been added. Mary went to the kitchen and retrieved a knife. She snipped the top stitch and opened up the small pouch to not only find the dried potpourri but also a small note that had been rolled up and tucked inside with the spices. It was a note from Liza.

They taken over the house. A captain named John Simcoe in charge. He seems fair and is nice to Sally. But we stay timid and keep our guard. They believe master Robert in New York is a Tory, so for now we stay safe. The captain has meetings in the house. I listen in and he don't know I do. I pray for you every day. Your friend, Liza

Mary walked out of the kitchen and went upstairs to her room, where she sat on the bed. She was thankful for the news, but it worried her. Although Liza's note did say the soldiers believed Robert Townsend—Sally and Phebe's older brother—to be a Tory, so maybe they believed the same about the rest of the household. As she thought of Liza, and the soldiers that were quartering inside the Townsend home, she wondered; could Liza give the Continentals information regarding the British military plans? Could Mary get involved? If anyone would know, it would be her brother or Lieutenant Caleb Brewster. When Nicoll had been home for the holidays, he'd talked about how Caleb took whaleboats up and down the sound near Long Island, to watch for the British. He said Caleb was sending reports of what he'd seen directly to Washington. If she could get word to Nicoll to tell Caleb about the British captain staying in Oyster Bay, maybe any information Liza could overhear would help the Americans succeed.

Mary walked over to her desk and opened a drawer. She removed a piece of paper and began to pen a note to Nicoll.

Dear Brother,

I've just received a lovely note from your treasured Phebe. She and a beloved housemate of hers made the loveliest sachets, and the scent is divine. She added a note about some unfortunate houseguests who might have overstayed their visit. She did say they have plans to continue their visit, as she hears all of their conversations being in such close proximity to her guests. And it just so happens young girls can be curious at times and somewhat nosey. But I digress. I would very much like to see you soon. We should discuss Phebe and make plans in person. I hope you are willing to take leave for a visit. Father and Sister will return from the city and will be home soon.

All my love and prayers go to you. I am your beloved sister.

Mary decided as soon as her father was home, she'd ask him to send her letter to Nicoll. From there she'd see what would happen next.

24

Germantown, Pennsylvania
Winter, 1777

Benjamin and his light-horse-dragoon troops had been scouring the country from the Delaware to the Schuylkill to keep watch on the British, hoping to prevent them from carrying supplies into Philadelphia. They couldn't tarry long in one place for fear of another attack like the one Lord Rawdon had carried out against them. At one point they went eighteen days without removing their clothing. But a break in routine came for Benjamin based on his talk with Caleb. Benjamin pulled together some men to ride with him toward the British lines, and to a tavern called The Rising Sun.

After dismounting his horse, Benjamin waited and watched for the female spy near the tavern's entrance while his men stood watch on the other side of the building. Soon he saw a young girl on horseback come riding out of the city. She stopped at the tavern and dismounted. When she came closer to where Benjamin stood, he was shocked by who he saw and said,

"Mary? What are . . . How are you?"

Mary placed a finger to her lips, not wanting Benjamin to be overheard. He took her by the arm, and they moved inside the tavern.

"Nicoll helped me into the city in order to gather some intelligence," she told him, "and to let you know about a Captain John Graves Simcoe who is quartering in the home of some friends of mine in Oyster Bay."

Mary's words were hurried and quiet. Benjamin stared at her in disbelief.

"This friend happens to be a kitchen slave," she continued, "and she and I are close friends. From working in the house, she learns quite a lot by overhearing things during important meetings that this captain holds. It's the home of the Townsend family. They are merchants. One of Samuel Townsend's sons, Robert, owns a shop in Hanover Square in New York. Because he has stayed with his business in New York City, he might be considered to hold Tory sentiments. I believe he will be of help in gathering information about British movement in New York. And so will my friend who lives in the Townsend home in Oyster Bay."

Mary glanced around the tavern and only saw the owner clearing dishes from a table. She continued in a whisper. "Not long ago, while walking through Philadelphia, I overheard a British officer talking about General Howe's plan to return to England."

Suddenly, one of Benjamin's men informed him that the British light horse were advancing. Stepping toward the doorway, Benjamin looked out and saw them approaching at full speed. They chased down one of Benjamin's patrols and captured him. Without a moment to reflect, Benjamin took Mary by the hand, and together they scurried toward his horse. He hoisted her up onto the saddle, then mounted himself. They took off rapidly, through considerable pistol fire, but escaped into safe territory. When they were at least three miles up the road, Benjamin stopped to let his horse rest for a moment. He was quite impressed with this young girl who never flinched, squealed, or uttered any expression of fear as they fled the enemy.

They both took a moment to catch their breath then Benjamin spoke.

"First, I'll say how incredibly brave you are," he said. "But war and the prospect of spying are beyond dangerous. It goes without saying that your life is at risk. Your father would never forgive me if something were to happen to you. I want to know how you came to be in Philadelphia. I know your father is not there, as Congress has been removed to a secure location. I'm much surprised to know your brother Nicoll was the one who helped you."

Mary adjusted herself in the saddle and turned around to face Benjamin. She nodded. "He provided a horse and safe transport in order to meet you. I can assure you I was never suspected, and I promise I can be of service. We have family on Long Island who are Tories, including my cousin Benjamin Floyd. I could pass as a Tory, just as I did to get here."

Benjamin shook his head. "Mary, I cannot encourage this. I appreciate the information. But it's too dangerous for you. We must get back to Patriot lines quickly."

The horse returned to a canter then a gallop as they continued their journey toward Patriot lines. Once they were near Trenton, they rested a few hours before traveling to Princeton. The next day, they were weary by the time they met up with Nicoll along the road to Morristown. After a much-needed rest, Benjamin re-saddled his horse so he could continue to the camp at Trenton.

But before he departed, Benjamin pulled Nicoll to the side and spoke quietly to him.

"I must ask that you take as much precaution as you can to protect your sister. She's most brave, and I find her efforts agreeable. But I cannot say I would accept the idea of her continuing in this manner. The dangers it holds are much too great."

"I agree with you, sir," Nicoll said. "But you don't know my sister well. She is more than stubborn and strong-willed. I would be afraid to see what she might do to the man who were to stop her. She's mighty clever, Major. I did everything I could to keep her from this mission, but it had no effect." The corners of Nicoll's lips turned up in a smirk. "I assure you our father is not to hear of this if I can help it. Mary will take it to her grave and will continue to play the role of perfect and favored daughter."

Benjamin glanced at Mary, who was watching them intently. Something inside him stirred. He might be feeling a bit beguiled—and somewhat enchanted.

"I see," Benjamin said. "Your sister has impressed me, it moves me to say, I may, in fact, be struck with rapture." Benjamin shook hands with Nicoll, then said, "Safe travels to you."

Benjamin tipped his hat to Mary, then mounted his horse and moved toward the road back to Trenton.

25

Middleton, Connecticut Winter, 1777

As Mary and Nicoll drew closer to their home in Middleton, Mary grew more anxious about what might take place once they arrived. A knot formed in her stomach, and she felt cold and more fatigued. Finally, they arrived on the road leading to the house. As they came nearer, all Mary could think about was getting off the back of Nicoll's horse and falling into bed. Out front, they stopped to tie the horse to the hitching post. As soon as they dismounted, Mary saw Jeb come around from the barn.

"Miss Mary, Master Nicoll," he greeted. "It's good to see you. I'll take your horse to the stable and get him fed. Will you be needing him later today, Master Nicoll?"

"No, Jeb. But thank you. I will be staying the night and will leave by sunrise tomorrow. I'll need him ready then."

Jeb nodded, took the horse by the reins and led him around back.

Before Mary and Nicoll could make it to the porch, the front door swung open, and Mary's mother bolted from inside.

"Mary Polly Floyd!" she cried. "How dare you leave us for days on end without us knowing where you were. For two days we thought you were ill—with your sister playing her part in this charade of yours. Finally, I demanded to come into the room to see you, and what do I find? Blankets and pillows folded into the shape of a sleeping body on your side of the bed! It was a good thing Cora followed me up. She caught me when I fainted."

Then Mary's father came up behind his wife and took her by the arm. "Now, dear, let the child come into the house. Let's not make such a fuss where others could hear."

William ushered Mary inside after her mother, and Nicoll followed. William closed the door. Kitty was waiting inside, and Mary could see Cora and Joli standing in the doorway of the kitchen, but they soon went back to whatever they'd been doing.

"Both of you have a seat," Mary's father said and pointed to the couch. He sat in one of the tall wingback chairs in front of the fire. Hannah sat in the chair opposite, and Kitty remained where she was. All eyes were on Mary.

"I should start by asking where you two have been, and I want the truth," William began. "Nicoll, since you are the young man in all of this, tell us, please, why your seventeen-year-old sister has been gone for six days and has just come riding up to the house with her older brother, who we know should be in Fairfield running support across the sound for the Patriot cause."

Nicoll looked to Mary then to his father. "She contacted me about wanting to relay information to Major Tallmadge, sir."

"What possible information would Mary have that she needed to tell Major Tallmadge?" their father asked.

Kitty giggled. "I can think of something."

"Catherine Floyd!" her mother shouted. "It's bad enough you kept us in the dark that Mary had plans to sneak away with Nicoll for some unknown reason. We don't need your twaddle now."

Kitty blushed and shrank down in her seat.

"And you thought it was a good idea to allow your sister to cross enemy lines in order to see Major Tallmadge?" Mary's Father asked.

Nicoll shook his head. "No, sir. I did not think it was a good idea. I told Mary it was dangerous, and she could be hanged as a spy if she were caught."

"A spy?" Hannah gasped. "Oh, Lord, Mighty, divine, Heavenly Father." She looked as if she might faint.

"But yet, you proceeded?" William asked.

"Obviously," Kitty said.

"Catherine!" Hannah shouted.

Nicoll nodded. "Yes, sir. Mary told me it was of utmost importance that she be the one to relay the information to Major Tallmadge. And she wanted me to personally escort her to meet him. First, though, I sent word through Caleb Brewster that there would to be a girl in Philadelphia who had information regarding the British, sir."

"And did Mary tell you what this information is?" William asked.

"She did not. She said it would remain a secret and she would only relay the news to Major Tallmadge."

William looked at his daughter. "And did you, Mary? Relay this important news to Major Tallmadge?"

"Yes, sir. I did," Mary said.

"And how did you come about this information?" asked her father.

"Through correspondence with an old friend in Oyster Bay."

"I see," her father said. "If it's that important, maybe you should tell us what it's about."

"I've relayed the information to Major Tallmadge. That was what I intended to do. I've done that. Now, I'm tired and would like to rest. May I be excused?"

"Be excused?" Her mother looked confused and annoyed. "We cannot excuse your behavior, that's for sure. This is an outrage! William, this is all preposterous, is it not?"

William stood and walked over to where his wife sat. Gently, he took her hand. "Preposterous it is not. Unusual, yes. And quite dangerous. But if Mary thought it necessary to go to as much trouble as she did to give information to Major Tallmadge that might serve as useful intelligence to General Washington, then we should let her be excused for now, seeing as to how she and Nicoll have had a long journey."

William moved to where his daughter sat, then extended his hand to her. After Mary took hold of her father's hand, he said,

"You should have come to me first, Mary. I can get information to the right people."

Mary stared into her father's eyes briefly, then nodded.

Cora and Joli came into the room with a tray of tea and plate of cookies. They set their offerings down on a table near Mary. Then Cora asked, "May I fix you a hot bath, Mary?"

Mary nodded then stood. She walked past Kitty and started toward the stairs. As she made her way up, she could hear her mother begin to cry. When Mary got to her room, she started to close the door, but Kitty stopped her and came into the room. Mary sat down on the bed and began to take off her shoes and stockings. Kitty sat next to her.

"I held them off as long as I could," Kitty said. "But by the third day, Mother insisted upon coming into the room. I couldn't stop her. Cora was with her, and I think Cora had an idea what you might be up to. She's keen to how you and Liza write secret notes to one another. And we all know that life on Long Island with soldiers quartering in people's homes. . ." Kitty shook her head. "I'm sure it's terrifying. She placed her hand on Mary's shoulder. "I think what you did was brave. And if I can help again, if there is a next time, I will be glad to."

26

Spring/Summer 1778

Benjamin walked past Washington's aide-de-camp, John Laurens, who was holding open the flap to the general's tent.

"You wanted to see me, General?" Benjamin asked.

"Yes. Sit down, Major." Washington pointed to a seat at his table.

A map was unfolded in front of the general, held open with rocks placed along the edges.

"As you know, the British are preparing to leave Philadelphia, and I believe General Henry Clinton will go back to New York. But along the way his armies could strike at any moment. If they take the road through Monmouth, we will cross the Delaware at McConkey's Ferry. I plan to have General Lee engage them until the whole army can press Clinton at all sides."

Washington moved his hand across the map, stopping at each place mentioned.

Benjamin nodded.

"The French fleet is underway and should arrive within the month," Washington continued. "I'll have you and your light dragoons stationed along the sound in Connecticut—Westchester, no-man's land. If General Clinton readies his army for a new attack, we will need to know his movements along the sound and along Long Island. If he were to get up the Hudson to West Point, he'd be able to completely cut us off from all contact between our northern colonies and our southern colonies. Communication between our armies and residents in our southern colonies would be affected."

Washington's piercing blue eyes met Benjamin's hazel-flecked light brown ones. "We can't allow him to control the Hudson. I've received important dispatches with intelligence from Lieutenant Brewster. His reports from Long Island along the sound have been helpful. Since you are also from Setauket, I would ask that you set up a system for gathering intelligence. Find those you can trust to collect information and get it to me quickly. If that be through whaleboat and Lieutenant Brewster, then so be it. We need to know the enemy's movements, what supplies they have, the number of troops, and, of course, we need to figure out their next moves."

"Yes, General."

Washington paused. His stare was intense. The air in the tent felt as if it had thinned. Benjamin watched as the general pushed his chair away from the table and stood. Quickly Benjamin jumped to his feet, his eyes never leaving his commander in chief.

"It goes without saying that our correspondence will remain private in this matter, as will your arrangements with your agents," Washington said. "You must find intelligence agents with good reason to be traveling into New York City."

"I assure you, sir, I will only recruit those I can trust with my life."

"Very well. Thank you, Major. You are dismissed."

Benjamin gave a short bow to the General, then turned to leave.

"Oh, and Major," Washington said.

Benjamin turned around. "Sir."

"General Gates has left this." Washington picked up a note and handed it to Benjamin. "I believe he's invited his commanders to a Fourth of July party."

Benjamin smiled. "Thank you, sir."

27

Setauket, Long Island Summer, 1778

Benjamin met up with Major John Clark, Washington's spy, who had been working in and around Philadelphia. Together they left camp at sunrise and rode from Durham to Fairfield to meet Caleb near the sound, arriving at sunset. When they reached the Continental camp, Nicoll took their horses from them.

"I'll feed them well," Nicoll said, then led the horses away.

Benjamin and Clark walked down Harbor Road, where they met Caleb on the banks of the river.

"We'll cross once the sky hits its peak darkness," Caleb instructed. "Don't make any sound as we cross. News from Setauket is Captain Hewlett's taken Selah Strong captive, thinking he's a spy. He's been imprisoned on the Jersey. British soldiers are camped in his house. Because of that, his wife, Anna, and their children have moved out of the main house into the guest quarters out back, near the water's edge. Anna has always been good about leaving a signal on her clothesline that hangs near the water's edge, alerting me which cove to hide in. We'll look for her signal. The number of items hanging from the line will show which cove Abraham will meet us in."

In near silence, with only the slight splash of the oars gracing the water, the three men crossed the sound in just over four hours. When they arrived along the bank in Setauket near the Strongs' property, Caleb took note of the number of napkins on the line, signaling they were to meet Abraham near the Strongs' property. He steered the whaleboat into the brush along the edge of the bank. Soon, the men could see a figure coming close to where they were.

"Caleb," Anna said in barely more than a whisper.

"Aye," Caleb answered and exited the boat. Anna's dress was all black, and with her dark hair pulled into a tight bun at the nape of her neck, she blended well with the night sky. When Caleb saw that Anna was alone, he signaled for Major Clark and Benjamin to step ashore. The four of them gathered near the thick brush along the bank, and in whispered words, Anna told them about Abraham's recent arrest for trying to smuggle goods grown on his farm into Connecticut.

"Abraham is being held in a Patriot prison in Connecticut for illegal trading of British goods—selling things he's obtained in New York and potatoes from his farm," Anna said.

Benjamin and Clark looked at one another. Benjamin's thoughts turned to concern for his friend Abraham.

"Well, to be a spy, he has a good cover as a smuggler of goods," Major Clark began. "But I know Washington will be concerned that he'd take proper measures to curb any passion for gain."

"I assure you, Major Clark," Benjamin said, "Washington should have no concern over Abraham Woodhull's loyalty. I know him to be reliable and more motivated by his support for the Patriot cause than any interest in filling his pockets."

"I can affirm that too," Caleb added. "We've all grown up together here in Setauket. I can vouch that Woodhull is from good Presbyterian stock."

"Once we are back in Connecticut," Benjamin explained, "I will ride out to the place he's being held and see to it that Abraham is released. In order to do that, I must speak with Governor Trumbull on Abraham's behalf. Once Abraham has been released into my custody, and if he agrees to take part in this private correspondence his excellency is in dire need of, we shall all be duly empowered to carry on the Patriot cause, however endangered or unguarded our lives might be. Justice and liberty can only be gained by the bravery we summon within ourselves and from our cognition that we serve a just God who presides over our destinies."

The others nodded in agreement.

"Correspondence must be kept among us," Benjamin said. "Our identities must remain unknown. Code names and numbers will be used. I will prepare a codebook."

"Keeping the intelligence from enemy eyes will most definitely require a variety of careful considerations," Major Clark said, "and even though I will continue my secret measures in my other posts as directed by his excellency, if there comes a time I am needed in this new operation, you may implore me for my services. And if you are interested in a name for this private correspondence, Washington has told me on several occasions about his time as a surveyor in Culpeper County, Virginia. Perhaps that could inspire a name."

"We must not tarry too much longer," Anna said. "British guards will make their rounds soon. I must take leave of you."

She quickly turned to walk back toward her quarters, leaving the three men standing in the brush. They watched carefully to see that she made it safely back. After they determined everything was clear, they swiftly climbed into the boat, pushed off, and made their way silently back across the sound, to Patriot territory in Fairfield, where they would find their horses were well rested and well fed.

28

Middleton, Connecticut, 1778

Benjamin learned from Governor Trumbull that Abraham was being held on house arrest in the home of Jehoshaphat Starr in the town of Middleton. He guided his horse down Main Street to the corner where the Starr family's large two-story colonial stood. As he made his way down the road, he passed the Floyd home and turned to see if anyone was about. He thought he might stop for a short visit with the Floyds once he was able to get Abraham released.

At the Star home, Benjamin tied up his horse and walked toward the guard.

"I have papers signed by Governor Trumbull for the release of Abraham Woodhull into my care," he said.

The guard took the papers from Benjamin and read them. When he handed them back, he turned and opened the door for Benjamin to enter. Benjamin was then stopped by a captain who was sitting behind a makeshift desk near the entry. Benjamin handed over the papers.

The captain looked at Benjamin and asked,

"Is this a friend of yours, Major?"

"Sir, do you mean the governor or Mr. Woodhull? Both happen to be respected friends of mine. I would appreciate it if you would get Mr. Woodhull."

The captain smirked at Benjamin but said nothing; instead, he left the room and returned with Abraham. When Abraham saw his longtime friend and rescuer standing near the door in full uniform he appeared to be overwhelmed with emotion.

"Benjamin," Abraham said, "I'm more than grateful for you. Thank you."

Benjamin saw the emotion in his friend's face and eyes. "It's good to see you too, brother."

Together they walked outside. Benjamin gathered his horse's reins and began walking down the street with Abraham by his side.

Benjamin pointed. "William Floyd's home is near the end of the road. We can stop and refresh there. There is something of great importance I need to share with you. Once you learn of it, I implore you to join with me. What I will ask of you will be dangerous, but it may also be a deciding factor in whether we will gain victory in the cause of freedom."

Abraham simply nodded. But what he heard in his friend's voice was an intensity and a sense of valor. Abraham wasn't sure what would be asked of him, but what he did understand was that his longtime friend needed something important. As they approached the Floyd home, Benjamin led his horse around to the back, and the men made their way toward the stables.

As they got closer, Jeb came out from where he'd been cleaning a stall and met them.

"Master Tallmadge," Jeb greeted Benjamin. "Good to see you. Can I take your horse for you? Will you be staying the evening?"

Benjamin handed the reins to Jeb. "This is my friend, Abraham Woodhull. We only require some refreshments and will only visit for a while. We are meeting someone at the river later tonight."

Jeb took Benjamin's horse into the stable, and Benjamin and Abraham walked to the well. After each took their turn taking a drink and washing his hands and face with the cool water, Abraham spoke.

"Tell me, Benjamin. What is this question you wish to ask of me?"

"I've been asked to take up a private correspondence with General Washington," Benjamin began. "This correspondence will be secret and will be for the purpose of creating a network of passionate friends willing to fight for and defend our right to freedom. It will mean creating a system of close-knit communication regarding the movements of the British troops, the numbers of their ships and guns, and updates on their supplies, along with any ideas of what their plans might be. This information will be collected and personally carried across the sound by Caleb or his men. It will then be given directly to me or to one of my dragoons, who will get it to me, then I will get it to Washington. The information must move quickly in order for me to get it to Washington in time for him to react."

Abraham looked up at Benjamin, who was several inches taller than him, and searched his friend's eyes. "Spying?" Abraham asked.

"Yes," Benjamin said. "Gathering intelligence. Since your sister lives in British-occupied New York City, she and her husband might be good contacts to begin with."

Reacting to a nearby sound, both men looked toward the house, where they could see movement in one of the open kitchen windows. The blur of a woman's dress had caught Benjamin's eye. It had been light red with some type of pattern on the fabric. Suddenly, the back door opened, and Benjamin saw Mary Floyd in the doorway wearing a dress that matched the flash of colors he had seen. He wondered what she might have overheard.

29

Middleton, Connecticut Summer 1778

Mary's heart leapt into her throat when she passed the window and saw Benjamin Tallmadge splashing water from the pump onto his face. Standing near the window, she was able to catch some of the conversation, and what she overheard was more than intriguing. She waited near the window until the conversation ended, then walked to the door and opened it.

"Major Tallmadge, it's so good to see you again," Mary said from the open doorway. "You and your friend are welcome to come inside."

Benjamin and Abraham made their way up the back-porch stairs and into the kitchen, where they could see Cora and Joli busily baking bread.

"Miss Mary," Benjamin said, "It's good to see you as well. This is my friend, Abraham Woodhull."

"Nice to meet you," Mary said to Abraham. Then she realized he was the friend of Benjamin's she had seen at her uncle's home years ago.

"Please have a seat," Mary offered. "I'll get you some refreshment."

"Thank you," the men said in unison.

They moved to sit at the small table in the kitchen. From the next room, they could hear the fortepiano being played.

"Kitty's practicing," Mary said. "She's always practicing."

"It's most entertaining," Benjamin said.

Cora set tea and biscuits in front of Benjamin and Abraham, and said,

"We will have supper in about an hour. Will you be sta—?"

Mary cut her off. "They will," she said.

Cora nodded, and Mary noticed Abraham glance at Benjamin. Benjamin only smiled and went back to eating. Mary enjoyed a cup of tea and pleasant intercourse with both guests. Soon the piano playing stopped, and Mary could hear the front door open as her father and mother returned from an errand in town. With them was a guest from Congress her father had invited for supper.

Mary excused herself from the table and stood near the doorway. "Father, Mother," she called, "we have guests for supper. Major Tallmadge and a friend of his have stopped by."

William and Hannah walked into the kitchen to greet Benjamin and were introduced to Abraham.

"Always good to see you, Benjamin. Please join us in the other room," William said. Then they all retired to the larger room near the front of the house to visit with their other guest, who at the moment was holding a pleasant exchange with Kitty.

"I'm sure you know each other, Major Tallmadge, Colonel Madison," William said.

Benjamin and James Madison greeted each other with short bows. Benjamin's taller frame seemed to tower over the much shorter Madison. Kitty had told Mary that one thing she did find attractive about Colonel Madison was his sharp, clear blue eyes. But Kitty had also told Mary that she was easily bored by Madison's talk of the war and his love of politics.

"This is a dear friend of mine from Setauket, Mr. Abraham Woodhull," Benjamin said.

Once the introductions were completed, they all sat in the parlor and the small talk began.

"Colonel Madison has brought a copy of the paper from Philadelphia," Kitty shared, holding out the newspaper. "Apparently, a British officer, a Major John André, has held one of the largest social events ever in the city. It's been called the Mischianza, and it began with decorated barges that floated down the river, each carrying a general. Then there was jousting."

"Oh my," Hannah exclaimed.

Kitty giggled and, with bubbly enthusiasm, read from the newspaper an account of the extraordinary British party. "When it was time for them to enjoy the feast," she read. "the artfully concealed doors were opened to reveal a two-hundred-and-ten-by-forty-foot magnificent salon filled with flowers, three hundred candles, and twelve hundred dishes. Can you even imagine?" Kitty asked. "Then there was dancing, fireworks, and balloons. Oh, how the British celebrated their beloved General Howe," she gushed. "And this Major André who threw the party, he must be something of a charmer." Kitty beamed with delight as she turned to James Madison. "Have you met this Major André?"

Madison looked vexed. "No, I have not. I've heard he stole articles from Benjamin Franklin's home where André had been held as a prisoner."

"Now he's in charge of espionage for the British," Benjamin added.

Mary quickly glanced at Benjamin and caught his eye.

"The British have definitely been in a celebratory mood while holding Philadelphia captive," Benjamin continued. "It will be a good day when they remove from there."

"And we get our city back," Mary added.

"It will be good for Congress to resume meeting in Philadelphia," William said.

Cora came into the room. "The meal is ready."

"Thank you, Cora," Hannah said and stood. "Please, honored guests," she said, waving an arm in the direction of the dining room.

Mary watched as Benjamin placed his tall, regal hat on a table, removed his sword from the holster on his hip, and placed it next to his hat, then the men followed Hannah into the next room, where she offered them each a seat. William took his place at one end of the table and Hannah at the other. An extra chair was brought in and placed at the table next to Benjamin, and Mary made her way to it. Kitty sat next to Colonel Madison. Cora had prepared chicken and made a broth from the drippings. A bowl of broth sat in front of each guest. William passed a plate of bread around, and everyone took a piece, then William asked everyone to bow their heads before he began a prayer of thanksgiving for the food. For several minutes after the prayer ended, all was quiet around the table as everyone enjoyed their food.

Kitty was the first to speak. "I am looking forward to returning to Philadelphia."

"Mm, yes," Madison said. "I am certainly looking forward to joining the discussions in Congress, and it will feel most natural to be back in Philadelphia."

"Colonel Madison has impressive ideas for our country once we gain liberty," William said. "Central government and state and local governments."

"Do explain, Colonel," Hannah said.

Madison nodded. "It is of great importance that we have a union of states to hold us together. Being as one as opposed to remaining separate countries if you will—to afford us victories. The government should have certain responsibilities, but these should be limited, allowing the states certain privileges. We must trust the people by giving them power to enforce regulations, rules, and laws. Ambition must be made to counteract ambition and keep the government stable."

"How will the government ensure liberty and prosperity?" Benjamin asked.

Madison looked excited by the question. Kitty looked bored to tears at the turn of conversation. Mary was enthusiastically curious to hear Colonel Madison's explanation.

"The entire construction should emphasize the best parts of each state's constitution, which will guarantee the people's liberty and prosperity and will act as a deterrent to a tyrannical, overpowering government. A large republic is the best way to prevent fractions, with voters having a larger pool of candidates to choose from so that a competent representative will be selected."

The men at the table nodded in agreement.

Mary was still curious as to how a new government would be constructed, but Kitty changed the conversation to more talk of the elaborate Mischianza and the interesting Major John André.

When the meal was completed, Cora and Joli removed dishes and offered coffee to be prepared and brought into the great room, where Kitty proffered to play a song on the pianoforte. Everyone seemed thrilled, and Kitty was glad to entertain as she perched on the bench at the piano and began to play "Fantasia and Fugue in A Minor" by Bach. At the end of the song, Kitty bowed to the group's applause.

Benjamin stood, bowed to Kitty, then turned and bowed to Hannah then to Mary.

"It has been a most lovely evening, but we must take our leave," he said.

Abraham stood and also gave a gracious and thankful farewell. Colonel Madison and William stood, and the men exchanged handshakes as they bid each other a good evening. Suddenly, Mary stood and offered Colonel Madison dessert.

"Let me bring you a sampling of some of the wonderful desserts Cora has made this week."

She scurried into the kitchen, where she mumbled something to Cora about taking dessert to Colonel Madison. Then she rushed out the back door and quickly fell into step with Benjamin, who was making his way to the stable to get his horse. She noticed that Abraham was walking toward the outhouse.

"Major," she called, and he turned to face her.

Mary always acted before thinking, and—again—she had no idea what she was about to say. She just wanted Benjamin to know she wished to be of service if the opportunity revealed itself.

"I wanted to remind you," she began, "that I am willing to help if the occasion should arise and information can be gathered. Please allow me to be of service."

Benjamin's eyes glistened with interest. His features softened as he held Mary's gaze.

"Dear Mary, you are most enthusiastic, and for that I am grateful," he told her. "I wish that no harm should ever come to you, and for that, I may not be able to grant you my endorsement."

Mary stepped closer to Benjamin—so close that the edge of her dress skirted his pant leg.

"I understand your concern, and it delights me. But this is something that I feel compelled to do—an obligation, a desire deep in my heart. Please don't tell me that because I am a woman, I have no business or right to help our cause, because I won't hear of it!"

This made Benjamin smile. He reached to gently brush his fingers over Mary's cheek. When his fingers lightly pressed against her skin, she jumped, startled by the sudden intoxicating feelings his touch stirred within her. But without thinking, she reached up and covered his hand in hers, pressing it onto her cheek. Then she closed her eyes, entranced by her feelings for the major. When she opened them, she and Benjamin stood in silence, both held captive by their devotion. Their eyes were locked on to one another's as if their souls had joined. And in that brief moment, Mary knew her fondness for Benjamin Tallmadge had grown beyond the admiration she'd felt for him over the years.

The moment was broken when they saw Jeb coming from the stable with Benjamin's horse. Quickly they backed away from each other. Abraham then returned from the outhouse and joined Benjamin. Mary curtsied, bid them both farewell, and ran into the house. From the kitchen window, she watched Benjamin and Abraham as they climbed onto Benjamin's horse. She heard Benjamin say thank you to Jeb, and to Abraham he said, "We are less than a mile from the river, where we'll meet Caleb."

30

Summer/Fall, 1778

Abraham and Benjamin followed the road to the river where they planned to meet Caleb. Along the way, they came up with code names to use in their intelligence correspondence.

"Washington did surveyor work in Culpeper County, Virginia," Benjamin told Abraham. "You could use the name Culpeper."

"That's a little long. We can shorten it to Culper."

"Then how about 'Samuel Culper'?" Benjamin asked.

"Yes," Abraham agreed. "I will become Samuel Culper."

Benjamin nodded. "And I will be John Bolton. Our double lives will begin the moment you leave with Caleb to go back to Setauket and I head back to my troops."

"I can't afford for Washington to know my true identity ever," Abraham said with a serious tone. "With my two older brothers dead, my elderly parents at home on the farm, and my youngest sister there, my family looks to me for support. I cannot leave them unprotected as the British raid our cities and our country. I must remain anonymous. Promise me, Benjamin, that no one will ever know I'm Culper."

"You have my word. I will not reveal your true identity to anyone. It will be known only in our close-knit group. You can trust me with your life, as I trust you with mine."

When they approached the riverbank in the light of the moon, they saw a boat. Drawing closer, they recognized it was Caleb coming toward them.

"It's good to see you two together again," Caleb said.

"Aye," Abraham agreed. "Benjamin rescued me. And offered me the opportunity to help Washington with intelligence in hopes of winning the war. Together let us serve our Patriot cause—although in secret and without reward. Reward will be gained by all Patriots once we complete the job at hand with God as our guide, our protector, our defender, and our shield."

In unison, Caleb and Benjamin replied, "Aye."

"I must leave you," Benjamin said. "To go back to my troops in Westchester, but I pray a safe journey for you both. I will plan to instruct some of my men to retrieve your correspondence once Caleb receives it and crosses the sound again. Before we part, let me leave you with words from Psalm nineteen." Benjamin placed his hands on the shoulders of his two friends and recited verses one through seven as a prayer over both men. "'The heavens declare the glory of God; the skies proclaim the work of his hands. Day after day they pour forth speech; night after night they reveal knowledge. They have no speech, they use no words; no sound is heard from them. Yet their voice goes out into all the earth, their words to the end of the world. In the heavens God has pitched a tent for the sun. It is like a bridegroom coming out of his chamber, like a champion rejoicing to run his course. It rises at one end to the heavens and makes its circuit to the other; nothing is deprived of its warmth. The law of the Lord is perfect, refreshing the soul. The statutes of the Lord are trustworthy, making wise the simple.'"

Benjamin mounted his horse, Caleb saluted him. Then Benjamin watched as Caleb and Abraham climbed into the boat to cross the sound in the darkness back to Setauket. As he left them, he prayed for the success of this new venture. He made it back to camp in Durham, Connecticut, then later he chose to make his station at Greenfield, where he could easily connect with Caleb along the sound. From there, Benjamin began to receive a steady stream of reports which gave him a clear picture of British deployments and departures.

The British had already destroyed forts in Huntington and Setauket and now started erecting a bastion in the Huntington area, as well as constructing a stronghold near Mastic, which they christened Fort St. George. On the north shore in Oyster Bay, Colonel John Graves Simcoe had built an encampment to protect food and firewood for transport into New York. But the Crown's most powerful fortification was situated along the western edge of Lloyd's Neck, a small peninsula jutting out from Huntington, where General Oliver Delancey's Loyalists could command the entrance into both Oyster Bay and Cold Bluff Harbor. This was protected by Tory whaleboat raiders. The British had given it the name Fort Franklin in honor of Benjamin Franklin's illegitimate Tory son. Benjamin soon identified Fort Franklin as the key to the British operations in central Long Island and as a staging area for British whaleboat raiders. Not too far in the future, Benjamin and his men would be sent to defend the coastal Connecticut town of Norwalk after a British pillage in the seaport cities of New Haven and Fairfield.

31

Winter, 1778

Even though the winter months in Connecticut felt bleak to Mary with the bitter cold and snow, her spirits perked up when she received a letter from Benjamin stating that he would once again be joining her family on New Year's Eve.

Benjamin's troops had been stationed in Connecticut, and he had been making trips to and from the coastal cities collecting the intelligence Caleb was bringing over from Long Island. Benjamin, his men, and Caleb had also been keeping a close eye on the raiders along the Long Island Sound. Benjamin had written to Washington lamenting that the marauders on the Connecticut shore made no distinction between Whig or Tory and that the pirates continued to jeopardize his intelligence operations.

Washington responded that he would ask Governors Clinton and Trumbull to take steps to halt the whaleboat raiding and marauding. But, unfortunately, the sound and the bordering coastlines were too vast for the civil or military authorities to control. Benjamin sought approval from Washington to capture the perpetrators and hand them over to New York authorities for trial. "John Bolton" and "Samuel Culper" corresponded about the best ways to control the plundering.

With all of this on his mind, Benjamin was grateful for the small respite he found whenever he visited the Floyd home. On New Year's Eve he was welcomed at the door as the sweet smells of baked goods filled the air and a fire roared in the large stone fireplace in the next room.

Hannah ushered Benjamin inside and closed the door to the wind and snow. "Do come in, Major Tallmadge. It's good to see you."

Benjamin bowed and followed Hannah into their large main room, where the fire crackled in the fireplace.

"I'm afraid Mr. Floyd has returned to Philadelphia," Hannah explained. "He left a day ago. He and a few other men went to see about the damage done by the British, and Congress is planning to reconvene at the State House."

Kitty walked into the room and greeted Benjamin before sitting down. Benjamin bowed then sat in one of the large wingback chairs next to Hannah.

"I'm sure it's taken a toll on you having Mr. Floyd gone so often," Benjamin said. "Maybe there will be time to visit with him again in Philadelphia."

"I do have plans to go back," Kitty replied. "Father said he would write soon about returning to the boarding house. But we don't know about its condition or what might have happened to the owners. It's unknown whether they fled for their lives from the city during the British occupation. And Father did say it's quite possible some who owned property might not return."

"Mm." Benjamin nodded. "It's also quite possible some businesses and properties may be for sale."

"Oh," Kitty said in a high-pitched, excited voice. "Might Father buy property in Philadelphia, Mother?"

"I don't know, dear," Hannah replied.

Cora stepped into the room and set down a tray of tea. When she turned to go back to the kitchen, she noticed a rider coming toward the house. "Miss Mary is back," Cora said.

Benjamin moved to the window and watched as Mary rode her horse past the front porch and around to the back of the house.

"I'll go and see about helping Mary put her horse in the stall," Benjamin said to Hannah.

"Oh, no," Hannah said. "There's no need for that. Jeb is there to help with the horses." Hannah stood and walked to the front window. "Jeb's already come by and gotten your horse from the post. No need to worry about the horses. Come back and sit and enjoy your free moments with us."

Kitty noticed that Benjamin seemed a bit reluctant to sit down again. And she was curious about whether the major's feelings fell in line with those she knew her sister held for the handsome officer.

"Oh, Mother, it's fine," Kitty said. "Major Tallmadge might enjoy helping tend to the horses. After all, he is in charge of the Second Continental Light Dragoons. Horses are of importance to him." Kitty waved her hands at Benjamin. "By all means, Major, please feel free to go to the stable and check on things."

Benjamin bowed. "Thank you. I would enjoy that. Excuse me."

He walked out the front door and made his way around back. When he stepped into the barn, he saw Mary working to tie up her horse, and Jeb was carrying a pitchfork full of hay into the stall where Benjamin's own horse was. Jeb was the first to notice Benjamin.

"Good day, Major Tallmadge," Jeb said. "Can I get your horse for you now?"

Mary turned and saw Benjamin making his way toward her. Her heart skipped a beat.

"Major Tallmadge," she said breathlessly.

"Hello," Benjamin said. "Thank you, Jeb. I will be here a while yet. I came to help Mary with her horse."

Jeb nodded and continued with his business. Benjamin stepped closer to Mary and began helping her unbuckle and remove the saddle. "You've been in town this morning?" he asked as he took off the saddle.

Mary nodded. "Yes. I had to pay for the post and retrieve a package from Oyster Bay. I also wanted to do a little shopping for fabrics and thread. Mary gathered the pouch containing her items and held it as she watched Benjamin drape the saddle across the ledge of an empty stall.

Jeb walked over and took her horse by the bit.

"I'll clean the hooves, Miss Mary," Jeb said. "And I'll get some water and hay before long."

"Thank you, Jeb," Mary said. She turned and faced Benjamin. "I'm concerned about the contents of any mail I get from my friend in the Townsend home in Oyster Bay." She removed the package from her bag. "You might be too."

Benjamin nodded and watched Mary take the brown paper off, revealing a small tin.

Mary recognized the old snuff box from the time she'd mailed the decorated egg to Liza. She removed the lid, and inside was a new egg. This one was decorated with leaves that looked like a trail of ivy. It was light in her hand, and Mary knew it was hollow. She looked at one end and could see the smoothness of hardened, white icing barely visible to the eye. Liza had done a good job making it almost unnoticeable. Mary looked up at Benjamin, who was watching her intently.

She held out the egg for him. "It's hollow. The yolk has been drained. Years ago, I sent an egg like this to Liza, and I placed a note inside to let her know we had fled our home for fear the British would kill Father and everyone else if we were found."

Benjamin took the egg and looked at it carefully.

"Here," Mary said and pointed to the bottom. "This is icing. Once it dries, it covers the hole."

Benjamin carefully rubbed the icing with his thumbnail. Bits came off in small flakes to reveal the small hole. He shook the egg slightly to expose a note that had been rolled thin and placed inside.

"May, I?" he asked.

Mary nodded and watched as Benjamin removed the missive. He handed it over to Mary, and she unrolled it. It was written in the simple words and style Liza knew, and Mary was thankful Liza had learned to read and write. Mary had always perfectly understood Liza's communications. She read the note aloud to Benjamin.

Mr. Robert came home at Christmas for a visit. He upset with things and Simcoe men here. Robert went back to work in New York, but I know he afraid of what go on. One of Simcoe mens say they thinks spying near Setauket. Someone going across the sound. Then I hear Simcoe say to one of the other girls in the kitchen to prepare for a friend of his who coming. I don't know when he come but whoever he is he must be important, I saw some mail a name on it say John André.

"Could this information be of help to you?" Mary asked.

"Indeed. 'Tis most helpful, Mary. Will you reply to her and ask that she pay close attention when Major John André is there, to listen in on any conversations she can, and to try to send you that information?"

Smiling and filled with admiration for Major Tallmadge, Mary was more than overjoyed he was here now and that he thought she might be of service. He must believe her to be trustworthy and accomplished enough to carry out a mission, no matter how small it might seem. But what if it could be of great importance, and Mary finally had her chance to serve the Patriot cause? So many were dying and giving up everything for the freedom they wished for. And Mary had never wanted to just sit by and watch it happen. She knew there were other women like her willing to step in however they could. Mary put the note back inside the egg and carefully placed the egg inside the snuffbox.

Benjamin offered her his arm, and together they strolled back to the house to join Hannah and Kitty for the evening meal and to celebrate the end of another year.

∞∞∞∞∞∞∞∞

The following morning Mary woke early in hopes of seeing Benjamin off, but when she walked into the kitchen just before sunrise, he had left.

"You missed him," Cora said. "He must have left a few hours ago. But he left this." She pointed to a note with a slim black ribbon tied around it. Mary's name was written on the outside. She picked up the missive, carefully untied the ribbon, then unfolded the note.

Dearest Mary,

I'm sorry to have missed saying goodbye to you. There is business I must attend to, and as you know, I have limited time. Your home is always a most gracious place and I enjoy the company immensely. If I can say how I truly feel, Miss Mary, I especially find you to be most favorable. I shall wish to see you again soon.

I am your Dear Friend, B

Upon reading Benjamin's words, she was overcome with emotion. Her face lit up with a smile and she placed the note to her chest. Her heart pounded. Her breath became rapid. Filled with energy, she flew up the stairs before Cora or Joli could ask her about the note.

"Kitty," Mary whispered. When Kitty didn't move, Mary walked to the edge of the bed and tapped her sister on the shoulder. "Kitty," she said again.

Kitty opened her eyes, blinking at Mary as she tried to focus.

"Is something wrong?" she asked. "Is mother feeling ill again?"

"Uh, no. I, uh . . . not that I know of. Here!" Mary thrust the letter at Kitty. "It's from Benjamin Tallmadge. He left it on the kitchen table tied with this ribbon."

Kitty took the note and read it. As she did, her hand came to rest atop her lips. She breathed deeply and said, "He fancies you, Mary!"

Mary nodded, the smile on her lips and the gleam in her eyes lighting up the dark room. Mary took the note from Kitty and twirled around the room with it held close to her chest.

"Is this what it feels like, Kitty? To be in love? It's a grand feeling. Like I have gained the world. It's as if nothing could ever make me feel sad. It feels like I'm floating on a cloud and my heart will explode with joy."

Kitty sat up and watched Mary twirl around the room. "I think so. I've not felt it as strongly as you have yet. I am fond of Colonel Madison. Father says he may ask for my hand in marriage. But I had thought I would marry Mr. William Clarkson. We've been apart for so long now, only writing to each other, so I don't know how I really feel about William anymore. But I am certain that I am happy for you, and I do wish the war would end and we could all find our happiness—

or at least have the opportunity to pursue our own joy. I do wish to return to Philadelphia soon."

32

Late Winter through Summer, 1779

Benjamin met with Washington at headquarters, where he handed him the latest piece of intelligence from Long Island. When the general was finished reading it, he looked at Benjamin and said,

"Culper's account is a good one and makes me desirous of a continuance of his correspondence. But the information must somehow get to me faster without compromising the security of those involved in the process. Major Tallmadge, I charge you with the task of developing a method for expediting the delivery of Culper's intelligence. And how is the codebook coming?"

"I've just finished the codes and will be delivering copies to both Brewster and Culper." Benjamin handed over a book, along with more correspondence. "And this is the latest intelligence from Lieutenant Brewster, sir."

Caleb's missive contained further information on the activity of British troops throughout Long Island.

Gen. Erskine remains yet at South Hampton. He has been reinforced to the number of 2500. They have three redoubts at South and East Hampton and are heaving up works at Canoe Place at a narrow pass before you get into South

Hampton. They are building a number of flat bottom boats. There went a number of carpenters down last week to South Hampton. It is thought by the inhabitants they will cross over to New London after the Continental Frigates; Colonel Hewlett remains yet on Lloyd's Neck with 350 wood cutters included. Colonel Simcoe remains at Oyster Bay with 300 foot and Light Horse. There is no troops from Oyster Bay til you come to Jamaica. There is a 40-gun British ship in Huntington the brig HMS Halifax in Oyster Bay, with other vessels at shipyards to the west as far as New York City.

When Washington finished reading Brewster's correspondence, he said to Benjamin,

"Set up an officer as a dispatch rider in Fairfield to gather Culper and Brewster's intelligence and get it to me. Possibly dispatch officers every fifteen miles. You don't have time to continue this yourself. And I need the missives faster."

"I'll see to it, sir," Benjamin replied.

The next thing Washington reviewed was the codebook Benjamin had prepared. Upon opening it, Washington saw Benjamin had created code numbers to represent each participant. For Benjamin's code name, John Bolton, the number was 721. Washington had been given the number 711, Caleb was 725, and Samuel Culper was assigned 722. The general's eyes moved quickly across the pages as he read more code numbers for locations and common words. He saw that Long Island was 728, New York was 727, Setauket was 729, and England was 745. "Infantry" was assigned 309, "importance" 317, "ships" 592, and "camp" was 73. The general realized from reading Benjamin's codes there was even a way to scramble letters using a particular order when there was a need to disguise someone else's name. Washington closed the book.

"Very good, Major. You are dismissed."

∞∞∞∞∞∞∞∞∞∞∞∞∞∞∞∞

A few months later, an early warning came that British commander Henry Clinton was building transports. Writing as Culper, Abraham had more news that the general was on eastern Long Island looking to hire crews of Loyalists to raid the Connecticut coast. Washington told General Joseph Reed that one of his most intelligent correspondents had reported the enemy to have some enterprise in view in the region. Washington also advised Colonel Rufus Putnam in Connecticut to reinforce militia and fortifications along the coastal cities there. Later news came that Henry Clinton had backed off and returned to New York.

British New York Governor, William Tryon, then dispatched three thousand troops and a naval force to distress the seaports of Connecticut. He landed in New Haven and pillaged the town. His armies then moved to Fairfield and burnt everything. When it became apparent that Tryon was bent on inflicting such utter devastation, Benjamin and his men were dispatched with a light infantry to aid the militia in defending Norwalk, the next town hit by Tryon's troops.

Benjamin and his troops endeavored to protect the town as it was reduced to ashes and residents fled for their lives. Afterward, the troops encamped on both sides of the Hudson, where they kept a close watch on General Clinton thinking, he might have his eye on the fort at Stony Point. With only a meager number of Patriots to defend Stony Point, the enemy easily defeated them and soon began to make the fort at Stony Point a well-defended one, or so they supposed. They soon placed within it a garrison of select troops about six hundred strong. Washington spied the enemy through a telescope from atop nearby Buckberg Mountain, where he watched the British construct fortifications. As Washington watched from afar, he designed his plan of attack and began selecting his troops to lead the battle. He placed General Anthony Wayne in charge, and Benjamin and his troops were part of the Continental army's force of thirteen thousand men who would be engaged in the attack.

Benjamin met his commanding officers in Washington's tent. The air inside the tent on that mid-June day was hot and muggy. Benjamin swatted away flies and mosquitoes as he listened to General Washington and General Wayne plan the attack. Benjamin and other commanders stood along the outer edge of the table where Washington and General Wayne had laid out a map of the Hudson showing the location of Stony Point.

"We shall plan for a surprise attack," Washington said. "It should take place after midnight. The men should carry unloaded muskets, and attack using only bayonets and maintain complete silence."

Washington pointed to a location on the map near the southern shore. "It's best to start here at low tide," he continued. "The main attack could be here. But also, secondary attacks could be made along the north shore." Washington turned from the map and looked directly at Wayne.

"General," the commander in chief said. "you have my permission to modify the plan as necessary."

Benjamin noted that permission to modify the plan might be unusual for Washington, but it was obvious that Washington believed strongly in Wayne's tactical abilities.

Washington continued his instructions as he told his commanders to give their men their rum rations and pieces of white paper to place on their hats in order to tell each other apart in the darkness.

The following evening before midnight, Benjamin and his men began making their way to the fort at Stony Point. The Patriots moved with stealth, and the British were unsuccessful at repelling the attack. The British cannons could not be lowered to an angle low enough to sufficiently fight off the men scaling the hill. Within minutes the garrison was captured by the Continental troops, and the British bastion on the Hudson was destroyed.

After this was accomplished, Benjamin's regiment took their station in the region of White Plains, and North Castle. With the destruction of the British stronghold at Stony Point, Washington suggested the Second Dragoons establish a base at Bedford near Westchester to protect Whig inhabitants from British attacks.

During his next meeting with Washington and Colonel Sheldon, Benjamin expressed his fear that Bedford would be difficult to defend with only ninety men available.

"There are several roads leading into Bedford," he explained. "We should remain eastward and take up a position near Pound Ridge."

Colonel Sheldon agreed and said, "I'll scout for quartering nearby and send for Major Eli Leavenworth and his militiamen to join us."

"Should we also send for Moylan's Fourth Dragoons for backup?" Benjamin asked the colonel.

"Yes," Colonel Sheldon agreed. "Send word to Colonel Moylan that we require his Fourth Dragoons to engage with us in securing the region."

Sheldon then took off in search of safe quarters.

Later, when Sheldon returned, he immediately found Benjamin.

"We can quarter in the home of Major Ebenezer Lockwood," Colonel Sheldon informed Benjamin. "He's a member of the county committee of safety and a militia officer. There's a Presbyterian Church across the road for the rest of the men. He is also able to provide us one hundred local militia."

The commanders then led their men to the new location and set up camp. Benjamin wrote a missive to Washington letting him know of their location and sent one of his men off with the dispatch. This dispatch, however, would be intercepted and given to General Clinton, who would act on this new intelligence by calling for his most aggressive, bloodthirsty, and ambitious military leader, Major Banastre Tarleton, to unleash a devastating assault on Benjamin and his dragoons posted at Pound Ridge.

The evening before Tarleton planned his raid on Benjamin's camp, a Patriot spy by the name of Luther Kinnicott went to Pound Ridge to warn the American commanders of the imminent British attack. Not only were the Americans warned, but heavy winds and rain lashed out at Westchester County and slowed Tarleton's progress.

Before the break of dawn, just a few miles from his target, Major Tarleton stopped when he saw a man standing in his dripping, rain-sodden doorway. John Crawford was one of the few Loyalists in the area, and he told Tarleton and his group to go south. But, somehow, Tarleton misunderstood the directions and led his men north on the wrong road.

The rain stopped at dawn, and the Green Horse troops, led by Tarleton, moved through the wet and muddy countryside toward what they thought was the Rebel camp. They went half a mile before realizing the mistake, and Tarleton turned his column of horsemen around.

Back at the Continental camp at Pound Ridge, Colonel Sheldon posted mounted sentries on the roads north of the town and put Major Ebenezer Lockwood's militia on alert. Major Eli Leavenworth's infantrymen took positions on the road to the west.

By dawn, with no British forces in sight, Colonel Sheldon allowed his men to unsaddle and let their horses graze. Just as the soldiers relaxed, the mounted sentries who'd been on watch near Stone Ridge Road galloped into camp.

Panting and out of breath, one of the sentries relayed what he'd seen. "Sir, he began then stopped to catch a breath. "There's a cavalry column headed toward Pound Ridge."

Sheldon asked, "Can you tell if it's American? We're expecting Colonel Moylan's Fourth Dragoons."

"No sir, not for sure. They were far off still."

"Very well," Sheldon said. He then turned to command his men to re-saddle their horses. "Prepare for action!" he shouted. He found Benjamin and said, "Take a detachment with you and find out if the approaching column is British or American."

Benjamin took off with his small detachment of mounted horsemen and headed north.

As the British rode south to Pound Ridge, Benjamin and his men were riding north on the same road. The two columns rounded a bend and ran headlong into each other about half a mile from the Continental camp.

Tarleton shouted, "Charge!" and the Green Horse troops of the Seventeenth Dragoons advanced full force. "Surrender!" Tarleton commanded.

Benjamin turned his horse around and commanded, "Head back!" He and his men galloped full speed back to camp.

Tarleton stood in his stirrups at full gallop, waving his sword above his head. "Surrender, you damned traitors ! Surrender!" Tarleton yelled. He continued on at full speed, lapping at the heels of the Continental horses.

At the approach to Lockwood's farm, Colonel Sheldon and his men were ready and waiting, and the bloody battle began. The clash of clanging swords and sabers was violent. The Americans, who were just under one hundred men, held their ground against the 360 Green Horse troops as long as they could.

"Withdraw!" Colonel Sheldon finally yelled to his troops and the town's militia.

The Americans withdrew south into the countryside, but Tarleton did not let up on the charge, intent on capturing the Rebel cavalry. He and his army continued to rain musket fire upon the fleeing Rebels. Then Tarleton closed in on an American private, John Buckholt, and shouted,

"Surrender, you dirty Rebel, or I'll blow your brains out."

The pistol shot that followed grazed Buckholt's head and knocked off his cap.

Tarleton sat higher in his saddle and steadied his horse. "There, you damned Rebel, you, see?" he mocked. "You will die by my hand or surrender now. A little more and I would have blown your brains out."

Buckholt shouted back, "Yes, damn you, and a little more and you wouldn't have even touched me."

With that, Buckholt sped away while another fleeing Rebel, Jared Hoyt, received a saber cut to the head. Hoyt swung his own sword, slashing his attacker's face in two.

Tarleton tried to encircle the fleeing Americans, but the ground had become too rocky and unstable to continue the pursuit on horseback. Tarleton turned back and headed toward the Lockwood farm.

"Burn it to the ground," he commanded.

But inside the farmhouse, surgeons from both sides were treating the wounded, and two of the British doctors protested Tarleton's orders. Tarleton then ordered his wounded men be moved.

"And search every inch of this house and the barn," Tarleton demanded.

As his men were searching, they found all the baggage and equipment belonging to the Second Light Dragoons, including Benjamin's saddlebags that held dispatches for

General Washington. They also found the dragoon regimental colors. Realizing these belonged to a Patriot officer, they kept the flag and Benjamin's saddlebags as war trophies.

"Now, burn it to the ground," Tarleton yelled. "And torch their meeting house too."

The British were preparing to burn another home in the town just as the American militia began to fire upon them, driving them away. Major Leavenworth's infantrymen continued their advance to cut off the British retreat. When Tarleton realized he was about to be surrounded, he decided his raid was complete. As his men rode out of Pound Ridge and came upon Bedford, the citizens began shooting at the passing British troops. This angered Tarleton even more, and he burned their church and set fire to a Patriot tavern on his way out of town. Sheldon's dragoons and Leavenworth's infantrymen continued in hot pursuit as far as North Castle but were unable to overtake them.

Ten American soldiers were wounded, and four soldiers and civilians were captured, including Major Lockwood's son-in-law. Also significant was the capture of the colors of the Second Dragoons and the loss of the saddlebags, which included correspondence with Washington about activating a new spy in New York and sending ten guineas for Culper. That Washington had agents in New York was probably not news to Clinton, but the name of spy George Higday most certainly was news, as was the request for Benjamin to recruit him. Washington's use of the real name was an uncharacteristic blunder.

The fight at Pound Ridge was not the only sizable action Benjamin and the dragoons were involved in. Colonel Moylan's Fourth Dragoons finally arrived, and Benjamin got a taste of success when he and a hundred of his men from the Second and Fourth Dragoons skirmished with British Major Delancey's men near Maurrassian. There, the Continentals took thirty prisoners and considerable plunder. This success strengthened Benjamin's determination to take the fight to the enemy, and he devised a plan to spring a trap. But he came to discover the British had their own network of spies and informants who had been warned of his approach. Delancey had set up an ambush of his own on the road Benjamin was expected to use. Benjamin countered by falling back, hoping his retreat would entice the British to follow, but they refused the bait, and Benjamin and his men returned to North Castle.

33

Summer, 1779

Tension was high on Long Island, and Abraham Woodhull became more anxious about his trips into New York City, afraid of being stopped at checkpoints. He worried the British would question his need to go into the city so often. His excuses were that he was visiting his sister and her husband or selling crops from his farm in Setauket. Deep inside, he knew he would have to change something before he was caught.

Upon arriving in New York, one summer day, Abraham made his way to the boarding house owned by his brother-in-law, Amos Underhill, and Abraham's sister Mary. He pulled his wagon up to the post and tied his horse close enough to the trough that the horse could drink his fill.

It was early in the morning, and he didn't see anyone around when he walked inside. A moment later, he saw Amos.

"Brother, it's good to see you again," Amos said. "I have the things you've asked for in the back room."

Abraham followed his brother-in-law into a large closet at the end of a hallway. Abraham closed the door, and the two men stood in the darkness face to face, only inches apart.

"I've placed the missive inside a tomato jar," Amos said, pointing to a small wooden crate filled with jars of fruit. "We can only spare a few things this month. I removed the liquid from one of the tomato jars, folded the note, and placed a square of linen over it before placing it under the lid. Just in case the jar is turned over. I hoped it would be saved that way."

Abraham nodded. They heard someone coming and stood still as stones as they listened. When Amos realized it was his wife, he slowly opened the pantry door. Mary had just walked past them into the kitchen.

"Have a seat at a table. We'll get you some food," Amos offered.

Abraham followed Amos to an empty table, where he sat. Amos went to tell his wife that her brother was there. Mary returned with coffee for Abraham and filled a cup.

"Is anyone else here this morning?" Abraham asked her.

"Two British soldiers upstairs. They got roaring drunk last night. I put them together in the largest room. I haven't heard a sound coming from their room since Amos helped them up there last night."

Abraham nodded and sipped his coffee. "Did you hear anything before they passed out?"

"I overheard them mention a name a few times, but I don't know if it means anything. It was about a Major André who's just been stationed in New York." Her words were barely a whisper. "Also, I've told the shop owner around the corner that you would be seeing him today. He's expecting you."

Amos arrived at the table with a bowl of oatmeal and two figs for Abraham. After setting them down, he said, "We'll put you in the room next to the officers once you're finished with breakfast."

Abraham said, "Thank you." Then he picked up his spoon and started eating.

A few minutes later, Mary led him upstairs to his room. She unlocked the door and walked with Abraham inside. Then she handed him an empty glass and whispered, "You can place it against the wall and put your ear against it to see if you might hear anything."

Before leaving the room, she said,

"I'll be back with a fresh pitcher of water."

Mary returned to find Abraham sitting against the wall holding the glass against it with his ear pressed onto it. Mary poured fresh water into the bowl on the table so he could wash up later, then quietly walked over to Abraham.

"Anything?" she whispered.

Abraham shook his head. "Not yet."

"Robert Townsend's shop should open within the hour. Amos has moved your horse and wagon to the barn and settled the horse in. You can walk to the mercantile from here," Mary reminded him.

Abraham nodded, and Mary left the room.

A few minutes later, Abraham could hear the soldiers getting up, but their talk was about nothing more than returning to their post. Not long after they left, Abraham could hear his sister in the next room cleaning. She hummed a song to herself as she worked. Abraham knew it was her signal to him that the coast was clear. After freshening up at his water basin, Abraham prepared to walk down the street to Hanover Square and speak to the mercantile shop owner, Robert Townsend, with hopes of recruiting him to be a spy.

When Abraham walked into the mercantile, he noticed the shop owner working with a customer. When the lady left the store, Abraham went over to the counter and got Robert's attention.

"Excuse me, sir," Abraham said. "My sister, Mary Underhill, recommended your shop. I'd like to purchase a ream of quality paper. I've quite a bit of important correspondence to do." Abraham smiled at Robert.

With a knowing look as to what Abraham might be hinting at, Robert replied, "I've just the thing for you in the storeroom. Would you join me, and we'll see if it works to your liking?"

Abraham followed Robert into the back room. There, Robert reached up to a top shelf and pulled a ream of packaged paper down, then waited for Abraham to speak.

Abraham pulled a note from the inside of his sock and handed it to Robert.

"These are instructions from General Washington." Abraham's voice was quiet. "We're a small, tight group. We all grew up together in Setauket, and I would trust each of them with my life. Major Benjamin Tallmadge has been put in charge of intelligence. No one is to know our true names." He stepped closer to Robert. "I'm Samuel Culper, code number 722. Tallmadge is John Bolton and is 721. Washington, 711. Your name will never be used. You would take over gathering information here in the city. If you decided to help us, you would become Samuel Culper, Jr., 723. Lieutenant Caleb Brewster is 725 but is the only one who chooses not to use an alias."

"I see," said Robert. "Shall I ring this up for you?"

"Please," Abraham replied. "And I'm staying at my brother-in-law's boarding house. I'll be there until the morning. If you would like to give me your response then."

Robert nodded and moved back into the front of the store, followed by Abraham. He went about ringing Abraham up but only charged him half the normal price for the pack of paper.

"Thank you, sir," Robert said and handed him the package.

"I hope to see you again," Abraham said as he turned to leave.

∞∞∞∞∞∞∞∞

Later that evening, Abraham was sitting alone at a table in the boarding house eating a bowl of stew, when Robert walked in. Abraham saw him, the two locked eyes, then Robert made his way over to Abraham's table. Only a few other patrons were in the room. A table of British soldiers sat opposite Abraham's table playing a rowdy game of cards. None of them noticed Robert walk inside.

Robert stood at the edge of the table next to Abraham.

"May I join you?" he asked.

"Please. Have a seat."

Robert sat in the chair across from Abraham.

"Can I take it this is a good visit?" Abraham asked.

Robert nodded. "My father knew your cousin, General Nathanial Woodhull. We heard he had been mortally wounded at the Battle of Brooklyn. My sincerest condolences. He was married to Ruth Floyd, William Floyd's sister. William Floyd's brother Richard is a very dear friend of my father's." Robert leaned across the table, and in a whisper, he said, "I've only been home to Oyster Bay a few times since the Revolution started. My heart bleeds for the cause."

Abraham nodded then told Robert his room number. Abraham pushed his bowl of stew toward Robert and stood. He then made his way to the stairs leading to the second floor. Abraham went inside his room to wait. A few minutes passed, then he answered the knock at his door. Robert stood alone in the hallway. Abraham ushered him inside his room, then asked,

"Did you read Washington's note?"

Robert nodded. "I did."

Abraham went to his bag, which he pulled from under the bed, and retrieved a small Bible. He walked back over to Robert and opened it. Tucked in next to the beginning pages of the book of Job were papers with the code names and numbers. Abraham showed the notes to Robert.

"You'll need to learn these," Abraham instructed. "We will need a courier to help speed the missives through to 711. I know of one—another friend in Setauket. Maybe he could best Paul Revere's ride."

The two men laughed.

"Austin is his name, 724," Abraham said. "A tavern owner who would have reason to get supplies from your store and a reason to be in the city. We've only just spoken about it recently. Everything is approved by 711."

Robert placed the papers inside his coat, then turned to go back downstairs, where he sat back at the same table. Mary appeared with a pint of ale for Robert. She smiled and set it down in front of him.

"Enjoy, sir," she said. Satisfied that all seemed to be going well, she went to check on the other customers.

After a while, Robert finished his ale. He stood, nodded briefly in Mary's direction, then left.

Back in his own room, Robert retrieved the papers Abraham had given him and read the instructions again from General Washington. He already had some useful information from working with and being in close proximity to the British and Loyalists. He sat down and put pen to paper.

Christopher Duychenik former chairman of the Committee of Mechanics is among you and is positively an agent for David Mathew, former mayor. He is posing as a Patriot and working for the former Loyalist mayor. These particulars must be kept a profound secret, as few persons but myself know them and it is known that I do.

∞∞∞∞∞∞∞∞

The next morning, Abraham rose early to leave the boarding house to head home to Setauket. The crate of jars filled with fruits—one holding a piece of intelligence—sat by the door to his room. He gathered the package of paper and placed it inside the crate, then opened the door and made his way down the stairs. There he found Amos waiting with a cup of coffee and an apple.

"For the road," he said.

Abraham set the crate down in order to take Amos's offerings. "Thank you," he said. He looked around and saw no one nearby.

"I should expect Towns—" Abraham realized his mistake and made a quick correction. "I expect Culper, Jr. to prepare his report," he explained. He then glanced around the room again to make sure no one was around. "He's been given the information from Washington and knows there will be a courier, a tavern owner from Setauket, who will frequent his shop to gather the missives. The courier will return with them to Setauket, where I will add my report, then Caleb will arrive to transport them across the sound to Connecticut."

Amos picked up the crate. "I'm glad that is settled. It gives me great relief."

Together, they walked to the barn to retrieve Abraham's wagon and horse. Just before Abraham was set to leave, Robert approached with a book in his hand.

"I thought you might need this," he said. Abraham took the book from him.

"I'm sure it will be of great importance to me and my friends. Thank you." Abraham replied, then made his way to catch the ferry.

He prayed his travels would be without incident. But for Abraham, nothing would be easy. Upon returning home, he found his father barely alive. He'd been beaten almost to death by Simcoe's Rangers. Someone had tipped Simcoe off that there was a spy in Setauket by the name of Woodhull. When Colonel John Simcoe arrived with his men at the Woodhull farm in Abraham's absence, neither Abraham's parents nor his sister knew anything about his secret efforts for the cause. Simcoe sent a warning by hurting his father, which made Abraham more anxious than ever and even more in need of someone to travel with him to New York who could pass as a Tory, removing some of the suspicion from himself.

34

Fall, 1779

Benjamin had long held on to the idea of capturing enemy fortifications in Long Island's Suffolk County and driving the British from there. It was from those locations the British drew vast supplies of forage, grain, and fresh meat. Benjamin was more than ready to inflict payback for Tryon's raid on the Connecticut coastal towns and the plundering along the sound. He knew Fort Franklin to be the key to British operations on Lloyd's Neck, and he earmarked a mixed force of dismounted dragoons, assorted Continental troops, and fifty boatmen for his plans to raid and capture the fort.

He became more than invested in his idea to not only destroy the enemy's supply chains on Long Island but also to put a stop to their constant plundering of personal property. They didn't care whether a property owner was a Whig or Tory; they simply took from all.

A letter from Culper, Sr. implored Benjamin not to forget to urge 725 of his duty. In his missive, Abraham seemed to be implying that Benjamin and Caleb might stop the plundering.

Night before last a most horrid robbery was committed on the houses of Colonel Benjamin Floyd and Mr. Seaton, by three whale boats from your shore by Joseph Hulce and Fade Danolson, and the one other mast of a boat name unknown to me. 725 can well inform you of their names. From the best judgement I can form they took the value in money, household goods, Bonds and Notes of three thousand pounds. They left nothing in the house that was portable. They even took their clock and all their looking glasses . . . I cannot put up with such a wanton waste of property. I know they are enemies to our cause, but yet their property should not go amongst such villains. I beg you would exert yourself and bring them to justice.

Benjamin sent his reply straight to Washington, informing him of the need for force in this matter. He added his opinion that Benjamin Floyd could be of service to the Rebel cause. He knew Floyd had been taken prisoner by the Continentals in Connecticut. Abraham seemed to agree with Benjamin that Floyd should be released and protected. After being robbed by his own side, Benjamin Floyd might be willing to help the Rebel cause, and they could possibly use him as a spy.

When the time came to put into place Benjamin's plans to raid Lloyd's Neck, he and his men waited until the night was completely dark, then they started across the sound, making landfall at ten p.m.

"Thirty men should stay and guard the boats," Benjamin instructed one of his captains. "The rest of the men will quickly move upon the camp in a surprise attack. Captain Edgar will take fifty troops to capture and seize the first group. I'll lead the rest of the troops. Captain, move in fast and as quietly as possible so as not to alert the guards at Fort Franklin. Take prisoners and supplies."

At Benjamin's command, they moved swiftly toward the houses and huts inside the camp. At first all went as planned, and the two houses were taken, but the Tories sheltering in the huts nearby recovered from the surprise attack and opened fire. The resistance was brief, and Benjamin secured the camp and set about collecting prisoners and supplies. Some of the Tories, however, escaped to the swampy land nearby, and the sounds of musket fire alarmed the Redcoats stationed at Fort Franklin. With the element of surprise now lost, Benjamin knew the bigger prize of taking Fort Franklin was no longer possible.

Knowing time was running out, he next directed his men to set fire to the Tories' camp and their boats. "Take the prisoners to the boats, and burn the camp," he shouted.

Back on their own boats, Benjamin's crew began to row back across the sound. One of the prisoners was Captain Ezekiel Glover, a Tory refugee from Connecticut who was captain of the Loyalist militia at Lloyd's Neck. Benjamin charged Glover with plundering the property of friendly inhabitants. He also seized a document written by Colonel John Simcoe stating that Captain Glover had been reconnoitering in Connecticut.

Although Benjamin hadn't lost any of his troops in the raid, his inability to take Fort Franklin and destroy the British stronghold taunted him.

Benjamin and his crew arrived in Connecticut just before daybreak with boats filled with prisoners. Once the prisoners had been unloaded and secured inside the Patriot camp at Fairfield, Benjamin found Caleb.

"I was unable to take down the fort," he lamented to his friend.

"Aye," Caleb answered. "But you took prisoners and did damage."

"I won't rest until I can carry out a formidable operation with success."

Caleb handed over the latest dispatches. "As winter approaches, things will slow," he said.

Benjamin placed the dispatches inside his coat.

"My dragoons will leave in the morning for Wethersfield," he said. "I need to revitalize my men and gather supplies and fresh horses, new uniforms, and equipment. I will visit with an old friend, Colonel Wadsworth, as Jeremiah is the Continental Commissary in Connecticut. He's always been supportive and a voice on my behalf to the governor and Congress." Benjamin clapped Caleb on the back. "Before I leave, let's have a drink."

Together, they walked to the makeshift mess tent and sat on a bench. Caleb poured them each a cup of ale. Benjamin took the dispatches from Culper, Sr. from his jacket and read through them, sharing the information with Caleb.

"At my suggestion, and because Abraham needed to find a source within the city, he has been able to secure the help of a store owner named Robert Townsend, who will be Culper, Jr. And he says when he arrived home from New York City, he found Simcoe's men had been looking for him, suspecting him to be a spy. They beat his father in his stead."

"Aye. Abraham told me. He wants someone with him the next trip into the city. A Tory, someone who can take the suspicion away from him."

Benjamin nodded and took a sip from his cup. To his mind came the need of getting Washington to release Colonel Benjamin Floyd, and he pondered for a moment how they could use Floyd for their cause. An idea came to him, and although it might work, he wondered if he dared to think on it further.

He couldn't go through with it—or could he?

35

December, 1779

  The first of December was marked by Mary's father's return from Philadelphia. For a few weeks, they would be together as a family once more. It was a good thing her father was home since Mary's mother had been sick and in bed for a week. Mary and Kitty hoped with their father's return, Hannah would start to feel much better, and within a few days, her spirits indeed seemed to lift. She was able to sit up in bed and work on her sewing. She even started a new project, making hats and bonnets for her and the girls.

  A few weeks before, Mary had received a reply from Liza. Mary's last note to her had been sent inside a kerchief, rolled tight and inserted into the hem along the edge. Mary had created a rolled edge all the way around so any lump would not be noticeable. Mary had told Liza about her talk with Benjamin and how she'd described to him Liza's unwanted guests and the visit from Major John André. She'd asked Liza to keep listening for information that might be of service to the Patriot cause.

  Liza's reply had come hidden withing the decorations of the most beautiful hair comb. Liza had taken small pieces of lace and fabric and sewn them onto the edge, then she'd taken small, tightly rolled papers and created a design in the shape of a flower. The piece was so beautifully crafted that Mary had not wanted to take it apart to get to the note. Fortunately, she was able to gently slide the missive from a bit of the rolled paper without disturbing Liza's other careful work.

The contents of the note were disturbing to Mary. Major André had made several visits to Oyster Bay, and now Simcoe and his Rangers planned to reconvene in New York City. Liza wanted to go with them, saying she might be able to sneak away. The rest of her letter explained that she'd overheard them talking about someone in the American forces they planned to convert to their side with the help of someone in the city.

Mary wanted to get this information to Benjamin somehow, and she also wanted to plead with Liza to stay in Oyster Bay. How could she sneak into the occupied city with an army and stay safe? Where would she go? Mary needed to come up with a new way to send her missives: something as unique as Liza's hair comb design.

Her thoughts were interrupted by her mother's voice.

"Mary, Kitty!" Hannah called.

"Here, Mother," Mary said, walking to the doorway of her mother's room.

When Mary approached, her mother was sitting up in bed looking cheerful. She smiled at Mary. "Come see," she said. "I've just finished these new bonnets for you and your sister. Where is Kitty this morning?"

Mary took a bonnet her mother indicated was for her. "It's lovely, Mother. I can't wait to wear it." Then she walked into the hallway and paused at the top of the stairs. "Kitty," she called. "Make haste; come see what Mother has for you."

"Coming," Kitty replied. Her mouth was full of candy that Cora and Joli had been preparing for Christmas. Kitty brought a handful with her when she came upstairs.

"Look," she said when she entered her mother's room. "Caramels so sweet you will surely rot your insides with their decadent, savory goodness." Kitty held her hand out so her mother and Mary each could take one. They were wrapped in crisp baking paper, twisted tightly at each end.

"Wonderful," Mary said, unwrapping one of the candies and popping it into her mouth. "Mm, so good."

"You mustn't eat them all," their mother told them with a laugh. "Cora and Joli won't have any left for Christmas. "Here, Kitty," she said, holding up the bonnet she'd made for her oldest daughter.

"Thank you, Mother," Kitty replied. She moved to the mirror to try on her new hat.

"I'll take these downstairs," Mary said, picking up the extra candy Kitty had set down.

Mary wandered downstairs and into the kitchen, where she found Cora and Joli wrapping and rolling more of the caramels.

"Can I help?" she asked.

Cora nodded. "We'll place the hot caramel on the tray. Before it cools, roll it, starting at one end, and roll it toward the other. Once it cools down, we'll slice it into smaller bits then place the pieces on these papers and twist the ends."

As Mary worked, an idea came to her about how she'd hide her next letter.

"Could we make more candy?" Mary asked. "I have a feeling we will have visitors at Christmas and on New Year's Eve."

Cora smiled and nodded. "We could, but let's finish these for now. We can talk about making some more tomorrow." She let out a brief chuckle. She knew who Mary's visitor might be.

∞∞∞∞∞∞∞∞∞

Mary's candy-wrapped missive must have reached Benjamin because he arrived late in the afternoon the day after Christmas. Mary leapt from her chair; the book she was reading fell from her lap. She'd heard his horse let out a loud whinny, and she watched as the handsome officer dismounted his fine horse. Her breath caught in her throat, and she felt her stomach turning flips.

"Who is it, Mary?" Kitty asked.

Mary didn't answer. She hadn't heard her sister's question; all her attention was on the major, who was tying his horse to the post in front of their house.

Kitty moved to stand next to her sister at the window. When she saw who it was, she smiled and gave Mary a knowing look.

"Stand away from the window," Kitty instructed. "You don't want him to see you watching. That's far too unladylike.

"Oh, what must I look like?" Mary said before running up the stairs to her room to primp.

Their father came out of his room, where he'd been napping.

"What's the commotion?" he asked.

Kitty met him at the bottom of the stairs.

"Major Tallmadge is here."

"Wonderful," he replied. He walked past Kitty and into the hallway toward the front door, and as he did, there came a knock. William opened the door, greeting Benjamin and welcoming him into their home.

Benjamin and William shook hands, then William showed Benjamin into their sitting room and offered him a seat next to the fire. Before he sat, Benjamin greeted Kitty with a short bow then looked around the room as if he were expecting someone else.

"A brandy to warm you?" William offered.

"That would be nice. Thank you."

William moved to a table situated along a wall, opened a decanter, and poured two glasses while Benjamin removed his cape, his sword, and his plumed dragoon hat.

"Mother, Cora, and Joli have been preparing Christmas leftovers," Kitty said. "I'll bring refreshments."

But instead of going in search of offerings in the kitchen, she snuck upstairs to check on Mary. When she walked into the room they shared, Mary was powdering her nose and gazing at her reflection in the mirror.

"Make haste, Mary," Kitty urged. her voice was barely louder than a whisper. "What's taking you so long?"

"I feel uneasy," Mary whispered back. "A queasiness in my stomach. Oh, what is wrong with me, Kitty? My palms are so sweaty."

"Stand up," Kitty instructed. "Take a deep breath. I've never known you to be afraid of anything, Mary. Where's my bold sister, the one who races horses to beat her older brother and mock him for losing to a girl? Where's the girl who caught the biggest fish from the creek back home? The girl who was never afraid of spiders. And the one who talked Nicoll into sneaking into Philadelphia to spy on the British—and who was shot at as she and her handsome officer escaped on his horse. *That* handsome officer is downstairs now, and he's waiting for you."

"Is he? Waiting on me, you think?"

Kitty nodded and placed both hands on her sister's shoulders. "There is no room for fear; that's what you've told me before. He favors you because he's seen your boldness.

He's captivated by your fearlessness and your selflessness. You don't have to charm the opposite sex with song or entertain them on the piano. You have something more unique. He's seen it, and my guess is he appreciates it. Now go."

With both hands Kitty shooed her sister out the door.

Later, when the family sat to eat, Kitty made sure Benjamin was seated next to her sister.

"We're so glad you could join us this evening, Major Tallmadge," Mary's mother said.

"It's always a pleasure to be here," Benjamin replied.

"You should visit Congress in Philadelphia soon," William suggested.

"Mm, I just might. Thank you for the offer. I've wondered what is talked about and discussed. I'm always ready to reserve and proffer supplies for my troops. It would be in my interest to learn how decisions are being made."

"I'll be heading back in a few weeks' time," William said. "A boardinghouse we've stayed in is for sale, and I have plans to purchase it."

Benjamin nodded. "A wise choice."

"Have you seen much of Nicoll?" Hannah asked. "We hear so little from him these days."

"Yes, ma'am, I have," Benjamin replied. "He works closely with a dear friend of mine. If you have news or anything you'd like me to share with him, I'll be glad to get that to him."

"Can you tell us anything of the progress of the war or of your dragoons' activities?" William asked. "We've heard bits and pieces shared in Congress. So I know you have led some very brave operations."

Benjamin nodded and began telling them about the bloody battle against Banastre Tarleton, then about leading the siege at Lloyd's Neck. Mary sat enthralled. His bravery seemed unmatched, and Mary's heart melted even more for the daring officer. She thought of him on his fine horse leading a charge and fighting bravely during battle. Mary watched Benjamin as he used his hands to describe the scene at Fort Franklin. Then slowly her eyes followed his arms up to his broad shoulders, to the stubble on his cheeks, and then to the bit of hair that curled near his ears; the rest was pulled into a low ponytail at his neck and tied with a black satin ribbon. Being so close to him, Mary could smell saddle oil, leather, earth, campfire smoke, and the sweetness from his glass of brandy. She wondered what it would be like to be held in his strong arms, to touch his cheek, his full lips . . . or to maybe even kiss them.

Suddenly, Cora set a slice of pie in front of Mary, and she jumped, startled by the motion. Her mind was jolted back to reality. What had she been thinking? How could she even think such thoughts? Surely she would need extra time in prayer this evening.

When they'd finished their meal and enjoyed the delicious pie, they removed to the sitting room. Kitty played a Christmas tune on the fortepiano, and they all joined in with the singing. When they tired of that, Mary's father offered a game of chess to Benjamin, and the ladies sat quietly. Hannah and Kitty sewed; Mary read her book.

"Ah, I believe you have me beat, Major," said Mary's father in a booming voice. He chuckled and then stood. "I shall take my leave. Major, feel free to have another glass of brandy."

Benjamin stood and gave a short bow as William turned to leave the room. Mary's mother stood and said, "Good night, Major Tallmadge. There are fresh sheets on the bed down here. I'll make sure Cora has brought fresh water for the basin."

William held his arm out for his wife to take, and together they left the room. Cora appeared in the hallway and assured Hannah the guest room was ready. Mary could hear her mother telling Cora to make sure she and Kitty went to bed soon and to prepare some extra food for Benjamin and some for him to take to Nicoll. Mary noticed Benjamin was resetting the chess table as Cora walked into the room and reminded her and Kitty it would soon be time to retire.

"I'm almost finished with what I'm working on," Kitty said. She glanced at Mary and winked. This was Kitty's way of giving Mary more time to talk with Benjamin; Kitty understood they would not be allowed to be alone together.

But Mary couldn't let Kitty overhear what she wanted to tell Benjamin; she never wanted to endanger her family with knowledge of her spying.

"I shall pack Major Tallmadge some food for his journey so it's ready for him when he takes his leave in the morning," Mary said. She stood and walked past Cora into the kitchen.

Kitty looked surprised and stood up. She wished Benjamin a good evening and made her way up the stairs. Cora said good night to Benjamin and went into the kitchen to see what Mary was putting together. A single candle was lit and sat in the middle of the small table in the center of the kitchen. Mary stood at the counter along one wall, placing apples and oranges into a small basket. When she heard a noise behind her, she quickly turned around.

"Oh, Cora, it's just you," she said breathlessly.

Cora nodded. "I can take care of packing food for Nicoll and the major. You go on to bed, Miss Mary."

Mary shook her head. "Please, Cora, just let me speak to Major Tallmadge alone for just a minute."

Even in the darkness, Cora could see the pleading look in Mary's eyes.

"All right, child," she said. "But I'ma be watching and listening for anything upsetting. I worry about you. But I trust the major. He seems like good folk. But I's still be close. I'm not going to my cabin yet. When I knows you safe, I will."

Mary whispered, "Thank you."

Cora left through the back door, and Mary set the basket of fruit on the table. Then she walked back to the sitting room. When she got there, Benjamin was making his way around the room blowing out the candles. He only had three left to go.

"Wait," Mary whispered urgently.

Benjamin set a candlestick down, then turned to see whose face was behind the voice.

Mary rushed over to him. When she got closer, their eyes locked, their bodies casting large shadows along the walls in the dimly lit room.

Benjamin cocked his head to the side, curious as to why Mary was standing before him.

"You received the candy I sent?" she asked.

"Yes."

"And the note?"

"I did. Thank you." His tone was supple and gentle. His soft hazel eyes held her gaze. "The information from your friend in Oyster Bay has been helpful," he told her quietly. "My agents have been kept abreast of the news."

"I don't think Liza should sneak away with Colonel Simcoe and his men. I fear for my friend."

Benjamin nodded. "That's understandable," he told her in a low voice, then stepped even closer to Mary. "We can't always make others do as we'd want them to. Each of us has our own will. Even Divine Providence doesn't interfere with our choices, no matter how bad those might be. Maybe your friend wants her freedom, or she may want to continue to help by finding out more. She may plan to seek out her owner's son, Robert Townsend, once she's there. She could be of great benefit to the cause and go completely unsuspected."

Mary broke the gaze and looked down. That was not what she wanted to hear. She wanted him to say he'd find Liza, that he'd save her.

Benjamin must have understood her thoughts. He reached out and tenderly took her hand and held it. The gesture made Mary jump, and she looked up to see Benjamin's eyes searching hers.

"Decisions about this business of war—and about spying—are not easily determined, Mary. Your boldness is an anthem to me." He squeezed her hand, and her stomach leapt to her throat. "I have spoken with your cousin, Benjamin Floyd, and he is willing to provide my agent on Long Island safe passage into New York. Whether or not your cousin still holds his faith in the Tory cause is uncertain. But he has been robbed twice by the British, which might be the reason he is willing to be of service. He might also be entangled in the same circles as Major André, and he might overhear something that could become our gain."

Mary's face brightened. "That's good news then. I've heard Major André has been one to throw lavish parties. What if I were to visit my cousin Benjamin and attend one of these parties as his guest?"

Benjamin took a deep breath but didn't let go of her hand. "Oh, my dear Mary. What you suggest is as brilliant as it is treacherous. If it were anyone but you risking their life, I would be jubilant to respond. You must know how hard it is for me to answer you."

He lifted their clasped hands to his lips, closed his eyes, and tenderly placed a kiss on Mary's hand.

Mary gasped aloud. Her stomach turned endless flips, and her heart pounded wildly in her chest. She trembled with desire from the gentle touch of his soft lips.

"I must bid you good evening, my dear Mary."

With that, he let go of her hand, and walked away, leaving Mary stunned and trying to catch her breath.

She blew out the rest of the candles then rushed up the stairs and into her bedroom, shutting the door quietly. She leaned against it, her heart pounding as if it would burst from her chest. Then she decided she must make plans right away to visit her cousin on Long Island.

36

Fall, 1779

Liza snuck out of the Townsend home and onto the back of Colonel Simcoe's wagon, managing to escape unnoticed amid the hustle and bustle of the army scurrying to leave. She rode curled up inside a trunk that had been packed with a few extra uniforms. She propped the lid open by hanging a sleeve of a uniform over the edge and settled in for the long ride to Staten Island.

Liza had confessed to Sally Townsend her desire to leave when Colonel John Graves Simcoe and his Queen's Rangers left Oyster Bay. Sally had flirted with Simcoe, and he had even given her a love poem. Liza had watched Sally play the part of a sweet, doting girl with Simcoe and the handsome Major André. Sally had acted like it didn't bother her that her home had been overrun by British soldiers or that they had taken whatever they wanted.

Sally had them fooled, and whenever they said something in front of her that might be helpful to the Patriot cause, Sally would mention it to Liza or to her sister, Phebe. Sally hoped Phebe would send a missive with information to Nicoll, her beau, who was with the Continentals. Liza, of course, wanted to keep Mary informed, thinking she would share the information with Major Tallmadge.

Liza had heard that slaves might be freed if they joined the British cause, but she didn't want to be with the Queen's Rangers or John Simcoe; she really wanted to be near John André. He was kind and funny, very handsome, and she liked it when he drew pictures of people. He had even drawn a portrait of her. She liked the way he smiled at her, the way he touched her hand when she brought him his tea, and the kind and thoughtful way he would speak to her. She wanted to be near him if she could, and if that meant risking her life to travel to New York, she'd do it.

When she told Sally and Phebe about her plans, they'd agreed to help however they could. Sally wrote a letter to a Tory family on Staten Island on Liza's behalf, explaining to them that she would be sneaking away with the Queen's Rangers near the end of October. Could they grant her safe passage into New York City and take her to Major André? Sally knew it was a great risk to even ask Christopher Billopp, the wealthy Tory whose home was the most obvious location for the Queen's Rangers to station themselves. Sally was frightened about what could become of her if anyone found out she'd requested help to sneak a slave into the city. She'd asked that the letter be burned once it was read. When Sally received an agreeable response, she explained to Liza that someone in the Billopp home would help her once the Rangers arrived on Staten Island.

Liza hated being in the trunk. It was the last item that had been loaded onto the supply wagon, so whenever she peeked out from the crack, she could see a little of where they were. But after several hours, she curled into a ball and went to sleep despite the frequent bumps and jostling. When the wagon finally stopped, she woke. She peeked from the crack to see the army preparing to set up camp for the night.

Sally had told Liza it would take them two days to get to Staten Island since most of the men were walking behind the wagon and there were few on horseback. Liza knew they would unload the wagon on this first stop to get to their cooking supplies. She quickly pulled the sleeve of the uniform inside the trunk. Then swiftly, she closed the lid and waited. Eventually the trunk was lifted from the wagon and set off to the side so the soldiers could climb in and out from the back to get to what was needed. When Liza saw it was safe, she crawled out and made her way behind a tree, and then into the bushes to wait for nightfall. She would have to make her way back into the trunk in the wee hours before sunrise in order to go undetected. For now, she'd continue to pray that she'd make it to her destination alive.

Later, in the darkness of the camp, with soldiers snoring loudly, Liza tiptoed out of the bushes, crawled back over to the trunk, and climbed inside.

"Who goes there?" she heard a man call.

Liza made not a sound. She continued to lift up silent prayers asking almighty God to grant her safe passage. After several moments, Liza thought the soldier must have decided there wasn't a threat, so she curled up and went to sleep. The next leg of the journey turned out to be not nearly as long as the one the day before. When the wagon came to a stop, Liza woke and snuck a peek, sensing they might be at their destination. But she knew she'd be in the trunk much longer since she'd have to wait for darkness to fall, so she settled in to wait.

Soon, she heard a female voice calling.

"Liza. Are you there?"

She wasn't expecting anyone to be calling for her, but she lifted the lid a bit higher and looked around. She saw a woman and a teenaged girl, and it seemed they were looking for her.

"Here," Liza said in barely more than a whisper. "I'm in here. The trunk."

The woman heard Liza and looked at the trunk.

"Quick," she said to the girl with her. "Cause a distraction so that I can help her without anyone noticing."

The girl walked over to a group of soldiers asking if they needed any water or food. As the girl continued to engage the soldiers with questions and conversation, the woman walked over to the wagon and motioned for Liza to come with her. After Liza quickly crawled from the trunk, the woman placed her arms on Liza's shoulders and together they walked to a nearby house.

"Go inside," she told Liza. "Hurry."

Liza went into the house and waited. She could hear the woman and the girl talking to the soldiers, then soon the two women made their way into the house.

"I'm Jane," the woman said to Liza. "This is my daughter Louisa. We will take you down to the basement. We have a storage room there that has a lock. You will need to stay there until they leave. It might be a day or so."

Jane led Liza down into the cellar and into the small pantry which had already been prepared for her.

"When we received the letter from the Townsend girl addressed to my husband," Jane explained, "there would have been no way for her to know he had just been captured by the Rebels and imprisoned in New Jersey. We wanted to help you. We have a young slave girl named Rosa; she will check on you."

Liza nodded.

Jane closed and locked the pantry door, leaving Liza in complete darkness. She was still fearful and unsure of what might happen, but at least she had some food, a blanket, and a place large enough to lie down. After eating a few bites from an apple and drinking some water, she was grateful to be able to lie down and stretch out. A few hours later, she heard the rattle of the lock. She jumped and scooted back as far as she could into the darkness for fear of who might be on the other side. What if the Rangers had found out? Would Simcoe or his men harm Jane or her daughter if they found out they'd hidden a runaway slave? Liza shook with fear and fervently prayed as the door to the cupboard opened and faded light poured in around her.

"I'm Rosa," the young African girl said. "I brought you some broth. It's okay. I'm on your side. The mens outside don't know you here. You safe with us."

Rosa walked closer to Liza, holding the cup out for her to take.

"Thank you," Liza said as she took the cup.

"Welcome." Rosa smiled. "I heard them talking. They planning to leave in the morning to Perth Amboy then go into New Jersey, thinking they'll ambush the Continentals there. I hope they don't. Colonel Billopp, the one who owns Bentley Manor—that's where we is—he in prison, caught by the Rebels."

Liza nodded and sipped the broth.

"I'm on the side for the Rebels, but no one here know that. It don't matter what side you's on though. I help you. Once they leave in the morning, Miss Jane says we goin' take you into the city. I best be getting back fo' anyone notice."

"Thank you," Liza said and paused. The two girls looked at each other with an unspoken understanding. "I'm grateful."

Rosa closed and locked the door. With her hopes up, Liza settled back onto the blanket and drank more of her broth. Tomorrow she might find Major John André.

At dawn Simcoe and his Queen's Rangers left Staten Island and made their way to Perth Amboy in New Jersey. A Loyalist named Jim Stewart guided the Rangers along the Raritan River. Another British unit landed at South Amboy to prepare an ambush in conjunction with Simcoe's Rangers to capture a Continental Army major and burn boats at Raritan.

Simcoe and his men posed as Henry Lee's dragoons as both groups wore green. Simcoe tried to pass himself off as a Patriot when they met a band of armed militia at the Frelinghuysen Tavern in Bound Brook. A bystander, however, recognized Simcoe and sent a rider to warn Governor Livingston in New Brunswick. Simcoe's men did not find the Continental major at the Van Horne house as they had expected. The Van Horne house, Simcoe had learned, served as the headquarters for several American generals. Simcoe's Rangers continued on to Raritan, where they blasted eighteen flatboats with grenades and set them on fire, preventing George Washington from attacking Staten Island. Simcoe had his men burn down a fifty-eight-year-old Dutch Reformed Church in Finderne, where the Continentals had stored additional equipment.

Simcoe continued his raid, burning a courthouse and adjacent houses. Militia around New Brunswick found out about the location of the Rangers from seeing the fires, and militiamen ambushed Simcoe on the morning of October 29. Knocked unconscious, Simcoe was taken prisoner and placed in the same jail where Christopher Billopp was being held.

While Simcoe and his Rangers were plundering New Brunswick, Liza, Jane, and Louisa were making their way to Liza's next destination.

That morning, Jane had given Liza fresh clothes to wear. Together the ladies traveled in the Billopp carriage into the city. Liza was grateful to this Tory family who had gone out of their way to help a slave girl they didn't know.

But when she started to thank Jane, Jane shook her head and took Liza's hand.

"We want you to be free if you can," Jane told her.

"Where should we take you?" Jane asked Liza on their way into the city. "Do you know anyone?"

"I know Major André is here. He stayed in the Townsend home a few times. I know Robert Townsend too, the son of the man who owns me. He owns a store in Hanover Square."

"We shall take you there then," Jane decided.

37

New York City, Early November 1779

Robert Townsend was walking to his shop from Rivington's coffeehouse when he saw a carriage pulling up in front. Two ladies stepped out, then Robert caught sight of a familiar face when a third figure made an appearance. Could that be who he thought it was? As he walked closer, he grew sure it was indeed Elizabeth, the young slave girl who had grown up in his home. What was she doing here?

"Liza?" he called out.

She turned toward the sound of his voice.

"Sir," the older woman said. "My name is Jane Billopp." She turned to the girl with her. "This is my daughter, Louisa. My husband is Christopher Billopp of Bentley Manor on Staten Island. Your sister Sally wrote to us about Liza."

"Please come inside," Robert said.

He unlocked the door to his shop and ushered the three ladies in.

"We can talk in the back," he said, and they followed him.

Robert went to a table and pulled out a few chairs.

"Mrs. Billopp, Louisa, Liza, please sit."

Then he picked up a stool, brought it over to the table, and joined them.

"You were saying Sally sent a letter to you?"

Mrs. Billopp nodded. "It was for my husband. But he's been taken prisoner by the Rebels. In the letter, she asked for safe passage for Liza, saying that Liza planned to escape when Colonel Simcoe and the Queen's Rangers left Oyster Bay. We wanted to help her. Louisa, myself, and our young slave girl, Rosa, are the only ones who know. I promise her secret is safe."

Robert looked at Liza, who was sitting quietly.

"I appreciate all your help," Robert said to Jane. "Can I pay you or offer you something from the store as a token of my gratitude?"

Jane shook her head. "That won't be necessary. Being able to help Liza is enough reward. We hope that she will find her freedom soon."

She and Louisa stood.

"We should be going," Jane said.

Liza stood. "Thank you," she told them.

Jane and Louisa smiled at Liza, then Jane moved closer to Liza and took her by the hand. "Stay brave. We pray this will all be over soon."

"I'll walk you out," Robert said.

Then he returned to the back room with a changed demeanor.

"You can't stay here Liza," he told her nervously. "I'm going to have to write my father and tell him not to worry about you. Having a runaway slave can be a serious situation."

"But I want to go with Major André," Liza said. "Can you take me to him? I believe he will grant me my freedom."

Suddenly, the shop's bell tinkled, alerting Robert someone had entered the store.

"Quick," Robert said. "Hide in here."

Unfortunately for Liza, it was another trunk.

As Robert was walking into the next room, he said, "I'll check on you periodically."

∞∞∞∞∞∞∞

At the end of the day, Robert closed his shop, and went into the storeroom to check on Liza. He helped her out of the trunk.

"For you."

He handed her some cheese and bread.

"I have correspondence to write; one of those letters will be to Major André. I'll request an audience."

As Robert sat at the table to write, he pulled from his coat a letter from home that had been delivered only an hour ago. He gestured to Liza to have a seat next to him. Robert looked at the letter; it was from his father. Robert glanced at Liza but kept his thoughts to himself about what he assumed would be in the letter, knowing his father must be concerned about his runaway slave. He knew he'd need to spare his father any further worry, but he had other pressing correspondence to attend to first. Earlier at the coffeehouse, he'd learned information he needed to convey to Culper. The British planned to counterfeit Continental currency.

The British think America will not be able to keep an army together another campaign because the currency will be entirely depreciated, and that there will not be provision in the country to supply an army for another campaign. That of the currency I am afraid will prove true, as they are indefatigable increasing the quantity of it. Several reams of paper made for the last emission struck by Congress have been procured from Philadelphia.

Robert signed the note Culper, Jr. then began to pen a note to his father. In the letter to Samuel Townsend, Robert had no intention of explaining Liza's escape plan or involving his sister Sally or Jane Billopp, who had burned Sally's letter upon reading it. He also didn't want anyone looking for Liza or claiming she was a runaway.

The Queen's Rangers are now beyond King's Ridge. When I see any of the officers will make inquiry for her—Tho' I think there is no probability of your getting her again—believe you may reckon her amongst your other dead losses.— I am surprised that Colonel Simcoe would permit her to go—he certainly must have known it when they left Oyster Bay.—I am

Dear Sir, Your dutiful Son Robt. Townsend

He sealed and addressed the missive to his father. Then penned a letter to Major John André that he would give to an officer in the morning when he went to Rivington's. It had become part of his new routine to visit the coffeehouse in hopes of overhearing information from the British officers who frequented the shop. For the Culper letter, he went to a shelf and retrieved a bag of coffee beans, dumped them out, placed the note inside, then replaced the beans. That would be given to Austin Roe, the courier, when he arrived for his weekly pickup of supplies and secret dispatches for Washington.

"Liza," Robert said softly, "you'll need to stay here and stay hidden until I have word from André about a meeting. Since I'm thought to have Tory sentiments and am often seen around British officers throughout the city, Major André may grant me permission to speak with him, but we must wait and see. The door will be locked when I leave. I'll return in the morning with more food."

Meeting Robert's eyes, Liza said, "I understand."

A day later, Robert received a note from Major André granting permission for an audience, and the address given was One Broadway. Robert knew that was the home where Sir Henry Clinton was headquartered, and it seemed reasonable that Major Andre would make his residence there also. Early the following morning, Robert gathered Liza, and together they walked the three blocks to the meeting. Upon reaching the grand house, Robert turned to Liza and said,

"I'll do what I can. But if he is not agreeable, I feel it may be best if you return to my father's home in Oyster Bay."

Liza nodded and watched as Robert went to the door and knocked. A very tall butler with skin darker than Liza's answered the door, allowing Robert inside, but he gave Liza a questioning look.

"I'm Robert Townsend. I own a store in Hanover Square and have been gifted permission to meet with Major André this morning." Robert turned to Liza. "Please permit her to enter as well."

The butler nodded to Liza. They followed the butler from the large foyer into a much larger and grander room on the right.

"Have a seat, Mr. Townsend. I will send for Major André," said the butler.

A moment later, another servant appeared with tea and offered it to Robert. Liza stood close by, feeling nervous and anxious. They heard footsteps in the hallway, and soon Major André appeared in the doorway.

"Greetings," André said. He stepped into the room, not noticing Liza.

.Robert stood and bowed.

"You must be Robert Townsend," André said and bowed to Robert. "I frequented your father's home in Oyster Bay. Your sisters were always most courteous."

André took a cup of tea from the tray in front of him, and when he straightened up, he saw Liza standing nearby.

"My dear." He looked from Liza to Robert. "This is a most wonderful surprise. How are you, Liza?"

"Good, sir," Liza replied, giving the Major a slight bow.

"Sir, can we speak in confidence?" Robert asked.

André sat on the couch across from where Robert stood and motioned for Robert to sit.

"Major André, Liza has requested to live with and work for you. She wishes to have her freedom and feels you can provide her with that."

"I see," said André. "But she is still owned by your father, I presume?"

Robert nodded.

"I have no problem with having Liza here. I would need to go through Sir Henry and also the housekeeper, Mrs. Mary Baddeley. But we can always use the help. I throw grand parties, and as the year comes to a close and a new one begins, there will be much to celebrate. I am very fond of Liza."

André glanced at Liza with the hint of a smile on his lips, causing heat to rise to her cheeks.

"If all is agreeable, I shall gather Liza and her things from you tomorrow." He paused. "As for freedom papers for Liza, that might be a possibility once we have won the war." André leaned forward. "I might ask a favor in return, Mr. Townsend."

"Sir," Robert said.

"I would implore you to join the Loyalist volunteers of the City of New York and stand guard as sentry in front of General Guy Carlton's headquarters here on Broadway near the Battery."

Robert nodded. "Of course, Major. However I might be of service." He stood and gave a short bow. "I own the mercantile shop in Hanover Square a few blocks from here. I shall look for you in the morning. Thank you, Major."

Robert turned to Liza, and together they walked into the hallway. The butler showed them to the door. Liza left with hope that André would come for her the next day, and Robert with the opportunity to spy on the British from General Guy Carlton's headquarters.

38

Setauket, Long Island, 1779

The Presbyterian church in the town of Setauket had been vandalized by the British months ago. Colonel Hewlett had ripped out the pews and made the church a stable. The enemy had plucked gravestones from the cemetery to make weaponry. The beautiful field in front where Benjamin and Mary had once been in attendance at a picnic was now filled with tents and supplies for the British.

But on fair-weather days, the Reverend Benjamin Tallmadge spoke to his congregation from the sloped lawn of his home along the bank of the sound. Today the congregants stood along the grassy bank near a large firepit that had been created for the outdoor services. The sun was bright and the clouds were sparse. A row of British sentries stood guard, as if a congregation gathering to worship was a reason for the British to be watchful.

Abraham and his sister Susannah were among those gathered. Abraham watched as Anna Smith Strong made her way toward the fire, her flock of children surrounding her.

"Anna," Abraham said to her in greeting.

Anna nodded to him. "Good morning, Abraham, Susannah. It's good to see you both. Is everything all right, Abraham? I haven't seen you lately."

Abraham shook his head. "Nay. I've British soldiers quartering in my home." He drew closer to Anna and then whispered so his sister would not hear. "It makes me too anxious to take pen to paper these days. Until they quit my place, I shall not write as Culper."

Anna's younger children ran in circles in front of where the two friends stood. Their laughter and joy were a diversion amid the tension gripping the adults.

Anna whispered back, "I will alert Caleb."

"I don't think you should dare. Not with a note in the dead drop. It poses the threat of exposure."

"I won't use the secret location to leave a note. Instead, I'll place only petticoats on the line. He will know from seeing those that I have news. If he finds me, then I will tell him in person. Austin still rides to the city?"

"I believe so," Abraham said.

"We will pray the soldiers leave you and your family's home soon," she said. "My prayers were answered when Silah was released on prisoner exchange. I am relieved he is now safe in Connecticut. Our oldest is with him now."

A young girl walked up to greet Anna.

"Mary Smith," Anna said, "this is my dear friend Abraham Woodhull."

Abraham and Mary nodded to each other, and Mary curtsied. Her smile was welcoming, making Abraham feel a little less troubled. He turned to introduce Mary to his sister. As the two ladies greeted each other, Reverend Tallmadge collected the attention of his congregation with a prayer then began a short sermon.

"In the word of God," the Reverend began, "the book of Romans, chapter three, verse ten says, 'As it is written, there is none righteous, no not one.' And let us ponder on verses twenty-two through twenty-four. 'Even the righteousness of God which is by faith of Jesus Christ unto all and upon all them that believe, for there is no difference. For all have sinned and come short of the glory of God. Being justified freely by his grace through the redemption that is in Christ Jesus.'"

The Reverend held his Bible high in the air. "It is not for us to not have troubles, for we know trouble will come. Like birth pains, things will get worse before they get better. If things aren't worse, you are not yet at the end. In the end God promises new life when we are all caught up with him in heaven. A time will come when he brings his righteousness to the earth, destroying evil once and for all. All will be judged, and a new kingdom will be established. Until that time, take heed from Mathew, chapter twenty-four."

Reverend Tallmadge turned the pages quickly and read them silently before he closed his Bible and spoke from memory. "And ye shall hear of wars and rumors of wars: see that ye be not troubled: for all these things must come to pass, but the end is not yet. For nation shall rise against nation, and kingdom against kingdom: and there shall be famines, and pestilences, and earthquakes. Then shall they deliver you up to be afflicted, and shall kill you: and ye shall be hated of all nations for my name's sake. Many shall be offended, and shall betray one another, even hate one another. And many false prophets shall rise and shall deceive many. Iniquity shall abound, the love of many shall wax cold. But he that shall endure unto the end, the same shall be saved. This gospel of the kingdom shall be preached in all the world for a witness unto all nations; and then shall the end come."

The Reverend paused and looked around at all who had gathered and said,

"Revelation, chapter two, tells us not to fear 'those things which thou shalt suffer . . . Ye shall have tribulation. Be thou faithful unto death, for God will give thee a crown of life.' Let us bow in prayer. Father God, make strong our faith in you, oh, Lord. Help us to not allow our suffering and affliction to separate us from your love; instead, let it bring us toward you. Let us praise you through our sorrow, for you knew us before we were conceived in our mothers' wombs, so you know our needs even before we ask. Let us remember to hold you sovereign above our own thoughts and desires, for you alone are holy. Amen."

A hymn was sung, then Reverend Tallmadge began walking around, shaking hands and giving hearty claps on the backs to the men within the crowd. He greeted each of his congregants with a blessing and a smile.

As Anna left to gather her children, she gave Abraham an understanding nod to show her sympathy for his current situation at home. Mary Smith and Susannah talked with one another, then Mary asked Abraham how his father was, and the conversation flowed freely, relieving some of the stress he'd felt. As their visit ended, Abraham's sister invited Mary and her family to supper later that evening. Mary accepted, and Abraham was very pleased she would be dining with them.

∞∞∞∞∞∞∞

A week later, Anna and Mary stopped by the Woodhull home to deliver a basket of canned goods. Anna handed one specifically to Abraham and said,

"I made this to your taste. I do hope you will enjoy it."

Abraham took it from Anna and said, "Thank you. I will."

After a few moments of pleasant exchange, Mary nervously bowed her head before glancing up at Abraham.

"Mr. Woodhull," Mary said, "I would be honored to return the gracious favor of inviting you and your family to our home for a meal."

Abraham beamed with delight.

"Miss Smith," Abraham answered, "I would be grateful to accept the invitation. And if my parents are unable to attend . . ." He paused and caught her eye.

"Certainly you and Susannah are more than welcome." She smiled and cleared her throat. "Even if Susannah is unavailable, Mr. Woodhull, we would be honored by your presence."

Abraham smiled broadly then nodded. "I'm much delighted, Miss Mary," he said.

When the two ladies left, Abraham was still holding the jar of strawberry jam Anna had gifted him. He carried it with him to his room, shut the door and opened the lid to find a note.

Caleb has brought over Benjamin Tallmadge. They wait for you in the wood along the far edge of your farm.

Abraham destroyed the note by holding it over a candle flame then brushed the ashes into a nearby bucket. He then took the jam into the kitchen, where he set it near the cupboard, and gathered his hunting rifle. At the door, he told his father he was going hunting and would return shortly. The soldiers who stood guard near the door overheard him, but before they could insist on tagging along, Susannah walked past carrying the laundry to hang on the line. The soldiers were easily distracted and followed her instead. As they trailed behind her to the clothesline, their chatter was loud enough to annoy Abraham.

With haste, he made his way into the woods near the sound, hoping Caleb and Benjamin would soon hear him approach. He wasn't careful to be quiet, but was, in fact, the opposite, allowing twigs to snap under his footsteps.

"Abraham," he heard from up ahead.

"It's me," Abraham answered.

Benjamin Tallmadge stepped from behind a large oak tree and greeted his friend with a hug.

"Good to see you ol' friend," Benjamin said. "Caleb and his men had to return to Connecticut. He left a few hours ago."

"When will Caleb come for you?" Abraham asked.

"I hope he can return within the week. I came because I've been worried. You haven't sent reports in almost a month."

"British soldiers are camped in my home. They have been for weeks. They suspect me, I suppose, even though Simcoe found nothing when he came to my farm with his men. I can only dare to sneak away at night to find you. I'll bring food. I am off hunting now, or so they think. I don't know if I will be able to return to the business you require. I fear going into the city alone."

"I have something Washington has given us to use," Benjamin explained. "A secret invisible ink rendered only visible with a counter ink. It was invented by John Jay's brother, James, a chemist. This ink will not become visible by heating it as some made from lemon juice do. Washington said Jay's innovation was years in the making. Only those with the counter agent will be able to reveal any message written with it."

Benjamin handed Abraham a pouch that held four vials. "There is enough for you and Culper, Jr. You will need to get it to him." He showed him which was the ink, and which was the agent. Then he handed over some money. "For any expenses you've incurred."

Abraham took the offerings from him.

"It is helpful to be able to write and not have the information visible," Abraham said. "But I still fear traveling into the city. Austin has been gathering the intelligence from

Townsend these last few weeks. I've checked the dead drop at least once and found this note there." He removed his shoe and handed Benjamin the missive.

"Austin can only go so often," Benjamin said. "But between the two of you, the information will arrive more quickly. I think there is a way to alleviate suspicion from you—using Colonel Benjamin Floyd, if he were to vouch for you. If you traveled with him in and out of New York, you would be seen with a prominent Loyalist, and it would become known that you have a connection to someone influential."

Abraham nodded. "I need to kill a few squirrels and make my way home with them. If I come back with food, it will be easier for me to sneak away at night." Abraham placed a hand atop Benjamin's shoulder. "I do appreciate you, my friend, for coming to check on me. In a few days' time, Caleb should return and not leave you stranded."

39

January, 1780

"I shall pack two sets of gloves and my new fan," Kitty rambled on. "The one Mother and Father gave me at Christmas, and I think two pairs of earrings. Do you like these?"

She turned away from the trunk she was packing to look at her sister. Mary was sitting at the desk in their room, focused on the letter she'd been writing. When Mary continued to ignore her, Kitty walked over and stood next to the desk.

"Are you listening, Mary? I'm trying to pack for Philadelphia. Father and I leave at dawn, and I want your thoughts on my selections. What are you so busy doing that you don't hear me?"

"What?" Mary asked, looking up at Kitty.

Kitty peered down at the paper that lay in front of Mary. Mary's hand still held the quill.

"Are you writing a love letter to Benjamin Tallmadge?" Kitty giggled. "Let me read it."

"No," Mary said. "This is not to Major Tallmadge. It's for Benjamin, our cousin."

"Cousin Benjamin? Whatever for?" Kitty asked. "What are you up to, Mary?"

"I want to see about visiting Benjamin on Long Island and making a trip with him into New York City."

Kitty gasped. "Oh, my skilamalink! I don't think Father will allow it."

"He shall if Cousin Benjamin is agreeable."

"Why do you want to go to Long Island and into the city? It's covered up with British." Kitty looked at her sister for a moment then said, "You look worried. You've been sitting there staring at the page for a generation. I don't think you heard anything I said when I was packing my trunk."

"I'm sorry, Kitty. Is there something you'd like to show me?"

With a dreamy look, Kitty said, "I'm excited to go back to Philadelphia. I hope to see William Clarkson again." Kitty smiled then wandered back to her trunk. She picked up a pair of earrings and walked back to the desk to show Mary.

"Those are lovely, Kitty. A good choice," Mary said, then turned back to her correspondence and began a new letter, this time for Benjamin Tallmadge.

Dear Benjamin,

My constant hope is always that you are well. I look forward to our next meeting wholeheartedly. I have just written to my cousin on Long Island. You are aware of Colonel Benjamin Floyd, as he is a known Loyalist of some prominence on the island. I feel it would be of benefit for me to pay him a visit and possibly make a trip into the city with him. Kitty and Father leave for Philadelphia tomorrow. She is filled with excitement to quit Connecticut and Middleton as this town seems to bore her. I find it quite charming here, although I sometimes still long for our home in Mastic. There was so much to explore. But I was also very young, and it seems like ages ago. Now, I fill my time by baking with Cora and Joli, riding my horse, Spot, and reading. I've just started a new book called Evelina by an English author named Frances Burney. I've just received it from Father as a Christmas gift. I don't think it would be something you'd fancy, because the character of Evelina is a young girl coming of age in London society. I find the story quite charming and humorous.

    I shall delight in receiving your next letter. Please know I pray for you daily, even nightly, and think of you continuously.

    Yours most sincerely,

    Mary Floyd

    Mary addressed her correspondence and went downstairs. She'd give the letter for Major Tallmadge to her father. He could mail it from Congress, knowing it would be safe in the hands of Continental dispatch riders. The one for Cousin Benjamin could be sent through the post. Mary decided if her cousin was agreeable for her to visit and even travel with him into the city, she'd send a letter to her brother and ask him to take her to Long Island. How, she wasn't sure, but she knew Nicoll and Caleb crossed the sound from Connecticut to Long Island often. The only thing that worried her was leaving her mother. She'd be here with Cora, Joli, and Jeb, but Mary was concerned because her mother's health had not been the best. But she knew her mother's cousin, Alice and her husband, Tom would be willing to come by and check in on her mother if she were to leave.

∞∞∞∞∞∞∞∞∞∞

    Two weeks later, the post arrived. Mary went out to retrieve it from the rider, gave him a coin, and quickly looked through the items. There was mail from her father for her mother, something from Kitty, and a letter to Mary from Cousin Benjamin. Nothing from Major Tallmadge. She went inside and sat on the couch to open the letter from her cousin.

Dearest Cousin Mary,

How great it was to hear from you and to learn you are all doing well in Connecticut. I can't say we are at our best here. As you might have heard, we've been plundered and robbed several times. For some, this war seems to be a way to gain an individual reward at whatever cost it might be to others. I can dare say I am in favor of the end and for that to come sooner rather than later.

You and your mother are more than welcome to come for a visit. We will prepare a room for you. Although I don't remember if you mentioned your mother coming. I do recall your father and Kitty are currently away in Philadelphia. Whenever it is possible for you to come, I shall enclose travel papers that will allow you to cross unharmed between the lines.

Your Cousin most sincerely,

Benjamin Floyd

Mary went to her room to pen a reply. Then she wrote to her brother, letting him know she would be receiving the papers signed by a British commander that were needed for safe passage into Long Island. She also asked Nicoll to meet her at home and travel with her, maybe he could provide a carriage.

Six days later, Nicoll arrived driving a small one-horse carriage. Mary and her mother were thrilled to see him, as were Jeb, Cora, and Joli. No one questioned why he had the carriage with him instead of just his horse. And Nicoll didn't realize Mary hadn't told their mother of her plans to visit their cousin on Long Island. After they settled into the kitchen and Joli had handed Nicoll some refreshments, Hannah asked,

"How long will you be staying?"

"Maybe a week?" Nicoll replied looking at Mary.

"I've just remembered something," Mary said. She stood and left the kitchen.

She flew up the stairs and penned a quick letter to her cousin, letting him know they were ready for the journey as soon as he could send the signed travel papers. She sealed and addressed the letter quickly, donned her cape, then made her way down the stairs and out the door to the nearest place to mail the missive. When she returned home, her brother was waiting for her.

"Mother doesn't know of your plans, does she?" Nicoll asked.

"I wasn't sure if things would work out." Mary stepped close to Nicoll and spoke softly. "I've just mailed Cousin Benjamin a letter asking him to send the travel papers. Once they arrive, I will have proof that we can travel and visit with him. I'll tell her I miss home and that since Kitty is in Philadelphia, I thought I might take a trip. Mother's cousin is close by and can check in on her. There wouldn't be any reason for her to worry."

Nicoll laughed. "There might always be a reason to worry where you're concerned, Mary. Long Island, as you know, is completely occupied by the British. It's not exactly safe."

Mary grinned at Nicoll. "But I'll be staying with a Loyalist family of whom I'm a part. It would be of benefit to go with Colonel Floyd into New York City. You know he has connections. I could be among the likes of John André at one of his grand parties. And, oh, what I might overhear while there!" Mary poked her finger into Nicoll's chest playfully.

Nicoll rolled his eyes and let out a breath. He shook his head at his sister. "I don't know what to say. You've been warned about this before. I will need to ride to camp and let Caleb know. He could get word to Benjamin Tallmadge, and they might come up with a more secure plan than anything you might have thought of."

Nicoll left on his horse, leaving the carriage in the stable with plans to return within a few days. Mary invited her mother's cousin, Alice and her family for dinner with the idea of sharing her plans with her mother during the meal. She knew her mother wouldn't say anything hasty in the presence of their guests. And who knows, they might be persuaded to bend Hannah's ear in Mary's favor. Kitty, after all, was enjoying more of a social season than Mary, and Mary felt she was due this trip.

40

January, 1780 Long Island

When Nicoll arrived back at camp, he found Caleb at the shore about to cross the sound.

"Wait," Nicoll called. "Let me go with you."

"Quick, climb aboard," Caleb said. "I haven't much time. Major Tallmadge has been stuck in Setauket almost a week. We must hope he is well."

A little over four hours later, Caleb steered his whaleboat to shore along the edge of Anna Smith Strong's property. Caleb and Nicoll waited in the bush several minutes as they watched the British on patrol. When it appeared safe, Caleb turned to Nicoll and said,

"Stay with the boat. We might need to leave with haste. I don't see Woodhull or Benjamin. I need to find Anna and speak to her."

Nicoll watched as Caleb crept along the bank to the back of Anna's house.

When he got there, he tapped the window, calling, "Anna" in barely more than a whisper.

Anna opened another window along the back of the house.

"Here," she said.

Caleb moved under the window. "It's Caleb," he said. "Where are Benjamin and Abraham?"

"The British are still quartering in Abraham's home. He barely leaves it these days. Benjamin is still hiding in the woods near the shore on this side of Abraham's farm near the cow pasture. Abraham has been sneaking food to him the past few days."

"Aye, I will find him."

Suddenly, they heard movement. Anna quickly raised the window enough to allow Caleb to crawl inside. The two waited inside near the window for several minutes as a British officer made his rounds across the property. The officer was alone on horseback and seemed to be in no hurry to be done with his job there and move along.

With Caleb being gone longer than they'd planned, Nicoll became nervous and ventured near the house, where he too could see the officer on horseback. When the guard wasn't looking, Nicoll crawled toward the house to the open window.

"Caleb," he whispered.

Caleb crawled out from the window and stood with Nicoll at the rear of the house. When the British officer came around again, Caleb lunged at him, pulling him from his horse.

The Lieutenant was young and began begging for his life.

As Caleb and Nicoll carried him toward the boat, Caleb stopped.

"We won't take your life this time," he said. He dropped the young lieutenant to the ground. "You're just plain lucky today."

Caleb took the officer's gun and his sword, while Nicoll tied the man's hands behind his back and took what he could find from his pockets. Their hope was that the lieutenant would assume they were thieves there to rob the house rather than being whaleboat men on a secret mission. They watched as the officer scurried away to find his horse. When he was gone, they fled to the bushes, got into their boat, and followed the shore toward Abraham's, where they hoped to find Benjamin Tallmadge alive and well.

Arriving at their destination, Caleb pulled the boat up onto the sandy bank. Again, he asked Nicoll to keep watch over the boat as he left to scout for Benjamin.

A few minutes later, Nicoll saw two figures coming toward him out of the woods. He breathed a sigh of relief when he saw they were Benjamin and Caleb.

"Ah, it's good to see you again, Major," Nicoll said.

"It's good to be found," Benjamin replied.

The three men got into the boat, and Caleb began steering them back across the sound.

"What news have you?" he asked Benjamin once they were away from shore.

"I gave Abraham the stain for writing the invisible letters. He is to give a supply to Culper, Jr. in the city. Although Abraham fears for his life to cross into the city again. And he feels he won't be able to leave unless the soldiers quit his home. We need a safe passage for him into the city. He needs a Tory escort."

"I think I know of one," Nicoll responded.

Benjamin nodded. "I've thought of one too. Colonel Benjamin Floyd. But we must come up with an excuse for him to travel with Abraham, and that is something I haven't fully worked out."

"I think we can come up with a good plan that might involve a lady," Nicoll suggested.

"Tell me," Benjamin said.

"As you may know, Colonel Floyd is my cousin."

Benjamin nodded. "Yes."

"It happens that Mary will be staying in his home in Brookhaven, near here, and wishes to travel with him into the city. Benjamin Floyd has received word that Major John André is planning another one of his elaborate social gatherings. One that will be held at British headquarters."

A look of disconcert fell across Benjamin's face. He stared at Nicoll then looked off into the distance before speaking. When he turned back to face Nicoll, his voice held a sense of trepidation.

"Are you certain Mary is willing to play the part of a Loyalist socialite? You know how I feel about putting her in any danger."

"And you must know how bullheaded she is. She is the one who wrote to me with the idea. We received travel papers signed by Colonel Floyd. I plan to deliver her to his home in the next few days."

Benjamin nodded. "I believe I do remember reading a letter from her before I left to meet with Abraham telling me she'd written to Colonel Floyd. But I can never comprehend her desire to get involved in our business. Although she insists. If it was anyone else, I would grant permission wholeheartedly. You must realize I have feelings for your sister and the utmost wholesome intentions toward her."

"I do, Major," Nicoll replied sincerely. "She understands what's at stake."

"Then, I shall write to the Culpers of the plan," Benjamin decided. "Culper, Jr. should obtain the information about this grand party and make sure the invitation list will include Colonel Floyd and guests. Culper, Sr. will go into the city with them to gather intelligence. He will be seen with a prominent Loyalist, which will give him a cover and should provide him with some relief about his situation. If all goes well, we may find out more by having the assistance of a 355, codename for "lady," who might be able to outwit the most wily of British officers and get them to release the most useful information for our cause."

41

January, 1780 New York City

The large house had an atmosphere that felt intimidating to Liza. Sometimes she would get lost and find herself heading down the wrong corridor. General Sir Henry Clinton's English housekeeper was Mary Braddeley, whose husband was away fighting alongside the British. That left Mrs. Braddeley and her young children in the unique position of living and working in such a grand home. Mrs. Braddeley had assigned Liza the job of keeping the fires going in all the rooms. Liza was also expected to help serve breakfast and supper. Today would be busy because there was a party planned that evening, a grand ball. Liza would hardly have time to breathe with all the preparations that needed to be done.

Before the sun rose, she made her way into the main house from the servant cabins. She gathered an armload of firewood before she entered and made her way into the main hall. When she approached Sir Henry's private office, the door was slightly ajar, and she heard a noise and then a moan. Liza wondered if someone was ill. She stopped at the entrance and peered through the slightly opened door to see Mrs. Braddeley splayed atop Sir Henry's desk. The housekeeper's skirts were above her knees, and her legs were bent and wrapped around Sir Henry's waist. There was much panting and gyrating.

Startled, Liza jumped away from the door and moved quickly down the hall, stopping at the corner to lean against the wall and catch her breath. As she set the load of firewood down, she wondered; what had she just witnessed? A moment of passion? Was Sir Henry Clinton in love with his housekeeper? What Liza had just seen made her feel odd, uneasy. But she mustn't dawdle. She had work to do, so with a few deep breaths, she closed her eyes then turned to pick up the wood. Before she bent down, she saw Major André approach.

"Hello, sir," Liza said.

"My dear, Liza. It's good to see you up bright and early."

The young major's smile made Liza feel warm and comforted. Nervously, she gazed at him, then glanced down at the load of wood on the floor next to her.

"Are you all right?" he asked.

Liza gave a slight nod; her eyes never leaving Andre's.

He then placed his hand on the side of her face. It felt warm and soft against her cool skin.

"You are exquisite," he whispered. "Vous êtes trés belle, ma chérie."

The foreign words flowed from his lips like liquid fire, heating up Liza's cheeks. She felt frozen as she continued to gaze into the handsome major's eyes. Her breathing became rapid. Then he leaned down and kissed her lips, lightly at first, before his tongue traced a trail across her bottom lip. Then softly he slipped his tongue into her mouth and moved it gently over hers. Soon Liza yielded to the desire that stirred inside her, and she kissed him back as their tongues danced together.

Just as quickly as the kiss had happened, Liza pulled away, gathered the wood, made her way quickly into the nearest room, and stopped in front of the fireplace. What was she to think? That passionate kiss had come from the man she so admired, the one who was so handsome, smart, and sophisticated—the one she believed would grant her freedom.

Liza looked at the fire, which was dying. She had to get back to work or she would be chastised. She took the poker in her hand to revive the fire and added one of the logs she'd carried in. Then she made her rounds to each room, doing the same.

The rest of the day, she kept busy, trying not to think about the kiss, but it was almost all she could think about. She hadn't seen much of Major André since that morning. He was busy supervising servants as they placed massive flower arrangements and floral garlands in each room. Liza had to replace all of the candles in each room, and she had no time to think about what had happened. She mustn't think of it; she had to keep working.

By sunset, a light snow had begun to fall. The torches were lit outside along the front of the house, and the other slaves were lighting the many candles in each room throughout the main floor. Carriages began arriving filled with ladies and gentlemen wearing the most gorgeous clothes and jewelry Liza had ever seen.

Liza had been given a job she hated but also had been gifted a new dress to wear, so at least she felt she looked nice. Her job tonight required standing mostly in one place in front of the door to the water closet, where she would have to assist partygoers upon entering, then emptying the used bowl once they exited. For Liza the job was a bore, and for a while, her thoughts returned to that morning and the kiss.

42

New York City, January, 1780

Mary rose early and took her time bathing, applying perfume, and powder, and putting on her jewelry. Her cousin's wife, Ann, had kindly offered to have two of her servant girls help Mary with her stays, her hair, and the new dress that had arrived a few days prior. Mary had enjoyed the past few weeks in her cousin's home. His younger children were a delight, and Mary enjoyed spending time reading to them. Even with the constant flow of British officers who frequented the home, Mary had been able to relax and play the part of Loyalist cousin well—or so she thought. She stayed alert for any information she believed would be of interest to Benjamin Tallmadge. And she pondered what she heard with plans to write him when she felt it would be most safe to do so.

As she pulled her shift over her head, there was a knock at the door.

"I'll answer it," said one of the servants.

"Allie, please tell Mary that I've gone to fetch Mr. Woodhull," Mary heard her cousin say. "I shall be back shortly. Make sure she is prepared for the five-hour journey into the city. The carriage will be waiting out front."

"Yes sir," Allie replied.

The girls continued to help Mary get dressed as they slipped new stockings onto her feet and up over her knees and tied them with ribbon. After she was dressed, they began working on her hair. The girls were experts with plaiting, and they created rows of braids along one side that they wound into the hair they'd teased and curled. Then they added shiny combs that sparkled with stones in the front and back of her hair. Mary stood before the mirror in awe. The dark-blue silk gown brought out the color of her eyes in the most flattering way.

"I don't know if I recognize myself," she said with a laugh.

The girls chuckled too. "You look beautiful," one of them said.

They helped Mary into her shoes, and handed her a drawstring bag for her wrist and a fan before opening the door for her. The children were gathered in the main room of the house, waiting to see her before she left.

"A princess!" cried the youngest.

The boys giggled, and Ann appeared from another room escorting her oldest daughter. Elizabeth, fourteen, would be joining Mary at the party that evening. Her gown of pale-pink silk matched the ribbon around her neck and the one in her hair.

"Two princesses!" said Elizabeth's youngest sister.

"You look stunning." Ann beamed at Mary. "Benjamin should be back any moment," she said.

Smiling, Mary said, "Thank you. I'm more than thrilled to be able to attend such a magnificent party. Cousin Elizabeth, you will have gentlemen fighting each other for a dance with you."

The two girls giggled.

∞∞∞∞∞∞∞∞∞∞∞

Colonel Floyd's carriage pulled up in front of Abraham Woodhull's home. Two British soldiers came quickly to the carriage to escort Colonel Floyd into the house.

"Is there a problem, sir?" one of the soldiers asked.

Benjamin shook his head. "No, no problem at all. Mr. Woodhull and I will be attending a party in New York at Sir Henry Clinton's home and headquarters. "If you'll excuse me, I must gather Mr. Woodhull and we'll be on our way." Benjamin stepped past the officers and made his way up the steps to the front door.

Abraham's father let him in, and Benjamin was also greeted by Abraham's sister and mother.

"Lovely to meet you both," he said.

Abraham approached the group and bowed to Benjamin.

"Sir, these are the finest clothes I own, he said, "but I fear they are not good enough."

He had put on his newest shirt and coat, shined his shoes, and pulled his hair into a low ponytail tied with a black ribbon. He looked quite proper and maybe even a bit dashing but nowhere close to the grandness of Benjamin Floyd or the two ladies they would be with that evening.

"Not to worry yourself, my friend. I have something for you in the carriage," said Benjamin.

He bowed to the ladies and Abraham's father. "We shall be on our way then."

Abraham followed Benjamin out to the carriage. Once they were seated across from each other, Benjamin held up a dashing new coat. "I had it made especially for you by a tailor in the city. Hercules Mulligan creates the most fashionable attire for the most selective of British Loyalists whether officer or gentlemen."

Abraham recognized the name. "Hercules Mulligan, you say?"

Benjamin tipped his hat, and his lips formed a knowing smile. "Major Tallmadge wrote me that he'd learned that Hercules Mulligan, who appears to be a Loyalist and heavy supporter of the British Crown, is known among the Continentals to secretly send missives filled with information overheard from the British officers who frequent his shop."

Benjamin opened the inside of the coat, ran his fingers down the lining and said, "Here, a secret compartment along the seam. No one will even know it's there. It can hold a missive or coin. And . . ." He turned the left sleeve up for Abraham to see. "Another small pocket is right here."

Abraham was shocked by both the gift and the ingenious features of the coat.

"I don't know what to say, sir. I am most grateful."

He took off his own coat, removed the pouch of invisible ink and the bottle of the agent, then tucked his old coat out of the way under his seat. Then he donned the new one, solid black with a hint of a floral pattern. It had large silver buttons down one side and a few more along the sleeves. It fit a bit loosely on the shoulders, but Abraham felt comfortable and quite handsome. He placed the small pouch inside the secret opening in the hem with hope that Culper, Jr. would make an appearance that evening. He glanced down at himself, very pleased with the new gift, and felt eager to wear it in the presence of Mary Smith if he could be so bold.

The carriage stopped at Benjamin's home to collect Elizabeth and Mary, then they were on their way to the city. With Mary and Benjamin seated across from Abraham and Elizabeth, introductions were made.

"Abraham," Mary said. "Do you remember attending a birthday party for my Uncle Richard Floyd? I remember you and Benjamin Tallmadge being there together. I believe your cousin, Colonel Nathanial Woodhull, was also there with his wife, who is related to my Uncle Richard."

Abraham nodded. "I remember." He laughed. "I wondered at the time who the strange girl was who ran after Benjamin as we were about to leave. You handed him something, I think."

Mary blushed and looked down, embarrassed by the memory. Then she looked up again and met Abraham's eyes. "I first met him years before at his father's church, the church you attend, the day before he left for Yale. Everyone had gathered on the lawn after the service for a fine picnic. Afterwards, I went to call for our carriage to be brought around, but I stopped when I saw my brother with a group of boys, and there was a wrestling match between . . . I think it might have been Caleb and Austin?"

Abraham chuckled at the recollection. "Aye, the wrestling match. I remember that day well."

"Anyway, I was standing close by, and when the wrestlers started toward me, the crowd opened up and I got knocked down. I fell into the mud, which ended up all over my shoes and dress. Benjamin was kind and gave me his handkerchief, which I still have. Earlier that evening, I had tucked his handkerchief into the purse my mother had given me to carry. When I saw Benjamin, I desperately wanted to speak to him." Mary paused. The thought brought a smile to her lips. "I had no idea what to say to him, so I pulled out his handkerchief and said, 'Here, I washed this for you.'"

"That's a lovely story," Elizabeth said. "Romantic even."

The two girls smiled at each other, and Abraham nodded. It was then Mary knew he understood her and knew one of the reasons she cared so much about tonight's mission. Her true feelings for Benjamin Tallmadge must be showing.

Several hours passed. The men fell asleep, and the two girls chatted anxiously about what they might expect at the party. They even reminded each other about the steps to the minuet. When they arrived at the ferry, they got out of the carriage and enjoyed a bit of fresh air as they crossed the water into New York. As the ferry disembarked on the other side of the river, a new carriage was waiting.

Soon, they pulled up in front of a grand house. A light snow had fallen earlier, creating a light dusting. To Mary, the image of the large house, flocked with snow and glowing with torches and candles, seemed like something from a dream.

Colonel Floyd offered Mary his arm, and Abraham offered his to Elizabeth. Then the four of them made their way up the steps. An officer stopped them at the door and asked to see their invitation. He was a British Sentry, and both Abraham and her cousin spoke to him briefly before, Benjamin Floyd pulled the invitation from his pocket and handed it over. Then, Abraham took something from inside his coat and gave it to the officer. The officer opened the door for them, and a trumpet sounded as their names were read aloud. From there, they followed a red carpet down a hallway lined with festive floral arrangements, stopping when they reached a ballroom.

Abraham turned to Elizabeth. "I am afraid I'm not much of a dancer, but I shall try."

Elizabeth giggled. "I love to dance. I have all the favorites set to memory. Don't worry, Mr. Woodhull. You will do fine."

Abraham bowed and led Elizabeth to the dance floor.

Colonel Floyd turned to Mary and said,

"Let me introduce you to Major John André."

Mary nodded, took a deep breath, and tried to relax. He was just a man, right? A very well-known and important one, but Mary knew she had a part to play. She would smile and flounce and flirt like Kitty did; she would giggle like the girl she thought these men would want her to be. Isn't that what Kitty said they liked? Because it would make them feel uneasy for Mary to seem clever, and men wanted to feel important and in charge.

She didn't think Benjamin Tallmadge felt that way. Benjamin Tallmadge *was* in charge. Mary could tell whenever she was around him; he easily commanded attention, and he didn't need to prove anything to anyone.

When they approached the seated Major André, they found several ladies on either side of him, and a group of gentlemen was gathered behind him. The major must have been telling a joke or funny story, because a roar of laughter rose up from the group. When Colonel Floyd and Mary moved to the spot where he was holding court, he glanced at Mary then stood up, bowing low.

"And who might this lovely creature be?" he asked.

"May I introduce you to my cousin, Miss Mary Floyd?" said Benjamin.

As Mary curtsied and caught the major's eye, she noticed the other ladies whispering among themselves.

"It's lovely to make your acquaintance, sir," she said.

"Will you do me the honor of dancing with me?" asked the major.

Mary nodded in response and held out her hand.

As Major André took her gloved hand in his and led her to the dance floor, a new song was about to begin.

"You must tell me everything about yourself, Miss Mary Floyd," he said.

Major John André was dashing; that much was for sure. He was gracious and poised. Mary thought he seemed like Benjamin Tallmadge in the confident, self-assured way he moved and spoke. Both men had the kind of confidence and grace that spoke volumes, qualities that told the world they had nothing to prove. And she knew she would bore him to tears if she engaged in simple flirting, acting like a silly girl. She would have to be clever and confident in order to keep his attention and learn more about this man.

The music began, and she curtsied to him.

The major bowed to her.

When the steps of the dance pulled them close to each other, Mary smiled at him. "Sir, telling everything might take up too much of your time, and there are always things a lady should keep to herself."

Major André seemed charmed by this statement. Then the prescribed steps of the dance required them to change partners, pulling them away from each other briefly. When they came together again, he replied.

"Well said, Miss Mary."

When the dance ended, he brought Mary's gloved hand to his lips and kissed it, his eyes never leaving hers. But this did not bring on the strong feelings Mary felt when Benjamin Tallmadge was near.

As the major walked with her off the dance floor, a young officer approached her, bowed, and asked,

"May I have the next dance?"

Major André bowed to Mary then to the young officer. "I shall hope to see you again, Mary."

Mary curtsied, and the young officer extended his arm. Together they made their way onto the dance floor. The officer was nice-looking but seemed nervous, and he was much younger than the major. As they danced, he introduced himself as Captain William Clinton.

"I'm Sir Henry's nephew."

Mary nodded and smiled. She had to keep him talking, understanding that in his case, this *would* require her to flirt and giggle, employing all her charms as she'd seen Kitty do.

Mary smiled, batted her eyelashes, and tried to appear nervous and shy. "You must tell me all about yourself, Captain. I would love to learn about your job and your position in the king's army. It would be such a pleasure to get to know you better."

"And with that, he began talking—and talking and talking. Mary continued to display an interest in him, interjecting a comment every now and then. When the song ended, she wanted to continue talking to him, as she suspected the eager captain might slip up and say something he shouldn't.

"Oh, it seems a bit hot, don't you think, Captain?" she asked.

She pulled her fan from the bag on her wrist and began to fan herself flirtatiously.

"Let me get you a refreshment," he said as he began to move away.

"Don't leave, Captain," Mary said. A look of endearment graced her face. "May I lean on you? I suddenly feel faint. I suppose it's all that dancing."

Quickly, he was back at her side, offering his arm for her to take. He was playing perfectly the part of a doting gentleman and falling into step with Mary's strategy. Once he had walked with her to get drinks, he led her off to the side near a group of officers, some of whom seemed to have had too much to drink.

Mary sipped her drink, "Mm, I feel so much better."

A woman and a man walked past them, and Mary had to move closer to the group of officers in order to allow the couple to pass. When she moved in behind one of the men in the drunken group, she heard him say, "If they turn him, he'll be able to give us—"

Suddenly a woman screamed.

"Fire!" someone yelled. "Her hair has caught on fire!"

The music and dancing stopped, and Mary moved to a place where she had a better view. Across the room, flames were engulfing a large feather tucked into the hair of a tall woman, and the fire was growing larger by the second. Someone plucked the feather from her head and began to stomp on it. Then someone else emptied a bucket of water onto her head. Then the weeping woman was led away by a man, maybe her husband. Mary was glad to see that although she was distraught, the woman was uninjured. Once everything had calmed down, the music began again. Mary couldn't help but giggle, which caused her new friend, the young captain, to laugh too.

"How awful," Mary said.

"At least she didn't catch the whole place on fire. Are you feeling better? Would you like some air? We could walk out onto the balcony."

Mary shook her head. "No, that won't be necessary."

He smiled at her and sipped his drink.

Mary moved a bit closer to William. "Tell me more about your exciting position in the king's army."

"The war will be won soon," He said with an air of confidence. "We'll have the French trapped before their anchors are even wet. Then they'll forget about their Rebel friends, and our army will easily conquer the Continentals. The Rebels will be put in their place soon enough."

Mary tried to smile at that, but instead she downed the rest of her drink.

"Shall I get you another?" William asked.

Mary shook her head. "That's very kind of you. I think I shall look for the water closet."

She curtsied, and he bowed.

"I will be glad to escort you," he said.

Mary held out her hand, and he took it. As they walked through the crowds, they found Elizabeth. Mary stopped to talk with her and introduced her to the young captain. When she saw how impressed Elizabeth looked while speaking with him, Mary excused herself and made her way into the hall. As she walked down the hallway, she saw a lady leaving a small room. A young servant girl was taking a bowl from her. The girl left to dispose of its contents, and Mary waited until she returned. When the girl came back, she offered Mary the bowl, then opened the door for her. The girl reminded Mary of someone. When she took the bowl from her, their eyes met.

"Liza?" Mary asked.

"Mary?"

Mary nodded.

"How? Why?" Mary asked.

Mary didn't know what to ask or what to say. Her dear friend Liza, whom she hadn't seen in years, was standing in front of her inside the home of Sir Henry Clinton. How could it be?

Liza held a finger to her lips. Then she moved toward the water closet, motioned for Mary to go in, then stepped inside with her. Liza closed the door and whispered.

"I escaped when Simcoe and his army left Oyster Bay," she said. "I knew Major André would be in New York, and I asked to work for him."

"Oh, my." Mary gasped.

"I'm safe here. I think Major André is special. He's very kind to me, and I believe he will grant me freedom. I plan to ask him for it soon."

"Why are *you* here?" Liza asked.

"I came with my cousin Benjamin Floyd and his daughter, and a man named Abraham from Long Island. I wanted to see if I could hear anything I could share with Major Tallmadge," Mary whispered. "I heard one of the officers start to say something that might have been important about how if they turned someone, that person would in turn give them something—but then a lady's hair caught fire, and I didn't hear him finish."

Someone knocked on the door.

"Uh oh," Mary said. "I really do need to go. One moment, please," she called out.

Mary pulled her dress up, then squatted over the bowl, continuing her whispered conversation.

"Is there anything you've heard since you've been here, Liza?"

"I know a lady named Peggy Shippen comes by often. I thought she liked Major André, but then I heard them talk about her marrying someone else. I've seen notes she's brought with her from someone named Gustavus or Monk, or it might be two different people. I don't know."

Mary handed the now-full bowl to Liza, fluffed her skirts, then leaned in and hugged Liza.

"It's so good to see you," she whispered. "Stay safe."

Liza nodded, her face and eyes alight from seeing her old friend, then she opened the door. When the two girls stepped out together, they received an odd look from the lady who was waiting to go into the closet. Mary and Liza glanced at each other and smiled.

"It will be just a moment, ma'am," Liza said.

43

Long Island, January, 1780

The carriage arrived back at the Floyd home a little past three in the morning. During the final hour of their journey, the four passengers had fallen asleep. As the carriage driver pulled up to the front of the home, they began to awaken.

Benjamin said to Abraham, "Stay with us. It's late. I can have the driver take you home after sunrise."

Abraham agreed.

Benjamin looked at Mary and Elizabeth. "Will you two share a room tonight, so Mr. Woodhull can stay?"

The girls agreed. "Of course," Mary said. "I'll just gather a few things from my room."

Mary walked quietly and quickly into the darkened house. In the guest room, she gathered a few things, then passed the desk on her way out. She set the items she was holding in a chair, picked up the quill, and began to scratch out a note for Abraham, hurriedly describing anything of note she could remember hearing at the party.

—heard an officer say, "if we can turn him, he'll give us. . .,?"

—a captain said they will have won the war even before the French fleet's anchors are wet.

—a "Peggy Shippen" frequents the house to visit with M. André with letters from a "Gustavus" and someone named Monk.

——355

She signed it with the code number her brother Nicoll had told her was used for the word "lady." She folded it and left it on the pillow, picked up her things, and met the others in the hall, where they said their good nights.

When Abraham got to the guest room, he removed his coat and went to lie down. Seeing the note, he picked it up and read it. He had also overhead talk from officers that night about a turncoat and someone named Gustavus. He smiled when he saw the code signature. He took the note and slipped it inside the secret hem along the inside seam of his new coat. Their plan to involve a 355 seemed to be a success. As he lay down, sleep came slowly as his mind stayed restless with thoughts about the possibility of the British recruiting a turncoat.

∞∞∞∞∞∞∞∞

The next morning when Colonel Floyd's carriage driver delivered Abraham to his home, there were no British soldiers anywhere around. When Abraham went inside, his sister greeted him with news.

"The British soldiers have left us, Abraham," she said. "I hope they never return."

"When did they leave?"

"Last night. I thought they had gone for supplies, but they've yet to return. I think if they had plans to come back, they'd be here by now."

Abraham nodded. Then a huge smile graced his lips. "That is such good news. I shall call on Miss Mary Smith and ask her to dine with us tonight."

"Oh, brother," Susannah said. "It's so good to see you smile again."

∞∞∞∞∞∞∞∞

Benjamin Tallmadge read over the missive from Culper, Sr. He had read this same note many times the last few days.

I do not think the vigilance will continue long so I intend to visit New York . . . and think by the assistance of a 355 of my acquaintance, shall be able to outwit them all.

Culper, Sr.

Each time Benjamin read the note, he also prayed over it; he prayed for his friend and especially for Mary Floyd. He had faith that the next dispatches from Setauket and New York would bring promising news.

It was more than a week later when he received some dispatches from Caleb with information from Culper, Sr. and Culper, Jr. One report included information about the capture and imprisonment of Colonel John Graves Simcoe, and the other had information his beloved 355 had written in her own hand. Culper, Sr. had also noted that the British had left his home and not returned and that he felt confident about traveling again.

Benjamin was grateful for the good news and sat down to put all of this information into a letter to Washington. He had received intelligence earlier from headquarters that Congress had been forced to take all its bills out of circulation and would be declaring bankruptcy in order to save itself from the upcoming British move to flood the colonies with fake money. Now Congress had need of help from a French subsidy and a Dutch loan to rescue the country's currency. Washington had again suggested to Benjamin a faster route for the Culper correspondence. Since Washington was now headquartered in Morristown, New Jersey, he was worried the Connecticut route was too circuitous.

Washington wrote,

It would be a very desirable thing if a channel of communication be opened across the North River, or by way of Staten Island. If C—— can fall upon a line which he thinks he may safely trust, I wish it to be adopted; but if this cannot be accomplished, he will continue his communications in the old channel, and make them as constant as the season will admit.

Benjamin penned a reply to Washington then a missive to Culper, Sr. and one to Culper, Jr. alerting them of Washington's new location and the request for a quicker route through Staten Island. He sent the letter for Washington with a dispatch rider, and the ones to the Culpers would be sent by boat through Caleb and delivered to Culper, Sr. The latter would then go into the city to deliver the information to Culper, Jr. or would have it delivered by Austin Roe.

Later, Culper, Sr. wrote he would plan to meet with Culper, Jr. to discuss a change in the route. But later, Benjamin and Washington found out that Culper, Sr. had forgotten to mention the route change to Culper, Jr., which angered Washington. In his next correspondence, Washington suggested Culper, Jr. correspond directly to him, but to write in a Tory style so that even if his agents were negligent, no discovery would be made.

Write a letter in the Tory style, with some mixture of family matters and between the lines and on the remaining part of the sheet communicate with the stain the intended intelligence.

Upon receiving Washington's request, Culper, Jr. decided to use his nephew James Townsend as a secret courier across the Hudson. Since that part of New Jersey was heavily Loyalist, James's cover was that he was a Tory visiting his family in a rebel-controlled area of New Jersey and was seeking to recruit men for the British side. Unfortunately, the young man partook of too much ale and behaved so suspiciously that he was taken to Patriot headquarters. The boy told the Patriot commander the truth, but they found on him only a bawdy poem since the intelligence was written at the bottom of the page in invisible ink.

When the information was given to Washington, he tried to render the note visible, but the ink had been applied sloppily and blurred when the counter stain was applied. The entire situation made Washington livid. It took the commander in chief's personal intervention to secure the young Townsend's release. Culper, Jr. was angry and embarrassed by the debacle he had caused by using his nephew. When Culper, Sr. found out, he was annoyed and felt Robert Townsend had gone behind his back in using a new courier, and he sent a letter informing him of such. This made Culper, Jr. more upset, and he replied he would no longer be sending information.

At this point, Benjamin planned a meeting that he hoped would smooth things over between the two spies. But Culper, Jr. canceled. A few days later, Culper, Sr. paid him a visit and was relieved to learn Culper, Jr. would at least supply verbal information if not written missives. Culper, Jr. was now too afraid to compile written reports that might be traced back to him if intercepted.

44

Summer, 1780

Several months had passed and Washington's anger toward the Culper spies had subsided, as had the annoyance the two spies held toward each other. Washington penned a letter to Tallmadge saying,

> *As we may every moment expect the arrival of the French Fleet, a revival of the correspondence with the Culpers will be of very great importance. If the younger cannot be engaged to give written information again, you will endeavor to prevail upon the older to give you information of the movements and position of the enemy upon Long Island.*

It took three days for Washington's letter to travel from his headquarters in New Jersey to Benjamin Tallmadge in Connecticut. Upon reading Washington's letter, Benjamin set out to find Caleb, who would take it to Culper, Sr. in Setauket.

When Caleb arrived at the shore, he pulled his boat up onto the bank and made his way up to Abraham's farmhouse. There he found Abraham was too sick to leave his bed. He then went to Austin Roe's tavern and had him immediately ride into the city to deliver Washington's note to Culper, Jr.

Upon reading Washington's missive, Culper, Jr. didn't follow his usual procedure of writing with the special ink either on a blank page placed between reams of paper or on page inside a book cover. Instead, Townsend wrote a letter to Colonel Benjamin Floyd with the important message written in invisible ink between the lines.

Sir,

I've received your favor by Mister Roe and note its contents. The articles you want cannot be procured, as soon as they can I will send them. I am your humble servant,

Samuel Culper, Jr.

Austin left with this note and rode back to Culper, Sr's farm. When he arrived, Roe insisted that he must see Abraham.

"I know he's ill, Susannah, but if you'll just allow me a short visit," he insisted. "I have news from a dear friend that I'd like to share with Abraham."

"Wait here."

Susannah left Austin standing at the door while she went to tell her brother who was there to see him. Abraham agreed to the visit, and she led Austin into the bedroom.

"Close the door," Abraham said to Susannah.

He sat up in bed, and Austin handed him the missive from Culper, Jr. After applying the counter agent and reading it, Abraham asked for pen and paper. He then wrote the most urgent note to Washington he had ever penned.

Sir,

The enclosed from Culper, Jr. requires your immediate departure this day by all means let not an hour pass for this day must not be lost you have news of the greatest consequence perhaps that ever happened to your country.

The information Culper, Jr. had written in invisible ink in between the letter to Benjamin Floyd warned that the British were aware of the French fleet's location and that British troops were carrying vital arms with the intention to ambush the fleet. British Admiral Thomas Graves was already on his way to Rhode Island with eleven ships to take on the French, whose fleet, the British thought consisted of only seven vessels. In fact, it was composed of seven French warships, each with two gun decks and designed to be positioned for battle in line with their other ships. The rest included four frigates along with thirty-six transport vessels carrying approximately six thousand French soldiers, commanded by Lieutenant General Jean-Baptiste Donatien de Vimeur, comte de Rochambeau, and their supplies. These ships had already arrived and were anchored off the Newport, Rhode Island coast. Sir Henry Clinton would not learn they had arrived for another week, but he had known the French fleet was on its way. That information had come from a turncoat with the code name "Gustavus" who also sometimes used the code name "Monk."

Clinton's thoughts were that General Rochambeau's French soldiers would be tired after their long voyage and that, unfamiliar with their new terrain, they would be camped out in the open, where Clinton's redcoat veterans could spring a surprise attack while the Royal Navy attacked the French ships. General Clinton thought such a bloody blow would prove embarrassing and would surely cool off Paris's love for her American allies, leaving Washington alone once again to face Britain's forces.

"Get this to Brewster so he can get it into the hands of Major Tallmadge," Abraham instructed from his sickbed.

Austin handed it to Caleb when Caleb returned later to collect dispatches.

"This is of the greatest importance," Austin said.

As soon as Caleb's boat arrived in Connecticut, he left on horseback for Benjamin's headquarters. When he arrived, he wasted no time and stopped the nearest dragoon, asking where to find Benjamin, but the dragoon was not sure where Benjamin was at the time.

"I have a most important dispatch that requires Washington's immediate attention," Caleb explained.

"I'm sorry, sir. Major Tallmadge is not here."

"Then you must go to Washington with it yourself and spare no time," Caleb insisted.

The dragoon mounted his horse and rushed toward Washington's headquarters. As soon as he arrived, he began asking for Washington, but was told the general was away.

The dragoon leapt from his horse and walked into Washington's office anyway where he was stopped by an aide-de-camp. "This requires immediate attention," the dragoon insisted, handing the missive over.

Alexander Hamilton approached the dragoon. "Give it to me," he said. Upon reading and deciphering the information from Culper, Jr, Hamilton was alarmed. With Washington still touring the lines, Hamilton made the decision to pen a letter to the French commander, Jean-Baptiste Donatien de Vimeur, comte de Rochambeau.

Le quartier général vient d'être informé que l'ennemi un embarquement dont ils pouraient menacer la flotte et l'marmée françaises. Cinquante transports auraient romonté le Sound pour prendre des troupes pour procéder directement Rhone Island.

After Hamilton wrote the note to the French commander, he translated it into English in a copy for Washington to have.

Headquarters has just received advice that the enemy is making embarkation with which they may menace the French fleet and army. Fifty transports are said to have gone up the Sound to take in troops and proceed directly to Rhode Island.

Upon completing the missives, Alexander rose from his desk and called for his fastest riders.

"Make haste," he urged the express riders. "Meet up with the Marquis de Lafayette, who is now on his way to Newport to rendezvous with Rochambeau. You must give this to him immediately."

Later that evening Washington returned to camp, and Alexander Hamilton met him as he approached.

"Sir," Hamilton began, "a dragoon arrived with important dispatch papers from Culper, Sr. that required immediate attention. It appears that General Clinton has been made aware of the French fleet's arrival and is preparing an ambush. I've sent express riders to warn the Marquis de Lafayette and Rochambeau."

"This may be an opportunity to launch a surprise attack against the British," Washington replied. "Clinton would have to remove troops from New York City, leaving it vulnerable. Alexander, call a meeting of my most senior officers. We shall examine the possibility of taking the city."

Hours later, the commanders stood around the table in Washington's headquarters discussing a plan to take back control of New York City.

"Sir," General Horatio Gates addressed Washington. "May I speak freely?" he asked.

"You may," Washington replied.

"I don't believe we have enough cannons or supplies to take on New York, even with most of their troops leaving the city for Rhode Island. We would need at least forty cannons, large amounts of ammunition, and a thousand artillery shells, plus another hundred for the mortars."

Washington considered his general's concerns, then decided that instead of planning a physical attack, he would create a clever subterfuge.

"We will allow them to think we have planned an attack on New York," he announced. "We will make use of a Patriot disguised as a Tory farmer, who will report the discovery of a saddlebag near his property. That bag will contain false dispatches that the 'farmer' will take to the British outpost. The documents found inside will give the British the idea that we have plans to ambush New York City."

Washington's plan was a success. Clinton took the bait when the dispatches reached his headquarters stating that twelve thousand Patriot troops planned an imminent attack on the city. Clinton ordered the lighting of signal fires along the northern shore of Long Island to recall his fleet. This allowed the French to establish themselves in Rhode Island unharmed.

In supplying the information that led up to this move by Washington, the Culper ring had provided its most important contribution to the war effort.

45

Summer, 1780

Mary and her mother sat together on their porch, as a light breeze blew through the trees. As they sewed, they chatted.

"What do you think Kitty will do?" Mary's mother asked.

Kitty had told them in a letter several weeks ago that James Madison had told her he wanted to ask for her hand in marriage. Although James had not made the request official, Kitty had sensed her admirer was fishing to see what her reply might be. Kitty's letter also mentioned that her suitor and Thomas Jefferson were both currently at the same boarding house as Kitty and her father. She believed James was seeking Jefferson's input about asking for Kitty's hand.

"I'm sure Kitty will make the best choice," Mary answered.

She knew her sister enjoyed the attention she was getting from James, but Mary often wondered if Kitty was more in love with William Clarkson. William had finished his medical degree and was serving in the Patriot army as a doctor. He and Kitty hadn't seen each other in years, and it was only through infrequent letters that the two had any communication.

So Mary was unsure how Kitty would answer once James officially proposed.

And Mary was glad that she didn't have to make a choice between two men. She loved one man and only one—although Benjamin might not realize what her true feelings were. They'd engaged in a fond correspondence, but the word "love" had yet to be mentioned.

Mary often wrote to Sally and Phebe Townsend asking about their "dear friend." She never mentioned Liza's name in the letters because Liza was a runaway, and she didn't want to cause Liza any trouble. Sally and Phebe had received a letter from their brother Robert telling them where Liza was. They knew she was living at Sir Henry Clinton's headquarters—but nothing beyond that. Mary would continue to write with the hope of one day learning more. She couldn't tell the Townsend sisters that she had seen Liza briefly; it would have been too hard to explain why Mary had been at a party at the headquarters of a British General where Liza made her home. Liza was always in Mary's prayers and always had been, and Mary fervently hoped her friend would stay safe, be happy, and one day gain the freedom she sought.

"Ouch," Hannah said after pricking her finger with her needle.

"Are you okay, Mother?" Mary asked.

Her mother nodded, but Mary saw that she looked pale.

"Let me see if Cora can make you some tea," Mary suggested.

She got up, went to the kitchen, and brought back a cookie and a cup of tea for her mother. When she stepped onto the front porch, her mother was slumped over in her chair. Mary ran to her and tried desperately to get her to wake up.

"Cora, Joli! Come quick!" Mary yelled.

Cora and Joli ran over to help, and together the three of them were able to revive Mary's mother. Then they helped her upstairs and settled her into bed. The next morning, Hannah woke feeling much better and insisted it had just been the needle prick or the sight of blood that had caused her to faint. Mary didn't really believe the reason her mother gave for fainting, because deep in her soul, she felt her mother might truly be ill.

At the end of the summer, Mary received a package from New York, and the return address showed it had been mailed by Robert Townsend. Mary opened the package to reveal a carefully wrapped hollow egg. Painted on one side was a crown. Mary's heart leapt to her throat, and feelings of joy overcame her.

She scraped the icing away from the concealed hole in the bottom of the egg and pulled out the rolled missive.

Dear friend Mary,

I am good. I hope you are. The woman I told you about married the Rebel General Benedict Arnold. Major André left for Oyster Bay. I think Simcoe went back there. And I think I'm going to have a baby. I may leave this house and get help from Mr. Townsend.

Although the letter was unsigned, Mary had no doubt it was from Liza, and she was concerned about her friend's possible condition. But the information about Major André's close Loyalist friend Peggy Shippen, who had married a Patriot general, might be of interest to Benjamin.

Mary took pen to paper and informed Benjamin she'd received a package "from a dear friend from Oyster Bay." She added lengthy information about her sister and the possible proposal Kitty might receive. And in between the bits of chatter about Kitty, she added another and most unusual piece of marriage news; that would be the marriage of Benedict Arnold to the rich Loyalist, Peggy Shippan.

46

Fall, 1780

Benedict Arnold had fought gallantly at Ticonderoga and played a distinguished role in the Battles of Saratoga, with the battle scars from a leg injury to prove it. It had long been evident that Arnold did not always follow the rules. He had been removed from field command after the first battle at Saratoga following several disagreements between him and General Horatio Gates that had often resulted in shouting.

Arnold had disobeyed Gates's orders and taken to the battlefield to lead attacks on British defenses, almost single-handedly preventing General John Burgoyne from escaping at the Battle of Bemis Heights, where Burgoyne surrendered. Arnold had also reinjured his left leg during the battle. Nevertheless, Arnold didn't receive the recognition or the promotion he thought he deserved. He became increasingly resentful that he was continually being passed over for promotion and not being given the honors he felt he was due.

While Arnold was recuperating from his leg injury, Washington put him in charge of Philadelphia, which might have been a terrible decision. Philadelphia was a rich and very politically divided city. Arnold was simply not qualified, especially with his tendency to become embroiled in disputes and his lack of political astuteness. Arnold lacked tact, patience, and fairness when dealing with people deeply distressed by months of enemy occupation.

It was in Philadelphia that Arnold became acquainted with Peggy Shippen, a beautiful and wealthy Loyalist almost twenty years his junior. He also accumulated a large dept to Congress, having borrowed large amounts of money trying to maintain his lavish lifestyle. Some within his military circles accused him of dishonest dealings, resulting in a court martial. After Arnold was acquitted, Washington tried to smooth things over with the promise of a future high command. This included the possibility of commanding West Point, which Washington stated was the most important post to keep under Patriot control that would keep the British from controlling the Hudson River.

But by that point, Arnold had had time to adjust to the waters in Philadelphia, fueled by his romance with the daughter of a prominent, wealthy Loyalist. Arnold had also become discomfited with the French alliance and more comfortable with Tory views. And for the next year, his calendar would include parties, social gatherings, and, most importantly, an introduction to Peggy's friend Major John André.

By the time Washington gave Benedict Arnold command of West Point, Arnold's thoughts had turned to treachery. Benjamin Tallmadge had become acquainted with Arnold during his years at Yale, and he did not think of Arnold as a man of integrity. Most thought Arnold was arrogant. But once the war began and Arnold fought with such zeal, gallantly capturing General Burgoyne, most seemed to forget his roguish tricks. But soon Arnold would become the most high-ranking mole in espionage history. And because most people focused on his undisputed martial talents, no one suspected he was capable of the worst imaginable treachery.

For the most part, British secret intelligence had lagged far behind that of Washington, whose Culper ring had surpassed anything Generals Clinton or Howe had put into place. When Clinton put John André in charge of espionage, he might not have made the best choice. André was graceful and artistic, a bit of a dabbler. Dilettante that he was, he was even a bit cunning. When Arnold became acquainted with Peggy Shippen, André began his scheme to turn him. And over the next year, Benedict Arnold would provide André with information about American deployments and other military plans. In return, Arnold asked for a great deal of money, a future high-ranking command in the British army, and a knighthood.

Sir Henry Clinton wanted to control the Hudson River to cut off the Patriot supply chain and cut the colonies' communications between the north and south. To that end, winning West Point became an important goal. It was late August by the time André and Arnold had an agreement on compensation, and a plan was beginning to form. For twenty thousand pounds, Arnold would turn over West Point to the British, and with that, Washington himself.

André, along with another British agent, Beverley Robinson, were set to meet secretly with Arnold to finalize the terms on September 11. But that plan was aborted when a British patrol boat fired on Arnold's barge as it neared Dobbs Ferry. On September 20 a second attempt was made, and André and Robinson sailed upstream aboard HMS Vulture. The following evening, Arnold sent his intermediary, Joshua Smith, a local resident, to collect André, bringing him ashore near Haverstraw on the west bank of the Hudson.

"Sir," Smith addressed André. "I'm to bring you to General Arnold. He's awaiting you just a mile north of here."

Arnold had told Smith that Major André was a merchant by the name of John Anderson. By the time the two met Arnold in the place where he was hiding, it was two in the morning.

"Go back to the shore and wait for me there," Arnold commanded Smith.

As soon as Smith was out of sight, Arnold and André began their secret negotiations. Arnold gave specifics about West Point, along with details about how the capture should go. After a while, the two realized the sun would be coming up soon, so they returned to Smith and the waiting boat that would take "John Anderson" back to the Vulture. It was then Arnold knew there might be a problem.

"I don't think we will be able to continue our talks aboard your ship tonight," Arnold said to André. "We can't row six miles upstream before daylight to get back to the Vulture. The sun will soon rise, and we'd be caught, especially with you wearing your red uniform. You'd be spotted by Patriot scouts easily."

"We can go back to my house," Smith offered. "It's not far from here. Then we can try to row you back to the Vulture again tomorrow night."

The three stayed in Smith's home for the night, and the next day André and Arnold continued their negotiations. They even went on a scouting mission to inspect some possible routes to West Point. Then as night fell, they made their way down to the river to send André back to his ship. But the Vulture had sailed away, having been spotted by Patriots; it was now making its way south and back to safety, which left André in American territory.

"Don't worry," Benedict said to André. "I'll grant you papers that will allow you to pass between enemy lines unharmed. But, as a merchant named John Anderson, you should change out of your uniform into plain clothes. Smith will get you a horse."

André knew he needed to rid himself of his British officer's uniform now that Arnold had given him papers to carry claiming he was a merchant. Anyone in the army caught behind enemy lines in plain clothes would be charged with spying and given a death sentence. But putting his fears aside, André agreed to change out of his uniform.

"I'll stay with him part of the way," Smith added. "To help him navigate the unfamiliar territory."

With that, Arnold took off back to West Point, leaving André to find his way back to the British. Smith and "John Anderson" spent the evening at a tavern before traveling the rest of the way through the American lines toward British-occupied New York City. In the early morning, André, having donned a floppy hat and a cape tied about his shoulders, traveled toward the bridge over the Croton River, which was the fastest route from American territory back into the city of New York.

It was at the bridge Smith bid his new friend farewell, handed him some money, and turned for home. André crossed the bridge and rode along the path in silence, now with no guidance or anyone to talk to. Around nine thirty in the morning of September 23, André stopped to consult a map. It was then that John Paulding appeared on the road and pointed a musket at him. In the bushes on either side hid Isaac Van Wart and David Williams both were also armed.

"State your name and position," Paulding demanded.

André, thinking, they might be British cowboys—marauders looking to mug Patriots or innocent travelers along the road—misjudged the situation.

"My lads, I hope you belong to our party," André mused.

"Which party might that be, Patriot or British?" Paulding asked.

"The lower," André replied, referring to the British side.

"That's too bad for you then, sir. For we are on the Patriot side."

Startled, André stammered, "Sir, I am an officer in the British service on particular business in the country." Then he mustered his senses enough to sit up straighter in the saddle in an attempt to look impressive.

"Dismount your horse," Williams ordered.

André dismounted and proffered the permit from Arnold.

"Damn your pass," Van Wart exclaimed. "Give us all your money."

Williams and Paulding took hold of André, pulling his hands behind his back and searching his pockets, taking what they could find.

"Look at his fine boots," Williams said.

As the men took off his boots, they found Arnold's devious plans for the capture of West Point hidden within their captive's stockings. Williams handed the papers to Paulding, who was the only one of the three who could read.

"This is a spy!" Paulding shouted. "We need to take him to the command post at North Castle."

"I'll get you even more money," André said. "I can promise to get you whatever sum you name as long as you take me to New York instead of a commanding officer's post."

"No." Paulding looked to the others. "We are taking him to the command office," he insisted. "He's a spy and we're turning him in."

The three men brought André to Colonel John Jameson.

"He says his name is Anderson," Paulding reported. "He said he had papers to pass. And he claims to be a British officer, but we searched him and found maps of West Point on his person."

Paulding handed over the maps and information Benedict Arnold had provided André. Jameson read over everything, including the pass Arnold had written. He was dumbfounded. This man dressed in plain clothes had a pass from Arnold—and maps of West Point hidden in his stockings. Jameson had recently received a letter from Arnold telling him to let a man named John Anderson pass through unharmed and to give him an escort of two horsemen. Now, here was a man claiming to be a British officer by the same name Arnold had provided. With the pass, the men should have let him go, but upon robbing him, they had found some papers which proved quite interesting.

"I shall send this information to Washington immediately," Jameson announced. "I am not sure if I should hold you captive, sir, or not," he said to André. "You speak like a genteel man; you are rational, and don't seem like a panicked spy to me."

"I only request to be escorted back to West Point, where General Arnold can explain everything, sir. He will be able to set the matter straight, I assure you."

Jameson looked at the man in his custody. Maybe he should send the man to Arnold—or else he might find himself on the receiving end of one of Arnold's famous outbursts.

47

Fall 1780

Benjamin Tallmadge had been out on patrol on a daylong scouting mission and had just returned to camp at North Castle, where he had heard some talk of the newly apprehended prisoner named John Anderson. Benjamin was more suspicious than puzzled. For more than two years, he had been dealing with reports and activities in a secret world where there was no such thing as coincidence.

Back inside his tent, he began reviewing the letters that had accumulated in his absence as well as others he had put aside before leaving. One of the notes was from Benedict Arnold and had been sent several days prior, alerting him that there would be a John Anderson who might pass through.

I have to request that you give him an escort of two horse to bring him on this way to this place and send an express to me that I may meet him. If your business will permit, I wish you to come with him.

To Benjamin it all made sense. He rushed to Jameson and demanded to see the prisoner.

"I'm afraid not, Major Tallmadge. For I've had him removed. He's been taken with escort to West Point, where General Arnold will deal with him."

"No!" Benjamin said. "Sir, I must point out to you the glaring atrocities revealed by this situation. I should take measure with the help of a unit of dragoons to arrest General Arnold for treason."

"What?" Jameson exclaimed. "You cannot suggest that General Arnold has committed treason. There is no proof. If you are wrong, sir, you would pay dearly for making such a terrible mistake."

"I understand you are unsure of the situation, sir," Benjamin stated. "But I must implore you to command the prisoner to at least return to North Castle until we can address the situation with General Washington."

"Very well," Jameson said. "But I am still sending the dispatch to General Arnold alerting him that we have John Anderson in our custody."

André and his guards were stopped en route to the Robinson house, where Arnold maintained his headquarters, and brought south to where Benjamin and his light horse dragoons would escort André to Lieutenant Joshua King. André would then be held at the home of Jacob Gilbert in the Hudson River town of South Salem for safekeeping. At this point, André now had three days' growth of beard.

"Lieutenant," Major André said when he was brought to King. "I have need of a shave. I shall require a man to shave me."

King was perceptive, noticing this Anderson had quite a lot of powder in his hair. This led him to believe their prisoner was no ordinary person. King brought this to the attention of Benjamin. As Benjamin watched this John Anderson pace back and forth, he made note of his gait and how he turned on his heel to retrace the course of the room. Benjamin knew this man had been bred to arms.

"Mr. Anderson," Benjamin began, "Information about your custody and what was found on your person has been sent to Washington. Once we have a reply, we will know your fate."

It was then André knew his cover had been blown.

"May I request pen and paper from you?" he asked. "I would like to write to General Washington myself."

Benjamin gathered the requested items, and when the man in custody was finished with his note, he handed it to Benjamin. As Benjamin began reading the missive, his agitation was extreme. The paper before him began with the heading, *Salem, New York, September twenty-four, the year of our King seventeen hundred eighty.* And as Benjamin's eyes fell over the words in the body of the letter, he saw the prisoner's true identity to be Major John André, adjutant-general to the British army.

Benjamin left André's holding room in a rush to pen his own note to Washington to go along with André's. Then he sent two express riders to take both letters straight to Washington. Unfortunately, Benjamin knew Jameson's letter would reach Arnold before Washington could lay eyes on his.

Washington had sent Alexander Hamilton ahead to Arnold's quarters at the Robinson house with the baggage to announce the general's arrival. And it was soon after Hamilton's entrance that Arnold received Jameson's letter. He was sitting at the table preparing for breakfast with Washington, who was expected at any moment. Upon reading Jameson's missive, he looked at Hamilton with distress.

"There is something urgent that has come up that I must see to immediately," he said.

Then Arnold flew up the stairs as fast as his wounded leg would take him to converse with his wife Peggy. Then he called for his horse and left with the horse at full gallop. He rode to his boat and demanded that he be taken to the ship The

Vulture which had sailed down the river and was safe in British territory.

When Washington arrived at West Point a bit later, no one knew where Arnold was. But soon the dispatches from Benjamin and André would arrive, and Washington would know everything. All of America would soon know the depth of Arnold's treachery. He was a traitor to one group and hardly a hero to the other; instead, he would become known as nothing more than a turncoat. But for now, he hoped to escape with his life.

48

Fall, 1780

Benjamin took André to West Point with a strong cavalry escort. Then the following day, he proceeded with his prisoner down the Hudson to King's Ferry and landed at Haverstraw, on the west side of the Hudson River where a heavy escort of cavalry awaited to accompany André to prisoner headquarters in Tappan, far enough away from the threat of a British rescue attempt.

As Benjamin was traveling with André, the two conversed, having a lot in common. Both were well-bred, educated gentlemen.

"What do you think will be my likely outcome?" André asked.

"There will be a trial. The evidence will be laid out," Benjamin began. "But it does not look hopeful for you. I had a dear friend at Yale. His name was Nathan Hale. We roomed together the four years we were students, and he was an officer in Knowlton's Rangers. When Washington requested that a spy be sent to Long Island to gather intelligence, Nathan volunteered. He was caught with documents and notes about British ships and transports, the number of soldiers, and such.

He was, of course, not in uniform. And he was hung as a spy. My prediction is that your fate would be similar."

Benjamin's answer troubled André, and it may have also caused unsettled feelings for Benjamin. But the two continued in easy conversation as they traveled. Benjamin found André to be someone of great accomplishment. Once they arrived at the place in Tappan where André would be held, Benjamin stayed there with the guards to watch over things until the trial. While he was there, a request came in for an exchange in order to free André. In response, Washington requested that Clinton turn over Benedict Arnold. But that was something Clinton refused to do, although the thought of losing his beloved André distressed Clinton greatly.

Even if Washington had wanted to spare André's life in exchange for having Arnold hung as a traitor, he had his army to think about. Now that one of his generals had become a turncoat, his men were becoming reluctant to trust their officers, some even losing faith in their commanders. And, of course, the public needed to be appeased, and someone needed to be punished for these actions if order was to be restored. With Arnold now safe behind enemy lines, André was the only possible candidate for punishment, apart from Joshua Smith, who had also been arrested after Arnold's flight to the other side.

Smith was a member of a prominent Whig family in New York and had requested an audience with general Washington to prove he was innocent. Smith told Washington that Arnold had told him that his only interest was to bring the war to an end.

André's trial took place on September 29 in front of several top officers of the Continental Army. He was sentenced to death by hanging. Afterward, however, André requested to be executed by firing squad, which was considered a more honorable death for an officer. That same day André penned a letter to General Clinton.

Under these circumstances I have obtained General Washington's permission to send you this letter, the object of which is to remove from your breast any suspicion that I could imagine that I was bound by your excellency's orders to expose myself to what has happened. The events of coming within the enemy's posts and of changing my dress which led me to my present situation were contrary to my own intentions as they were to your orders and the circuitous route which I took to return was imposed perhaps unavoidably without alternative upon me.

I am perfectly and tranquil in mind and prepared for any fate to which an honest zeal for my King's service may have devoted me.

In addressing myself to your excellency on this occasion, the force of all my obligations to you and of the attachment and gratitude I bear you recurs to me. With all the warmth of my heart I give you thanks for your excellency's profuse kindness to me, and I send you the most earnest wishes for your welfare which a faithful affectionate and respectful attendant can frame.

I have a mother and three sisters . . . It is needless to be more explicit on this subject; I am persuaded of your excellency's goodness. I receive the greatest attention from his excellency General Washington and from every person under whose charge I happened to be placed. I have the honor to be with the most respectful attachment,

Your Excellency's Most obedient and most humble servant,

John Andre, Adj Gen

At noon on October 2, Benjamin walked with André to the place of execution. The battalions of about five hundred men formed a square around the gallows, holding back an immense number of civilian spectators. Under the gallows stood a wagon holding a black coffin. Next to the coffin stood the executioner, his face smeared with black grease to obscure his identity. André showed no signs of fear or emotion, but he appeared startled when he saw the gallows, understanding his request to be shot had not been granted.

André turned to Benjamin, and with some emotion in his voice asked, "Am I not to be shot?"

"No," Benjamin responded.

"How hard is my fate! It will soon be over."

André then resumed his usual cheerful demeanor and took Benjamin aside.

"I am grateful for your kindness and for your friendship these last few days; they have meant the world to me," said André.

He extended his hand to Benjamin, and the two men shook. André then climbed onto his coffin and pulled the rope down onto his neck. When asked his last words, he replied,

"I have nothing more to say than this; bear me witness that I meet my fate as a brave man."

With that, André tied his handkerchief around his eyes, then Brigadier General John Glover, the officer of the day, gave the command, and the wagon was pulled away. André's body dropped with a swing. The gathered troops and civilians fell silent as they watched André's body twitch at the end of the rope; it seemed some time before it was totally still. For a moment, Benjamin felt he could not support André's death, having become deeply attached while holding him in custody. Was John André not an urbane and accomplished man, the type of gentleman and officer they all hoped themselves to be? Had not Benjamin's loyal friend, Nathan Hale, such a kindhearted soul, been a man no one would have thought to be a spy? Most thought spies to be untrustworthy liars, only out for themselves, but hadn't these men only wanted what was best for their countrymen?

Benjamin turned away from the scene; he could look no more as silent tears fell from his eyes.

49

Winter, 1780

Back at headquarters, Benjamin had time to write to Culper, Sr. and Culper, Jr. about the recent events. He wanted to make sure his spies were aware and took measures to see to their safety. After having failed to put West Point and Washington into the hands of the British, Arnold surely knew the demise of those plans had been due to the work of spies somewhere in the city.

Benjamin also now had time to process his feelings, and he poured his soul into a letter to Mary.

My Dearest Mary,

The events of the past week have been of great accomplishment for our side. They have also taken a toll on me emotionally for Major André was captured and hung as a spy. General Benedict Arnold was the mole. He is now on the other side, and I fear for those in New York whom we know might be a target for Arnold's wrath over his spoiled plans.

*For the few days of intimate intercourse, I had with John André, which was from the time of his being brought back to our headquarters to the day of his execution, I became so deeply attached to Major André that I can remember no instance where my affections were so fully absorbed in any

man. When I saw him swinging under the gibbet, it seemed to be as if I could not support it. All the spectators seemed to be overwhelmed by the affecting spectacle, and many were suffused in tears. There did not appear to be one hardened or indifferent spectator in all the multitude.*

The event brought to mind my dear friend Nathan Hale since he succumbed to the same fate. I felt the same kinship with André as I did with Nathan. For Nathan was Pythias, and I Damon. Do you remember reading this Greek legend? In Greek mythology it illustrates the Pythagorean ideal of friendship. In the story, Pythias is accused of and charged with plotting against the tyrannical Dionysius. Pythias asks to be allowed to settle his affairs, and this is agreed upon as long as Pythias's friend Damon is held hostage, to be executed in his stead if Pythias does not return. When Pythias returns, Dionysius is amazed by their love, trust, and friendship, and he frees them both. My heart has been broken by death many times, and yet I am still here. By what right am I allowed to live while my friends die? But such are the ways of war, love, or life.

My dearest Mary, I shall lament of it no more. Instead, I will remember my God is my sovereign, my absolute, and he alone knows more than my mind can fathom. I will reflect on these scriptures. —*For my thoughts are not your thoughts, neither are your ways my ways, saith the Lord. For as the heavens are higher than the earth, so are my ways higher than your ways, and my thoughts than your thoughts. Isaiah 55:8-9*

I shall not think that my thoughts are greater than those of Divine Providence, for I am only man, and man was breathed to life by God and created for his and only his Glory. Mary, I delight in our correspondence; it gives me great pleasure and peace. I pray for you and your family that you are well. Until I see you again, know you are in my thoughts and reside in a most intimate place within my heart.

Yours Sincerely, BT

In his letters to the Culpers, Benjamin warned them Arnold would not be finished sowing chaos even though he was tucked away on a ship in New York, enjoying the luxury of knowing that his wife and infant son were safe from harm since he'd asked Washington to give them secure passage to London. Washington had agreed, maybe because his feelings were that the sins of the father should not be forced upon the child. But Arnold would still be out for revenge.

The Culpers did not go completely dark. Culper, Sr. still forwarded information on the movements along Long Island. And in correspondence from the city, Culper, Jr. wrote to Benjamin,

I never felt more sensibility for the death of a person whom I knew only by sight, and had heard converse, than I did for Major André. I was not much surprised at Arnold's conduct, for it was no more than I expected of him. I am happy to think that Arnold does not know my name. However, no person has been taken up on his information.

But after Arnold's men began looking for spies in the city, a letter from Culper, Sr. to Benjamin revealed fearfulness for his own safety.

I am sorry for the death of Major André, but better so than to lose the post. He was seeking your ruin. The enemy are very severe, and the spirits of our friends very low. The imprisonment of one that hath been ever serviceable to this correspondence so dejected the spirits of C. Jr. I am sorry to inform you that the present commotions and watchfulness of the enemy at New York hath resolved C. Jr. for the present to quit writing and retire to the country. I do not think myself safe there for a moment, and as nothing is like to be done about New York, perhaps it may not be much disadvantage to drop the correspondence temporarily. If need requires, C. Jr. will undertake again, possibly in the spring.

Culper, Sr. was referring to the imprisonment of Hercules Mulligan, the tailor who had made the coat for him, complete with secret pockets at the request of Benjamin Floyd. With danger lurking and the fear of being caught, Robert Townsend felt he needed to close his shop for a while and return to Oyster Bay.

Washington, in the meantime made plans to kidnap Benedict Arnold.

With Major Henry "Light-Horse" Harry Lee, he discussed the possibility of capturing Arnold alive if Lee could find a man willing to embark on such a dangerous mission. If the man were to fail, the commander in chief's name could not be linked to such an unorthodox design.

Lee found his man in John Champe, a sergeant major in Lee's regiment. He was asked to make a pretense of deserting, and for it to look authentic. Also, Lee slowed his men's attempts at capture, allowing Champe to escape into enemy territory and join the British.

Brought before Sir Henry Clinton, Champe played his part well, telling Clinton that Arnold's defection was only the first of many among dispirited Rebels. Once finished with his inquiry, General Clinton sent Champe to Arnold, who was busy raising a regiment of deserters and Tories he felt would rise to the calling and help win the war for the British, thus making Arnold the hero he thirsted to be. Arnold took a shine to Champe and made him a recruiting sergeant.

For weeks afterward, Champe paid attention to Arnold's movements and habits. He found that Arnold liked to take a late-night stroll in his garden before going to bed, and that gave him an idea. Champe sneaked along the alley near the garden to loosen the boards in the fence enough for a man to pass through. His plan was to knock Arnold out and carry him away, making it appear as if he were helping a drunk friend get home.

But just as luck had saved Arnold before, he was transferred to new quarters before Champe could act. Arnold was to oversee the embarkation of his regiment, known as the

"American Legion," aboard naval transports, and Clinton issued emergency orders directing the legion to head for Virginia. Champe was now the one behind enemy lines; how would he ever find his way home and return to Lee?

Months went by with Lee not hearing from his man on the other side. Then one day a ragged, bearded Sergeant Major John Champe appeared in Lee's camp.

Meanwhile, Benjamin had grown increasingly chaffed by Arnold's treason, having received a letter from Arnold trying to persuade him to join him on the other side. Benjamin wanted to come up with a plan to raise the deflated spirits of the Patriots, especially his men on the inside who kept him informed. At the end of November of 1780, Benjamin was promoted to Colonel, and it was then he began preparing another raid on the British, this time on Fort St. George.

(* indicates a passage from Tallmadge's memoirs)

50

Fort St George, 1780

It had been Abraham Woodhull who mentioned to Benjamin in a missive that the British were stockpiling hay and other essentials in Coram, about eight miles from Setauket on Long Island. Benjamin needed more information in order to put a plan of action together for a raid.

At headquarters in Connecticut, he met with Caleb.

"I have the latest intel from Culper, Sr., sir." Caleb handed over the missive.

Benjamin read the information, then said, "See if Abraham will ride to Coram and have a closer look. If we can get more information, I will share it with Washington and ask that we put a plan in place for a raid that will loosen the grip the enemy has on this island."

Caleb agreed. "I'll see to it."

Within a few days Caleb returned with a map of Fort St. George. Benjamin informed Washington of his plans along with the details provided by Culper, Sr., and it was agreed they would relieve the British of their supplies for the winter.

In late November, Benjamin marched with just under one hundred mounted dragoons from camp at Stamford to where Caleb waited with whaleboats in Fairfield to embark on their risky journey across the sound. In order to avoid the concentration of British around Huntington, they landed after about five hours in a designated location that was far to the east of the British. A heavy rain forced Benjamin and his men to delay their cross-island march. He directed them instead to take cover.

"Pull the boats up onto the shore so they can be hidden," he instructed. "Take cover underneath, and we'll wait out the storm before we march. Before we strike, I will detach twenty of you to stay behind and guard our boats."

Once the storm had passed, they were ready to begin their mission, now under cover of night. Beginning at ten p.m., they marched until it was almost three in the morning. When they were just shy of two miles from their target, Benjamin stopped for a break and to give last-minute instructions to his men.

"The two detachments under Lieutenant Jackson and Mr. Simmons will get as near to the fort as possible without being seen," he said. "They will remain hidden until the main body, which I will lead, signals the attack. Simmons's command will keep defenders from escaping once the assault begins. And finally, men, we will not load muskets. We must advance with stealth, using only the cold, iron blades of our bayonets."

An hour before dawn, Benjamin advanced his men into Fort St. George.

A British sentry shouted, "Who goes there?" and fired.

But before the musket smoke had cleared from the man's vision, the sergeant who had been marching at Benjamin's side reached him with his bayonet, plunging it into him, and the sentry fell dead to the ground. At the sound of the fire, Benjamin's supporting troops sprang from their cover, shouting in answer to the sentry's question, "Washington and Glory!"

It took less than ten minutes for Benjamin and his troops to take the main fort, after which Benjamin stood in the center of the grand spectacle and surveyed the bloody scene. The stunned British struck their colors, raising flags of surrender. But defenders in one of the large houses fired a volley of musketry from the second-story windows.

"Load and return fire," Benjamin commanded. "Lieutenant Brewster! Use the axes and prepare a way for entry."

Benjamin led the whole of his men toward the house. Then as soon as Caleb and his axmen had broken through the entry, a column of Continentals burst through the shattered doorway. Confusion and conflict followed. Those who had fired after the fort was taken were thrown headlong from the upstairs windows to the ground below, and all would have been killed had not Benjamin ordered the slaughter to cease.

"Take prisoner anyone who has survived," he said. "Load what supplies you can carry and tie those onto the prisoners to haul back to the boats."

He then directed his commanders' attention to a vessel on the river in which some British troops were frantically attempting to set sail. The boat was full of supplies, including sugar, rum, and glass.

"Quickly," Benjamin shouted, "train the fort's gun on the ship and fire."

The ship's crew surrendered just as the sun began to rise, and Benjamin's men set fire to the fort's buildings and the ship. With most everything destroyed, the colonel sent the bulk of his men to begin their march with the prisoners and supplies back across the island.

"Caleb," Benjamin shouted, "appoint twelve men and gather all the horses. We will raid the forage of supplies in Coram next."

They achieved total surprise again and set fire to three hundred tons of hay and supplies before heading back to meet up with the rest of their command. Benjamin's mission had been a success, and with this bold move, a major British stronghold had been eliminated. In the process they had taken as prisoners three British officers, a surgeon, and about fifty enlisted men. By contrast, only one of Benjamin's men had been injured. The raid certainly raised the hopes of the inhabitants of Long Island who wanted independence, especially those in and around Suffolk County. Washington and Congress praised Benjamin for his efforts and issued an official resolution honoring the participants of the Mastic-Coram raid. Within the next several days, Benjamin removed his troops to Windsor to close the year and to settle into their winter quarters there.

51

Spring, 1781

    Robert Townsend returned to the city after his extended stay at home in Oyster Bay. He had closed his shop in Hanover Square and opened a new one in Peck's Slip. With his younger brother, William, and his cousin John, he signed a lease for an apartment above the shop and called the place "Bachelor's Hall."

    Robert had also been reunited with Liza, who had fled Sir Henry Clinton's home after finding out the fate of Major John André. Afterward, Liza's fear that she was pregnant was confirmed, and Robert arranged to purchase Liza from his father. She would be helpful to his housekeeper, but he was unsure what would happen after the baby's birth.

    Robert continued to see Culper, Sr. every so often to give him his verbal report, and he found out on one such occasion that his comrade was engaged to marry Mary Smith.

    Robert still frequented James Rivington's coffeehouse, which was often where he gathered intelligence on the British. He also continued his post as sentry at British headquarters. Washington had sent a man named McLane into the city to hopefully procure a copy of the British naval codebook, which Washington would give to the commander of the French fleet.

The British naval codebook was covertly given to Rivington, who took time away from printing his Loyalist newspaper to secretly make a copy of the codebook for McLane to take to Washington.

The British naval codes would benefit the Rebels tremendously during the Battle of Yorktown, and the copy of the codebook would be given to French Admiral Francois-Joseph-Paul, comte de Grasse.

Washington believed that the campaign of 1781 would be critical to winning independence. In May, he and Rochambeau met at a council of war in Wethersfield, Connecticut, where Washington pressed for a commitment to attack the British at their New York base. In contrast, Rochambeau thought the British were much more vulnerable at Yorktown. In the end the two generals agreed on a compromise. The French would march from Newport, Rhode Island, to Westchester, New York, and join Washington's army to form what would become the largest allied force in New York during the war.

While Washington was still in New York, he devised a scheme to conceal his plan of heading to Virginia thus keeping the British from sending reinforcements to Cornwallis. In a move that was similar to his earlier plan to throw the British off the trail, Washington leaked false documents, that led Sir Henry Clinton to think he planned to take New York City. This caused Clinton to order Cornwallis to send every soldier he could spare to the Northeast, leaving his troops in Virginia unequipped for what was about to take place.

∞∞∞∞∞∞∞∞∞∞

After the winter holidays, Kitty had not returned to Philadelphia as Mary had thought she would. Both girls knew their mother was unwell. It had been obvious when the family was reunited over the winter holidays, a time when Hannah had not seemed herself. Although Kitty had not been home to see the gradual changes in her mother's health, Mary had kept her well-informed through their correspondence.

Kitty wrote to James Madison, letting him know she would remain in Middleton, at least for the time being. And as winter gave way to spring, Hannah became more ill and remained in bed. Both Mary and Kitty sat down and wrote letters to family and friends letting them know their mother might only have days to live. William Floyd returned from Philadelphia, and once home he didn't leave his wife's side.

On the morning of May 16, 1781, Hannah Floyd didn't wake. She was buried the following day, during a small service for just her family.

Several days after the service, the girls and their father sat together in their large gathering room. The solemnness of the past days filled the air with heavy misery. Nicoll stood in the hallway, his things packed, ready to return to his post. The girls were the first to go to him. They hugged their brother close as their tears flowed silently down their cheeks.

Nicoll then walked over to his father and took his hand. "I'm sorry, Father," he said. "But it's time for me to return to my post."

William nodded, stood, and embraced his son. "I know, son," was all he said.

The girls walked outside and watched as Nicoll mounted his horse, then tipped his hat as he left. For several moments the two sisters stood together holding hands and watching as their brother's image grew smaller and smaller in the distance. Several minutes later, the postrider arrived and handed several letters to Kitty. The girls turned and went inside, where they sat near their father.

Kitty was the only one interested in the post.

She had received a letter from Madison, who wrote he was concerned about Hannah and Kitty both. His letter had been written prior to her mother's death.

"I don't know what I shall do," Kitty said. "It seems Mr. Madison is on his way here. He will be grieved to find out he has missed the funeral by a few days. Oh, Mary, I'm so heartbroken. I don't care that Mr. Madison is on his way. I don't feel he will be of any comfort to me. Maybe I shall forget about finding someone to marry. For now, I don't want to leave home. Maybe I shall stay with you and Father always."

Cora walked into the room with refreshments and set them on the table next to Mary.

"Child, there's no reason to go on with talk like that," she said. "Your mama loved you and lived a good life. You are young and are just starting yours. Don't hold on to the past. Remember how much she loved seeing you both happy. Nothing was more important to her than her family."

Mary stood and hugged Cora. "Oh, Cora. What would we do without you?"

Cora poured a cup of tea and handed it to William. "Thank you," he said.

She poured one for Kitty too and handed her the cup. Then there was a knock on the door.

"I'll answer," Cora said and moved to the front of the house.

The girls didn't think much about the news of a guest at the door since the past week had brought a slew of family and neighbors coming by with food and condolences. But when Cora and the gentleman caller walked into the room, they were shocked to see who was with her.

"Hello, Kitty," the man said.

Kitty glanced up at the sound of her name and gasped. Her teacup fell from her hands, and its contents spilled onto the floor.

"William!"

"I made arrangements to remove from my post once I heard your mother was gravely ill."

Tears fell from Kitty's eyes, and her shoulders began to shake. Her father stood and took her hand and held it between his own.

"Mother passed a few days ago," Mary said, breaking the news.

William Clarkson looked woeful. "I'm so sorry," he said and stepped further into the room.

"I'll have supper ready shortly." Cora headed to the kitchen.

A moment later, Joli came in to clean up the spilled tea.

"Please sit," Mary said and waved her hand toward an empty chair near the fireplace.

Clarkson glanced at Kitty, who was almost inconsolable. Then he glanced between the empty chair and Kitty, unsure whether to go to her or sit. When he took a seat, Kitty bolted from the room and ran up the stairs, and the others could hear the sound of her bedroom door closing.

"Excuse me," Mary said and went up the stairs to find her sister face down on the bed in tears.

Mary was unsure what to say. She knew William's visit was a shock to Kitty, who had not laid eyes on him in years.

Soon there was another knock on the door downstairs. Mary opened the bedroom door to see if anyone would answer. She saw her father walk to the front door and open it. When

Mary saw who it was, she quickly closed the bedroom door. Then she leaned her back against it and took a deep breath.

"Kitty," Mary said. "you have another visitor. James Madison has arrived."

"What?" Kitty whispered through her tears.

"Yes, Kitty. Both William Clarkson and James Madison are waiting for you downstairs."

"I shall say I'm ill. This is not fair. I don't know if I can compose myself."

"You can and you must. They are both here because they care for you. Our mother just died. They are bringing their condolences and well wishes."

"But William doesn't know that James wants to ask for my hand in marriage."

"And you don't know why William has arrived other than to give you his sincerest thoughts. I suppose you won't find out anything unless you go back down and talk to them."

"Yes. You're right, Mary. I just need a moment."

Kitty sat up in bed and wiped the tears from her cheeks then stood and walked to the dressing table to adjust her hair and dress.

"Please tell them I will be down in a moment," she said.

Mary nodded and left the room. Downstairs, she gracefully spoke to the gentlemen, who were now enjoying a pleasant discussion with her father.

"Kitty will be down soon," Mary said as she approached.

The three men looked at Mary with a sense of expectation. Joli came into the room, announced the meal was ready to be served, and asked everyone to remove to the dining room.

The three men and Mary stood around the dining table waiting for Kitty. A moment later, they heard her footfalls on the stairs. When she walked into the room and over to the table to sit, Clarkson quickly pulled her chair out for her. Madison then sat in the chair next to Kitty, and Clarkson took the seat across from her. Mary sat next to Clarkson and her father sat in his usual seat at the head of the table. To Mary it felt very odd to be entertaining visitors without her mother, and she looked at the empty chair.

"May I pray for us?" William Clarkson asked.

"Yes, thank you," Mary's father said.

The prayer was kind and heartfelt and reminded Mary of the prayers she'd heard said by ministers. It was graceful and full of praises to God for his watchfulness, care, and forgiveness. When Clarkson said "amen," Joli and Cora were waiting with plates filled with fresh fruits and vegetables. The neighbors had been generous with their gifts of food that week. Joli set down a plate of sliced tomatoes and a bowl of beans. Cora had plates of chicken, corn, and melon. Joli came back around and filled everyone's glass with mead.

"Tell us, Mr. Clarkson," Mary's father said, "will you stay in Philadelphia now?"

"No, sir, not yet. The French troops are now together with the Continentals and are gathered in Westchester. My plans are to offer my services as a surgeon and go with them to Virginia. Maybe even down into the Carolinas after that."

Madison nodded, then cleared his throat. "It is my understanding that Washington and Rochambeau's presence in New York is a threat to Clinton's hold on the city. And that Yorktown and the Virginia campaign may be only an alternative."

Clarkson smiled. "Congress, I am sure, is kept abreast of Washington's plans up to the minute. And I am just a doctor providing my services to the cause where needed."

Madison looked pleased with this response, then turned to his left to direct his next comment to Kitty.

"Will you return to Philadelphia with your father?"

He wore a hopeful expression, and Kitty smiled shyly at him.

"I don't know yet, Mr. Madison. I may stay with my sister here for a bit longer."

This comment made Clarkson smile, and Mary could tell the two men were vying for Kitty's interest.

Their father asked Clarkson about his plans for the rest of the week. "Will you be staying with us tonight, Mr. Clarkson? You are certainly welcome, as is Mr. Madison."

"No. With the days being longer, I can ride a bit farther toward Westchester this evening. I shall take my leave before sunset."

When the meal ended, Cora brought out apple pie. The smell of the buttery cinnamon and sugar would make anyone hungry, even after a big meal. After Cora served the slices, everyone was silent for several minutes as they devoured the dessert.

Then Clarkson leaned back in his chair and took a deep breath.

"This was the most wonderful meal I've had in . . . well, I can't even remember. Thank you all so very much. I'm grateful to have been able to visit with you, Mr. Floyd, Miss Kitty, Mary." He locked eyes with each family member as he said their names. "I believe I will go to the barn and gather my horse now. But" —he looked at Kitty— "can I ask you to walk out with me, Kitty?"

"Of course, Mr. Clarkson," Kitty replied.

"William, please. Call me William—like before." His face softened, and his eyes reflected his true feelings for Kitty.

Kitty giggled and smiled for the first time in weeks. "Of course, William," she said, standing up.

Mary watched Madison's face grow tense; his eyes dropped to the last bite of pie on his plate.

"Shall we play a game of chess then, Mr. Madison?" Mary's father asked.

Madison looked up from his plate and replied, "Oh, yes, certainly."

Those around the table stood as Kitty and Clarkson walked out the front door together. Mary watched from the window as they made their way around to the back of the house and then down to the stables.

Mary then went to the kitchen to help Cora and Joli with the dishes. All the windows were open throughout the house, and a slight breeze blew the curtains. Mary could hear bees buzzing near the bushes and even Kitty's laugh. She watched as Kitty and Clarkson walked, gazing at each other. Mary knew Kitty's heart better than anyone else did, and it was clear her sister was in love. Before the couple reached the barn, Clarkson stopped and turned to Kitty. By now, they were far away from the house, and Mary couldn't hear what he was saying to her. He took hold of one of Kitty's hands and got down on one knee.

Mary gasped aloud then moved to the doorway, where she could see them better. Cora and Joli followed.

I swanny," Cora said. "I knew it, I's just knew it."

Joli giggled. Mary just stared. Her breath caught in her throat.

The three women continued to watch as Kitty nodded. Clarkson smiled and stood. The couple embraced and held each other for what seemed like a long time. Then Mary watched as Clarkson lowered his head and placed a chaste kiss on her sister's lips. He took her hand, and together they walked into the barn. Mary watched as Jeb came around to help Clarkson saddle his horse. A few minutes later, Kitty and Clarkson walked his horse toward the road, and Mary went back to doing the dishes.

Later that evening when the two sisters retired, their father and Madison were still deep in conversation about the war. Mary was so weary of the war. As she and Kitty changed into their nightdresses, she decided to tell Kitty that she'd seen her and Clarkson from the window.

"Kitty," she began. "how do you feel about Mr. Clarkson as opposed to your feelings for Mr. Madison?"

Kitty shrugged. "I am fond of both."

"No, Kitty. How does William really make you feel? Do you get the feeling that butterflies are flapping their wings inside your stomach when he's close? Do you think about him all day? And, well, all night too? Do you long to just have him near you? Do you crave the way it feels when William touches you?"

These questions made Kitty blush, and she giggled. "Oh, my dear Mary." She took a deep breath. "I do feel all of those things for William. Not so much for Mr. Madison, although I believe him to be a fine man."

"I know, Kitty. I can tell that you are in love with William. I was watching you both from the window. Then I saw him get down on one knee. That's when Cora, Joli, and I moved to the doorway. We couldn't hear anything, of course, but we saw him kiss you, and we saw the way he held you."

Kitty looked shocked, almost horrified. "Oh," was all she said.

"Tell me, Kitty. What did William say?"

Kitty grabbed her sister's arm. "Oh, Mary. When he took my hand and looked at me the way he did, my heart leapt to my throat. I honestly thought I would die if I couldn't be with him. That my life would somehow be incomplete. Then he got down on his knee and asked, 'Will you wait for me, Kitty, until I return? I would like to ask for your hand in marriage. The past year, I've thought of you and only you, Kitty. He said, I'm more than fond of you. I'm in love. I love you, kitty.' Then he asked if I felt the same. I nodded and said yes. And I said to William, 'I'll wait for your return.' Then he kissed me and we held onto each other for what felt like forever until we knew it was time for him to leave." She gazed down at the floor. "And now he's gone."

"You do love him and want to marry him?"

"I do."

Mary's face filled with a look of sympathy and her voice sounded soft when she asked, "Are you afraid he won't come back? That he might be killed?"

Kitty nodded and her eyes filled with tears. "Yes," she whispered. "I am."

The next morning, Mary woke before Kitty. She dressed then went to the kitchen to see if she could help Cora and Joli with breakfast. When she got down there, she saw Madison coming from the outhouse.

"Good morning, Mr. Madison." Mary greeted him when he walked into the kitchen.
"Good morning," he replied.

"Would you like some coffee, sir?" Joli asked.

Soon Mary's father joined them at the small table in the kitchen, and then Kitty walked into the room.

"I believe I shall leave after breakfast," Mr. Madison announced. "To go back to Philadelphia. Kitty, I hope you will return in a few days' time with your father."

"We shall see, Mr. Madison," Kitty responded.

Cora brought biscuits and eggs to the table, and everyone ate their fill. Soon, Madison stood and walked over to where Kitty sat. When he got down on one knee, Mary couldn't believe her eyes. Kitty looked startled, and their father looked on with curiosity.

"Miss Kitty," Madison began, "in the presence of your family, I would like to pledge my undying love to you. I would like to offer you a life with me. Would you do me the honor of becoming my wife?"

Mary's father smiled. Cora and Joli stared, standing as still as icicles frozen into place. Mary waited with bated breath for what Kitty would say. For what felt like a generation, nothing happened. No one moved; no one dared to breathe.

And then Kitty said,

"Yes. Yes, Mr. Madison. I will."

Mary's fork fell from her hand to the table with a loud clunk. Her father clapped Madison on the shoulder, then the men shook hands after Madison got back on his feet. Kitty still looked stunned as Madison offered her his hand. She took it and stood. Madison hugged her, and she patted him on the back.

"You've made me a very happy man, Miss Kitty. I shall make you happy too," he said.

Kitty forced a smile and nodded.

Madison then said his goodbyes and walked out the back door toward the barn.

"I have some correspondence to catch up on before I head back to Philadelphia, the girls' father said. "I will see you two later. Congratulations, dear." He leaned in and kissed Kitty on the cheek before he went upstairs.

"Kitty," Mary hissed, "what have you done? You cannot be promised to two men, and they don't even know it. What are you going to do?"

Kitty shook her head. "I don't know."

52

Yorktown, Virginia Fall, 1781

The danger of having dispatches intercepted was always strong, especially when messengers were crossing the sound between Long Island and Connecticut. This was something Benjamin, Culper, Sr., and Caleb were always alert to. This time, however, they'd planned for dispatches to be captured by the enemy. The false missives between Washington and Rochambeau were captured and delivered to Clinton, alerting him to spies in his city, although under their Culper aliases, Clinton had no idea who they were.

In those intercepted papers were letters from Washington to Congress with the false information that allied forces were prepared to attack New York. But Washington had fooled the British once before by planting dispatches with false information. This was part of a similar strategy, and Clinton fell for it, believing he knew exactly what Washington's plans were. Because of that, Clinton did nothing to reinforce Cornwallis. By the time Sir Clinton understood the truth about the true plans for the Franco-American armies, it was too late for him to act. Washington and Rochambeau's combined forces were on the march to Yorktown, and Admiral de Grasse, with thirty-six ships prepared for battle and three thousand troops aboard, had landed in Chesapeake Bay. By the end of September 1781, the combined armies had reached their destination, and Washington commenced his siege on Yorktown.

Although Benjamin and his dragoons had not been needed at Yorktown, Washington had given him command of part of a force led by General William Heath that included seventeen New England regiments, the Third United States Artillery, and the New York militia. Their activities around New York might not have been as central as the battles fought at Yorktown, but they had been key in distracting Clinton and keeping him from sending any reinforcements to Yorktown.

About that time, Benjamin had received information that Benedict Arnold was planning an expedition and a raid on the Patriot coastal city of New London in Connecticut. This was also a plan to force the Continentals to detach men from the Southern campaigns in the Carolinas and Georgia. Arnold's plot to lessen forces in the South, could have been a way to give Cornwallis the advantage. Unfortunately, Benjamin arrived too late; Arnold had burned New London, which had been a haven for American privateers, and was where ships had brought in supplies for the Continentals.

All in all, Benjamin was glad to be back on the coast, where he still had plans to annoy the enemy and to stop their plundering along the sound.

Next, he received information from Culper, Sr. regarding the British bastion Fort Slongo, near Huntington on Long Island. Benjamin allowed Major Lemuel Trescott the honor of taking the lead on the raid at Fort Slongo. The Americans pulled off a surprise attack, and the Continentals quickly overran the bastion, captured its defenders, and set fire to its blockhouse, which was the main look-out post. Then they returned to Connecticut with the fort's strand of colors and twenty-one prisoners. This might have been a minor incident compared to Yorktown, but it was another piece of bad news for the British.

By October 17, Lord Charles Cornwallis had sent out a flag of truce in the form of a lone drummer boy beating 'parley' and a British officer waving a white handkerchief tied to the end of a sword. The officer was then blindfolded and brought inside American lines to secure terms of surrender for the British. Cornwallis asked for twenty-one hours to settle the preliminaries. Washington allowed twelve. On October 19, Cornwallis surrendered with an active army of 7,247. The total number, including the wounded, was around eleven thousand. Their mortification was great, as was the exultation and joy of the allied army. There was, however, not the smallest insult uttered to the prisoners.

Although the war was not yet over, the capture of Cornwallis at Yorktown, was a tremendous way to end 1781.

53

1782

    Benjamin received information that British commander Benjamin Thompson, along with six hundred light horse troops and infantrymen, had moved into the village of Huntington on Long Island. Thompson upon arrival forced the local militia to tear down the Presbyterian church and use the wood to erect a fort on the town's burial grounds. He then demanded the militia provide carpenters to prepare the bastion's defenses.

    When Benjamin's informant sent him word of Thompson's unnecessary, vindictive vandalism, Benjamin quickly wrote to Washington of his plans to answer Thompson's brutality. In that missive, he penned his most detailed report of the war, informing Washington that if he could defeat the British in Huntington, it would throw off their hold in Jamaica and Brooklyn. This would also be a destructive blow to the illegal plundering and stealing of goods along the Long Island Sound. These goods were later sold for profit in what was known as the "London Trade."

    Benjamin met Washington at West Point to discuss his plan of attack.

    "Sir," Benjamin addressed Washington. "I believe with an attack, the British would lose most of their cavalry, at least on central Long Island. It would also reduce the illegal commerce between Connecticut and Long Island."

Washington agreed. "With the British scaling down their New York operations, their forces on Long Island have become dependent on getting provisions and forage along the sound. Removing Thompson from his encampment at Huntington would certainly remove a large market for illegal operators."

Benjamin produced a map one of his spies had drawn of the encampment at Huntington. He laid it out on the table in front of Washington. As they studied the map, Benjamin reminded Washington of all the ways Thompson and his troops had brought misery and destruction to the innocent inhabitants of the town. Washington was convinced.

"This assault," Washington said, "will be even more daring than the one you launched against the enemy at Fort St. George. In conducting this business," he continued, "you will be governed by your own discretion. Set the date of destruction for December 5, unless an accident should intervene to prevent it."

"Sir," Benjamin said, "I believe this is to be the most impactful attack of my career. We will plan our landing at Eaton's Neck on the east side of Huntington. That way, we should be able to avoid any British ships in the harbor, and that plan will ensure a safe retreat if needed. I'll handpick my men and use four companies for the core of the strike. We will be reinforced by Connecticut militia, giving us seven hundred men in all."

Washington nodded, and Benjamin continued.

"I will muster the troops near Stamford and march them to Shippan Point, where the whaleboats will be waiting for us to cross."

"May God be with you," Washington told him.

Benjamin saluted his excellency and left to prepare for his attack.

54

Winter, 1782

It was a few days before Christmas and Mary had taken her horse to gather holly and Fraser fir branches to decorate the house. She wanted their first Christmas without her mother to feel warm and comfortable, the way their home had been when she was alive. She stopped along the road, dismounted, grabbed hold of a large sack she'd brought, and made her way through the snow to a large holly bush, where she began clipping branches. The crisp, cool air felt refreshing. She hummed a Christmas song to herself as she made her way over to a small pine tree and took clippings from it. Back at home, she'd add leaves from a tree in their yard to the mix and place the greenery along the fireplace, windows, and dining table.

After returning home, Mary opened up her sack and spread her clippings across the small table in the kitchen. She sorted the greenery and tied branches together with twine. Soon Kitty came to help.

Not long after that, Cora and Joli came inside from gathering eggs and commented on the lovely arrangements the girls were creating.

"Save me a few sprigs of that holly," Cora said. "I'll use it for garnish along the edge of the cake I'm going to bake."

Mary snipped a few twigs of holly from a larger piece and took it over to Cora.

"Here you go," she said cheerfully. "I can't wait to see how it turns out."

There was a knock on the door, and Kitty went to answer.

"It's the post," she called from the front room. She thumbed through the letters and found one addressed to her from William Clarkson. She carried it and the other mail into the kitchen and sat at the table to read her letter.

"I've just received a letter from William," Kitty said. Her voice sounded weak and trembled with emotion.

Mary set down what she was working on and asked if she was okay. Kitty looked at her sister with tear-filled eyes and nodded.

"It says he's coming home. The British have started evacuating the South, and he's coming home. Oh, Mary, what am I to do? I'm engaged to James Madison."

"You should follow your heart," Mary replied. "Father will have to understand. And Mr. Madison . . . well, I don't know. It will just have to be what it is. But if you've chosen to be with William, then you must write to Mr. Madison this instant and get that letter into the post."

Kitty stood and rushed to her sister, hugged her tight, and said, "I shall, Mary. I shall explain it all to Mr. Madison in a gentle correspondence."

She then went to her room to write a letter that would surely cause Colonel Madison heartbreak.

Mary wished for everyone's sake that Kitty hadn't put herself in the position to care for two men, be courted by two men, and now to be engaged to two men. Then Mary tried to put aside her worries, thinking the matter would soon be settled. And with the war seemingly coming to an end, 1783 looked to be promising. Mary finished with her sprays and bouquets and placed some along the front windows. She arranged the largest one above the fireplace and put two long arrangements down the center of the dining table. She had a few sprigs of greenery left on the kitchen table and decided to turn them into a bouquet to lay across her mother's grave. Once she had tied them with a large bow made from twine, she called for Kitty to come with her.

"I'm not yet satisfied with my correspondence to Colonel Madison," Kitty called from upstairs. "Go on ahead. I shall stay to finish this."

With that, Mary donned her cape, walked out to the stable to saddle Spot, and with her bouquet in hand, rode off to the cemetery. Mary tied her horse to a post then walked down the narrow path to her mother's tombstone. There, she stood and gazed at the lettering, reading it over and over in her mind. Then she placed a gloved hand atop the snow-covered arch-shaped stone. "Mother," she whispered. She bent down and brushed the snow away from the base of the tombstone, then she brought the bouquet to her nose, closed her eyes, and breathed in the succulent scent of fresh pine and red holly berries.

"Merry Christmas," she said and set the flowers down in front of the tombstone.

"Merry Christmas." The voice had come from behind her.

Mary turned and looked behind her. There stood Benjamin.

Mary gasped. "You're here."

Benjamin stepped closer to her.

"That I am. I'm sorry I could not be here when your mother died."

His eyes held sorrow, yet Mary noticed a glimmer of something more.

"I understand," she said. "You have a command and an army to tend to—and a war to win. Even though you couldn't be with me, your letters were enough."

Her last words came out as a whisper, and emotion overwhelmed her.

Benjamin held out a gloved hand for her to take. When Mary placed her hand in his, he helped her to stand and pulled her to him, then lowered his head until it was just inches from hers. Their breath danced before them in heated clouds, and a gentle snow began to fall as Benjamin brought his lips to hers. He pressed his mouth lightly to hers at first, then the kiss grew more intense, reflecting the yearning and long anticipation that had led to that moment.

"Mary," he whispered, barely breaking their kiss. "I love you."

Mary replied by pulling him closer; she wrapped both hands around his back, holding him to her like she would never let him go. Their kiss, heated and passionate, took them away to somewhere that was safe, a place where their souls joined, and their hearts became one.

After what seemed like hours, although it had been only minutes, Benjamin pulled away. He got down on one knee and looked up at Mary, who held a hand to her lips, now raw and chafed from their kiss.

"Mary," he said, "I can only hope that you feel for me the way I do for you."

"I've never doubted my feelings for you," Mary began. "I think I must have loved you all my life. For you are in my dreams and in my heart and in my mind. It has and will always be you. I am and will forever love you and only you, Benjamin Tallmadge."

"Then marry me."

Mary lowered herself to one knee so that she was eye to eye with her handsome commander.

"Yes." She nodded. "Yes. I will marry you."

He pulled from inside his coat a sprig of mistletoe. He held it over her head and kissed her again. Then he kissed her once more before they walked back to where their horses stood.

Together, Benjamin and Mary rode their horses back to her house, where she found Nicoll waiting, having ridden home with Benjamin from the Continentals' camp along the Connecticut shore. Soon, William Floyd arrived and, together with his children and one dragoon commander, he sat at the table to enjoy a decadent meal brought in by Cora and Joli, who had been cooking and baking most of the day.

The table was filled with laughter, joy, and stories of war as Nicoll described Benjamin's successful raids against the British along the Long Island Sound. He held his listeners rapt as he continued with a vividly told story.

"And then a violent wind, like a terrific squall, came up along the sound. We had to spend a rainy night huddled under the shelter of our whaleboats. The next day the sound was full of choppy waves." With a smile on his lips, Nicoll looked across the table at Benjamin. "That's when Colonel Tallmadge received intel that three Tory whaleboats had crossed. He was determined not to let them get away, regardless of the winds."

Everyone sat hanging on to Nicoll's every word. Mary glanced at Benjamin, who looked a bit embarrassed at his prominence in Nicoll's tales.

"Three of our boats were forced back to shore by the winds," Nicoll continued. "But Caleb carried on. He caught up with the Tories in the middle of the sound and closed in on two of the British craft—and a fight began. All the Tories were killed or wounded in the volley of musketry." Nicoll paused briefly as his emotions caught up with his words. "Caleb was shot in the chest."

Mary and Kitty gasped.

"Oh no," Mary said.

"The bullet passed straight through him," Nicoll explained. "And despite his wound, he managed to capture two of the British boats. The third escaped to the British outposts on Lloyd's Neck. And Caleb returned to our side victorious."

Mary started clapping, then Kitty joined in, and their father rapped his glass with his knife. Mary turned to her left and looked at the commander sitting next to her. She beamed with pride. This brave, handsome man loved her.

"We are grateful that Caleb came back and will live to tell his grandchildren about it one day." Benjamin chuckled. "Although, the raid wasn't as successful as I'd hoped it would be."

"Ah," Nicoll said. "There's still more up your sleeve, commander. I know you're not done yet."

When Cora brought in a beautifully iced white cake with sprigs of holly along the edges, everyone oohed and aahed.

But before she could slice it, Benjamin stood.

"I'd like to share some rather happy news."

He glanced at Mary, who was looking up at him with the deepest of adoration.

"I've asked Mary to do me the honor of being my wife, and she's accepted."

Cheers and squeals rang out across the table. Cora looked like a proud mother as tears brimmed in her eyes. Joli came running from the kitchen, where she had been preparing coffee, and joined in the celebration. Kitty came around the table to hug her sister. Mary's father shook Benjamin's hand and welcomed him to the family. And Nicoll said,

"I couldn't ask for a better brother. I'm glad to know the man who captured Mary's heart."

"Aye," William added. "As Mary's father, I always knew it would take someone very special to win my daughter's heart." He turned to his daughter and lifted his glass. "To Mary and Benjamin and to a happy life ahead. Your mother would be proud. I know she is with us in spirit."

Everyone lifted their glasses to cries of

"Cheers!"

55

Fall, 1783 New York City

Benjamin received reports that those aboard an American sloop called the Shuldham, commanded by Captain Isaac Hoyt, were smuggling British goods using the cover of their assignment to suppress illicit commerce. Benjamin requested that one of his agents get a copy of the ship's manifest.

When the sloop docked in Norwalk, Benjamin boarded and introduced himself to Hoyt.

"I'm Colonel Benjamin Tallmadge. I have in hand a warrant and a manifest and would like to search the ship for illegally imported goods. I believe, sir, this ship has been commissioned as a public American vessel to protect these waters against illicit trade but instead is engaged in the London Trade, which, as you know, is a crime."

The captain flew into a rage.

"I will have you thrown overboard for such accusations, Colonel."

"You must know the futility of such threats, sir, for you are addressing a commander of a much higher rank. Therefore,

I advise that you obey my commands and allow me to search the ship."

Hoyt turned away from Benjamin and yelled to his crew.

"Weigh anchor. Hoist the sails."

There was a wind from the northwest, which carried the ship away from its position.

"I order you to put back," Benjamin commanded.

The captain began to swear at Benjamin.

"Damn you. I will throw you overboard, by God." Hoyt spat out the words.

"If you make any such attempt, I assure you, sir, that I will take you with me."

Hoyt ignored Benjamin and continued his course toward Lloyd's Neck, where a British ship was anchored.

"Where are you headed, Captain?" Benjamin inquired.

Hoyt glared at the colonel. "I swear I will hand you over to the enemy."

"For such an offense, you would be given the punishment of death under martial law if you proceed. If you continue on this course, Captain Hoyt, I can assure you I will have you hanged as high as Haman." Benjamin was referring to Haman from the book of Esther, who plotted to kill the king but was foiled by Esther and hung from a fifty-foot gallows.

Things became more alarming as they were approaching the enemy, and Benjamin became angry.

"Put about this ship and turn it around now!" Benjamin commanded.

Hoyt hesitated a few moments before he ordered his crew to their posts, changed course, and steered the vessel back to the Norwalk harbor. As soon as it was anchored, the captain, was taken ashore, and Benjamin proceeded with his search for the contraband, which he found matched the manifest he had been given.

Several months later, there was talk of a cessation of hostilities as preliminary articles of peace had been received by Congress. This seemed to put an end to the further cascade of bloodshed, but Washington still asked Benjamin to obtain information from the Culpers in order to help him gauge the probable movements of the enemy. On September 3, the Treaty of Paris was signed in France by representatives of King George III and of the United States of America, officially ending the American Revolution. The commander in chief's final act at his West Point headquarters was the discharge of the Second Continental Light Dragoons, and he granted Benjamin a last-minute promotion to the rank of lieutenant colonel.

Benjamin was concerned his agents in the city might have a problem after the British left, and he requested that he and the officers in his legion be included in the official reentry of American forces into the city of New York. That day held the promise of triumph and zest, of a momentous celebration to be savored by those who had served through the dark days of the war, during which American forces had been driven from the city.

Benjamin wanted to pay particularly close attention to certain individuals who had carried out their duties for the cause of freedom but were thought by some in the city to be Tories. He knew they would not wish to have the true nature of their service to the American cause revealed. His agents had feigned loyalty to the Crown as a cover for their real work. To ensure none of them suffered reprisals on this account, Benjamin undertook a special mission into the city.

As he rode through the still-occupied city under a flag of truce—after leaving it six years before, he found himself surrounded by British troops, Tories, and traitors. But he was well-treated by the British army and naval officers. Sir Guy Carleton had been placed in charge of British troops in New York City during the last year of the war, and he invited Benjamin to dine with him. On that occasion, he introduced him to several very high-ranking officers of the Royal Army and Navy. Over the next several days, Benjamin contacted his agents and informants, and with the help of his new high-ranking acquaintances, he took measures to provide for the safety of his men.

Benjamin then returned to Washington and briefed him on the situation regarding his informants and his impression of the British high command. He let Washington know that he had been treated with the utmost civility. Then Washington himself prepared to enter the city of New York with much pomp and circumstance. On November 25, the British ferried their forces from the city over to Staten Island, where their transports waited. As the British embarked onto their vessels, Washington and the remaining Continental Army triumphantly marched down Broadway.

One of Washington's first acts upon entering the city was to recognize and reward those agents whose safety Benjamin had asked him to help secure. Washington had breakfast with Hercules Mulligan, tailor to the British, who had secretly passed on information he overheard to his former King's College classmate Alexander Hamilton. Washington then visited with James Rivington, the owner of the coffee shop and the British newspaper known as the Rivington Gazette, whose service Washington considered to have been of great value, especially the copying of the British naval codebook.

New York's governor, George Clinton, threw a dinner party for Washington and his officers. Victory and independence were celebrated with a tremendously moving and exciting display of fireworks. But the most emotional event took place on December 4 as Washington prepared to return to

Mount Vernon and take leave of his officers. Before he departed, he met with the group at Fraunces Tavern.

56

December 4, 1783, Fraunces Tavern, New York City

At noon on Tuesday, December 4, Washington made known to his officers that he intended to commence his journey home and retire from military life. He made an appointment to gather at Fraunces Tavern for a meal with his commanding officers. Benjamin and his fellow soldiers assembled in a large downstairs room inside the Pearl Street building.

They had not been assembled long before his excellency entered the room. His emotions were too strong to go unnoticed, and every officer present responded in kind to their leader. Benjamin noted that Washington, although poised and regal as always, displayed his emotions unapologetically. The weight of the war, his gratitude toward his men, and the jubilation of victory were reflected in the commander in chief's expression. After partaking in a meal in what felt like suspenseful silence weighed with the anticipation of this special time coming to a close, the general filled his glass with wine and turned to his officers.

"With a heart full of love and gratitude, I now take leave of you. I most devoutly wish that your latter days may be as prosperous and happy as your former ones have been glorious and honorable," he said, then lifted his glass into the air.

Once every officer had lifted his glass high, Washington continued.

"I cannot come to each of you but shall feel obliged if each of you will come and take me by the hand."

General Henry Knox, being the closest to Washington, turned to his excellency, who by then was flushed, tearful and no longer capable of speaking. Knox grasped his hand, and they embraced in silence. With the same affectionate manner, each officer in the room walked up to, kissed, and parted with his commander in chief.

Benjamin had never before witnessed such sorrow and weeping. The emotion in the room was tangible, and Benjamin took it all in, capturing the moment and the mood within his heart and his mind. He knew what their army had accomplished was far greater than anything this group of military heroes could fathom. Tears of deep, complex empathy shone in every eye; every heart was filled to bursting. No word broke the solemn silence that marked their final moments in each other's presence. They each found it hard to part from the man who had conducted them through a long and bloody war and under whose instruction the glory and independence of their country had been won. That they should see him no more seemed impossible to believe.

Benjamin approached Washington, and the two looked at each other. Washington's clear blue eyes pierced him so deep Benjamin felt it down to his soul.

"Sir," Benjamin said, "I am most grateful to you. But my words cannot summarize what cherished esteem I hold for you deep within my heart. I am and will always be your most humble servant."

Washington gripped Benjamin's hand and pulled him into a strong hug. Benjamin felt Washington's emotion, and it overwhelmed him even more.

But the time for Washington to leave his men had come. Waving his hand in farewell, he left the room. Passing through two columns of light infantry who were waiting to escort him, he walked silently and stately on to Whitehall, where his barge awaited. Everyone followed him to the wharf, where a large crowd had assembled to witness the departure of the man who, under God, had been the great agent in establishing the liberty and independence of these United States.

Once Washington was seated, the barge pulled away from the dock, and when it was out in the stream, the great beloved general waved his hat and bid his men a silent farewell.

Benjamin watched his noble commander's figure grow smaller, and his heart filled with boundless pride over having been a part of such greatness.

57

Setauket, Long Island, 1783

It had been almost seven years since Benjamin had been able to return home to visit with his father and stepmother. He now set out to pay his respects to his family and honored friends near Brookhaven and Setauket, where the community was enjoying their relief from the strife of war. Public notice had been given for everyone to celebrate on the green meadow across from his father's church in Setauket. With a roasted ox and a feast to celebrate, the town had proclaimed Benjamin as master of ceremonies.

He arrived with Mary, whose family was living once again in their home in Mastic. To the Floyds' relief, they had found their home still standing although in great need of repair. Nicoll and William, along with Jeb, Mary, Cora, and Joli, had begun the cleaning and reassembling of their home. Kitty had married William Clarkson a few months before the celebration in Setauket, and they were currently living near his family in Philadelphia with plans to move to the Carolinas.

Benjamin had collected Mary from her home in Mastic early that morning. Then their carriage made its way to Benjamin's father's Presbyterian church and the town green in front that had recently been a British camp. The enemy had taken all the pews from the inside the church and burned them for firewood, but repairs had begun, and soon Benjamin's father would return to the pulpit. Today, however, it was time to reflect and celebrate.

Acting as master of ceremonies, Benjamin greeted friends and community members with Mary by his side. When the ox had been fully roasted, the Reverend Tallmadge led the gathered in a prayer of thanksgiving. When the prayer was completed, he said to the crowd,

"My son, Lieutenant Colonel Benjamin Tallmadge, your master of ceremonies." He turned to his son. "Will you do the honor of carving the beast?"

Applause and cheers rang out, and Benjamin made his way over to the ox. He then carved the meat and distributed it to the crowd. After everyone had been served, he carried his own plate over to where Mary sat and joined her on the green. The two smiled at each other, and Benjamin said,

"All feels in harmony now. For everyone seems to be of one mind. A united family. I do not believe a Tory could live in this atmosphere one minute."

Mary giggled at his comment. "No, they most assuredly could not."

Soon, Selah and Anna Smith Strong came by to say their farewell since the sun was beginning to set and most were starting to leave. Then Abraham and his wife Mary stopped to talk. Austin Roe was next, and then Caleb appeared at their side. They all shook Benjamin's hand and congratulated him and Mary on their upcoming marriage.

Mary watched as each took Benjamin's hand, their eyes filled with tears and their faces full of gratitude and emotion. Mary looked out over the green field, the spot where almost fifteen years earlier she had first met Benjamin. A smile formed on her lips, and her heart filled with joy.

After Mary had been driven from her home so many years ago, it felt good to place her feet upon that same soil. Nicoll and Jeb had worked to rebuild the barn and stables. And Mary, Cora, and Joli had cleaned, painted, and replaced all the bedding and curtains. Jeb had even dug up the silver that had been buried next to baby Lucas's grave. The fence had been removed from around his burial stone, but Mary's father had plans to replace it. Once Mary's family home was put to rights, plans for her wedding began.

It was to be a grand affair and would take place on March 18. Engraved invitations had been sent to family and friends far and wide. Benjamin's father would conduct the ceremony. There would be dinner and dancing, flowers, and family gathered all around them. A true celebration of life and love.

Even though both Mary and Benjamin had been born on the island, they would make Connecticut their final home, it being the place where they had spent most of their years during the war. Benjamin had made an investment in a mercantile business with his younger brother near Litchfield. He had also purchased a large home near that business in the main area of Litchfield where the couple would live and later raise their family.

After their wedding, they planned to take a slow, farewell trip along the island to spend several weeks visiting with those they would greatly miss. There would be a special trip to the Townsend home in Oyster Bay to see someone near and dear to Mary's heart, her friend Liza, who had given birth to a baby boy.

On the afternoon of March 18 at three o' clock in the afternoon, Kitty handed Mary her bouquet of white flowers, then Mary and her father made their way past family and friends on a path of leaves and petals that had been spread out before them. At the end of the path was a pergola that had been built for Mary and Benjamin to be married under. Across the top, Kitty, Cora, and Joli had placed vines and branches. Under it stood the Reverend Tallmadge and his most dashing son, who was wearing his full uniform. Benjamin's hair was pulled into a low ponytail and tied with a black satin ribbon. Pinned upon his left breast was a white flower, matching those in Mary's bouquet.

William Floyd escorted Mary to her groom, following a path in the family's back pasture. Mary wore a pale green silk gown embellished with pearls along the collar and sleeves. Around her neck was the strand of pearls her mother had given her on her sixteenth birthday. Her mousy-brown curls were piled into a spiraling bun atop her head, and Kitty had loaned her the pearl earrings that matched the necklace. In her shoe was a sixpence, and she carried the handkerchief Benjamin had handed her the day they met, his initials, embroidered in blue thread in one corner.

Benjamin stood tall, smiling at his bride as she made her way toward him. Mary's father kissed her on the cheek, then took her hand and placed it upon Benjamin's arm.

Reverend Tallmadge asked,

"Who gives this woman to be wed to this man?"

"I do," Mary's father answered, then stepped back and moved to the side.

Reverend Tallmadge said, "Let us bow our heads in prayer. Father God, we come before you today with our hearts full of love. Filled with love and gratitude for you and for your grace. We are thankful to you, the giver of life and love. We ask that you grant a life full of happiness and hope to the two who stand before you today in the presence of family and friends and before you, oh, God. Grant them, a life of love and thankfulness. We ask your blessing upon them now and until you call them home. Amen."

He then addressed the congregation. "Let us now turn to scripture. First Corinthians, chapter thirteen, verses two through eight says, 'And though I have the gift of prophecy, and understand all mysteries, and all knowledge, and though I have all faith, so that I could remove mountains, and have not charity, I am nothing. And though I bestow all my goods to feed the poor, and though I give my body to be burned, and have not charity, it profiteth me nothing. Charity suffereth long, and is kind; charity envieth not, charity vaunteth not itself, is not puffed up, doth not behave itself unseemly, seeketh not her own, is not easily provoked, thinketh no evil; rejoiceth not in iniquity, but rejoiceth in the truth; beareth all things, believeth all things, hopeth all things, endureth all things. Charity never faileth.'"

After the vows were said, the festivities began. The fiddlers played, and the guests danced, toasted, ate, rejoiced, and laughed. Their lives had been restored, their hope reestablished, and their joy set free. For they too were free, as was their country, and it would become known as the land of the free and the home of the brave.

As the sun began to set, Benjamin pulled his bride to him, bent his head, gently kissed her lips, then whispered,

"Today, I feel as if I've won more than a war, and may I remain grateful to God for what he's granted us in this new endeavor." Benjamin's face hovered close to Mary's, his nose brushing against hers. "And, Mary, may this new country of ours become as great as the love I have in my heart for you."

Every post is honorable in which a man can serve his country. —George Washington

In addition to the protection of a merciful Providence, I would notice the peculiar marks of attention which I uniformly received from the commander-in-chief through the war. Having been early and personally acquainted with this great man, I held him in high veneration, and when he appointed me, or rather requested me to take charge of a particular part of his private correspondence, this brought us into frequent and intimate correspondence. His approbation to my conduct on many occasions, expressed both publicly and privately by letter, together with the favorable expression of Congress, afforded me the highest satisfaction that a soldier could receive.—

Benjamin Tallmadge

Author's Note

    I hope I did the life of Benjamin Tallmadge justice. My goal was to create a captivating read in which fact and fiction worked seamlessly together to weave stories about the Culper Ring and various families on Long Island with the facts about the war.

    I first learned of the Culper Spy Ring, around 2019. As I recall, my local National Society Daughters of the American Revolution chapter was reading a work of historical fiction called *355—The Women of Washington's Spy Ring* by Kit Sergeant. At the same time, I was watching AMC's TURN on Netflix and may have become a bit obsessed! Especially by the actor who played Benjamin Tallmadge, Seth Numrich. ☺ From there, I read everything I could find on the Culper Spy Ring and made my way to Setauket, where I had a wonderful tour with Tri-Spy Tours founder and owner Margo Arceri. I also went to Raynham Hall in Oyster Bay, Long Island, the home of Robert Townsend, and had a great time in their museum. I also had a chance to tour the home where Robert and a young slave girl named Elizabeth grew up. This was also the home where Colonel John Simcoe met with John André. I also hopped over to Litchfield, Connecticut, to snap pics of Benjamin Tallmadge's beautiful home, which is still a private residence.

    Then I went back to New York right before I started writing this novel to tour spy related locations in Manhattan with Karen Cherro Quinones, known by her fans as Karen Q. or Mrs. Q. Karen is the owner of Patriot Tours in Manhattan. In addition to running tours, she goes live on most Friday evenings from Karen Q's Patriot Tour NYC Facebook page, sharing facts and stories from the American Revolution. Then I went back to Setauket so that I could visit the Three Village Historical Society for a spy tour. I also enjoyed a Sunday service at the Setauket Presbyterian Church, where Benjamin Tallmadge's father was the minister for about ten years, beginning in the mid-1700s.

And I couldn't miss going to Tappan, New York, to The Old '76 House, which is the tavern where John André and Benjamin Tallmadge spent several days before André's trial and hanging. Today it's a beautiful restaurant in a unique historic setting. Also in Tappan, you can see the location where Major André was hanged, it's marked with a historic marker and the area is set apart with an iron fence. Near Tappan, in Terrytown, New York, there is a monument commemorating the three men who stopped André along the road—robbed him, found the plans and maps of West Point on his person, and took him in to Patriot headquarters. I hope you enjoy all the photos I've included of my tours; those are located near the end of this book. I've also included information on how you can learn more about all the tours I took. You will also find information on the books I used for research.

When I decided to write a work of historical fiction based on the life of Benjamin Tallmadge, I knew there was a question surrounding the identity of Agent 355. Everyone seems to have opinions about who she was—or could there have been more than one? So I, of course, had to write her into my story, and I hope you enjoyed my idea of who 355 might have been. Although I know it wasn't really Mary Floyd—or was it? ☺ I did alter her age for the story. I made her the youngest in the William Floyd family because I wanted the reader to fall in love with a headstrong, feisty nine-year-old girl at the beginning of the book.

And I wanted her to be friends with Liza, a character who was inspired by a real-life Townsend family slave. I became fascinated with her after reading her story in Claire Bellerjeau and Tiffany Yecke Brook's book, *Espionage and Enslavement in the Revolution*. I wanted to create a character or several characters for the reader to root for at the beginning of my book, and I took some liberties with their ages for the sake of the story. Liss, the real-life inspiration for Liza, may not in truth have ever met Mary Floyd, but I thought a friendship between the two would enhance the story. Even though we know Liss did escape to New York with Simcoe and the Queen's Rangers, we are not sure how she did it. You'll enjoy reading more about Liss in *Espionage and Enslavement in the Revolution.* I've included a short bio for almost every character on the next few pages so you can find out a little more about who they really were.

And lastly, as with all my books, I've included discussion questions. I myself love diving more deeply into topics I have read about with my book-club buddies and other friends. I hope this book inspires lots of fun and interesting discussions!

There are at least 198 surviving Culper Spy Ring letters. Although the spies asked that their identities remain a secret, even from Washington, the commander in chief did save the letters that made it to him without being intercepted. These letters can be found in the National Archives under the Culper aliases. In the following section, I've listed information on my sources for letters from or quotes attributed to Washington, Tallmadge, and the Culpers.

I have so many people to thank for helping me bring this book to publication. My beta readers read my first draft before edits to give me their ideas for additions, improvements, and changes. Included in my group of beta readers is an expert on the Culper Ring; Margo Arceri, owner of Tri-Spy Tours in Setauket, New York. Tri-Spy customers walk, bike, or kayak to all the "hot spots" in Setauket, where the members of our beloved Culper Ring lived and operated. Thanks as well to my other beta readers, Eileen Tucker, Tali Mullins, and Elizabeth Holcomb. And special thanks go to my wonderful and informative editor, Mary Beth Bishop. Extra thanks go to my husband Jeff for his love, support and help with any technical issues—and for making the journey with me to all the fabulous historic places I wanted to visit for research.

Quote Notes & Book Resources:

1. Chapter 9. Letter from Benjamin Tallmadge to Nathan Hale. July 9, 1773 (New York Public Library, Hale Collection)
2. Chapter 11. Letter from Benjamin Tallmadge to Nathan Hale. July 4, 1775 (Connecticut Historical Society)
3. Chapter 13. Letter from Benjamin Tallmadge to Nathan Hale. May 1775 (Connecticut Historical Society)
4. Chapter 19. Quote from George Washington speaking to Congress on February 9, 1776 (mountvernon.org)
5. Chapter 19. Quote from a speech by Governor Jonathan Trumbull (A Cloud of Witnesses by David N. Bell.)
6. Chapter 22. Letter from Benjamin Tallmadge to Jeremiah Wadsworth. July 9, 1777 (Connecticut Historical Society)
7. Chapter 32. Culper correspondence from Caleb Brewster to Benjamin Tallmadge. February 26, 1779 (Library of Congress)
8. Chapter 33. Culper correspondence from Culper, Jr. (Robert Townsend) to Culper, Sr.. July 15, 1779 (Library of Congress)
9. Chapter 34. Culper correspondence from Samuel Culper, Sr. (Abraham Woodhull) to John Bolton (Benjamin Tallmadge) regarding movement on the Long Island Sound and the robbery of Benjamin Floyd. October 29, 1779 (founders.archives.gov)
10. Chapter 37. Culper correspondence from Culper, Jr.(Robert Townsend) to John Bolton (Benjamin Tallmadge) concerning British plans to flood the colonies with fake currency. November 29,1779 (Library of Congress)
11. Chapter 37. Robert Townsend's letter to his father, Samuel Townsend, regarding their escaped slave.

	(Townsend family papers, Collection of Friends of Raynham Hall Museum)
12.	Chapter 43.Culper, Sr. letter to John Bolton regarding the assistance of a 355, —the code number for the word "lady." August 15, 1779 (founders.archives.gov)
13.	Chapter 43. George Washington to Benjamin Tallmadge requesting that a shorter route for the Culper correspondence be created by opening a channel through the North River and Staten Island. December 6, 1779 (Library of Congress)
14.	Chapter 43. George Washington to Benjamin Tallmadge suggesting that the Culper, Jr. letters be written in a Tory style. February 5, 1780 (Library of Congress)
15.	Chapter 44. George Washington to Benjamin Tallmadge on the need to revive the Culper correspondence in anticipation of the arrive of to the French fleet. July 11, 1780 (Library of Congress)
16.	Chapter 44. Coded missive from Culper, Jr. to Benjamin Floyd that appeared to be about items not being procured. The hidden message was that the British had learned the location of the French fleet. July 20, 1780. (Library of Congress)
17.	Chapter 44.Culper, Sr. to George Washington, the shortest Culper correspondence and the most urgent. July 20, 1780 (Library of Congress)
18.	Chapter 44. Alexander Hamilton given to Lafayette for Rochambeau regarding the French fleet. July 21, 1780. (Library of Congress)
19.	Chapter 47. Benedict Arnold's letter to Benjamin Tallmadge requesting passage for John Anderson (John André.) Fall, 1780. Malcom Decker, *Ten Days of Infamy: An Illustrated Memoir of the Arnold-André Conspiracy* (New York Arno Press; 1969)
20.	Chapter 48. Major John André's last letter before his execution, written to Sir Henry Clinton. September 29, 1780. (William Clements Library)

21. Chapter 49. Within the fictional letter from Benjamin Tallmadge to Mary Floyd, noted with asterisks is a quote from Tallmadge's memoirs on his recollection of John André's death.
22. Chapter 49. Culper, Jr. to Benjamin Tallmadge (John Bolton) regarding the news of André's death. October 14, 1780. (founders.archives.gov)
23. Chapter 49. Culper, Sr. to Benjamin Tallmadge (John Bolton) regarding the news of André's death and Arnold looking for spies in NYC. October 14, 1780. (founders.archives.gov)

Non-fiction Books on Benjamin Tallmadge and the Culper Spy Ring

Washington's Spymaster, Benjamin Tallmadge's Memoirs

George Washington's Long Island Spy Ring by Bill Bleyer

Espionage and Enslavement in the Revolution by Claire Bellerjeau and Tiffany Yecke Brooks

George Washington's Secret Six by Brian Kilmeade and Don Yaeger

General Washington's Commando, Benjamin Tallmadge in the Revolutionary War by Richard F. Welch

Washington's Spies: The Story of America's First Spy Ring by Alexander Rose

Nathan Hale: The Life and Death of America's First Spy by M. William Phelps

Lives of the Signers of the Declaration of Independence by Benson J. Lossing Reprint of the 1848 original

Fiction Featuring Culper Spies

355: A Novel: The Women of Washington's Spy Ring by Kit Sergeant

Rebel Spy by Veronica Rossi

TV Show

ACM's TURN on Netflix

Brief Bios

Benjamin Tallmadge: Born in 1754 in Setauket, Long Island, he was the second oldest son of Benjamin Tallmadge, Sr., the minister of the Setauket Presbyterian church from mid-1700s until 1786. Tallmadge entered Yale University at around the age of fourteen and graduated in 1773. At Yale, Tallmadge and Nathan Hale were good friends, and roommates. After graduation, Tallmadge accepted a position in Wethersfield, Connecticut, where he was a teacher and the superintendent of Wethersfield High School until 1776.

He began service in the American Revolution as a lieutenant, going on to lead the Second Continental Light Dragoons and received promotions to the ranks of captain, major and colonel. His last promotion was in 1783, when he became a lieutenant colonel. Tallmadge fought gallantly throughout the war and led many successful raids on British encampments and forts along Long Island. His best-known work in the Revolution was providing military intelligence under the direction of George Washington. Tallmadge organized the Culper Spy Ring, the most successful spy operation of the Revolution. Another major contribution came when he sensed something was amiss after Colonel John Jameson told him a prisoner named John Anderson was being held. Because of Tallmadge's quick thinking, Benedict Arnold's attempt to turn West Point over to the British was foiled.

Tallmadge married Mary Floyd of Mastic, Long Island, in March of 1784. The two settled in Litchfield, Connecticut, where Tallmadge operated a mercantile business. The couple had seven children. Tallmadge was appointed postmaster of

Litchfield. He was the first president of the Phoenix Branch Bank, a position he held from 1814 to 1826. He became a member of the House of Representatives in 1801 and served in Congress until 1817. He was an original member of the Society of the Cincinnati, established for Revolutionary War officers in July of 1783.

Mary Floyd Tallmadge died in 1805, and Tallmadge married Maria Hallett, the daughter of his friend, Joseph Hallett, in 1808. Tallmadge died in 1835 and is buried in East Cemetery in Litchfield. His beautiful home in Litchfield, is now a private residence. There is a National Society Daughters of the American Revolution chapter named for Benjamin Tallmadge in New York.

Mary Floyd Tallmadge:
Born in 1764, she was the daughter of William Floyd of Mastic, Long Island, New York. Mary was actually the second child of William and Hannah Floyd. However, for the novel, I have made her the younger sister because I wanted her to be a certain age in chapter one when she meets her future husband. She, in fact, most likely met Benjamin Tallmadge during the American Revolution, when he made visits to her father, who was a member of Congress. On several occasions, Tallmadge may have even stayed in the Floyd home in Middleton, Connecticut, during the Revolution. Mary Floyd and Benjamin Tallmadge were married in March of 1784 at her father's estate in Mastic. Tallmadge's father, the Reverend Benjamin Tallmadge, Sr. performed their ceremony. After an extensive honeymoon visiting friends on Long Island, the couple settled into a grand home in Litchfield, Connecticut. Mary and Benjamin Tallmadge had seven children. Mary died

in 1805. There is a National Society Daughters of the American Revolution chapter named for her, the Mary Floyd Tallmadge chapter of Litchfield, Connecticut.

William Floyd: Born in 1734, he was a politician and a signer of the Declaration of Independence. Floyd was a delegate to the Continental Congress. He was born into a wealthy family on Long Island and inherited his father's land and farm in Mastic. He was a member of the New York State Senate from 1777 to 1788. He was elected to the New York Society of the Cincinnati as an honorary member. In March of 1789, he was elected to the First United States Congress under the new Constitution as an Anti-Administration candidate and served until March of 1791. Floyd was a presidential elector in 1792, voting for George Washington and George Clinton.

Floyd, for whom the town of Floyd, New York, is named, became a resident of Oneida County in 1794 after giving his land and farm in Mastic to his son, Nicoll. In 1795, Floyd ran for lieutenant governor of New York with Robert Yates on the Democratic-Republican ticket, but they were defeated by Federalist John Jay. Jay was the brother of James Jay, the chemist who invented the invisible stain and counter agent used by the Culper Ring. Floyd was again a presidential elector in 1800, voting for Thomas Jefferson and Aaron Burr. He then served as an elector in 1894, voting for Jefferson and George Clinton. Floyd was a member of the state senate (Western District) in 1808.

Floyd married **Hannah Jones** in 1760, and together they had three children: Nicoll, Mary, and Catherine (known as Kitty). The family fled their

Mastic home by ship to avoid being captured by the British. While William was attending congressional meetings in Philadelphia, Hannah and the children often visited. Hannah died in 1781. After his wife's death, Floyd married Joanna Strong of Setauket, Long Island. Their children included: Ann, who was born in 1785 and married George Washington Clinton, the son of governor George Clinton, the first governor of New York and the fourth vice president of the United States. Floyd and his second wife were also parents to Elizabeth, who was born in 1789, and married Continental Congressman Zephaniah Platt.

Today the William Floyd House, located in Mastic Beach, is part of the Fire Island National Seashore and open to visitors. It consists of the home, grounds, and the Floyd family cemetery. Over the course of two hundred years, eight generations of Floyds have managed the twenty-five-room mansion and 613-acre property. Prior to the twentieth century, the estate was much larger.

Nicoll Floyd: Born in 1762, he married Phebe Gelston, in 1789. She was the daughter of David Gelston, the customs collector at the Port of New York. In the novel, Floyd corresponds with and has a possible romance with Phebe Townsend of Oyster Bay, Long Island, but that is part of the fiction I invented to serve the plot. Nicoll Floyd inherited his father, William Floyd's farm and land at some point after the Revolution. The property stayed in the Floyd family until 1975, when it was sold to the state and became a National Historic Landmark. Today it is owned by the National Park Service as part of the Fire Island National Seashore.

Nicoll Floyd was the father of US Representative John Gelston Floyd.

Catherine (Kitty) Floyd:
Born in 1767, she married William Clarkson who became a minister. She met James Madison during her stay at a boarding house in Philadelphia, where her father, Madison, and Thomas Jefferson were also lodging. Madison was a great deal older than Kitty, and he was very shy. After Madison fell for Kitty, it is said that Jefferson urged him to propose. Madison did, in fact, propose and Kitty accepted. The two even exchanged miniature portraits. But once the Floyds returned to their estate in Mastic, Kitty ended the engagement. Madison may have been too introverted and scholarly to suit her tastes.

Kitty married medical student William Clarkson, who gave up his plans to practice medicine to become a Presbyterian minister. The two moved to South Carolina and had two daughters and a son. Clarkson died in 1812, the same year Madison won his second term as president of the United States and celebrated the eighteenth year of his marriage to his wife, Dolley. After her husband's death, Kitty and her son and youngest daughter went to live with her oldest daughter in New York City.

Benjamin Floyd:
Born in 1740 in Brookhaven Town, Suffolk County, New York. He was the son of Richard Floyd III, who inherited the Pattersquas estate in Brookhaven and who was the brother of William Floyd of Mastic.

The Floyds of Brookhaven were wealthy Loyalists and members of the Anglican Church. During the war, Colonel Benjamin Floyd's grand home was robbed and looted by both Tories and Patriots, and he was at one point taken to Connecticut as a prisoner. But because of his Patriot connections, he was freed quickly.

His great-grandfather, Richard Floyd, Sr., came to America with Richard Woodhull, great-grandfather to Abraham Woodhull. Both settled in Suffolk County, in Setauket and Brookhaven respectively. Abraham Woodhull's cousin, Colonel Nathanial Woodhull, was married to a member of the Floyd family. Nathanial Woodhull was known as Suffolk County's first martyr for the Patriot cause. Although Benjamin Floyd's loyalties during the war might have looked weak, most feel he was helpful to the Culper Ring and to Abraham Woodhull.

Abraham Woodhull: Born in 1750 in Setauket. His father was a magistrate and potato farmer. Woodhull's two older brothers died, leaving him in charge of the family farm and estate. The Woodhulls' were some of the first settlers on Long Island and included Richard Woodhull, a wealthy settler in Setauket, and militia Brigadier General Nathanial Woodhull. Abraham Woodhull married Mary Smith in 1781, and together they had three children.

Around the time Caleb Brewster was sending important information about British activity to Washington through Tallmadge, the commander in chief asked Tallmadge to find someone on Long Island to assist in the operation. Needed was a reliable informant who could send reports on British movements, ships, weapons, and the size of the troops involved. In 1778, Tallmadge recruited

Woodhull, whose spy name became Samuel Culper. The name was inspired by work Washington had once done in Culpeper County, Virginia during his early years as a surveyor.

After the war, Woodhull became a judge in Setauket. He died in 1826, is buried behind the Setauket Presbyterian Church, and his grave is often visited by fans of the TV series TURN and those interested in the Culper Spy Ring.

Robert Townsend: Born in 1753 in Oyster Bay on Long Island to Samuel Townsend, a shipping merchant. Townsend was the third son of eight children. He owned a store in New York City and for a while lived in the boarding house owned by Abraham Woodhull's brother-in-law, Amos, and his sister, Mary Underhill. Woodhull asked Robert to spy on the British in order to help him gather information in the British-occupied city of New York. It was becoming harder for Woodhull to come up with reasons to explain his trips to the city, and Washington had requested that the information be brought to him more quickly.

After Benedict Arnold switched sides and began arresting those in New York he thought were spies, Townsend left for Oyster Bay and closed his shop in the city for a short time. Later, he returned and opened a new store in Peck's Slip with an apartment above it that he shared with one of his brothers and a cousin.

One of the Townsend family slaves, known as Liss, escaped with the Queen's Rangers when they left the family's Oyster Bay home. Liss ended up in New York City and eventually became pregnant.

She came to stay with Robert and his brother, and cousin until the baby was born.

Townsend posed as a Loyalist in the city and even stood guard at British headquarters. He took his identity as a spy to his grave, as did the other Culper members. It wasn't until 1930 that a historian named Morton Pennypacker was given a trunk belonging to the Townsend family. It was inside the trunk that Pennypacker found Robert Townsend's ledgers, and he realized Townsend had been a spy. Handwriting from Washington's Culper letters, along with Pennypacker's discovery, linked Townsend to the spy called "Culper, Jr." After more research, Pennypacker confirmed that Townsend was indeed Culper, Jr.

Townsend never married. It is believed that his brother and his housekeeper had a baby that they named Robert Townsend, Jr. In his will, Townsend left $500 to Mary Banvard, his housekeeper in Peck's Slip. Townsend died in 1838, taking his identity as Culper Jr. to his grave. Today the Townsend home in Oyster Bay is part of a museum called Raynham Hall. Robert is buried in the Townsend family cemetery in Oyster Bay.

Elizabeth, Known as Liss:
The inspiration for the character, Liza. Liss was born into slavery in the Townsend household in Oyster Bay. We know that Liss escaped when Colonel John Graves Simcoe and his Queen's Rangers left Oyster Bay. It is unknown whether anyone knew of her plans to escape or helped her in that endeavor. Mystery also surrounds the question of where she went once she arrived in the city of New York. We do know she had a child named Harry. Liss found Robert Townsend in the fall of 1782 and moved in with him and his two roommates, who were his brother

and cousin. It was around that time Robert paid his father for Liss.

More of Liss's story can be found in the book *Espionage and Enslavement in the Revolution* by Claire Bellerjeau and Tiffany Yecke Brooks. Bellerjeau has also started an educational nonprofit dedicated to the memory of Liss. The purpose of www.rememberliss.org is to educate the community about the extraordinary life and times of an enslaved Black woman from New York named Elizabeth or "Liss." The story of her bold and daring struggle for freedom can help us understand the founding of America through the eyes of a woman of color. More information can also be found at www.espionageandenslavement.com

Caleb Brewster: Born in 1747 in Setauket on Long Island, Brewster was a descendant of Mayflower passenger, William Brewster. Caleb Brewster was an officer in the Continental army and ran a whaleboat across Long Island Sound from Connecticut to Setauket, carrying intel for the Culper Ring as well as providing protection from the British ships and marauders along the sound. His unit during the Revolution was stationed in Fairfield, Connecticut. After the war, Brewster married Anne Lewis of Fairfield, Connecticut. They resided in Fairfield, where he had a blacksmith business. Together they had eight children. In 1793, Brewster joined the US Revenue Cutter Service, which was the predecessor of the Coast Guard. Caleb died in 1827 and is buried in Fairfield Cemetery.

Anna Smith Strong: Born into a wealthy family in 1740 in Setauket, New York on Long Island. She was also known as Nancy. She married Silah Strong, who was a captain in the New York militia and a delegate to the First Provincial Congress in colonial New York. He was thought to be a spy and was imprisoned on the HMS Jersey. Anna, with the help of Tory relatives, was able to bring food to the ship and eventually get him released through a prisoner exchange. It is said that Anna helped communicate with Caleb Brewster by hanging certain items on her clothesline. If there was an important message for Brewster, she would hang a petticoat. Abraham Woodhull could see Anna's clothesline from his farm, which sat a little higher than Anna's property. The number of napkins Anna hung on the line would indicate to Woodhull which cove Brewster had sailed into. The spies took their secret to their graves, but Anna's clothesline story has been passed down through generations as a hometown legend and piece of family folklore.

After Silah was released from the prison ship, he remained in Patriot-protected Connecticut with his oldest son. Anna and the couple's nine other children stayed in Setauket. Today, their graves can be visited, and they face Long Island Sound. There is a National Society Daughters of the American Revolution chapter in Setauket, New York named for Anna Smith Strong.

Austin Roe: Born in 1748 in Port Jefferson, New York, just to the east of Setauket on Long Island Sound. Roe was asked to be the courier for the Culper Spy Ring in order to help Abraham Woodhull (Culper,Sr.) bring back messages from Robert Townsend (Culper, Jr.) in New York City.

Because Roe owned a tavern in Setauket, he had an excuse to go into the city for supplies and could easily get past the British checkpoints. Because he traveled more than a thousand miles over the years for the Culper Ring, he became known as the "Paul Revere" of Long Island. At some point after the war, Roe and his family moved to Patchogue on the south shore of Long Island. Roe died in 1830 and was buried in the family graveyard. His body was later moved to the Cedar Grove Cemetery in Patchogue after the town was founded by one of Roe's descendants and incorporated in 1893.

Benedict Arnold: Born in 1741 in Norwich, Connecticut, he joined the Continental army in 1775. His activities in the war included the surprise attack and capture of Fort Ticonderoga and defensive and delaying tactics at the Battle of Valcour Island on Lake Champlain in 1776, which allowed American forces time to prepare to defend New York. Around the time of the Battle of Ridgefield, he was promoted to the rank of major general. He suffered a leg injury in the pivotal Battles of Saratoga in 1777, which halted his combat career. Arnold repeatedly claimed he was passed over for promotions by the Continental Congress while other officers were given credit for some of his accomplishments.

He also borrowed heavily to maintain his lavish lifestyle. When Washington put him in command of the Philadelphia military after the British withdrawal, he developed a relationship with eighteen-year-old Peggy Shippen, the daughter of wealthy Loyalist, judge, Edward Shippen III. It was also around this time that Arnold became acquainted with the British spy leader Major John

André, who was friends with Peggy Shippen. Soon, Shippen was giving André information about the American army, and together André and Shippen began the process of turning Arnold to the British side. Arnold was feeling rejected by his own army, he had a jealous personality, and he was in debt. He may have even had doubts that the Americans would win. He began dealing with André, and the two came up with a plot to take West Point and hopefully capture George Washington in the process. In order to give the British West Point, which Arnold had been given command, he asked for 20,000 pounds, a high command in the British army, and a knighthood. Their plot was foiled when André was captured in Patriot territory and brought to the nearest command post. Colonel Benjamin Tallmadge felt something was amiss and asked that Colonel John Jameson bring André back to camp until Washington had time to be briefed. Washington had planned to meet with Arnold at West Point, but Arnold received information about André's capture from Colonel John Jameson and fled to the British ship the Vulture.

Afterward, Arnold remained in British territory, and André was eventually hung as a spy. Benedict Arnold received a brigadier general's commission with the British army. He died in 1801 and is buried at St. Mary's Church in the Battersea area of London. As a result of a clerical error in the parish records, his remains were removed to an unmarked grave during church renovations a century after his death. His funeral was without military honors.

John André: Born in 1751 in London to wealthy Huguenot parents. His father was a merchant from Switzerland, and his mother was from Paris. During the early part of the American Revolution, André was captured at Fort Saint-Jean and held prisoner in Pennsylvania. In 1776 he was freed in a prisoner exchange. André was a favorite in colonial society, both in Philadelphia and New York. He had a friendly, lively personality and was skilled at drawing and music. He was a prolific writer and handled most of Sir Henry Clinton's correspondence. In addition to his other talents, André was fluent in four languages. He planned the grand Mischianza when General William Howe, Sir Henry Clinton's predecessor, resigned and was about to make his return to England.

During the nine-month British occupation of Philadelphia, André stayed in Benjamin Franklin's house and is known to have removed several valuable items, including a portrait of Franklin, on the orders of Major General Charles Grey. Grey's descendants returned Franklin's portrait to the United States in 1906.

In 1779, André became adjutant general of the British army in North America with the rank of major. It was in that year he took charge of the British secret service and soon began plotting to turn his friend Peggy Shippen's romantic interest, Benedict Arnold, to the British side. With the help of Arnold as an important leader of the Patriot cause, André and Shippan began to secretly solicit intelligence about the Continental military. Their secret correspondence eventually led to the plot to turn West Point and Washington over to the British, ending in André's capture and Arnold's escape to the British side. After a trial, André was hung as a spy on October 2, 1780, in Tappan, New York. The location of André's hanging is marked by a fence and sign. The Old '76 House, also located in

Tappan, now a restaurant, and is the location where André was held before and during his trial. Today you can see a portrait he drew hanging above the fireplace. The cover of this novel depicts the Revolutionary flag hanging from the roof of The Old '76 House, and I took that photo while I was there having lunch and conducting my research.

Alexander Hamilton:
Born in 1755 or 1757 in the British Leeward Islands known today as St. Kitts and Nevis. Hamilton was born out of wedlock. His mother had been in an arranged marriage to a wealthy man she did not love. She fell in love with Hamilton's father, a Scotsman who was the son of the laird of Grange, Ayrshire. Hamilton's mother died when he was around nine. He was brought to America by a very wealthy man and sent to King's College in New York, now known as Columbia University. It is thought that his birth year may have been altered to allow him to enter King's College. Hamilton began the American Revolution as an artillery officer in the new Continental army. In 1777, he became a senior aide to General Washington. He returned to field command during the Battle of Yorktown. After the war, he was elected as a representative from New York to the Congress of the Confederation. He resigned to practice law and founded the Bank of New York before returning to politics. He helped to ratify the Constitution by writing fifty-one of the eighty-five essays known as the Federalist Papers, which are still used as one of the most important references for interpretation of the Constitution. As part of Washington's first cabinet, Hamilton led the Department of Treasury. When Aaron Burr ran for president, Hamilton campaigned against him. Taking offense, Burr challenged him to a duel on

July 11, 1804, during which Hamilton was shot, and the wound resulted in his death. He is buried in lower Manhattan at Trinity Church Cemetery next to his wife, Eliza Hamilton.

James Madison: Born in 1751 in Port Conway, Virginia. Madison was from a prominent family. He served as a member of the Virginia House of Delegates and the Continental Congress both during and after the American Revolution. He helped John Jay and Alexander Hamilton write the Federalist Papers, and he was a close advisor to President George Washington during the early 1790s. Madison served as secretary of state during Thomas Jefferson's presidency from 1801 to 1809. During that time, he supervised the Louisiana Purchase. Madison won the presidential election in 1808. He led America into the War of 1812. Madison was reelected in 1812. He retired from public office in 1817, returned to his plantation, Montpellier, and died there in 1836.

Madison married Dolley Todd, a twenty-six-year-old widow, in 1794. Madison had been introduced to Dolley by Aaron Burr. The two never had children, but he adopted Dolley's son. Before he met Dolley, Madison had fallen in love with Catherine (Kitty) Floyd. The two became engaged to be married, but Kitty called off the wedding by writing Madison that she was really in love with William Clarkson. Later, Thomas Jefferson sent Madison an old letter he'd kept in which Madison spoke of his love for Kitty.

Nathan Hale: Born in 1755 in Coventry, Connecticut. In 1769, Hale and his brother, Enoch, were sent to Yale University. Nathan Hale was a classmate and roommate of Benjamin Tallmadge. The Hale brothers were members of the Linonian Society of Yale, whose members debated topics in the areas of astronomy, math, and literature, as well as ethical questions surrounding slavery. Hale graduated from Yale in 1773 at the age of eighteen and became a teacher. After the American Revolution began, he joined the Connecticut militia as a lieutenant. Hale's company participated in the Siege of Boston, but Hale remained behind in his teaching position. After receiving a letter from his former classmate and good friend Tallmadge, Hale was inspired to accept a commission as a first lieutenant in the 7th Connecticut Regiment under Charles Webb. Hale was also part of Knowlton's Rangers, a reconnaissance and espionage detachment of the Continental army established by George Washington. It was named for its commander, Thomas Knowlton. The unit was formed in 1776.

In 1776, after the Americans were defeated in the Battle of Long Island and the British took over (Manhattan) and Long Island, Washington was seeking spies to go undercover in and around Long Island and New York City. Hale volunteered and was ferried across the Long Island Sound to Huntington, New York, on British-controlled Long Island. As he gathered intelligence, Hale disguised himself as a Dutch schoolteacher looking for work, but he did not travel under an assumed name. He traveled with his Yale diploma as proof of his qualifications to teach. Hale was noticed in a tavern near Huntington by British spy and Queen's Ranger Captain Robert Rogers. Rogers struck up a conversation with Hale to find out more about him. In doing so, Rogers was able to trick Hale into thinking he was a Patriot and asked to meet with Hale the following morning.

Hale fell for the trap and was captured by the British and brought into New York City. He was taken to Post Road Park of Artillery, which was next to a public house called Dove Tavern. Situated at what today is 66th Street and 3rd Avenue, this is where he was hung as a spy on September 22, 1776. There are no official records of Hale's last words. It has traditionally been said that his final words were "I only regret that I have but one life to lose for my country," which is similar to a quote from the famous Whig play by Joseph Addison titled Cato.

Hale's body was never found. His family erected an empty cenotaph in Nathan Hale Cemetery in the South Coventry Historic District, of Connecticut. A statue of Nathan Hale stands on the grounds of the CIA headquarters, and another keeps watch in Manhattan in City Hall Park next to the entrance to city hall. He is considered to be America's first spy.

Colonel John Graves Simcoe:

Born in 1752 in Cotterstock, Oundle, England. He was one of four children, and the only one to live past childhood. His father was a captain in the Royal Navy. In 1770, Simcoe entered the British army as an ensign in the 35th Regiment of Foot, and his unit was dispatched to the American colonies. He saw action in the Revolution during the Siege of Boston. Afterward, he was promoted to captain of the 40th Regiment of Foot. Simcoe commanded the 40th Grenadiers at the Battle of Brandywine. Legend has it that Simcoe ordered his men not to fire on three fleeing rebels during the Battle of Brandywine and that among them was George Washington. Simcoe sought to form a Loyalist regiment of free negros from Boston but was offered the command of the Queen's Rangers, which was formed on Staten Island in 1777. Simcoe led many attacks during the Revolution, but his most famous is known as Simcoe's Raid. On October 26, 1779, he and eighty men launched an attack on central New Jersey from southern Staten Island. The attack was launched from what today is known as the Conference House; during the Revolution, it was the Billopp home. It resulted in the burning of Patriot supplies stored in the Dutch Reformed Church in Finderne. He also released prisoners from the Somerset County Courthouse. Simcoe was captured but later released. He rejoined his unit in Virginia and participated in a raid on Richmond with Benedict Arnold in 1781. He was also in the Battle of Yorktown.

Simcoe wrote a book on his experiences with the Queen's Rangers, titled *A Journal of the Operations of the Queen's Rangers from the End of the Year 1777 to the Conclusion of the Late American War.* It was published in 1787. He served as inspector general of recruitment for the British army from 1789 to his departure for Upper Canada two years later. He became lieutenant governor of Upper Canada.

During the American Revolution, Simcoe quartered in the home of Samuel Townsend in Oyster Bay, and it was there he was visited by Major John André on several occasions. He is noted to have written the first Valentine and gifted it to Robert Townsend's sister, Sally.

Christopher Billopp: After years of distinguished service in the Royal Navy, he came to

America in 1674. He was granted a land patent on the southernmost tip of Staten Island. He built his home on the site in 1680. Billopp named the estate Bentley Manor after his ship. Legend has it that Billopp was on Staten Island, just across from Perth Amboy, New Jersey on board a two-gun vessel called the Bentley. Billopp was selected for the Duke of York's challenge to complete a voyage of more than thirty-five miles within the duke's time frame of twenty-four hours. Billopp reasoned that if he packed the deck of his ship with empty barrels, the extra surface area could harness more wind to give his ship a boost in speed. Billopp won the race and secured Staten Island for New York. He was awarded a total of 1,163 acres of land, which is where he built his house, named for the ship on which he had secured his victory in the race. Today his former home is a museum known as the Conference House. The house was passed down to his great-grandson, also named Christopher Billopp, who was commissioned as a colonel and led Loyalist forces against the Colonials in the American Revolution.

In September of 1776, Colonel Billopp hosted an informal diplomatic conference with the goal of bringing an early end to the American Revolution. Lord William Howe, commander in chief of British forces in America, arranged to meet with representatives of the Continental Congress for what is known today as the Staten Island Peace Conference. Benjamin Franklin, John Adams, and Edward Rutledge rowed over from Patriot-held Perth Amboy, New Jersey. The meeting lasted for three hours with the Americans politely declining the diplomatically handcuffed offer. The British representatives would not consider independence from England a negotiable term, and the congressional representatives had been authorized only to negotiate terms that included their independence. The failure to come to an agreement led to another seven years of conflict.

Colonel John Graves Simcoe and his Queen's Rangers were encamped on the Billopp property just prior to Simcoe's Raid. In the later part of 1779, Christopher Billopp accused one of his female servants of spying on him for the Patriots. He thought this slave girl might have tipped off the Patriots, leading them to his capture and imprisonment in New Jersey. The servant denied his charges, and this enraged Billopp, who then grabbed her and threw her down the stairs. She died of a broken neck, but Billopp was never accused or tried for murder. It is said that the ghosts of Billopp and this slave girl have haunted Billopp House—then known as Bentley Manor—today it's called The Conference House. For the past 243 years, the ghosts of British soldiers are also often reported on the property. With this as the case, how could I have not included it as the location where Liza is assisted in her escape by the wife, daughter, and servant girl of Christopher Billopp when she arrives with Simcoe and the Queen's Rangers? Billopp's property is also mentioned in the journal of Major André. The house is located within the Ward's Point Conservation Area and was separately added to the National Register of Historic Places in 1982.

General George Washington: Born in 1732 in Popes Creek Virginia. Washington had three brothers, two sisters, and one half sister. He was raised in an Anglican-Episcopalian household and had no formal education. At the age of eleven, he was left ten enslaved people in his father's will. He would go on to inherit, purchase, rent, and gain control of at least 577 enslaved people by the end of his life. He took on work as a surveyor at age sixteen.

In 1754, Washington led a surprise attack on a small French force at Jumonville Glen. His subsequent surrender to French forces at the Battle of Fort Necessity helped to spark the French and Indian War, which was also known as the Seven Years' War. Washington served in the Virginia House of Burgesses from 1758 to 1776. He married a widow named Martha Dandridge Custis in 1759. They were married for forty years but had no children. Together they raised two children from Martha's first marriage.

The famous house and property known as Mount. Vernon were inherited by Washington in 1761. The mansion was first constructed in 1734 and underwent major expansions in the 1750s and 1770s. The mansion is 11,028 square feet with twenty-one rooms. John Augustine Washington III was the last private owner before the property was purchased by the MVLA—the Mount Vernon Ladies Association in 1858.

Washington was selected as commander-in-chief of the Continental army in 1775, and he would go on to raise a ragtag, inexperienced militia that would go up against the greatest army in the world. Washington lost more battles than he won during the American Revolution, but with resiliency, leadership, guts, a winning strategy, a superior spy ring, and the help of Divine Providence, he won the battles that mattered most. With some of the most brilliantly executed plans in military history, his

Patriot fighters shattered the illusion of British invincibility. Thus the dream of a new nation became a lasting reality with the birth of the United States of America.

Washington presided over the convention that drafted the Constitution. He was elected the first president of the United States on April 30, 1789. In 1790, Washington made a special trip to Long Island. Although he did not personally meet with any of the members of the Culper Spy Ring due to their desire to remain anonymous, never wanting to be discovered, his choice of locations for his itinerary surely was a nod of thanks to his courageous spies. Washington served two terms as president at an annual salary of $25,000, an amount that today would be around, $800,000. Washington died of a throat infection on December 14, 1799, at the age of sixty-seven. In his will he made provisions to free all of the enslaved people he directly owned. He is buried in the Washington Family Tomb at Mount Vernon.

Birth of a New Nation:
Thirteen divided states chose to unify rather than go their separate ways due to the leadership of a small group of visionaries. Those leaders understood the lessons of the past and sought a new, more representative form of government—a more perfect union. They believed that government existed to protect fundamental rights. When those rights were violated, they believed that government could be and should be overthrown. But what should fill the void? Giving too much power to a government could lead to tyranny, but having a government with too little power could lead to anarchy. So the new government, they understood, would have to be

created with the perfect balance, including within it a system of checks and balances.

During the Revolution, the colonies came together under the Articles of Confederation. Each state had sovereignty and its own currency, it was a union in name only. After the war, a national Constitution was needed. The colonies needed the leadership of the only man known and trusted throughout the states, George Washington. In 1786, angry mobs marched through Massachusetts, led by Revolutionary War veteran Daniel Shays. They protested high taxes, threatened the army, and closed courthouses. A widely held view was that the Articles of Confederation needed to be revised as the country's governing document, and the events of Shay's Rebellion served as a catalyst for the Constitutional Convention and the creation of the new government. Shay's Rebellion was brought to a halt, and Congress rallied for a national convention to be held in Philadelphia to create a new Constitution and a true national government. Fifty-five delegates served at the convention, which was overseen by Washington. James Madison took diligent notes, as this was behind locked doors, with attendees sworn to secrecy. It was here the House of Representatives and the Senate were formed. Madison proposed that the powers of a single head of government be balanced by a representative legislature and a judiciary system.

By the time the Constitution was ready to be signed, it consisted of seven articles that defined the branches of government, created checks and balances, and outlined the relationship between the states and the federal government. Also outlined was the process for making amendments. Nine states had to approve the new Constitution in order for it to be ratified. Those who favored the new Constitution were known as Federalists. But some felt the proposed new government needed to better safeguard individual rights, and a free press as well as protecting citizens from unlawful prosecution; those became known as Anti-Federalists. Even though nine states did vote to ratify the Constitution, a request was made for a Bill of Rights to be added.

Washington's leadership carried a new government. A nation was built by the once feuding states, ensuring that the great American experiment would continue. Today, almost two hundred and fifty years later, the US Constitution has endured to become the world's oldest representative constitution in existence. It remains the democratic bedrock of a more perfect union.

I'm beyond grateful to have ancestors who helped create the state of New Jersey and fought bravely during the American Revolution. I'm more than thrilled to share my work of historical fiction with you, and it's my wish that if you enjoyed the story— and maybe learned something new about our nation's history, you'll leave a review on Amazon or Goodreads. Please reach out to me personally for speaking engagements at perrietuck@mac.com. Now, on the following pages, please enjoy some photos from my tours and research.

Benjamin Tallmadge's home in Litchfield, Connecticut, is a private residence.

Benjamin Tallmadge's childhood home on Long Island Sound in Setauket, New York Today is a private residence.

Photos of Setauket Presbyterian Church, where several of the Culper Spy Ring members once attended services. Benjamin Tallmadge's father was the minister here from the mid-1700s to 1786. During the Revolution, the British used the church as a stable.

Abraham Woodhull's grave, located behind Setauket Presbyterian Church is often visited by Culper Spy fans.

Abraham Woodhull's wife, Mary's grave sits to the left.

Graves of Anna Smith Strong and Selah Strong in Setauket, New York

Selah and Anna Strong's graves face the Long Island Sound.

The gravesites of Anna Smith-Strong and Selah Strong, visited during my Tri-Spy tour in Setauket with Tri-Spy Tours owner, Margo Arceri.

Caleb Brewster's home in Setauket, New York.

The Townsend home in Oyster Bay, Long Island, is now part of the Raynham Hall Museum. In this room, Colonel Simcoe met with Major John André.

Robert Townsend's home in Oyster Bay, Long Island, New York.

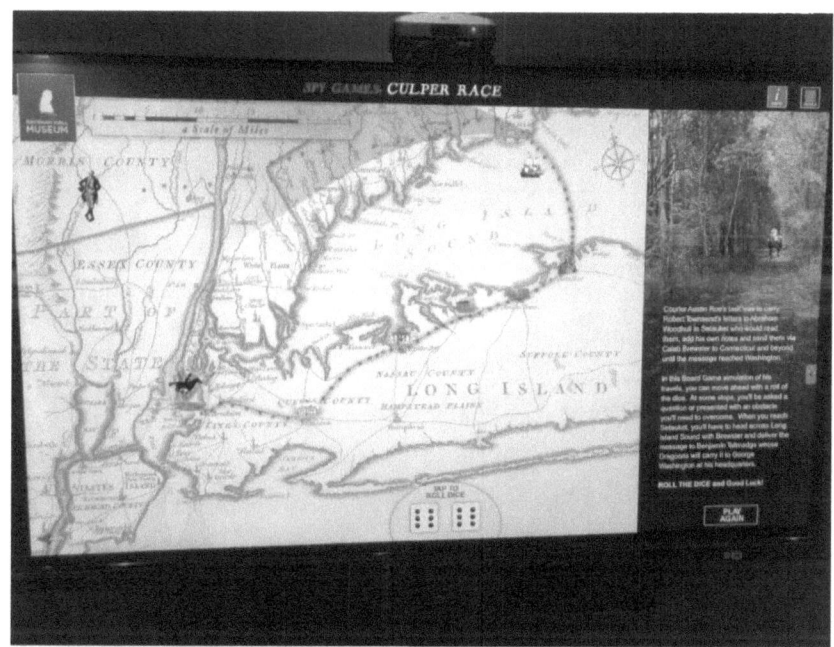

The Culper Spy route from Long Island to New York City, and from Setauket across the sound to Benjamin Tallmadge in Connecticut. Photo taken at Raynham Hall Museum, Oyster Bay.

Patriot Rock Plaque provided by the Mayflower Chapter

Patriot's Rock, where Caleb Brewster set the cannon during the Battle of Setauket. Plaque provided by the Mayflower Chapter National Society Daughters of the American Revolution in acknowledgement of the Battle of Setauket during the American Revolution.

Me and Margo Arceri, founder, and owner of Tri-Spy Tours on Long Island Sound in Setauket.

Tour website: www.culper.com Instagram: culperspyringtour Customers choose a walking, biking, or kayaking tour to all the Culper Spy locations, such as Abraham Woodhull's gravesite, the Brewster home, Benjamin Tallmadge's childhood home, and other spots.

Patriot Tours owner and guide Karen Quinones. New York City. www.patriottoursnyc.com Choose from several historical guided walking tours. Sites include Hanover Square, where Robert Townsend owned a shop, and the statue of Nathan Hale outside of New York City Hall.

In front of Fraunces Tavern with Karen Quinones, owner and founder of Patriot Tours in New York City. Facebook: Karen Q's Patriot Tours NYC. Instagram: @mrsqnyc You can purchase signed copies of Karen's book *Theodosia Burr: A Teen Eyewitness to the Founding of the New Nation* from her website. You can also purchase a copy from Amazon.

Inside the second-floor museum of Fraunces Tavern with Claire Bellerjeau, co-author of *Espionage and Enslavement in the Revolution*. Website: www.espionageandenslavement.com The portrait on the wall depicts the goodbye scene in Fraunces Tavern with Washington and his commanders. Claire's book is available on Amazon.

Nathan Hale statue in front of city hall steps in lower Manhattan, and directly inside City Hall Park, New York City.

Fraunces Tavern on Pearl Street in New York City.

The Old '76 House was the location where Major John André was held prior to his trial and execution. Today, the historic building is a lovely restaurant featuring many relics from the American Revolution, including a hand-drawn portrait, André drew of himself during his imprisonment.

Inside The Old '76 House, a hand-drawn portrait by John André hangs above the fireplace. The major drew this while he was being held before his trial and execution, and it was left in the building.

At Three Village Historical Society where there is a special tour dedicated to the Culper Spies. Tour Website: www.tvhs.org

Facebook: Three Village Historical Society Instagram: @threevillagehistory

The William Floyd estate in Mastic is now a part of the Fire Island National Seashore. It is available to tour, and the grounds surrounding the estate have lovely walking trails. The Fort St. George site is located nearby. Find out more:

https://www.nps.gov/places/the-william-floyd-estate.htm
www.nps.gov

About the Author

Perrie and her husband live north of Atlanta with their three rescue fur babies. Having raised two children, Perrie has more time now to write novels and tour the country doing research. Perrie is a graduate of the University of Alabama and loves to cheer on the Crimson Tide during football season. Her first novel, *Walking the Crimson Road,* is set on the UA campus, as are the two books that followed, *My Blood Runs Crimson* and *All the Crimson Roses*.

Perrie is a member of the Descendants of the Founders of New Jersey and her local chapter of the National Society Daughters of the American Revolution (NSDAR), in which she holds three positions. Perrie helps facilitate her neighborhood book club, leads a ladies' Bible study group, and hosts a podcast for which she interviews other authors. The Talking Book Atlanta Podcast can be found on Spotify and the Anchor podcast app. The Talking Book Atlanta Podcast also has a Facebook page; The Talking Book Podcast (Atlanta) and the Instagram handle is @thetalkingbookatlanta

Leader of Liberty is Perrie's fifth novel and her first work of historical fiction. Perrie's books can be found on Amazon as well as in selected bookstores. Signed copies of her books can be found at Ernest & Hadley Booksellers in Tuscaloosa Alabama, and John's Creek Books and Gifts in John's Creek, Georgia, as well as The Bookworm Box in Sulphur Springs, Texas. Her website is www.perriepatterson.com. Her email is perrietuck@mac.com You can find her on Instagram at @always.n.style, on Facebook at Perrie Patterson Author, and TikTok at @authorperriepatterson.

Perrie would love to connect with her readers through social media, and if you would like her to attend a book-club meeting or speak at an event, please send her an email. And if you enjoyed this book, please leave a review on Amazon or Goodreads.

Books by Perrie Patterson

Walking the Crimson Road, Book One in the Crimson Trilogy—New Adult Romance, for ages 13+

My Blood Runs Crimson, Book Two in the Crimson Trilogy —New Adult Romance, for ages 18+

All the Crimson Roses, Book Three in the Crimson Trilogy —New Adult Romance, for ages 18+

Hit Zero—A Young Adult Sports Romance, for ages 13+

Leader of Liberty: A Culper Spy Ring Tale — Historical Fiction Romance, for ages 13+

Discussion Questions:

1. Did you find yourself rooting for a particular character?
2. Did you find that you had a favorite character or a favorite scene?
3. Did you know about the Culper Spy Ring before reading this novel? If so, what had you read or watched on the subject, and how much did you enjoy the book in comparison?
4. Did you enjoy the romance aspect of the story?
5. Did you have an idea about who Liza's baby's father was? Discuss Liza's story arc and how she might have felt when she found out she was expecting.
6. Which part of the story did you find the most interesting?
7. What surprised you most about the lives of the characters or this time in history?
8. What else did you learn about the American Revolution that stands out in your mind? Is there something specific that you learned after reading the story?
9. Is the American Revolution a favorite time in history for you?
10. Do you think high school students would enjoy having this book as an option to read for a project or paper in Advanced Placement American History? Explain why or why not.
11. Did the story make you want to plan a trip to Long Island to see Setauket and Oyster Bay and take some of the tours listed in the author's notes?
12. Did you find the mini bios and the information in the back of the book helpful and interesting?

You might be interested in joining an ancestry-based historical society if you have an ancestor who fought or gave aid to the American cause during the American Revolution. There are forty committees in the National Society Daughters of the American Revolution, and one might be waiting for you to chair or co-chair. With so many committees to choose from, and ways to volunteer, there is a place for you! The male version is the Sons of the American Revolution (SAR) and there is an organization for children called Children of the American Revolution (CAR). Each of these ancestral organizations supports veterans, active military, protects historical sites, provides scholarships and student awards, and preserves our American history for future generations. www.dar.org

 May God bless America!

www.ingramcontent.com/pod-product-compliance
Lightning Source LLC
LaVergne TN
LVHW041738060526
838201LV00046B/851